THE
SILENCE
FACTORY

BRIDGET
COLLINS

b
THE BOROUGH PRESS

The Borough Press
An imprint of HarperCollins*Publishers* Ltd
1 London Bridge Street
London SE1 9GF

www.harpercollins.co.uk

HarperCollins*Publishers*
Macken House,
39/40 Mayor Street Upper,
Dublin 1
D01 C9W8

First published by HarperCollins*Publishers* 2024
1

A catalogue record for this book is available from the British Library

Hardback ISBN: 978-0-00-842404-6
Trade Paperback ISBN: 978-0-00-842403-9

This novel is entirely a work of fiction.
The names, characters and incidents portrayed in it are
the work of the author's imagination. Any resemblance to
actual persons, living or dead, events or localities is
entirely coincidental.

Typeset in Meridien by Palimpsest Book Production Ltd, Falkirk, Stirlingshire

Printed and bound in the UK using 100% Renewable Electricity
by CPI Group (UK) Ltd

MIX
Paper | Supporting
responsible forestry
FSC™ C007454

This book contains FSC™ certified paper and other controlled sources
to ensure responsible forest management.

For more information visit: www.harpercollins.co.uk/green

Part I

Nr. Telverton, June 182 —

Last night I could hear them again. They make so little noise that I do not understand how it can carry through the corridors of this house. But carry it does. It is hard enough to sleep, gravid and swollen as I am; and once I hear it I cannot turn my thoughts away from it. So when that silken whisper began to tug at me I dragged myself to my feet to answer the summons. I drew on a wrapper, because the half-hearted English summer night did not warm me past the top of my skin, and padded on naked feet down the stairs and through the dim passages until I came into the orangery. The moon was full, dazzling among the foliage of the olive and lemon trees, glinting through the stinking juniper. If it had not been for the walls and windows I might have thought myself transported — and I caught myself thinking: *home*. But that Mediterranean island was not home; it was never home, no matter how much I longed to belong there, no matter how I yearned to lose myself forever in the midday shade of the evergreen forests. I should have remembered that I am an Englishwoman, a Christian, alien and pale-skinned and above all James's wife. If I had held tight to those undeniable facts — if I had kept faith — then . . . Oh, but it is done, it is over, it is no good now.

I stood shivering and barefoot on the threshold, staring at the shimmer of reflections at the far end of the room, where

3

the glass cases stand half concealed by the greenery. The moonlight and shadows were so deceptive that I could make out nothing but my own wan face peering back at me through leaves, my thin shoulders and bony neck above the shocking mass of my breasts and belly. It was not until I stepped forward into a band of darkness, erasing myself, that I could make out the contents of the nearest vivarium: the branches dry on the dead stones, the scatter of fallen pine needles, the scabrous bundles that hung like limbed fruit from the webs that spanned from one side to the other. I could smell putrefaction. The sound that had woken me grew louder – or did it? Perhaps it was an illusion, perhaps it is always, ever, an illusion – and seemed to swirl about the room, coming from new directions or from every direction at once. It is neither a song nor a susurrus, not a call nor a creak nor a command; and yet it is all of those. It cut my breath and made my innards roil. I found my legs carrying me towards the tank, until I was barely a hand's width from the glass.

Within the tank, something moved. At first it was hardly perceptible, a little trembling in the cobweb, a glint of moonlight too brief to fix my gaze upon. Then, with its peculiar darting rush, the spider was poised in front of me. Its abdomen glistened like a polished mineral; its precise legs were dotted with vivid red at the joints. I was glad of the pane between us. But as I kept my gaze steadily upon it, I grew conscious of more movement, from every side: until at last I glanced up and across, and saw that in each tank a spider was emerging from its corner or crevice, advancing into the dense heart of its web. It must have been my footsteps across the floor, or some other variation in vibration, temperature or humidity – indeed, let us be rational, James would cry! But to my sleepless mind, it had the deliberate improbability of a nightmare. I could feel the hostility, the reproach in every eye – and there were so many of them. So many eyes, and each one turned on me . . .

I said, although not aloud, Forgive me.

I said, I did not mean to bring you here.

I said, Are you hungry? I shall bring you more food. I shall bring it to you alive. And I meant it, even though it made my gorge rise to remember the long sea voyage, and the looks that the sailors turned on me when I begged them for live rats at any price. I had not known I could be so fierce, so devoid of womanly tenderness; I had not imagined that I could sacrifice my finer feelings so entirely. A rat's panic is surprisingly like a man's, I discovered, and yet if it was necessary to lean over the opened lid of a glass tank and drop a wriggling, squealing, scratching and biting victim to certain death, I found that I could do it without blenching. I saw in James's expression what I had become. He would have said that he approved, that he had commanded me to keep the spiders alive, that it was the least I could do to atone – but his frown belied him. He never said so, but I think he looked at the rats, caught in their cauls of silk and sucked dry, and wondered whether, under different circumstances, I would baulk at greater crimes.

I said, What can I do?

The roaring in my ears rose. It was like the sound of the surf against the shore, the night we left. I know perfectly well (yes, let us be rational!) that the noise is made not by the spiders themselves, but by their silk – and indeed that it is not exactly the silk either, that the sound is a mere reflection, no more innate in the silk than the colours of iridescence can be distilled out of a beetle's shell. But that did not protect me from the shuddering impression that the spiders remembered that night, too, the night we left Kratos – that they could follow

5

my thoughts, that they were deliberately imitating the hoarse crash of the waves on the sand, in furious reproach.

I was too sick, afterwards, to set it down here: but perhaps I will, now. All that I can remember, at least . . . I remember a wallowing bed beneath me that became the hard slats of a dinghy; I remember vast nausea that overcame me as I raised my head, so that I vomited helplessly into something that I only began to realise was the sea. And I remember dim shapes of stone overhanging the water as we went further along the shore, and James sitting rigid opposite me, a whitish blur resolving slowly into his double-flickering face, wearing a smile that I did not yet understand. Behind him, a dark figure moved like an automaton, and I heard the dip and splash of oars. I do not recollect whether I was obliged to gasp out an enquiry, or whether James was pleased to volunteer, as I retched, the information that we were, at last, on our way back to England; that I should become a good wife again, or reap the consequences; and that it was not only his intention but his absolute conviction that he should become a wealthy and respected man. I do not think that any of those pronouncements made much impression on me, at the time. I was too bewildered, too absorbed in trying to fix my eyes upon the lurching cliffs. I had not said farewell to Hira. I felt as though some deep root of me had been wrenched from the anchoring rock and was withering already in the salt air. I wish I had launched myself out of the boat, desperate and ill as I was: I would have made landfall, or drowned. But I had not the presence of mind. I was carried, like a good wife, on the tide of another's desire, even though it bore me away from everything I held dear. Well, not everything, I suppose; but I did not know then what else the tossing boat carried. I could not even keep a steady gaze on the line of the shore; a moment later the nausea took hold of me again, and everything about me blurred and spun.

Perhaps James took pity on me, for when the spasms receded and I was able to catch my breath, he took my hand. 'Let us pray,' he said. 'Almighty God, look upon your servant Sophia and lead her to repentance. Chastise her as a father would, until the black taint of sin is washed away by her tears. And carry us both in your hands, back to your blessed land of England.' He looked at me for a moment; when I began to retch again, he said, clearing his throat sharply, 'Amen.'

'I must go back,' I said, when I could speak. 'I must see Hira.'

He shook his head.

'James,' I said, 'please, I cannot leave like this, without a word. I cannot. It is wrong – it would be unbecoming.'

I landed upon the word without thinking, for it is one of his own favourite epithets; how many times has he condemned the villagers for their lack of proper English decorum and manners? But he jerked his head as though it were a bee sting. 'You dare to say so!' he said. 'Well, pardon me if I do not quite believe in your high feelings. You will come to understand the depth of your transgressions in time, I hope. As for seeing that— for seeing *her* again . . .! No, naturally we will not turn back now. We are fortunate to get away just before the autumn storms. Wipe your face, hold your tongue, and bend your thoughts on Him who sees and judges you.'

'A farewell,' I said, 'only a farewell . . .'

'It is out of the question.'

I could see from James's face – which hung as flat and white as a mask – that no pleading, no abasement would make him relent; but I cried, in desperation, 'Then if not for a farewell, then because I am sick! Can you not perceive that I am not fit to travel? Give me a day – an hour – to recover, on dry land—'

'It is nothing,' he said. 'It will soon pass. It is only the after-effects of a soporific. I was obliged to ensure that you would come with me without fuss.'

He was looking down at me as I have seen him look at whores. I could not bear it. I closed my eyes, and against the weltering flesh-dark of my eyelids I saw him as he was when we first came to that shore: full of energy and grace, a little ambitious to be sure, but a good man. That man was long gone: murdered, I thought, by this one. And I was filled with such rage and hatred that I leapt to my feet in the swaying boat, not knowing what I intended.

Perhaps, after all, I am glad that a wave flung me down again; I do not want to dwell on what might have happened, if I had struck out. (Am I, as James would have it, a woman who would give in to a terrible impulse, a woman who must be protected from herself? Oh, it does not matter, it does not matter.) I crashed backwards, and found myself rolling in the foul-smelling water at the bottom of the boat, while the pain in my ribs took my breath away. James said, 'You will hurt yourself if you do not master your agitation.' He did not offer me his hand, this time.

I groaned and covered my face. As I drew my knees towards my belly my feet struck against something with a peculiar resonance. It made a hollow wooden sound, but with an elusive, harmonic edge, like the knell of a sunken ship's bell. James snapped, 'Careful, there!' and slapped my ankle away. As I raised my head I discerned several boxes wedged under the seat of the dinghy: they were about the size of my clasped hands, or a little larger, and all were wrapped in sacking and tied with leather thongs. James pushed his leg forward to protect them, contorting himself as though he was at once afraid for, and afraid of them; as though they were both precious and loathsome. I think it was not the sound they made, but the expression on his face, that revealed to me – like a curtain being drawn aside – what they contained.

'What is in those boxes?' I said, although I knew.

'I am taking as many specimens home as I can,' James said, and coughed suddenly as though he had swallowed a fly. 'For the most part I have commanded them to be loaded at the port where we will board the *Prosperity*. I have high hopes that they will survive in the West Country; the climate is kinder than Sussex. I intend our garden to be renowned among both landscapists and Classical scholars.'

'But they are not seeds, in those boxes,' I said.

'There were a few species that are too localised to be ordered and collected elsewhere. Come, come, Sophia, there is no need for histrionics. I have merely taken a few of either sex, to breed . . .'

I do not think I answered. I do not think I was capable of it. I wondered how James would respond to the trampling of religious texts underfoot – to the burning of Bibles . . . No doubt he would think the analogy sacrilegious.

I bent my head.

'They are only spiders, for pity's sake, Sophia! Interesting ones, I grant you. But it is mere superstition . . .'

I should have asked him the difference between religion and superstition, except that the former is what he believes, and the latter what I believe. I should have—

Oh, let it go. Let it go, Sophia. It is bootless, it is gone, it is over. He followed me to the sacred place, and looked with hateful eyes upon what happened there; and then, later, he drugged me. He strode into the forest and plucked the spiders from their webs as though he had every right; he stuffed them into boxes as if they were inanimate trifles; he took them miles from their proper place without a second thought. But there is nothing to be said, because no Englishman would regard this as extraordinary. If I myself, ten years ago, had encountered a white woman who objected to the reasonable collection of specimens for the education and enlightenment of the English public (who are surely more interested in the lands of Homer and Ovid than those who actually live in them) – well, I should have blinked and bitten my lip, and marvelled a little at her benighted views. Now . . .

Sometimes I think I cannot bear it. How much I miss Hira! As I stood in front of the spiders last night I wrapped my arms around my belly, trying to conjure her solid female strength. Perhaps all she felt for me was pity; but I would rather have her pity than James's esteem. Even now – no, especially now. Now that I am – as James might say – *in a delicate condition*, or, as I prefer, *pregnant*: pregnant as a prophecy is pregnant, brooding as a romantic hero broods. If she were only here to rub my back with oil, to murmur those half-songs that promise an easy deliverance, to feed me segments of lemon to quell the churning of my innards. And, when the time came, to take my hand and lead me to the silk tent where I might cry as loud as my lungs would let me – and emerge, as Misia did (or was her name Mila? already my memory betrays me), gingerly into a new-made world, a baby wrapped between my milky breasts . . . I should not have written that. It makes me think too clearly of what lies before me here: confinement and strangers and cold hands forcing me apart. I remember an aunt telling me once that they would not open the box that held the doctor's instruments until she had been blindfolded.

I am afraid. There is no way out. There is nothing to do but wait.

I reached out and laid my hand against the glass. Perhaps the touch of flesh against the pane stilled some resonance, because the ocean-roar in my ears quietened to a kinder hiss, like slow spring rain. I said, We are all exiles.

The eyes went on looking at me, all of them. If the tank that I was touching had been large enough I might have stepped into it, dragged the cobweb up and around my shoulders like a shawl, and lain down. I might have stayed there, singing to the spiders, singing to the child that weighs like a stone in my womb, until I fell asleep, drunk on the echoes. What would I have dreamt of, before they drained me dry? What would my child?

Wait, we must wait. I have so few things left to which I can be faithful. I can count them on my fingers, as though I am looping a thread over each in turn: the child, the spiders, the memory of Hira. And – perhaps – the memory of the island itself, hot and wild as the beginnings of the world, and its skies and pines and the smell of the sea. In comparison England is cold and bare as a painted nude, keeping her arms crossed over her narrow breasts – breasts meant to be coyly glimpsed, to please men's eyes, not to nourish. Hira would despise this country, the men who own it and the women who love them – or, no, she would only be mystified, amused and a little sad, as she often was when she understood where I came from and who I was.

No doubt she is not amused any more. What did they do, when they saw that the holy places had been desecrated? Did they blame James? Did they blame me? Did Hira think that I had crept away willingly, that I deliberately kept my silence when I should have cried out to wake and warn them all? Or worse, that I helped James, that he knew the way there not because he had crept after me but because I had shown him? Did she curse me?

That is the only thing for which I pray: that she did not curse me. I do not know to whom I am addressing that prayer. It is not James's God, that ever-judging, ever-merciless father like an Englishman in his celestial study. Neither is it the vindictive raptor gods of the old stories. Sometimes I wonder if it is the spiders. Please, I say to them, please. Please do not let Hira hate me. If there is a curse, turn it aside. Do not let it touch me, or the child. Or you. It is a paradox, to pray to them for their own safety: it must mean that I do not truly believe they have any power. That my prayer is only superstition, and James is quite right.

And last night, I said to them again, what can I do? I will do anything.

They did not answer. I put one hand on my belly and willed the child to quicken, but she is obstinate, she waits for something, some voice that she has not yet heard. With the other hand I leant hard against the glass – certain and yet not certain that I would not press hard enough to break it.

I said, I will keep you alive. Whatever comes, you and your children will stay alive. I promise.

One

Henry was polishing the whorls of a silver ear when the shop bell jangled; or, rather, he was holding the ear and a smeared rag while he stared at the rain falling against the windows. He watched the dusk close in, his thoughts very shallow, noticing the tracks of raindrops on the panes and the slow darkening of the sky above the crowded London roofs. It was only the chime of the bell that hung above the door and the noise of the traffic in the street outside that returned him to himself. He jerked upright. As he did, he fumbled the ear and it skittered over the counter to fall at the feet of the man who had entered.

The man stooped for it and straightened up, turning it over in one hand while he took off his dripping hat with the other. From his gait, Henry had thought him young; but now, in the lamplight, he could see that he was in late middle age, although his head of hair was still full and his eyes were as merry as a boy's. He said, 'What an extraordinary thing. A hearing aid, I suppose?'

'An historical one,' Henry said, 'designed to replace the natural pinna of the ear, if it is absent. It's decorative, really.' He wrapped the ear in the grimy rag, and put it in a drawer under the counter. When he looked up again, the visitor

13

was pivoting slowly, his dripping coat leaving a circle of water on the carpet.

'What a charming establishment. I feel as though I have stepped into a collection of curios.'

It was true that the ranks of mahogany and glass cabinets looked at their best in the warm gleam of brass and lamplight. In the shining cases every object was set apart from its fellows, as though it should be touched only with reverence; and certainly many were both outlandish – the auricles, the audinets, the cornets and the *apparitor auris* – and ostentatious, plated or thinly veneered or lacquered, so that to the uninformed eye they would seem both rich and strange. It was the sort of shop where asking for a price was generally a roundabout process, if money were mentioned at all. Argyll had often said, 'It is not a *shop*, Latimer, it is an *emporium*.'

'Mr Argyll would be very glad to hear that you approve, sir,' Henry said.

'Your father?'

'No,' Henry said. He was too weary to feel the old flash of resentment when he thought of the & *SON* that Argyll had had added to the gold lettering on the frontage, without consultation. 'My father-in-law, as it happens. My name is Latimer.'

'Ah,' the man said, and smiled. It was a wry, complicit sort of smile, and for a moment an answering spark of warmth jumped in Henry's chest, not quite strong enough to ignite. 'Well, it is very intriguing.' He put his hat on the counter and strode to the furthest corner of the room, tilting his head to scrutinise the conch-spirals of an elaborate French trumpet. A few seconds later he moved on, while his breath lingered, evaporating slowly from the glass. He stopped in front of the shelf of invisibles – the nearest set were gold-plated – and tapped on the case as though the little objects might squirm on their bed of crimson plush. 'What are these? These things like buds on a stem?'

'Those are not especially effective,' Henry said. 'They are designed to hold open the walls of the external auditory canal, but in fact that is very rarely a solution to the problem.' As the man moved on, he added, 'I take it you are not— That is, are you looking for yourself, sir?'

'On behalf of my daughter.'

'Then, perhaps over here . . .' Henry gestured to the case which held the ladies' auricles, with their flowered head-bands and coiled nacreous shells.

The man nodded, but he did not move in the direction Henry had indicated. He took out his watch, consulted it and put it back in his pocket. 'Do you ever feel as if they are all listening to you?'

'All the time,' Henry said, 'but I never say anything worth remarking.'

The man laughed. 'I find that hard to believe, somehow.' He went on looking at Henry, and although his grin faded, the light in his eyes did not. 'Funny, isn't it? You sell sound, and I sell silence. We are two sides of the same coin.'

Under that intent gaze Henry felt his face grow warm; and yet it was oddly exhilarating. He cleared his throat. 'You sell . . . ?'

'Oh, did I not . . . ? Forgive me. My name is Ashmore-Percy. I have an appointment with Mr Argyll.'

Henry fumbled for the memorandum book that was kept beside the till. The man had announced his name as if it should be familiar, and in fact Argyll had said something at luncheon – and there it was, *Sir Edward Ashmore-Percy at half past four o'clock*. Henry should have been expecting him. 'I shall find Mr Argyll directly. Will you come through to our consulting room? Shall I ring for tea?'

'Thank you.'

He showed the man – Ashmore-Percy – through the doorway into the consulting room. It was dimmer in here, and in spite of the fire in the grate the air was chilly. He gestured to the deep winged armchair, set a lamp on the table and turned to leave, letting his eyes slide past the shrouded piano with its empty stool and unlit candles. Argyll was already in the doorway. 'Get some tea,' he said, *sotto voce*. 'I sent Townsend to post a letter.' But as soon as he stepped forward his voice changed, taking on a new unctuousness: 'Sir Edward,' he said, 'this is a pleasure. An honour. I do hope my son-in-law has not kept you waiting long.'

Henry did not hear the reply. By the time he returned, bearing a loaded tray, they had clearly got down to business. He caught the end of Ashmore-Percy's sentence: '. . . love her dearly,' he said, and Argyll responded with a *mm-hmm* that dripped with sympathy. 'She simply must learn to speak. She must! Otherwise she will be a prisoner in her own life. You can imagine my feelings, as a father—'

Henry stooped to pour the tea and passed a cup to Ashmore-Percy.

'Thank you,' he said, with a swift look at Henry. 'So, you see, Mr Argyll, I must do everything I can for her. I would like to know what you suggest.'

'Well, Sir Edward, I am very glad you have come to me. Doctors are useful people, of course, but their range of solutions is limited. It has sometimes happened that apparently incurable cases have been helped immeasurably by mechanical means – and *we* are the experts in those. I can promise nothing, you understand – but there is still hope, oh yes, I venture to say that you may continue to hope.' Argyll smiled.

'That is excellent news.'

'The only difficulty is that the young lady is not here for

me to assess. Our service tailors the auricle to the ear, you see. It is a skilled job. Thank you, Latimer, you had better go and watch the shop.'

Henry felt both men's eyes follow him as he went. Behind him, he heard Ashmore-Percy say, 'Ah. I see. There is no use my buying anything now, then. Well, never mind. Thank you anyway.'

'That said, I am sure some arrangement might be made—'

'No, indeed, I understand your point entirely. How can you tell what would be effective, unless she is in your presence? I appreciate your candour, Mr Argyll.'

'Ha,' Argyll said, and Henry heard a note of ill-concealed regret in his voice. 'I am a professional, Sir Edward. I pride myself on my integrity and rigour. But we can certainly find a way. Many of my clients prefer to receive me in their own homes—'

'I will not occupy any more of your time today. We are both busy men, I dare say.' There was a rustle of upholstery as the visitor got to his feet. 'Good afternoon, Mr Argyll.' Then he strode out into the main shop. He paused when he saw Henry, as if he might add something, but in the end he only nodded a farewell. He opened the door with a jangle and stepped out into the rainy blue dusk.

'Blast it!' Argyll said. He stood in the doorway of the consulting room, grimacing. 'I thought I had him. A man like that – money to spend, and high hopes . . .'

Henry said nothing. He had felt his own pulse of chagrin when the door shut, but he could not exactly identify why; certainly he did not care very much about the loss of business. But now the shop seemed colder.

'Blast,' Argyll repeated, but more softly. As he passed Henry to go back into the office, he glanced sideways into the consulting room. There was a fractional hitch in his step, and a sudden fixity in his expression. Henry followed his gaze: he was looking at the piano, with its unlit candles and empty music-stand. For the first time that afternoon Henry felt something other than resentment for the older man. But before he could speak – if he had thought of anything to say – Argyll had already mastered himself, and a moment later he had disappeared through the door behind the counter.

Henry passed his hands over his face. The bell jangled again. He drew a weary breath and raised his head.

'My hat,' Ashmore-Percy said, pointing to where it still sat beside the memorandum book. His hair was wet, and a streak of moisture was running down his temple.

Henry fumbled for it. 'Here.'

'Thank you.' He took the hat from Henry's outstretched hand, but he didn't put it on his head. Instead he was looking at Henry's sleeve, and the black armband. When he met Henry's eyes, he was not abashed – as most people were, when they were caught staring – but quite self-possessed. 'Was it your wife?'

'Yes,' Henry said. Of course, he would have seen Argyll's armband, too.

'I'm sorry.'

Henry had heard that sentiment, or variations on it, more than he cared to remember. Even if anyone truly was sorry, it made no difference, it was no consolation, Madeleine would still be dead . . .

But Ashmore-Percy was watching him, his mouth a little quirked, his gaze level; and to Henry's surprise it came to him that after all it was something, it was like meeting someone else on a road that had seemed the loneliest in the world.

'Take heart.'

Henry opened his mouth to reply; but suddenly, humiliatingly, he felt his throat tighten, and he did not dare acknowledge the other man's unlooked-for comfort. He said, grasping desperately for a new subject, 'You said, sir – you said you sold silence. What did you mean?'

There was a little silence then: as though the word *silence* were a flask that had broken, and let its essence spill into the space between them.

Ashmore-Percy said, 'But I thought—?' and broke off with a rueful grimace. 'Perhaps you haven't heard of me,' he said, 'and why should you have done? One becomes accustomed to being recognised, but of course outside one's own *petit monde* hardly anyone knows or cares that one exists . . . I do sell silence, quite literally! But you needn't look like that, I'm not a blackmailer or an assassin. No, I own the factory that makes Telverton silk.'

Henry raised his eyebrows. He was conscious that he was expected to show some definite reaction to this, and already he did not want to disappoint this man. 'I see,' he said.

'Ah, you haven't heard of that either. A pity. I wish more people had heard of it, and saw fit to drape their drawing rooms with it, too. But let me enlighten you.' He laid his hat on the counter, fumbled in his pocket and drew out a square of glimmering white fabric. He pushed it into Henry's hand. 'Now,' he said, with an intent, smiling look in his eyes, 'what do you think of it?'

For an instant Henry had the sense that he heard high notes in the air – or rather, *had* heard them, like the aftermath of a dream. Obediently he looked at the little scrap of silk in his fingers. It was so thin he could hardly feel it; supple as oil, light as air, and with a lovely watery lustre that made the coils of silver and mother-of-pearl on the

19

shelves around him seem suddenly dull in comparison. It was as if the light around him had been quenched; and a different, unearthly radiance was welling through the threads of the silk. He said, 'It is beautiful,' but before the last syllable had left his lips he started and glanced over his shoulder: he was sure he'd heard an answering whisper, just at the edge of audibility.

Ashmore-Percy laughed. 'Put it to your ear,' he said. 'No, the other way up. Here, let me.' He turned it over in Henry's palm with warm fingers. 'Now try.'

Henry lifted it, cupping his hand. He did not know what he was expecting: perhaps the shh-shh of a seashell, or a softening as though a curtain had been drawn between his mind and the outside world. In spite of what Ashmore-Percy had said, he was not expecting silence. Or, at least, not this silence. Not utter nothingness; not an absence as complete as an earful of clay . . . He jerked it away, and the familiar noises of traffic and rain flooded back. 'What is it?'

'Astounding, isn't it? Keep it, if you like. Recommend it to anyone who wants to cut out the noise of the street. I suppose it's in your line of work, in a way.'

Henry stuttered, 'That's very kind,' because he could not think of anything else to say.

'Spider silk,' Ashmore-Percy said, rocking back on his heels like a boy. 'From *Pseudonephila graeca sireine*, the silver orb-weaver, only found on Kaphos – no, Psaxos . . . oh, I forget. Some remote Greek island, anyway. We breed them down in the West Country and draw out the silk to weave in the factory there. My father set up the factory for lace, you know – he made his fortune adapting knitting machines – but I was the one who turned the whole place over to spider silk. We've been doing it for nearly ten years now. And it has been— It promises to be a great success. In another year or so, you'll hear Telverton silk talked about everywhere you go.'

'I don't doubt it.' Henry opened up the square of silk and smoothed it flat on the counter. As his hands passed over it he caught another almost inaudible murmur.

'That is the wrong side. It's warp-knit, not really woven, you see. The sides have different effects. To attain silence it must be hung with the other side outwards.'

'And – this side?' Henry smoothed it again. It was so subtle, so fluid, that he could hardly feel friction against his palm; and yet it gave off that faint tintinnabulation, a kind of crackle that was at once melodious and queasy.

'It seems to create some sort of unpredictable vibration. We call it turbulence. If there's a lot of noise, it gives some people a bit of a headache. But it's nothing, a minor inconvenience. The price you have to pay for perfect silence, I suppose.'

'Turbulence,' Henry echoed, and he seemed to hear the deeper notes of his voice lingering for a moment before they died away.

'We don't know exactly how it works,' Ashmore-Percy said. 'But isn't it extraordinary? Tell everyone you know, won't you?'

Henry nodded. He had never been so conscious of the hearing instruments around him, the ranked cones and spirals and pinnae of pearl and silver.

'Well, I must go. Good day, Mr Latimer.'

'Good afternoon, sir.'

There was a sudden rise in the volume of the rain as the door opened, and then the noise was muffled again. Henry bowed his head over the silk, staring into its silvery depths as if it were water. He rolled a corner of it between his fingers, and as the silent side was uncovered it seemed to make a hole in the fabric of reality, a place where every sound was swallowed.

He swept it off the counter and into a drawer. He locked it, and pocketed the key. Then he raised his eyes to the shop, with its endless shelves of dead, disembodied ears.

Since Madeleine's death Henry had dreaded the moment when he was obliged, every night, to lay his head on the pillow and close his eyes. It was not that the house was quiet; it was that a few particular silences – beside him where Madeleine should have been, in the dust-sheeted room above which should have been a night nursery, and the passage where a nursemaid's footsteps should have come and gone – drew his attention to the noise. The ticking clock in the study, the whine of a dog in the next-door yard, or the distant cries of a drunken brawl some streets away would jerk him without fail out of the beginnings of rest. He lay with clenched fists, cursing London and everyone in it; and once he had allowed himself to reach this pitch of fury – irrational, he knew, and yet irresistible; all he wanted, by heaven, was unconsciousness! – he knew that even if the sounds were to cease entirely it would still be hours before he could sleep. During the day he gritted his teeth to hear the organ-grinders and the street sellers outside, and had to restrain himself when Argyll slurped his soup; but it was at night, as though the darkness amplified every creak and yell, that he thought he might go mad. If only Madeleine had been there to mock him gently, and fold a sleep-warm arm about his neck; or if he had heard her voice overhead in the nursery, murmuring a lullaby, or her footsteps pacing up and down . . . He would not have minded that. Or even a child squalling – even less, a child squalling . . . He pressed his hands over his ears until his arms ached. He almost envied Argyll's elderly clients, with their frowns and their hearing trumpets. What a blessed relief it would be, never to be troubled by noise again.

So that night, when as usual he could not sleep, he found himself dressing, descending the creaking stairs and letting himself into the shop to pull open the drawer and slip the glimmering square into his pocket. He had meant to leave it untouched – there had been something too like enchantment about it, when he laid it upon the counter – but now, in his gritty-eyed sleeplessness, he could see that his qualms were childish, based on nothing but superstition and distrust of novelty. If it might prove a remedy . . . He remounted the stairs with a soft tread, in case Argyll too was awake. Then he undressed and lay down in the fading warmth, and turned his head so that one ear was buried in the pillow. He fumbled for the silk, hesitated so briefly he could deny it even to himself, and laid it over the other ear.

It was like a spell, or a miracle. The dog, the man, the ticking clock were extinguished as cleanly as a mirage. After a moment he clutched at the cloth, unnerved, in case the whole world had disappeared; but when he was sure that he could still hear, and the cacophony of the city continued regardless, he let it fall again. He felt the silence flood into him like a long, easy breath. It eased the tension in his limbs and the soreness behind his eyes; and at last it swept him away like a warm current, into a dreamless dark.

All through the days that followed, he felt an unfamiliar peace. He put the silk (rolled into a twist so slender it could have passed through a wedding ring) into his pocket, and kept it with him. When he was trapped in the consulting room, making an effort to speak tactfully and clearly, 'And is *this* an improvement . . . ? And this? And this? Ah, then shall we try the flowered auricle? It has a certain elegance, perhaps for evening wear . . .' Even when his gaze caught the piano with its dusty candles – and in spite of himself he remembered Madeleine's snatches of Beethoven, and the way the old men would lean back and sigh, letting the hearing tubes dangle from their wrinkled hands as if after all their deafness was neither here nor there . . . Even then, he could drag his thoughts away. Nothing had changed; Madeleine was still dead; his days were as monotonous, his horizons as limited as before. But there was, now, the possibility of retreat: as though the silk were a way out. Or was it even simpler? Not only the silk, but the man who had given it to him. *Take heart*, Sir Edward Ashmore-Percy had said; and for the first time since Madeleine's death, Henry had not felt alone.

But slowly, as he grew habituated to its presence, the silk – and the memory of Sir Edward's smile, easy and brilliant as a struck match – became less remarkable. Things drove it from his mind: Townsend's monthly tantrum, the customer who tried to sneak out with a gold-plated telescopic trumpet in his pocket . . . And the latest missive from his cousin in the North, which was terse and dutiful, as always, and which Henry read twice, his toast drying to leather on the plate in front of him, before he held it out over the breakfast table to Argyll.

Ordinarily the older man took it without a word and ran his eyes over it briefly before passing it back, but this morning he was absorbed in his own letter, one written on crested, gilt-edged notepaper. At last, with a sigh, he leant back in his chair. 'It seems that I shall have to leave you for a few days,' he said.

'What?'

'I have been summoned by Sir Edward Ashmore-Percy, do you remember him? He came into the shop to ask about a hearing aid for his daughter. A charming man. Well, it appears that he would like me to go and visit, so that I can see her in person.'

Henry stared at him.

'He lives in Devon. A very fine house, I believe. Newly built, best of everything. He is known for his prodigality. I seem to recall he is working on some new invention to make his fortune – or replenish it. What's the matter, laddie?'

Henry drew back his hand, which was still holding his cousin's letter, and laid it carefully down. He thought of the square of silk in his pocket. He had not told Argyll of it. He turned his eyes to the windows. Below a grey sky the winter-worn garden was narrow and dim; the louring clouds created the illusion that the walls were creeping inwards. He said, 'Might it be easier for me to go?'

Argyll passed his hand across his eyes. 'I know,' he said, 'that in the past you have shown a certain . . . talent, with customers. Given your initial reluctance to join the business, you do not acquit yourself badly. But since Madeleine . . .' He coughed. 'I do not think you would represent Argyll and Son at our best.'

Henry drew a breath, resisting the impulse to correct *son* to *son-in-law*. 'Sir Edward would welcome me. I am sure of it. He spoke to me, in the shop. We had a long conversation.' He added, to give credence to the claim, 'He gave me some of his silk.'

'Indeed? To what end?'

'As a gift,' Henry said, and then added, honest in spite of himself, 'or as a sample, really. He thought our customers might be interested in anything that helped reduce extraneous noise.'

'They might, at that,' Argyll said. 'And it is a long journey for an old man . . .' He sighed. 'You'll do it properly, mind? You must give the impression that you are a studious, scientific young man, not an idler.'

'I am not an idler.'

'Well. Not a – a *poet*.'

'I have not written— I have not *read* any poetry for months.'

'And you must be very patient with the child. God knows if—' Argyll cleared his throat, as if he had embarrassed himself. 'That is, she will certainly be backward, and probably ill-disciplined. If she lost her hearing before she began to speak . . .'

'Was it an illness?'

'An accident, from what I gather, although he does not go into detail. Clearly it is a painful subject for him. To be frank . . .' Argyll sighed. 'I do not necessarily think we will find an instrument that answers. It may well be a difficult case.'

'Yes,' Henry said. 'I see. Is she— I suppose she is capable of making her wishes understood?'

'Up to a point, I gather. It seems that at the moment she can say very few words at all, and relies greatly on miming and pointing.'

The image in Henry's mind flickered between a little cherub, grateful for any key to her silent prison, and a feral, tangle-locked scrap. 'Very well,' he said. 'Perhaps you might ask for more details, so that I can—'

'It would be extremely ill-mannered,' Argyll said. 'It is obviously a very delicate subject and a source of sorrow. I will set aside everything you might want. You shall have to take several cases of instruments. I will work on a list.' He got up stiffly, and nodded good day.

'Thank you,' Henry said, and bent his head over his empty plate, trying to quell the sudden elation that swept through him.

On the day before he left, Henry was so restless that he slipped out of the shop after luncheon, in spite of the bleak bitter day, locking the door behind him. There were no appointments, and Argyll would not be back until nightfall. On impulse he made his way west, towards Oxford Street.

But the girl in the mercery department of Marshall & Snelgrove only shook her head when Henry asked for Telverton silk. 'It has a – an acoustic effect,' he said. 'It is spider silk.'

'*Spider* silk? Our usual customers do not care to buy cobwebs, sir. If you are looking for cobwebs, I suggest you ask your housemaid.' She turned to follow another customer's gaze. 'That is both elegant and hardwearing, madam, but have you seen this *faille française* . . . ?'

He fumbled for the square of silk in his pocket, and held it out. 'Look,' he said. 'Sir Edward Ashmore-Percy himself—'

'If you wish to present a sample for our consideration, please apply to the manager,' she said, over her shoulder. 'Ah, madam, but your complexion is so fine – perhaps our new shade of mauve . . .'

He shoved the silk back into his pocket and spun on his heel. He had come out of mere curiosity; how dare she treat him like a salesman? He strode away through the displays of mantles and gloves and furs, and emerged a few moments later into the driving sleet. He set his teeth and walked into the wind. Never mind. It had only been a whim. And tomorrow he would be far away, on his way to Cathermute House and Sir Edward's deaf young daughter.

He entered a little alley that led between two tall houses.

The light was failing. Ahead of him a church and an overgrown graveyard shimmered through the veils of sleet. Madeleine's tomb was a long way away, the other side of Holborn Hill: he did not know why he slowed now to stare over a tumbledown part of the wall at a rain-blurred angel. A gust of wind brought ice and water pattering around him, harder than ever. And he thought—

He turned. Through the echoing hiss of the rain he had heard a voice, singing: *Hush, my love, hush, my dove* . . . The edges of his vision rippled, like a gauze waiting to be drawn aside. Surely . . . but the lullaby rose and fell, and when he stepped forward it softened until he could not be sure he had heard it at all. He swallowed, straining his ears through the rain and the odd clamour of the wind in the narrow space. Of course he had not heard Madeleine; maybe some woman at a window close by . . .

But it had been like her, so like her. Those were the words she had murmured as she stroked her belly, with that lovely, private light in her eyes . . .

He looked around, queasy with – what? Not hope, exactly, nor fear, but something in between. His eye caught a glimmer on the ground, and he stooped to look more closely.

Somehow the square of Telverton silk had fallen from his pocket. He must have pulled at it unconsciously, he thought, knotted it around his fingers and let it drop. Now it lay wrinkled and wet in a puddle, but still with that lustrous gleam, still bright enough to catch his attention in the wintry dusk. He bent for it.

As he did so, the voice he had heard rose again. He scooped the silk up and whirled round; but as his grasp closed over the fabric, the world steadied itself, solid and real. Cautiously he opened his hand. As soon as he did, it was there again: a creeping, haunting note, almost imperceptible.

He took a deep breath, listening. Sir Edward had said that the silk caused unpredictable vibrations – *turbulence*, he had called it – but Henry had not realised that it would sound so uncanny, so . . .

But no. It was not heart-rending. It was merely unfamiliar, so that naturally the human brain searched for the quickest way to render it intelligible. It was an acoustic phenomenon, not a supernatural one: intensified, no doubt, by the sibilant rain and the high brick walls, producing an effect that was liable to be mistaken for other things.

With a shiver he pushed the damp square into the depths of his pocket, and wiped the wetness from his face with his sleeve. Then he set off again, his head lowered, resolutely thinking of the next day, and the task that awaited him in Telverton.

Two

As the train rattled in towards the station, Henry shifted in his seat and turned his head from side to side. Something had changed: it was as if they had climbed steeply, emerging abruptly into a dazzling space above the clouds, where the altitude made it hard to catch his breath. He leant back, trying to identify the sensation. There was a ringing, like distant bells on the wind, and a slight giddiness when he moved. He stared past the rags of smoke and steam blowing across the window. Nothing in the grey vista of cinder-yard and warehouses rushing past was out of the ordinary, and yet he could have sworn that there was a kind of sparkling in the air – a lack of shadows and solidity, one dimension too many or too few – that his physical senses could not perceive.

The portly widow opposite him leant forward, proffering a rattling tin in a lace-mittened hand. 'Do try one, dear,' she said. 'Is it your first visit?'

With an effort he focused on the label. *Maddison's Incomparable TELVERTON NUMMS. A Sovereign Remedy for All Sickness, Confusion and Megrims, especially the new TELVERTON MALAISE.* 'No, thank you.'

'It's the factory noise and the silk everywhere, it can give you a terrible headache, if you are unaccustomed to it—'

'Really,' he said, 'you are very kind, but I am quite all right.' He turned back to the window, and was relieved to hear her settle back into her seat in a rustle of bombazine. Earlier he'd seen her eyes slide from his black necktie to his hatband, and she had an eager, motherly look: both were danger signs, and today of all days he had no desire for a stranger's sympathy.

Thankfully, in any case, the train was slowing now, rattling in a long curve under a footbridge and past the bulk of a gasworks. He got to his feet and grabbed his luggage, avoiding the widow's bright gaze as he piled the cases of instruments onto the floor between the other passengers' legs. A sudden shaking of points beneath made him lurch like a drunkard, and he reeled into the man opposite. 'I beg your pardon.'

'No need.' The man was a Quaker, sharp-eyed and dressed in grey. As the train rounded the curve in a graunch of brakes he too stood up, swaying with the movement of the train, and reached past Henry to open the carriage door. He paused, waiting for the final halt, his arm tense as though he begrudged every instant of delay. At last – as the train jolted to a stop – he swung the door open, glancing behind him as he did so. 'Yawn,' he said, and stepped out onto the platform.

'I'm sorry, I didn't quite—?'

The man tapped his own temple, in front of his ear. '*Yawn*,' he said, as if more syllables would be an expensive luxury. 'Opens the Eustachian tube.' Then, without waiting to see if he'd been understood, he disappeared into the growing crowd of people on the platform.

But Henry had no time to make sense of it; he had a strange, vertiginous feeling that the few steps to the door and onto the platform had stretched into miles, and that the train would bear him off again before he had time to disembark. He stooped, gathering the cases into his arms, and stumbled forward. Then, once he was safely out of the carriage, he set them down and stood still, letting other passengers move past, not quite trusting his legs. How absurd, it was as though he were drunk! Distantly he heard the door slam behind him – and more, others, a ragged tattoo of noise all along the length of the train – and the engine gathering steam to depart. Voices called out goodbyes, hellos, good wishes, mingling into an echoing cacophony. He blinked until the station came into focus.

A porter materialised at his shoulder. 'Help you with that, sir?'

'No,' he said, automatically, 'they are fragile.' The porter walked away with a sniff, and immediately Henry regretted it; surely he was more likely to drop them himself. He lifted them again – the instruments in their cases wedged against his chest, one finger looped painfully through the handle of his suitcase – and staggered carefully towards the ticket office. He had to wait for a group of women in rustling skirts to allow him to pass, but at last he found himself outside the station. In front of him was a Clarence, with a coat of arms on the door. A bored-looking coachman was leaning against the front wheel, whistling through his teeth.

'Mr Latimer? Going to Cathermute House?'

He hesitated; he had expected a hansom or a pony-trap. Then he nodded as though he were perfectly accustomed to gilt and grandeur, and clambered past the coachman into the dim padded inside of the carriage. The windows had curtain panels of Telverton silk, strung on wires to keep the fabric taut, and as the door shut behind him the bustle of the station and the grinding noise of traffic were extinguished. The blood started to flow back into his stiff fingers, and he sank back into his seat, limp with relief. So that was the Telverton malaise: a sliding disorientation, subtle but unmistakeable, like the first moment of over-indulgence. In fact, like over-indulgence, it was not unpleasant – but no doubt he would become accustomed to it, and the heady novelty of it would wear off.

As the carriage began to move he shuffled closer to the window, but the fabric across the glass was semi-opaque, like fine shell or mother-of-pearl. Yesterday, in Yeovil, he'd pored over the entry in Bradshaw as though the terse text (*Telverton, Devon line. Inns: the Angel, the Rose, the Rising Sun. Market day: Wednesday*) was some kind of code; but even the brief mention of the factory had told him nothing that he didn't know already. In Yeovil the innkeeper had warned about the Telverton malaise – then laughed and added, 'Only joking, sir, it's not much more than a headache, if you don't hang about next to the factory,' – but Henry had not anticipated its strangeness, the glittering aura that had descended so swiftly as the train approached the station. The relief he felt inside the carriage was tempered by an inexplicable urge to step out again. It was a fascinating phenomenon, one that made him conscious that he was somewhere new, somewhere entirely different from London – as though Telverton were an undiscovered country and the malaise the necessary sea-sickness of an explorer . . . He smiled a little at the thought, and drew a deep breath, hardly noticing the bitterness of soot in the air. Yes, that was it: he had washed up on a new shore, ready to begin a new life, far away from Argyll and the shop and the empty rooms above it. He had escaped. And here, under new, West Country skies, he would begin again. He would win Sir Edward's approval – no, why stop there? His friendship – and prove himself as the saviour of Sir Edward's little deaf daughter; he would show Argyll that he was worth his keep, after all; and he would—

He thought of Madeleine, and the smile on his face faded. Surely she would have encouraged him – she would have leant forward, taken his hands, and murmured, 'My dear, you must take every opportunity . . .' She would even, he thought, have understood his eagerness to leave Argyll and the absence where she and the child should have been. He was not betraying her – she would not have wanted him to suffer – and she was dead, for heaven's sake, it was not as if he could bring her back! But suddenly his throat was aching, and his eyes stung.

It was best not to dwell on it. He turned determinedly to the window, pulled the side of the silk panel away from the glass with one finger and squinted through the gap.

He caught a glimpse of a goods yard on the left. They passed a footbridge, a green, a row of new-built villas. A little further on was a terrace of low brick houses, and then shops, and then narrower, denser streets, while the tang of smoke and chemicals in the air grew stronger. Faint sounds of industry began to seep into the enclosed silence, through the chink between the silk and the window: the thump and groan of a distant engine, the low beat of ranks of machines . . . An unfamiliar taste began to spread across his tongue, and the pressure mounted again in his temples. Now they were trundling along a wider street past brickwork black with smuts, a glimpse of brownish water between high walls, dark cinders trodden into the mud. Then they swung around a corner and – through some peculiar trick of perspective – abruptly the factory chimney was there, materialising against the grey sky like magic, too tall and close for Henry to see the top. Just then, the confluence of traffic brought the carriage almost to a halt. He craned his head sideways to see as much as he could. The main buildings were visible as well above the walls, their windows like blank mirrors in the daylight, six storeys high. And the noise! Even through the small crack in the silk, the machines rumbled and thundered until his teeth hummed.

He stared for as long as he could, until the carriage wheels ground slowly around a corner, and the vision was hidden from him – although the sound still sang in his head, insinuating itself between the plates of his skull. Then, quite suddenly, they were driving through a slum. The traffic sped up as they passed a grimy row of cottages, so that he only caught a glimpse of two children gesticulating furiously at each other, their hands flying every which way as though carving threats from the air. A door slammed, just ahead, and a young woman stumbled into the street. She paused, sagging against a lamppost, her hand covering her face.

The carriage had already moved on, but in that brief moment her misery had been so clear, so desperate, that Henry spun round, peering, unable to dismiss what he had seen. 'Stop,' he said. 'Please, excuse me, *stop*,' before he realised that the coachman couldn't hear him. There was a bell-pull beside him – naturally, there had to be – and he tugged at it. A second later, reluctantly, the carriage ground to a halt.

'Are you quite well, sir?' The coachman jerked the door open and peered at him as though he was an invalid.

'Yes,' Henry said, pushing him aside. 'But that woman – she is in need of help. Wait here.'

'Best stay inside if you've got the echoes, sir. There's too many around here who need help.'

Henry waved him away and hurried back the way they had come, past a man slumped alone in a doorway, his mouth open and slack. But his attention was on the young

35

woman who was leaning against the lamppost, her chest heaving. 'Here,' he said, 'you are in distress. Is there anything I can do for you?'

She was dark-haired, full-mouthed, her skin pocked with little scars. She blinked, and more tears rolled down and dripped from her chin. Before she could speak, a bell rang. Another seemed to answer it, reflected from the opposite rank of houses – then more, coming from all directions, prolonged and brittle, as though the chimes were hammers against the glass hemisphere of the sky. Then, miraculously, they died away, and with them the terrible drone of the factory. Suddenly the world was wider, clearer, as though more blood had suddenly flooded into Henry's brain.

'That's the dinner bell,' she said, and her accent was strange, thickened, as though she were drunk, although her breath smelled only of decay. 'Let me go – when the shift changes they'll notice—'

'But are you all right? Here,' he said, and fumbled for a handkerchief to offer to her. His hand met the slippery square of silk in his pocket; but that was precious, he could not give her that. He tried his waistcoat. 'You are weeping,' he said. 'Has someone hurt you? If I can help . . .'

Her mouth twisted. 'No,' she said, 'you cannot. I must go.'

'I am sorry,' he said, helplessly. What had possessed him to want to comfort her? Only that something in her stance had made him think of Madeleine, reaching for the nearest support, when the birthing pangs began. Madeleine had been so brave, so absurdly gentle to him, as though he were the one suffering . . . At first, anyway, until the pains had got worse, and— But he did not want to remember. His fumbling hand found a few coins, and he pushed one into the young woman's hand. 'Take this,' he said. 'It is the least I can—'

'And what do you want for it, sir?'

'Nothing – no, for heaven's sake, nothing at all,' he said, feeling the heat rise in his face. 'Merely to help you.'

She raised her eyebrows at him, with a long look; and then she swung away, wiping her face on her sleeve as she went.

He might have followed her, but at that moment a few men appeared at the corner of the street, shouting and gesticulating. Then, all at once, the pavement was full of people jostling, yelling to one another, spilling forward in a human tide. Henry flattened himself against the lamppost, afraid that he'd get swept up by the oncoming press of bodies. Was there some emergency, some riot? But no, he realised, these were the factory workers going home for their dinner. There was something about the accent that grated on Henry's ear, and surely their voices were shriller and more piercing than in London. A group of older men walked in morose silence, until one stumbled in front of another; even then none of them spoke, but resorted to clumsy gestures that turned swiftly from hostile to violent. Henry had no wish to become embroiled in a local brawl, and in any case, the woman he had wanted to comfort had disappeared. With a mingled sense of failure and relief, he turned back before the surge of workers reached where he was standing.

The carriage was where he'd left it, and the coachman standing beside it. 'Got a pretty bad case, haven't you? Of the echoes,' he added, at Henry's look. 'Can hardly walk straight.'

'Nonsense. I am perfectly all right.'

'That's when you have to watch yourself, sir, when it just feels like you've had a few. There's a box of Numms under the window, you have one of those and relax – once we get out of Telverton you'll feel—'

'I thank you for your solicitude, but really, I do not need it,' Henry said, and swung the door shut on the coachman's reply.

The carriage began to move. He watched angular shadows pass over the gauze covering the windows. He wished he had waited till the mob had passed, and then followed the woman, insisted on assuaging her sorrow, somehow . . . But if he closed his eyes what he saw was not the woman but the factory, a glittering edifice, raw and shining. It was magnificent, as a torrent or a glacier was magnificent; it was unlike anything he had ever seen. He imagined the silk taking shape on the looms, growing inch after miraculous inch; he imagined great lengths of it being rolled onto bales, as rich and fine as anything in the world. He imagined the lovely whispering that rose from it when the wrong side was touched, like a phantom singing – but no, in the noise of the machines, it would not be a whisper but a roar, bone-shaking, the glorious thunder of a many-piped organ. So much pure sound: so much silk to answer it, echo it, transform it . . . It was absurd to call the effect a 'malaise', when it was closer to the thrill of hearing an orchestra in full voice. Beside it, the small human miseries of the slums were insignificant – or commonplace, at least . . . He hesitated, longing to ask the coachman to turn back.

But he was on his way to Cathermute House, and gradually, as they drove, the thought of the factory loosed its hold. After a while the shadows that crossed the windows grew sparser, and the light brighter. Now and again a tree came close enough to tint the inside of the carriage green, and Henry could smell a difference in the air – not so much a scent as a lack of one. His head cleared; he slid a finger between the curtain and the window and peered through again. Outside there were fields and oak trees and hedge-rows, expanses of leaf-green and the rust-red of West Country soil. Masses of cow parsley swayed beside the road. There was no noise but the wheels of the carriage and snatches of birdsong. He caught his breath, and abruptly he felt happier than he had since before Madeleine had died.

Now they were driving through the outskirts of a village. He pulled the curtain further away from the window, until his finger threatened to break the wire that held it in place – clearly, whoever had designed this carriage had no interest in looking out – and stared at the cottages with their neat, colourful garden plots, a stone bridge over a river, the lych-gate of an old church. At last the carriage turned and went through a great wrought-iron gate and past a handsome, newly built gatehouse. For a few moments Henry twisted in his seat, pleased by the neatness of the walls and the rosy stone; then he looked forward again as the drive rose grad-ually through wide parkland, swinging through a generous curve until the house came into view.

It was impressive. As he disembarked – trying to note with detachment the sudden creep of sweat in his palms and the acceleration of his heartbeat, now that he was really here – he forced himself to pause for a moment and look around, taking it in. The place had the same forceful newness as the gatehouse, built in the same rust-red stone, but it was huge – as grand as a church, with high windows, a deep porch and a square tower with a crenellated top. He gazed up at the tower and thought of adjectives: bold, masculine, splendid. In spite of himself, he added, in mental parentheses: expensive.

The coachman said, 'There.' He pointed.

Henry said, 'Yes, thank you,' and strode, his arms aching with the weight of his cases, in the direction the coachman had indicated. He hardly had to wait at all before the door was opened, and the maid led him along a little passage so quickly that he had to break into a staggering run to catch up. 'Mr Latimer, isn't it? Your room is in the east wing. Dinner will be on a tray.'

'And Sir Edward . . . ?' he said, panting a little.

'What about him?'

'Will I see him tonight, or . . . ?'

'He's on business. You're to see the girl tomorrow morning, after breakfast.' She pushed open a door and started up a staircase, and they came out into one of the main corridors of the house. He caught a glimpse of a tapestry, a frieze of roses and nightingales in a medieval style, and bare stone-work with neat new-hewn edges. He would have liked to look more closely, but the maid whisked along and it was all he could do to keep up. She took him along one corridor and another, until he'd quite lost his bearings; then they climbed a steeper, narrower set of stairs and emerged into a dim passage that seemed to run the whole depth of the house. She opened the door at the far end. 'This is your room.'

'Ah. Thank you.'

She nodded, and withdrew. He exhaled, feeling as though he had suddenly disembarked from a merry-go-round, and looked about him. The room was neither grand nor especially shabby: there was a wrought-iron bedstead, an armchair, a rug, a washstand, a desk and chair, and two low windows that looked out over the lawn on one side and a formal garden on the other. A few botanical prints hung on the walls, and the screen in front of the fireplace was embroi-dered with dusty ferns. It reminded him a little of his rooms in Cambridge: and it was a good feeling, the memory of when he was young and free, before he met Madeleine, before he gave up his dreams of poetry and success. Now his dreams were more mundane, but worthier: he would help a little girl to hear again, and be thanked by her grateful, aristocratic father . . .

He sat down at the desk, and as he looked around he caught sight of something glinting in the crack between the desk and the wall, like a blue gem. He bent down and picked it up. A corner of cobalt glass, seemingly broken from an octagonal bottle, like the ones that held laudanum. He turned it over in his fingers; there was a dusty brown residue on it, as though the bottle had been full when it was smashed. He was not sure what to do with it. As he cast around for a wastepaper basket, he noticed that the leg of his chair was splintered, and where the rug had slipped askew under his feet there was another stain on the floorboards. Both injuries were old; the raw wood of the chair had dulled with time, and the stain was faded by scrubbing and only just visible. When he slid the rug further sideways, he saw a pattern of marks as though paint had spurted out of a tube, or ink sprayed from a thrown inkwell – or some other liquid, once bright as carmine and thick as oil . . . He shook his head, trying to drive away the memory of Madeleine, and the blood that had soaked through her sheets, pattering onto the floor—

He shoved the rug back into place with his foot. Outside in the corridor he heard footsteps, and he got up and peered out. But the woman at the top of the stairs was not the maid, returning; it was the full-lipped, dark-haired girl who had wept in the street near the factory. He stared at her, and she tilted her head and stared back, without smiling.

'It's you,' he said. 'What are you—?'

'I do not believe we have met.' And they had not. He could see that now, as though her cool, precise voice had broken a spell. There was a similarity in her gait and the shape of her face, but that was all; and as he stared, even that seemed to evaporate.

He hesitated, taken aback. 'I mean—'

'No,' she said again. 'I'm afraid you are mistaken. Good day.'

Who was she? She was dressed soberly and without frivolity, but not like a servant. Then she opened a door on the other side of the landing, and he caught a glimpse of a bare room beyond and heard a snatch of birdsong coming through the open window. Was she the little girl's keeper? A maid, or a gaoler? As she stepped through the doorway she raised her hand, gesturing to someone out of sight, while the door swung closed behind her.

Henry took a few steps, as if to follow her, and then came to a halt. Abruptly he was conscious that he was travel-stained and crumpled, and he had hardly slept the night before. Tomorrow, he thought, tomorrow would be soon enough.

He went back into his room, shut the door, and bent to open the smallest case. He drew out Madeleine's picture, which he had wrapped carefully and packed last. It was a double frame, hinged in the middle: on one side was a watercolour of Madeleine as a little girl, while on the other a photograph of the Madeleine he had known, already a little thin from the sickness of early pregnancy, stared at him solemnly. The older and younger Madeleines might have been mother and daughter. He thought of Madeleine's own child – his own child – that he would never know, now, would never watch grow up—

He did not set the frame on the desk, as he had meant to. After a long moment he wrapped it again and pushed it back into the case. Then he drew the square of spider silk from his pocket and laid it out, silent side upwards. It shone like a pool of faint light in the shabby room. He shut his eyes, and let himself remember the giddiness that had swept over him as the train drew into the station, the magnificent thundering of the factory, and the echoing, glittering veil that had seemed to lie over the Telverton streets and sky. It did not drive away his sadness, but it eased it; and mixed in was something more elusive, so fragile that he hardly dared to call it hope.

Three

As Henry knocked on the door of the child's room after breakfast he heard the hour chime, and then, a few seconds later, another bell and another: as though the clocks at different ends of the house had held to the old way, instead of keeping new-fangled railway time. He turned his head, listening to the clanging music, the melodious disagreements between long-acquainted timepieces, and smiled. He had slept well – surprisingly well – in this new place, and now he felt light-hearted and determined, ready to begin his task and succeed. No matter how backward or ignorant the child was, he would be patient; and this very morning he would begin the long task of ushering her into civilised society.

The brown-haired woman opened the door, with the same level, uncompromising expression that she had worn the previous day. 'Yes?'

'I am Henry Latimer,' he said. 'I hope you are expecting . . .' He stopped. Behind her, the room was flooded with sunlight. At the far end there was a blackboard, with words on it: *river*, *lake*, *ocean*, *cloud*, *rain*, *flood*. In front of it, sitting at a bare wooden table, was a little girl – of five or six, perhaps, although Henry had never known any children and did not trust his own guess. She had paused in the middle of drawing

44

a picture on her slate, and was watching him with bright, inquisitive eyes.

'Yes,' the woman said. 'Come in. I am Miss Fielding, and this is Philomel.' She stepped aside, holding the door open like a footman; with the other hand she made a quick gesture to the little girl, who gave him a wide, beaming smile. It made her so like her father that Henry stared at her, entirely – absurdly – taken aback.

There was a silence. With an effort he wrenched his gaze away and looked around for somewhere to put his cases.

'You may set those on the table, if you wish.'

He obeyed. He brushed a fleck of dust off the lid of the top case, as if it endangered the instruments inside. He had thought himself prepared for every eventuality, but not this, not an ordinary, neatly dressed little girl, delighted at the interruption to her schoolwork . . . Argyll had said that she could hardly speak. But then, how could she be . . . well, as she was? He had never met a deaf-mute child; from the stories he had heard, they were sullen and feral, on the edge of idiocy, hardly human. This little girl, with her white-frilled pinafore and chalk-smudged cheek, left him entirely at a loss. She was a child like any other; a child like the one he and Madeleine might have had . . . He felt Miss Fielding watching him, and straightened up. 'Hello, Philomel,' he said, making the shapes of his mouth as clear as possible. 'I am Henry. I am delighted to meet you.' In the corner of his eye he saw Miss Fielding make another gesture. He said to her, 'What are you doing?'

Miss Fielding shook her head, but her cheeks were tinged with pink. 'She is learning to read the shapes of words on my lips, but you are unfamiliar, and she is still very young. Now, Philomel,' she added, turning to face the little girl, 'what do you say?'

The little girl took a big breath. 'H-ow – do – oo – do,' she said. She was looking past Henry, with the fixed frown that showed she was repeating a lesson. Then, abruptly, her face lit up again, and she began to gesticulate, touching her fingers together in a complicated pattern. But a moment later, in response to something Henry did not see, she subsided, biting her lip, and looked wide-eyed from him to Miss Fielding.

'What was that?'

'Nothing.'

'But—'

'I am afraid that sometimes she forgets we are forbidden—that we do not use fingerspeak any more. Philomel, you know we must use English now.' Miss Fielding angled her body away from the table, and Henry was almost sure he saw her make some signal to the child, half hidden by her skirt. 'Her father is determined that she should learn to speak aloud, so that she can participate in society. She cannot be limited to conversations with other people who can sign. Better that she should say a few broken words to the people who matter, than express herself perfectly to those who do not. True speech is what distinguishes us from animals, is it not?'

'I— Yes, I suppose it is,' he said, with the sense that it was not the right answer.

'But Philomel was brought up with fingerspeak – that is what I call our language of signs – so she sometimes reverts. Please don't tell Sir Edward about her lapses. It isn't disobedience, Mr Latimer, it's only that it is hard, when she is used to communicating freely . . .'

'Yes,' he said, automatically, 'it must be.'

'Thank you.' She smiled reassurance at the little girl, before turning back to Henry. 'You are a doctor, I take it? Or a miracle-worker?'

'I am an aurist. That is, I sell hearing aids,' he said, when she tilted her head. 'Or rather my father-in-law— Never mind. I have brought a selection of them, for her to try.'

'How do these hearing aids work?'

'The mechanisms are quite simple,' Henry said, glad to be on familiar ground. 'They take advantage of the natural laws of acoustics to amplify the vibrations of any sound. Sound, you see, is merely the compression and relaxation of a medium – generally air – which is conveyed to the ear, through the ear to the aural nerve, and thence to the brain. The instruments collect and concentrate the waves, to make it easier for the ear to hear them. In some cases, they use the bones of the teeth and skull to conduct the sound. If the problem originates in the middle ear, that can make an enormous difference.'

'I see,' Miss Fielding said.

'We'll try all of them and see what works best. How much hearing does the little girl have?'

'None at all.'

He stared at her. '*None?*'

'No. None. Did you imagine she was merely a little hard of hearing?'

He bent his head over the case, pressing his tongue against his teeth. 'Very well,' he said, after a moment. 'That decreases the chances of success, significantly.' Argyll must have known, and decided in advance that it was hopeless. No doubt that was why he was so quick to let Henry go in his place . . . But damn it, he would not be defeated, he would show Argyll that he was more than capable. 'And how long has she been deaf?'

'Since before she was born.'

A congenital malformation, then. Argyll had said it was an accident; had that been a deliberate lie? But he could not ponder it now. He could feel both pairs of eyes – one bright and enquiring, the other faintly antagonistic – on him, waiting. 'Never mind,' he said, 'we must not lose heart – there is still hope. It may take a little more application, that is all. Let us see what we can do.' He took out the top layer of instruments: a large, simple ear trumpet, a japanned trumpet, a double curve trumpet, and a dipper trumpet, and set them out on the table. The little girl stared at them, chewing her lower lip; they were, of course, Argyll's most expensive exemplars, and they had ornate edges and engraved flowers.

'Oh – excuse me,' Miss Fielding said. 'I must get my workbasket. I may as well use the time fruitfully.' There was an edge to her voice, as if the trials were a waste of time. She disappeared through the far door beside the blackboard.

In another case, packed on top of the audiphones and auricles, were a small whistle, a drum and five tuning forks. Henry took these out too, and laid them in a row along the table opposite the trumpets. Gradually he grew conscious that the little girl was waving to get his attention. At last there was a squeak as she wrote something, painstakingly, on the slate, and then a small chubby hand pushed it into view. *I MADE A POFM*, it said.

'A – what does this say?' Then he understood. A poem, indeed! And she was already getting to her feet, beaming, for all the world as if she were going to recite it. He said, 'That is very – I mean, there is no need . . .'

But she had not seen him speak, or if so she had not understood; she gave herself a little shake, assumed a very serious expression, and began to gesture.

At first he thought she was miming – was she pretending to walk, to open a gate, to pluck a flower from an over-hanging branch? Then he saw that it had something in common with the gesticulation of the factory workers. But it was not the brief primitive back-and-forth he had seen the older men use; he began to suspect that in fact there was a grammar to it, a complexity that eluded him entirely. She spun in a pirouette, twirling her finger at the same time so that he almost saw the circles within circles. Was she blown by an imaginary breeze, or embodying the play of a fountain? Now she had paused, her hand crushed to her cheek as though it held a rose. *Come into the garden*, he thought suddenly, *I am here at the gate alone* . . . He had loved to read Tennyson to Madeleine, until poetry became a reminder of all his defeated ambitions. And in spite of himself, the words beat in his head: *Beginning to faint in the light that she loves – to faint in his light, and to die* . . .

He said, 'I am afraid I don't understand . . .' But naturally she did not hear him. And he could not look away: there was something painful in his chest, to see the child so joyfully abandoned to – to what? It was not poetry, surely, it had no music, no cadence – and yet that garden was all about her, she moved through it as deftly as a dance, sure-footed, her hands grasping at invisible vines and blossoms . . .

She cupped emptiness softly between her palms, and then threw it upwards. For a moment he thought he saw the flash of wings, or the spray of petals falling around her.

There was a silence. He could not speak; he could not have gestured, either, even if he had known the right signs.

He heard a voice behind him. 'Philomel! Sit down, please. Remember, we must not use signs any more. My apologies, Mr Latimer.' Miss Fielding walked past him and set a shabby workbasket down on the table. She took hold of the little girl's shoulder and piloted her gently back to her seat. If anything passed between them, Henry did not see it; he had swung his gaze away and was staring blindly at the window. 'Shall we begin, Mr Latimer?'

'Certainly,' he said, and without looking at either of them he drew up a chair, wrote the date at the top of a piece of paper and reached for the first trumpet.

Later that morning he shut the schoolroom door behind him and stood for a moment with his eyes closed. His head was aching. He had worked methodically, note by note, trumpet by trumpet, resisting the temptation to leap ahead; but the child had shown not the slightest flicker of a response, and after an hour or so she had started to yawn, twisting one foot around the other ankle and squirming as if she needed to use the pot. Miss Fielding, who until then had been watching impassively, had said, 'I think you must let us pause for a moment, Mr Latimer. Philomel has a glass of milk and some bread and butter at eleven.'

'Yes,' he said, 'in fact it might be better to leave it there, for today.'

'If you say so,' Miss Fielding had said. 'Tomorrow morning, then?'

He had nodded and begun to pack away his equipment, trying to master his disappointment. Tomorrow he would surely make more progress; just because his work had yielded no results today did not mean that the whole endeavour was hopeless. He owed it to the child to try everything. Watching her break into a smile or swapping a few half-concealed fingersigns with her governess, he had felt a renewed rush of determination: if she was delightful and charming now, with no hearing at all, what a joy she would be when she could converse in English! How pleased Sir Edward would be – how pleased he, Henry, would be, to know that he had given her the gift of music, the ripple of running water, the call of a nightingale . . . Yes, he must persevere. He must not be discouraged; this was his great opportunity, and he must grasp it.

But now the rest of today stretched in front of him, empty. He lugged his instruments into his room and put them on the floor beside the stained rug. Then he made his way down the stairs. When the maid had shown him to his room he had seen only sidelong, enticing glimpses of the house, and now he was curious to see more: he remembered Argyll saying, *newly built, best of everything* . . . But by the time he had reached the bottom of the staircase his resolution was faltering. Although he was not an intruder, he felt like one. The house was grand, as rich as cream, with the soft gleam of gold and velvet and polished stone; but it was the stillness that made him tread as lightly as he could, hardly daring to breathe. It was not the total silence of Telverton silk: it was the easy, expensive hush of distance and prosperity. The soft busyness of servants, the liquid trill of birdsong, the distant scrape of a rake on gravel – all of that only drew attention to the gracious absence of other noise, the proclamation of ownership that extended to the air itself. He felt the soles of his feet tingle as if he were treading mud into a Persian carpet.

To his right, a little passage led round to the rooms – he assumed – at the front of the house; across from where he was standing, he could just make out a high, long space framed by a dark arched doorway. He would have liked to see the room beyond, but a scrubbing-brush was scraping back and forth, and after a second the maid grunted and paused in her work, breathing heavily before she resumed. Instead he turned the other way, towards the back of the house. The doors were ajar, and he eased them wider, ready to retreat at the first movement or sign of occupation. The

first door opened onto a dining room, full of sombre panelling, deep colours and blurred shadows. Just below the dark
wood ceiling with its painted beams and medallions, a frieze
ran round the room in medieval lettering. Over the high
stone bay window he caught the words, *WELCOME AGAIN*.
The next door led to a morning room, with crimson walls
above more panelling. Then, finally, he opened the door of
the library, and after a moment stepped inside.

It was lighter than the other rooms, papered in ochre and
raw sienna, and daylight lay softly on the gilded spines of
books in their spired cases. The ceiling was thickly painted
in a medieval pattern, and punctuated with inverted golden
domes like jelly moulds. Every surface was rich with colour,
well made, expensive; the wood gleamed like satin; the very
air was like perfume.

Henry glanced around, taking in the ornaments and *chinoi-
serie*. Opposite him, in an alcove, hung the portrait of a
young man and his wife, dressed after the fashion of forty
or fifty years ago. He moved towards it. It was certainly
arresting; but after considering it for a moment Henry did
not, he thought, very much like it. The tableau of husband
and expectant wife was conventional enough, but if the
artist had tried to flatter them he had failed. The woman
was heavy-eyed and gaunt, clutching her swollen belly with
bony hands, and although the man who stood beside her
was undeniably handsome, he had an unyielding, arrogant
aspect. He was resting one hand upon a globe, and with the
other he gestured to the shadowy, autumnal landscape
behind. Among the ragged, twisted trees in the distance
there were other foreign plants, so that it was impossible to
tell whether it represented a real place or some deteriorating
Arcadia. Henry brought his face close to the canvas to see
if he could make out the signature of the artist, and recoiled.

There was a blotch just in front of his nose, which at first he had taken to be a patch of age-darkened pigment – but now he saw that it had legs, and a fat furred abdomen, and tiny eyes that sat on its head like raindrops on waxed cloth. A spider. And beside it – dipping behind the gilded frame – the artist had painted a fat pale purse with a greasy sheen on it, clinging to a twig. Was it meant to be a wrapped carcass, or an egg sac? Whatever it was, it had no place in a painting – bulging like a fungus, with that strange sliding light over it, as though it were liquefying . . .

Then Henry realised, and laughed. Surely it was meant to be the Telverton silk, and the spider – the *Pseudonephila*, or whatever its name was – that spun it; and that slick greying shine was only a bad attempt to render the silk's magic loveliness. Instinctively he reached into his pocket, drew out his talisman square and held it up to the painting. Yes, he could see it now – but how over-ambitious the artist had been. As he went to put the silk back into his pocket, he heard something, and paused. Of course it was only the reflected echo of his own breath, distinct as a whisper in this quiet room; even so, he closed his eyes, overwhelmed by a sudden longing to hear it again.

He jumped as a voice broke in on his reverie. This time it was a man's voice, gruff and unmistakeably real. It grew louder as it said, 'Yes, and how long have you been making it? Ten years now, I believe. And most of it is still sitting in the warehouse. How much of the Ashmore fortune have you poured into that factory? Good God, man, you are wasting your father's legacy.'

Henry whirled round, pocketing the silk, but it was already too late to advertise his presence. On the other side of the room, Sir Edward Ashmore-Percy and another man strode to the window and stood with their backs to him. The unknown man – a stout, ruddy, handsomely dressed gentleman – went on, 'For you – *you*, John Ashmore's son! – to be begging for investment – it defies belief! In a younger man it would be impertinence, in you, well! Shall I call it desperation?'

Sir Edward did not flinch. He said, 'It is hardly that, George. I do not think it a crime to be ambitious.' Henry had forgotten the timbre of his voice, and its charm.

'Oh, ambition is all very well, if it is well placed! But no. This Telverton silk is a novelty, I grant you, but that is all. Your father would be—'

'Dear God, must I still be in my father's shadow? If he had died when any reasonable man would have . . . No, George, I know you loved him, but I am fifty, I am no longer a young man. If I had come into that legacy thirty years ago—'

'Go back to lace. There is good money to be made in lace. Recoup your losses, if you can. Spiders, indeed! The whole thing is unworthy of you. The silk is trumpery. Too expensive, and no market for it. It is a mere gimcrack.'

Henry heard himself say, 'Forgive me, sir, but you're wrong.'

There was a silence. He had not meant to betray his presence at all; still less had he meant to speak, and so bluntly. What on earth had made him come to the silk's defence – unless it was his host that he had meant to defend? But now there was nothing for it but to step out of the alcove into the centre of the room. The two men stared at him, their expressions identical, full of surprise and disdain. But as Henry opened his mouth – meaning, God knew, to proffer excuses – he found himself addressing the older man. 'I did not mean to eavesdrop, sir. But I can see from your dress and demeanour that you are a successful man – an important man. I would venture to guess that you live in a house which befits your station. An ancestral seat, surrounded by parkland, perhaps – a gracious setting, with an atmosphere of quiet dignity and contentment. A place where you are lord of everything you survey.'

The man gave him a long look. Then he grunted.

'And if you are disturbed by something – a barking dog, or a crying child, or a madman shouting outside your window – you can easily remove it. You wave your hand, you ring for a footman . . . Even,' Henry plunged on, appalled at his own audacity, 'even the chatter of your wife and daughters can easily be avoided, by simply moving to another room.' Was that the hint of a smile on the man's lips? But Henry could not afford to hesitate to be sure. His palms were clammy. 'But you must not think that because you have attained a certain station, a certain power, all men are like you. You are quite correct that in a habitation like yours the silk is only a pretty trifle, not worth the expense. But that is because you have as much silence as you need already.'

Another pause. Sir Edward's eyes slid from Henry to the other man, and back again.

'I think, sir, you might be doing me the honour of considering what I have said. If so,' Henry said, breathless now, 'I am grateful. But think how much harder it would be if, instead of birdsong, all you could hear was the screech of traffic and the cries of street vendors, or the endless rumble of machinery. Silence is not only silence, sir, it is attention – it is sanity. It is sleep for infants, medicine for invalids, rest for the working man – it is money for the man who must think or starve. We build walls to shelter our bodies from the world, but we leave our minds open to assault on every side. The Telverton silk, sir, is not a gimcrack. It is the greatest discovery of our age.'

No one spoke. The heat in Henry's face spread upwards

until he felt the tickle of sweat crawling in his hair. At last the man sniffed, sonorously. 'Who are you?'

'Forgive me. Henry Latimer, at your service, sir,' Henry stammered, and bowed. 'I am an aurist – I am here to—'

'A natural philosopher, are you?'

Henry began to say, 'Well, I am not exactly—'

The red-faced man did not wait to hear Henry's answer. 'Remind me, Edward. Ten guineas a yard, was it? Or more?'

'I am a poor man and I would pay it, sir. Gladly,' Henry said. 'And I am not the only one. Once people know what it is, the price will be no object.'

'Hmph.'

There was a pause. Henry slid his gaze sideways. Sir Edward was watching him, his expression oddly set; but as soon as their eyes met, he said, 'Come, George,' and gestured towards the door. 'I apologise for my employee's impertinence. You have been quite definite in your refusal, and I know you have business in town. Let me ring for your carriage, and while we are waiting we shall talk of other things.'

'Ye-es,' the man said, as though he thought he had been the victim of some trick. 'Very well then.' He nodded to Henry with the same resentful unease, and stalked to the door. Sir Edward followed him.

Henry thought, until the last moment, that Sir Edward would at least acknowledge his presence; it was only as the door was closing that he stammered out, in sudden desperation, 'I am very sorry, Sir Edward – I did not mean to embarrass you—'

The other man stopped and looked at him for a long moment through the gap between door and doorframe, as though he were checking a length of material for flaws. 'No?'

'No, certainly not – only, the silk *is* extraordinary,' Henry said, hearing his voice rise. 'I could not help myself, when I heard him say— That is, I only wished to please you – and I have been treasuring the piece of silk you gave me—'

'What silk?'

'You gave me a square of your silk,' Henry said. 'When you came into the shop. Argyll's shop. You said . . .' *You said: take heart.* But the words died before they reached his tongue. The man looking at him now was not the man who had felt like a fellow traveller: his expression was icy. 'I am very sorry,' Henry repeated. 'I am so grateful to be here . . .' He forced himself to stop talking.

'I had forgotten that. You had better give it back, I suppose.'

'Give it . . . ?'

'Didn't you hear him? It costs ten guineas a yard. Did you think it was a gift?'

Henry swallowed. But he could not refuse; he could not do anything except reach numbly into his pocket and hold out the square of silk. He had washed it since he'd dropped it in the street, but now he saw a faint line of grime clinging to the edge.

Sir Edward plucked it out of his hand as though it were sackcloth. 'Knowing the difference between eloquence and bombast is a useful skill,' he said, soft as snow. 'As is knowing when to hold your tongue.'

Another surge of heat boiled over Henry's face and scalp. He knew now that he had looked forward inordinately to seeing Sir Edward again – had hoped for . . . what? For another one of those smiles, certainly; a moment of easy complicity; or even – oh Lord! – friendship . . . And he had ruined it, recklessly, foolishly. If only he had kept his mouth shut. 'Yes – of course.'

Sir Edward nodded. 'If you borrow any books, make sure

to put them back, won't you?' He seemed to hesitate, as though he might add another humiliation; then he drew the door closed and left Henry alone.

Part II

Kratos, 21st June 182—

We arrived yesterday, in a blur of heat and exhaustion and turmoil. I do not remember very much of our journey, save James's fury at the boatmen who demanded more money than we had agreed before rowing us the final stretch to the shore, and my growing misery as it became clear that none of the men who gathered on the beach understood James's schoolboy Greek or spoke the slightest word of English . . . I thought for a while that we should be left to sleep where we dropped.

But at last one of the men shrugged and gesticulated, indicating that we should follow him; and while the oars of the departing boat splashed behind us, we took the most precious of our baggage and trudged up the rocky path. After a long climb, the way curved and brought us to an outcrop of white houses. I halted to catch my breath, but our exertions were not at an end: the man pointed up to a low house some distance above the others, half overgrown by some clinging plant and overshadowed by holm oaks and a tall cypress. I could have wept at the prospect of another ascent, but as I bit my lip, conscious that such frailty would incense James even further, I caught sight of a figure in the doorway. It was a woman, dressed in black, her head covered and her arms at her sides. The afternoon sun shone upon her face and upon the bronze hair peeping out from under her veil (I believe it is called a *himation*). She did not move as we advanced towards her. Her face— I was going to write, was like a mask; but her gaze was more alive than any I have seen, entirely concentrated upon us, entirely free of fear or desire. I slowed to a stop. In my fatigue I felt an absurd impulse to fall to my knees.

'Hey, you!' James called. 'I am James Ashmore. I have come to visit Montague Gritney. I am looking for accommodation for the night. Is there an inn?'

I bowed my head, a little ashamed – oh, Sophia, ashamed of your own husband! – that he should address her like that. But to my surprise I heard her answer in clear, almost unaccented English. 'Here,' she said. 'This house is empty. It is where Mr Gritney lived.'

'Lived?' James said, with an outraged look at me, as though this excursion had been my idea, and not his. 'Is he no longer here?'

'He died long ago. You may stay in his house if you wish.'

'I wrote letters—'

'I do not read your language.'

There was a silence, full of James's harsh breathing and my own racing heart. Finally she moved out of the doorway and towards us. I thought she would say something as she passed; but although she nodded to me she did not pause, and I heard her sandals click on the stony ground as she disappeared into the green shadows of the forest.

'Well!' James said, and stood shaking his head as though a child had spat at him in the street. 'What are we to do? What a nuisance that the old man is dead, I so hoped—'

'I know, my love,' I said, and laid my hand upon his shoulder. He did not appear to notice. 'But if his correspondence is reliable, the island itself might be worthy of—'

'Ugh,' he said, pushing out his lower lip, 'I do not wish to stodge about by myself, without direction. He might quite easily have told me everything, and then I need only have sent out a few villagers to collect samples. I suppose the odd excursion, now and then, properly equipped and provisioned . . . but I was relying upon Gritney's cooperation.'

'You still have his essays, and his correspondence. They were what brought you here – perhaps, reread in the light of . . .' I looked around, forgetting what I had meant to say: for although I had not meant a literal light, I was struck by the sunset glow that fell so richly upon the dust and touched the vines and the humble little house with gold.

'Oh, curse it all,' James said, and kicked the suitcase beside his foot; then, catching my eye, he winced and held out his hand. 'Forgive me, sweetheart. Well, if this is our lodging for the night, let us go inside. I will help you make it homely.'

I did not want to go inside, at least not until the sun had disappeared, taking its vivid alchemy with it; but I could see his weariness, and how fragile his obvious resolution to be cheerful. 'Of course,' I said, 'we shall be like the grasshoppers in the Bible, camping in the hedge,' and for his sake I feigned girlish excitement as I pulled him towards the low doorway.

The house is barely a house – only a few rooms, bare and dirty, stripped of almost all furniture except the rotting rope-bed and scattered piles of Mr Gritney's books. I cannot say that when I opened my eyes this morning I was pleased to remember where we were, and why. We have stayed in other unpleasant places – oh, that lodging-house in Athens, where I thought I should suffocate with disgust! – but this was so entirely mean, so devoid of all comfort, that I could not bear to remain in it a moment longer. I slid from under the sheet without disturbing James, and crept out of the house.

I have often found that the more exhausted I have been, the earlier I awake: and so it was today. When I stepped into the open, I discovered that the world was shrouded in the blue half-light that precedes dawn. There was a sweet coolness in the air, and the sound of the sea; but otherwise a perfect quiet lay upon everything, like a kind of enchantment. We have seen so many different places – such sublime vistas of mountains and ruins, cliffs and shores, cascades of white water and green grottos, bare rocks baked hard in the blinding sun . . . Not to mention the towns, all of them more or less noisy and stinking, and the gamut of humanity that washed back and forth along every street. I am so weary of new landscapes – it has been so long since the pleasure of arriving in a new place has seemed worth the trouble! And yet today, alone in that blue lucency, I felt my breath rush into my lungs as though I had not inhaled for months, and I found myself drawn irresistibly down the path towards the village and the sea.

As I made my way between the square white houses, I saw no one, and heard nothing but the waves – and something on the edge of perceptibility, a distant note which was probably a goat-bell but made me think of the old stories of shipwrecks and drowned lands. I passed a covered well, surrounded by red flowers; a dog that slept on a doorstep and yawned, licking its chops; a patch of cultivated ground, where climbing plants clung to makeshift uprights. I saw a child's sandal discarded by the side of the path, and remembered some mythological hero who lost his shoe in carrying a goddess across a river and was forever blessed.

'You will be hungry. Here.'

I whirled around. It was the woman we'd seen the previous day, the one who spoke English almost like an Englishwoman. I made some incoherent noise of surprise, but she only held out a split loaf of bread and waited for me to take it.

I had not realised I was ravenous until I had food in my hand. I cannot even remember whether I thanked her before I tore into it with my teeth. The bread was an unleavened kind, tough and sour and wonderfully good, and inside it was cheese, wet and salty and peppery with olive oil, and green fragrant herbs, and pickled flowerbuds that burst on my tongue.

She smiled at me. 'Good?'

'Yes.' I began to stammer something about the stale bread and fish I had managed to barter the evening before from a squint-eyed widow in the nearest house, but then I was afraid of sounding discourteous.

She began to walk. I did not know whether she expected me to follow her; but when I took a few hesitant steps in her wake she paused, waiting impassively for me to catch up. She led me – whether desirous of my company or not – along a hidden track around the furthest houses and downwards. The sound of the sea grew louder, and the way steeper, weaving between little oak trees; then we came suddenly out onto a ledge, and there the sky and sea hung in front of us, the sky splendid in rose and copper and ivory, the sea a pale reflection as though the same colours were seen through a veil.

A dolphin leapt, close to the shore, and disappeared in a swirl of milky fire.

'Oh,' I said, 'it is so beautiful – so beautiful . . .'

We stood there until the sun had peeled away from the horizon, and I had to lower my eyes, dazzled. Then the woman laughed, and turned away.

'I must go back,' I said, gasping a little that I had forgotten James so completely. 'My husband might wake up and find me gone . . .'

'You are entirely free,' she said, without looking back, and in a moment she was half out of sight, picking her way down a rocky gulley with swift ease.

On my way back to James I have never felt less free; but then, perhaps she did not mean exactly that.

Kratos, 23rd (I think) June 182—

A few days have passed since I wrote the last entry: days, as usual, full of drudgery and frustration. James has been consumed by indecision; he swings from a desire to take the next boat back to Athens, and thence to somewhere more civilised, to a conviction that after all he was quite right to come here, and he will make his name from Mr Gritney's discoveries. It is a little wearing.

However, through my efforts the house is more habitable, and I have managed to negotiate a daily delivery of bread, cheese, eggs, olives and fruit, with the promise of an occasional chicken. This arrangement I owe to the help of the woman who speaks English, whose name is Hira. (I thought 'Hera' at first, but she scratched out the name laboriously in Roman characters when I asked.) I cannot quite understand who, or what, she is — among the other villagers, I mean. I think she must have been Mr Gritney's servant (she must certainly have learnt her English from him, and no other villager speaks a single word). She keeps somewhat apart from the others, and although they call upon her for salves and tinctures and help when a bone is broken or a child falls ill, it is difficult to know whether she is respected, feared or disdained. She is treated differently from the other young women, and she does not seem to have a husband. She is the closest thing to a friend I have had for many weeks — which, oh! is a painful admission, since if I am honest she is far from a friend, she merely tolerates my company when I manage to snatch a few moments away from James. Yesterday afternoon I found her in the patch of garden beside the house, clearing the earth around the herbs: when she straightened up, seeing me, I stammered a few words of thanks, and she gave me a brief, heart-stopping smile. I said, 'We will not stay long enough for that to matter – that is, you are very kind . . .' but she went back to her digging without a word, as if she knew better.

Kratos, July 182—

James has been in a rage all evening. For once it was cloudy today, and the light lay like gauze upon everything – the village, the forest and flowers and stony ground, the sea – so that all the shades of green and turquoise and rose were touched by a soft pallor. I longed for a walk, and as this morning he had been quite cheerful I thought I might safely leave him for a few hours. But when I returned he was scribbling in his memorandum book and grinding his teeth so that I knew I must anticipate a squall. I made our dinner as quietly as I might, and then sat with my hands in my lap, hoping not to aggravate him. At last I ventured, 'What is the matter, my love?'

He slammed down his pen. 'This is a fool's errand,' he said. 'This place is a perfect desert, populated by savages – not a sign of civilisation anywhere! I am sick and tired of it.'

'I thought you had found Mr Gritney's notes very useful? You said yesterday—'

'The man was a fantasist. It is all a mania, the inventions of a phrensied brain. I should have known. The birthplace of Harpocrates, indeed! The land of roses and silence! Utter nonsense. I believe God is punishing me for paying such attention to pagan myths.'

'But the spiders—'

'They do not exist. The villagers laughed at me. *Laughed,* Sophia! I explained that of course I did not believe in the

Olympian gods and so on, but that I suspected there was some basis in scientific fact, and that it might be the spiders Gritney described in his correspondence. I asked to be led to them. The men are such cretins it took hours to explain what I meant, and then—!' He leapt from his chair and strode to the window. There was quiet; the distant sea must have been as still as a millpond.

I went to stand beside him and put my head against his shoulder, and after a moment I felt him press his lips into my hair. 'Shall we go home?' I said.

'Having discovered nothing and written nothing, with my name as obscure as it was when I left? To be lorded over by my mammonish sinner of a brother?'

'Or we might go on,' I said, repressing a sigh. 'There are more islands. If this is not the one . . .'

He laughed, a little grimly. 'You are a good wife to me,' he said, 'I know you are homesick, and exhausted.'

It is true that I have been homesick for months; but the pang I felt at the thought of England was not as sharp as it generally is. I did not know how to answer.

'We will rest for a few days,' he said. 'I will scour the old man's papers for anything I might have missed, and trust Providence to direct my next steps.' He kissed me. 'You long-suffering little woman,' he said, and drew me closer, 'I do test your endurance, don't I? Never mind, we will not tarry here long.'

I did not correct him. It was unscrupulous to let him console me for a misery I did not feel; but his caresses are rarer these days than they once were, and in any case I could not adequately have explained my state of mind.

It has been weeks since I last wrote. I am afraid that James is sinking into despondency. For several days he spent long hours poring over Mr Gritney's books and diaries, and once or twice he disappeared for an hour or so and returned dirty and sweating, cursing the heat and the steepness of the paths into the forest; so I concluded that he had not entirely lost hope of finding the spiders. But his efforts, unrewarded, have dwindled. He still passes the greater part of every day with his books, but I have noticed that he seldom turns a page. My presence irritates him, and I have taken to dawdling on my way to and from the village. Sometimes I meet Hira, and sometimes she tells me I may come with her to visit the villagers. I have drunk *tisanes* with a widow and a young mother with a babe at her breast, and eaten sweet almond cakes with an elderly man, and watched Hira smear a pungent paste over a little boy's rash. The villagers accept me without particular interest, as though I were a tame animal trailing in her wake. It is the first time since leaving home that I have not felt conspicuous and ill at ease.

I cannot decide why she is being kind to me. She has the serene detachment of a priestess, and it is inconceivable that she is lonely – and yet I am not sure, either, that it is only pity. This evening I slipped away from the house and took the path down to the sea, savouring the fragrance of dew and pines and salt. I came out from under the last evergreen oak, and stood upon the sand. The sea was grey-green-blue and as flat as silk.

There was a sound behind me, but I did not startle; I only turned slowly, knowing by some irrational instinct that I should see Hira there. Then I did catch my breath, and felt the blood rush to my face, for she was naked. I had not the presence of mind to look away; instead (for shame!) I stared, utterly taken aback, at her bare breasts and belly. Heaven knows I have seen enough statues not to gape – and yet the shape of her was so unlike those stony Athenes and Aphrodites, sculpted by men for other men . . . She smiled, and wiped the water from her skin, and reached for her robe.

'Excuse me – I was not expecting . . .' I stammered, and finally dragged my gaze away. In the corner of my eye I saw the black cloth drop down over her body.

'If you want to bathe,' she said, 'I will wait for you. It is foolish to swim alone in a strange place.'

'Oh! No, I cannot.'

'No one will see.'

'I mean I dare not. I cannot swim,' I said, feeling a renewed heat in my cheeks. 'I do not know how.'

'You came a long way across the sea,' she said. 'Were you not frightened?'

'Yes.'

She looked at me for so long I could hardly bear it. Then she threw her head back and laughed, with an odd note of admiration. 'Very well,' she said, at last. 'I will teach you.'

'You are very kind, but honestly I have no desire—'

'I have seen how you look at the sea,' she said. 'Tell me when you are ready. Good night.'

She walked away, and I closed my mouth. James told me once that Plato said a man who could not swim was as ignorant as one who could not read; but he has never cared to help me remedy my incapability.

I sat down upon a rock, and watched until sea and sky and sand merged bluely together like bands of molten glass. The breeze that carried the scent of pines carried a sound too, an elusive shimmering chime that raised the hairs on my arms. I do not know if this is the birthplace of silence, but I am sure that there is something strange here, something of which I should be afraid. But I am not.

I lingered there until it was nearly dark; I did not want to leave and go back to James.

Oh, how that admission makes me wince, now that I see it written down! I have sadly neglected my prayers since arriving here, and this is the result. I will put down my pen now, and turn my mind to the Almighty and His endless help and mercy, and to His commandment that a wife must obey her husband.

Four

Henry would have given anything to take back his outburst in the library. Granted another chance, he would have bitten his tongue clean off before he said a word. But it was too late; all he could do was redouble his efforts with Philomel. That, after all, was why he had come: once he had succeeded he would be forgiven, and . . .

And – *what*? Whenever he tried to put it into words, Henry only thought of Sir Edward saying, *take heart*, and the smile that had felt like a kindled flame. Was that what Henry yearned for? No – or rather yes; that, but not only that. He would shake Henry's hand, and invite him to stay a little longer, and . . . But here Henry's inspiration invariably ran dry, and he opened his eyes to find himself alone in the shabby room in the east wing, and the pile of papers on the desk as criss-crossed with the marks of failure as ever.

For failing he was, so far. In spite of his determination he made no progress on the second day, and by an hour into the third morning it was clear that both Philomel and Miss Fielding were weary of his presence. Doggedly he worked on, unwrapping a pretty audiphone painted like a Japanese fan and showing the little girl how to rest the edge of it against her teeth. Behind him, he heard the huff of Miss

Fielding's breath and the squeak of a finger on glass; she was doodling on the window pane. Philomel set down the audiphone, began a question in fingerspeak before remembering that Henry would not understand her, and subsided, kicking the leg of the chair.

'You tighten the cords like this,' Henry said, demonstrating. 'Now, put it back in your mouth and let me strike another note.'

She shrugged, pointed to her ears and spread her hands. He was not sure it was fingerspeak, exactly, but the meaning was unambiguous. She might as well have said aloud, '*I – can't – hear – anything.*'

'We must be comprehensive,' Henry said, and twisted to look at Miss Fielding. In truth, he was hoping that she would agree as well as translate, but her gesture to the little girl did not reassure him. 'Truly, Philomel, it is in your best interests for me to do this properly – we must not lose hope.'

Philomel got to her feet. She stood beside her chair, wrapping one foot around the other ankle, but she did not look defiant so much as helpless. It *was* a lot to ask of a child; there were elderly customers who had cast up their hands at less and stalked out of Argyll's consulting room, refusing to continue. Abruptly Henry remembered his own schooldays, and the shattering weight of boredom on a spring day when he had twenty Latin verbs to conjugate and the clock seemed to have stopped. But it had to be done – he owed it to them both to plough on . . .

He stood up too. Philomel frowned, but he turned away, already leaning across the table to drag the two remaining cases towards her. He threw back the lids and said, 'There. Let us try another approach.'

She blinked and glanced at Miss Fielding. Then, at last, he saw a smile spread across her face, and she leant over the nearest case, dug her hands into the cotton waste and pulled out the wrapped instruments; tentatively at first, and then with abandon, for all the world as if it was a bran tub at a fair. She exhumed an auricle made of inlaid brass, and then one of mother-of-pearl, which she lifted eagerly onto her head like a crown. Henry reached for his tuning fork and struck a note, watching her for any response, but she twirled in front of Miss Fielding, oblivious and beaming. Then she cast it aside, rushed back to the table and reached for an audinet engraved with mythical animals.

'When will you admit defeat, Mr Latimer?'

He looked round with a jolt. Miss Fielding had turned her back to the child; but naturally she had not lowered her voice.

'I beg your pardon?'

'How long,' she said, 'do you intend to waste your time, and ours?'

He stammered, 'It is not a waste of time – we must try everything—'

'These instruments,' she said, 'they are all variations on the same principle, are they not?'

'To an extent. Some work by amplifying the sound waves by reflecting and concentrating them, some by using the structure of the teeth and skull to convey vibrations to the auditory nerve.'

'I understand that. But when the nerve itself—'

'There are differences. Subtle differences, I grant you, in some cases. But the smallest change might . . . that is, if we perceive the slightest glimmer of hope . . .'

'But we do not perceive it. That is my point. She – hears – *nothing*.' And perhaps unconsciously she echoed with her hands the gestures that Philomel had made.

'It is not that simple. When the auditory nerve is left

without stimulus it atrophies,' he said, conscious that he was quoting Argyll. But it was true, damn it – why should he feel like a charlatan? 'When some power to hear is restored through mechanical means, the nerve must rehabituate itself not only to perceiving but to recognising the phenomenon of sound. There have been cases where it took many sessions to educate both the auditory nerve and the brain, before the subject understood that an improvement had taken place.'

'Improvement?' she murmured, and turned to look at Philomel. He followed her gaze. While they had been talking, the child had taken a small wooden horse from the shelf, and was now holding it over the audinet as if to introduce it to the engraved unicorn.

He said, raising his voice, 'I want to help her. I want her to hear. Surely you understand that. If there is a chance that one day she will hear birdsong, speech, music . . . ! I cannot give up while there is still hope. How can I?'

'I admire your persistence, Mr Latimer. And you have been kinder to her than many of the others. But it is not right, or kind, to persevere beyond the bounds of—'

'The others?'

She raised her eyebrows. 'Naturally there have been others. Doctors, specialists, even a mesmerist. He is indefatigable. Since Phil began to resemble him, and he realised that in spite of everything, Lady Cecilia – his wife – had been faithful to him . . .'

Henry stared at her. 'Why on earth—?' he started, and then stopped.

She met his eyes with a wry flicker; then she took a pace towards the window and said, quite steadily, 'Never mind that. Until he was sure, I was enough, you see. The schoolmaster's daughter, who could read and write and use fingerspeak. I was top of my class and I could mimic a lady's accent so that I would not be an embarrassment to the household. I was not a proper governess, but I would do. What did it matter if Philomel never spoke like a civilised person, as long as she was cared for and out of sight? But then she grew so like him that it did matter, and the doctors started to come . . . I think he must know by now that no one can cure her, but he keeps trying.'

Henry said nothing. He watched Philomel gallop the wooden horse over the table, her face glowing as if she were seeing green fields and freedom.

Miss Fielding said suddenly, 'I should not have told you that. You must not repeat it. There is no doubt about her parentage now. Philomel—'

'Of course I shall not.'

'I want the best for her. She is all I have.'

Henry swung round. 'But you want me to fail. Don't deny it, please! How can you say you want the best for her when you are doing everything you can to persuade me to leave?'

She looked at him, unsmiling. 'If you could restore Philomel's hearing entirely,' she said, 'so that she could learn to speak English as well as she speaks with her hands, then I should feel nothing but gratitude.'

'And if I manage to make some small improvement, just enough to enable her to converse with ordinary people?'

'That would be the worst of all!' She said it so passionately that he flinched. But she did not apologise, or soften her voice. 'That would content Sir Edward. He wants to stop her using signs; he would rather she said nothing. But I could not – I *will* not see her reduced to a mumbling simpleton, surrounded by people who think she is incapable of thought as well as speech, left with a few barely comprehensible words! She is lucky to have learnt fingerspeak – I do not think you realise *how* lucky – and in time, when the Telverton children grow up, deafness will be so common that the whole town will speak as she does. She is clever, and funny, and perfect exactly as she is.'

'But . . . for her to learn words . . . cadence . . . poetry—'

'She already *has* poetry! She has more poetry in her hands than her father has in his whole body.'

That was not true, he thought, remembering the deft masculine fingers that had offered him the silk, but it would have been pedantry to say so. He turned away. The room felt colder, and darker. If he gave up now, he would never redeem himself in Sir Edward's eyes. He would return to London and be found wanting, again; return to Argyll and the & *SON* over the door; return to Madeleine's silent piano, and the shut-up nursery. He could not bear it.

Miss Fielding said nothing more. Philomel glanced up at them both, sensing perhaps that their voices had ceased; but without making a sign she went to the side where the brown paper was kept, took a pencil out of a drawer, and sat down again to take an impression of the unicorn on the audinet. There was no sound but the soft rhythmic scratch of the pencil lead over the paper. No one, Henry thought, would know that there was anything wrong with her at all. And if what Miss Fielding said was true . . . *Reduced to a mumbling simpleton.* The conviction came to him, starkly, that he could not go on. He had failed his own daughter utterly, in the few hours he had had her. He could not let his own ambition and loneliness blind him to the harm he might do Philomel, if he stayed.

'I shall go to him now,' he said, 'and tell him that my presence here is useless.'

Miss Fielding did not move, but he felt a tension leave her. She said, 'Thank you.'

He did not trust himself to answer. The only thing worse than this ache of misery would be for her to see it, and pity him. It was absurd, after all: his hopes had been a mirage, no more substantial than a candle flame. He had dreamed of beginning again, and he had awoken. There was no more to be said. He allowed himself one last look at the schoolroom, at the sunshine that fell on the varnished wood, at the ranks of books and toys, and at Philomel. She had almost finished her unicorn now. There was grey dust all over her pinafore, and tendrils of hair were escaping from her plait.

Miss Fielding moved to the door, and opened it. Numbly he followed her. 'My things . . .' he said, on the threshold.

'I shall have them packed up and put in your room.'

'Yes. Thank you.'

In spite of himself he glanced again at the little girl. Perhaps Miss Fielding liked him better now that he was leaving, for she followed his look and smiled. 'Do you have children of your own?'

'No.' His throat closed on the word, threatening to betray him, and he saw her eyes slide to his black armband. Rapidly, before she had time to ask anything more, he said, grasping at the first observation that came into his head, 'Philomel is a very pretty name. I have it in my head that it means nightingale – at least, that there is some connection . . .'

He had thought the observation an innocuous one, but for some reason it made Miss Fielding's smile fade. 'Yes. Philomel was transformed into a nightingale. In Ovid, I think. Other sources say a swallow. Do you think it's a pretty story, to go with the pretty name?'

'I – hardly remember. Did she weave a tapestry? Or is that Penelope?'

'Yes. She was raped, and then her tongue was cut out, so she wove the tapestry to tell her sister what had happened.'

There was a silence. Henry stared at her: she had used the word *raped* as though it bore no special weight, as though it was the sort of word anyone might use, at any time.

She held his gaze without flinching. 'Can you imagine telling such a thing, in embroidery silk?'

'I . . .' he said, then began again, 'I cannot imagine telling such a thing at all.'

'No. Perhaps it would have ended more happily for them all if she had not. It would certainly have been more convenient. For the men, and the gods.'

She had said *men* as if she meant all men. He said, 'Surely they were not thinking of that story, when they named her?'

She shrugged. It was not a shrug of insouciance, but of resignation. 'This is a strange house, Mr Latimer. You are lucky to be able to leave it.'

He did not have time to reply before the door shut in his face. He closed his eyes, trying to fix the last image of the room: the globe and blackboard, the little girl sitting at her work, looking up to smile at her governess – a sorrowless, sheltered, sunny little world, a world he had been part of, however briefly . . . But already it was not quite exact, as though it had never existed at all; and he knew, with a sense of loss that he dared not examine, that by the time he was in London the details would have blurred past recognition.

There was no answer when he knocked at the door of the study, but a maid dusting nearby directed him to the library. He hesitated outside the closed door, listening to the murmur of voices, but then, with a fatalistic resolve, he forced himself to knock. He could hardly disgrace himself more than he already had. It would be over quickly, and then he would never see Sir Edward again, and tomorrow he would be on his way back to London.

'Come.'

Sir Edward was standing at the desk, flipping over the pages of a thin volume; as Henry entered he glanced up, with a preoccupied, pleasant look of enquiry. The man beside him was much younger – only a little older than Henry himself – and ginger-haired, with patchy whiskers and a greasy complexion. Sir Edward said, 'This looks fine to me. Yes, Mr Latimer?'

Henry said, making sure he was looking straight at him, 'May I speak to you, sir? It won't take long.'

'You don't have time now, sir,' the other man said, 'I must get back to the factory, and if I must speak to the printers on the way—'

'Yes, yes,' Sir Edward said, 'I know, Worsley, but I dare say one day will make very little difference to my eventual ruin.' He said it lightly, but the younger man bared his teeth without the smile reaching his eyes. 'Go on.' He pointed to the door, and Worsley slunk away, giving Henry an unpleasant look as he went. 'Forgive him. He was brought up in the docks of Bristol, but he has his uses. What is it, Latimer?'

Henry took a breath, digging his fingernails into his palms. The older man's expression was amiable; he hardly seemed the same one who had plucked the square of silk out of Henry's hand and dismissed him so coldly. Perhaps he had decided to give Henry another chance. Yes, that was it: he was expecting news of Philomel's progress, and expecting to be pleased.

Henry's prepared speech faltered on his tongue. He looked about blindly; then he found himself striding across the rug to the window, as though he might break through the glass and escape onto the lawn. But as he cursed himself for his cowardice, Sir Edward sauntered to his side and stood looking out. The day had clouded over. Beyond the trees the park sloped down into the valley, and the haze of Telverton was just visible, the smoke rising to meet the grey sky. Sir Edward pointed. 'There,' he said, 'that's the factory chimney. That thread of smoke, you see?'

He could not put it off any longer. He blurted out, 'I am sorry, sir, but I'm afraid my experiments with Philomel have failed. I hoped to be able to help her, but – well, it is no good.'

It was a relief to have said it, at first. But the pause stretched on. Henry sneaked a sideways glance: Sir Edward was staring at his boots, his expression unreadable. At last he said, 'That is a pity.'

'Yes.' It was like the worst dressing-down at school; no rebuke could be worse than the silence of someone you had wanted so badly to please. He said again, 'I am sorry. Mr Argyll had the highest hopes. He will be disappointed in my failure.'

'*Your* failure?'

'Well – yes—'

'Is it due to your shortcomings? Or is it simply that my daughter is deaf?'

Henry stammered, 'Well – I suppose – I did my best, what anyone else would have done.'

'Quite.' Sir Edward blew air through his lips, and moved away. He paused by the desk and flipped a page back and forth with his index finger, until Henry thought it might tear. At last he said, 'So you will return to London, I take it?'

'Yes.' He tried not to think of London, and Argyll's shop, and the empty rooms.

'Ah.'

'I must apologise again for embarrassing you—'

At the same time Sir Edward said, 'Before you go, I have a favour to ask you. At least . . . a task. A test, if you will.'

Henry stared at him.

'I won't deny that the other day you were impertinent. Breaking in like that on a private conversation . . . it took me by surprise, rather. I thought you'd ruined everything. But as it turns out, it may have done the opposite. I think old George might be coming round.'

Henry opened his mouth, struggling for words. At last he said, 'I did not mean . . .'

'I'm afraid I was unkind. Will you forgive me?'

'Forgive *you*, sir?' Henry's head was spinning. He met the other man's eyes and was obliged to look away again; he had that look, the warm, humorous glint that Henry had imagined – only not like this, he could never have imagined being asked for *his* forgiveness . . .

'When I think about it, it was a masterstroke when you told the old bastard he was wrong. I do not think there was anything more calculated to shock him into paying attention. And then the flattery . . .'

'Honestly,' Henry said, 'I spoke without thinking. I had no intention—'

'Well, splendid,' Sir Edward said. 'Anyone would think you were an actor. I don't suppose you have a theatrical background?'

'No. I had ambitions to be a poet,' Henry said, and immediately wished he had not. He could remember Argyll's face, full of genial malice, when Madeleine mentioned the verses he had slaved over; the way the old man had broken into 'A wee, sleekit, cowrin, tim'rous beastie!' and then added, chuckling, 'You'll never outdo that, laddie.'

But Sir Edward did not laugh; he raised his hand in wry

acknowledgment. 'I should have known! That passion, that cleverness, that divine fire . . .' He smiled, but it was not mockery. 'Well then – here is my request. Will you say a few words at dinner tomorrow? Just the same sort of thing, to make my guests sit up and pay attention.'

'Yes – certainly – if I can be of any use.'

'Then that's settled. And if you do it well, we shall see . . .'

There was a pause. Finally Henry had to turn away; he did not know why, or whether what he felt was delight or fear. The blood drummed in his ears: *a test, a test.* If he did well . . . If only he could guess the end of that sentence! He blinked, and found he was staring at the old portrait that hung in the alcove.

'That is my great-uncle, James Ashmore,' Sir Edward said, in a different tone. 'He was the one who brought the spiders home from Greece.' He moved to stand at Henry's shoulder. 'I like to tell the story, when people ask me what's so special about Telverton silk. Some old opium-eater wrote about having found the birthplace of silence, and Great-Uncle James, being ambitious – and disinclined to what my father would call *real* work,' he added, with a glint, 'decided to go in search of it. He travelled all round the Mediterranean, I gather, like Odysseus. He starved and struggled and suffered to bring the spiders back. They are his legacy to the world.'

'Yes,' Henry said; although his eyes moved to the face of the woman standing next to Sir Edward's great-uncle, and the misery that he thought he could see there.

Sir Edward crossed in front of Henry to stand in front of the picture. 'That was painted just after he returned. He turned into a devilish old man. When I was a boy I used to have to visit him – he lived in the village, just the other side of the park – and he scared me to death. He made me throw live rats into the spiders' tanks.' He rolled his shoulders, as if he had put on a clammy shirt. 'You had to wear gauntlets or they'd scratch you to ribbons. After a while it was oddly fascinating, but—'

'Live rats?'

'Oh yes. The spiders are quite voracious – particularly the female of the species. Although they're not as large as you'd think. The silk does all the work of trapping their prey.' His mouth twisted. 'He went on and on about the silk, he was sure it would make his fortune. Kept breeding the spiders. My father thought he was a crotcheteer. It was I, you know, who saw that it had potential. I was the one who adapted the machines, and expanded the factory.'

Henry nodded. The spider in the picture watched him with its glistening eyes, hungry.

'I made another artist add the spider in later, just to make the point. But I'm not sure it's quite right. It looks – well, *alive*, somehow.' Then he added, with a strange note in his voice, 'He disappointed me, in the end. The artist, I mean. I didn't pay him for it.'

Henry hesitated; but at last he said softly, 'It is wonderful. The silk, I mean. You were right – you *are* right to go on making it. It is magnificent.'

'You think so?' Sir Edward swung round to look at him. 'Old George – not to mention most of my father's friends – thinks I am a fool.'

'Of course I think so. You must not listen to them. It will make your fortune, I am sure of it.' He hardly knew what he was saying; he was too conscious of the space between them, and the older man's gaze. *A test, a test, a test*, his heart said.

'Is that so?' Sir Edward frowned, as though Henry were a page to be deciphered. 'But you say I *must* not? "Must"?'

Henry said, horrified, 'I didn't mean—'

'Ha! Oh, come now, I'm teasing you,' Sir Edward said, chuckling, and laid a cajoling hand on his shoulder. It might have been the gesture of an adult to a child – comforting and oddly intimate – but for a split second his fingers tightened painfully, and a sudden heat ran down Henry's arm. 'Well, I suppose I should summon Worsley back, or he will sulk,' he went on, dropping his hand. 'He is keen to get this catalogue sent to the printer.'

Henry stepped closer to look at the book on the desk, but it took him a moment to focus his eyes on it. The title was printed on the cheap cloth in dark ink: *TELVERTON SILK*, it said, between clumsy curlicues.

Sir Edward flipped over a few pages, showing engravings of draperies, the lustre of the silk rendered flatly with concentric loops and lines. 'We have a few patterns of curtains that can be made up, different weights and widths and so on.' But there were only a few pictures before he came upon the price lists, and he shut the book with a snap. 'We're going to send a new one of these to every draper and haberdasher in the country. I want to get Telverton silk spoken of everywhere.'

'Quite right,' Henry said. He was a little calmer now. How foolish, to be so disarrayed! But he had come into the room expecting to be icily dismissed; it was only to be expected that he would be grateful for the older man's indulgence. Gratitude, that was all; and admiration, and relief that after all he had not missed his chance.

'Ring the bell, will you? Or – no, wait.' He crossed the room and flung open the library door. 'Ah, Worsley, you're there. Thought you might be. Very well, come in.'

Worsley came in with such swiftness that it was clear he had been eavesdropping. He did not exactly scowl at Henry, but his dislike blew off him like a foetid wind. 'I'm afraid it is too late for the printers now, sir.'

'Then take it to them on Monday. Well, I must dismiss you, Latimer. Worsley and I have other things to discuss.'

'Of course – and thank you,' he stammered, suddenly aware that he had not expressed anything of what he felt. 'I will do my very best – you don't know how glad I am—'

'Oh, pish.' Sir Edward waved his words away. Behind his arm Henry saw Philomel running across the lawn. Miss Fielding was hurrying after her, holding a diminutive hat in one hand, while under her other arm she clutched a blanket, a portfolio and a wooden case. 'Go and help her if you want,' Sir Edward said. 'Do you sketch?'

'Not . . . exactly.'

'Compose a few poems, then. Or better still, work out your little speech for tomorrow. The park isn't at its best at this time of year, but the formal garden is coming along nicely.'

'Yes,' Worsley said, with that tooth-baring un-smile, 'go and play. We have important things to do here.'

Henry drew breath, searching for a suitable retort. But Sir Edward met his eyes and then – impossibly, marvellously – winked.

Henry almost laughed out loud. He nodded to both men, made his way into the passage and stood on the terrace, breathing the clean air in great heady gouts, before he called out to Miss Fielding to offer to carry Philomel's baggage.

Five

Although it was not yet dark outside, the drawing room blazed with candles. They gave a papery tinge to the flowers in their silver bowls and softened the newness of the walls and panelling. The dark red of the walls was velvety and thick as an arras, and muted gold gleamed from the mouldings in the ceiling and the capitals of the pillars in front of the windows. There was an elusive scent of honey in the air, and a fire in the great Gothic hearth.

If it had been empty, it might have been a room from a fairy tale, a palace from a time that never existed. Its occupants, however, were emphatically of their own century: a dozen or so men in dinner suits stood sipping topaz-coloured wine, some already in conversation, a few apparently having drifted away to warm themselves by the fire or examine a picture. Henry paused on the threshold, his heart thudding. He had the sensation he had had as an undergraduate, before his final exams: his knees felt weak, and his palms prickled with moisture. How could he impress these men – he, Henry, half their age, a poet *manqué*, a mere shop clerk? His speech, which had seemed satisfactory when he'd read it over in the privacy of his room, felt as flimsy as the paper he had written it on.

'Latimer, come in, come in. Don't stand on ceremony.' Their host was standing beside the window with another man. He beckoned, and gratefully Henry approached them. 'This is William Hinshaw,' Sir Edward said, and the man he had been conversing with stepped forward into the light.

It was the Quaker who had spoken to Henry on the train, the day he'd arrived in Telverton. This evening he was dressed in black rather than grey, but there was still a quaint, old-fashioned cut to his clothes that marked him as different. He nodded at Henry. 'I am pleased to see thee again,' he said, 'and looking steadier.'

'I was unaware that you had met,' Sir Edward said, with a swift look at Henry.

'Only briefly,' Hinshaw said, 'at the railway station. So thou art a guest here, I take it?'

'Yes,' Sir Edward said, before Henry could answer. 'In fact, a friend. Although in truth it is the silk that brings him here, not the desire for my company. Is it not, Latimer?'

'Yes.' *Friend* . . . He could hardly correct the older man, and he did not want to. 'I am very grateful indeed to be here.'

Sir Edward laughed and passed him a glass of Tokay from the nearest tray. 'You are impeccably polite,' he said, 'it is very charming. Now, Hinshaw, excuse me, I must have a word with Colcastle before we go in.' He slipped away to accost the porcine young man who was squinting at the engraving on the wall beside the fireplace.

'An investor, art thou?' Hinshaw asked. 'Or a prospective one?'

'No! No,' he repeated, jolted into a laugh. 'I'm afraid not.' Sir Edward clearly did not want him to reveal the truth of why he was here; now he grasped feverishly for something that was neither truth nor falsehood. 'I am certainly interested in the silk. I am an aurist, y-you see.' He stumbled a little on the pronoun, and Hinshaw smiled.

'Do not worry thyself,' he said. 'I say "thee" and "thy" for my own sake, being a Friend. What thou choosest to say is between thee and thy God.'

'Yes. Well. I advise on hearing aids. So, you see, it excites my professional curiosity.' The almost-lie came more fluently than he had dared to hope.

Hinshaw regarded him. He had no wine glass, and Henry envied the self-possession with which he let his hands hang at his sides. 'Thou art *not* a guest, then.'

'Well – I – I am hopeful that – I mean, Sir Edward is being kind to say so—'

'Hmm,' Hinshaw said.

Henry did not know how he would have gone on, if another man had not appeared at Hinshaw's elbow. This man was greying, with a pointed, silvery beard and an abstracted air. 'Ah, Hinshaw,' he said, looking past them both. 'I hope Rachel and Hannah are well.'

'They are well, I thank thee. And thine?'

'Oh, as you would expect – costing me a fortune in fripperies and novels. I wish they would convert to your religion.'

'Thou might'st be surprised how much a plain bonnet can cost,' Hinshaw said, with a glint of amusement.

Henry took a mouthful of wine, gave them both a polite unseeing smile and moved away. He did not want to listen to them speak comfortably about their families, with that shared camaraderie – as though to have a living wife and child was the worst kind of burden. But he must not think about Madeleine – no, he must think about the here and now, think about what he had to do . . . His nerves, which had subsided, rose again. More than anything he wanted to draw his notes from his pocket and rehearse his speech; if only he were alone! He had planned to begin with thanks – thanks to Sir Edward for inviting him to speak, and to the listeners for, well, listening – and then, perhaps, some topical comment, a pleasantry. *Thank you, gentlemen, for your attention. As brevity is the soul of wit* . . . But his stomach was churning, and he could not remember what came next. Behind him someone said, in a moist, braying voice, 'Sheer naïvety. It wouldn't be the first time that someone has spent more than he can afford, to bluff his creditors.'

'I admire ambition,' another man replied, 'and there is no advance without risk.'

'But is that a sound basis for business?' There was a wet smack of lips. 'The father was a sensible man. But this one, what's *he* done? Spent the inheritance, that's all I can see. And his wife's, poor woman. Expanded the factory, built this grotesque house, splashed money about. And for what? No one has heard of the silk outside of Telverton. The malaise, on the other hand – oh yes, *that* is well known. I heard you can buy Telverton Numms in Dover, for sea-sickness!' Another gulp. 'And I heard the insurance hasn't been paid for months,' the man went on. 'Dicing with ruin, he is, to let that lapse when the warehouse and the factory are both so close to the Tell. Another flood like '53 and he'd be penniless. And the workers are restless. Hinshaw says when the Quakers visit the workhouse, they hear rumours. The town is seething with hatred, they say. Seething.'

'Respectfully, my lord, workers are the same everywhere. Bring in the Irish, that's what I say.'

He grunted. 'I just don't know, Reeve. My innards don't like it. Don't like *him*,' he added, without lowering his voice.

Henry clenched his jaw; he must not turn and glare, he must keep his expression pleasant, his stance relaxed. He was glad when they moved away and he could resume his interior monologue: *Thank you, gentlemen, for your attention. As wit is the soul of— As brevity—*

But he had got no further with his silent rehearsal when they were called into the dining room. The table was set with candelabras and bowls of hothouse flowers, and the silver and crystal shimmered like a mirage. He sat, as he was bid, opposite his host and Hinshaw, and beside Colcastle, who turned to his other neighbour and launched into conversation without acknowledging Henry. The dinner was served *à la Russe*, and Henry ate quickly, with his head lowered – more to occupy his hands and mouth, to cover his inability to join in the conversations on either side, than out of appetite – and had to make an effort not to drink more than was wise. It seemed an eternity before the table was cleared for dessert, and he had to raise his eyes and look around.

Opposite him, Sir Edward did not meet his eyes. Hinshaw was cracking walnuts, and there was some sort of argument at the other end of the table. Other guests leant back in their chairs, satisfied, stifling belches or yawns. There was the munch and pop of someone eating grapes. Henry wanted time itself to pause, so that he would never have to speak in front of all these unfamiliar men; or to jump forwards, so that it was already over.

Just then there was a natural lull in the conversation – an angel passing overhead, as Madeleine would have said. Sir Edward said, '. . . trying to persuade you, you're no fool, Colcastle,' and then looked around, laughingly conscious that he was speaking into silence. He raised his voice. 'And neither is any one of you here, gentlemen. Let us not pretend that I haven't invited you here to ask you to invest in my factory. I am very glad of your company, but I should be gladder still of your money. Is that plain enough for you,

Hinshaw?' he added to the Quaker, who smiled a little as he picked fragments of nutmeat out of a walnut shell. 'But I shan't apologise. Why should I? I am no beggar. I do not ask you for a favour; I am offering you an opportunity like no other.'

The thin old man shifted in his seat, and Colcastle spat a few grape seeds into his napkin. No one else moved.

Sir Edward leant back, smiling at them all. 'But you need not take my word for it,' he said. 'There is a man here – an expert in the science of hearing – who can speak without prejudice. Let me introduce Henry Latimer, a medical man, a specialist in the disorders of the acoustic nerve, who has treated some of the most illustrious men in London. After I gave him a sample of the silk, he came to visit me; it is my good fortune, I hope, that he happened to be here to attend this dinner. Latimer,' he added, and raised his glass in a gesture that was both toast and invitation.

Henry drew in his breath. It was not true – not exactly true – and yet he wanted to recognise himself in that description. He wanted to be that man. A wave of fear broke over him: this was the test, at last, and he could not move or open his mouth. The moment of silence seemed to go on and on, until he could not believe that the men had not got bored and resumed their conversations.

Then his heart thumped again – went on thumping – and he knew his hesitation had lasted only a split second. 'Thank you, Sir Edward,' he said – and almost added, fumbling for his notes, 'Thank you, gentlemen. As brevity is the soul of wit . . .' But something stopped him, just in the nick of time: some unidentifiable instinct that knew better. He dropped his hand and looked around, taking in the raised eyebrows and stifled yawns of the other men. And suddenly, with an odd, dangerous thrill, he found that he could speak fluently.

'Gentlemen,' he said, 'a few days ago I went into Marshall & Snelgrove to ask for Telverton silk. The shop-girl told me that if I wanted cobwebs, I should ask my housemaid.'

There was another silence, thicker and stiller than the last; then Colcastle gave a whinnying peal of laughter. A ripple of more decorous chuckles spread out, until it seemed that there was a smirk on every face; every face, that was, except Hinshaw's, which was full of tranquil interest, and Sir Edward's, who had leant forward, his hand tight around his wine glass, his jaw clenched.

'She was ignorant,' Henry said, shrugging. 'But why should we blame her? No one has heard of Telverton silk. I hadn't. No – I am unjust – some people have heard of it, some people have already bought it, there is *some* demand. Our host has himself used it to insulate his carriage – I have had the pleasure of riding in that vehicle, and enjoyed the sensation . . . But perhaps you will agree with me that Sir Edward's use of it is not an unbiased testimonial.'

Another silence: as though he were delving down through strata, each one harder and deeper than the last. With a sharp crack Hinshaw broke another walnut into pieces. He did not seem to notice the heads that turned to him; he took a perfect nut from its wooden brainpan and chewed it thoughtfully.

'And it is expensive, I believe,' Henry went on. 'I have not seen the factory, and I am certainly no businessman myself, but it does not take a genius to realise that stuff like Telverton silk – fine, rare, exquisite – is not cheap to make. So as I understand it, gentlemen, the proposition Sir Edward is making is that you should lend him more money, so that he can continue to produce, at great expense, something that no one has heard of, and no one wants.'

It took every piece of determination he possessed to lean

back in his chair and raise his glass; he hoped they could not see how much his hand was trembling as he moistened his lips and set the glass down again, turning it as though he watched the light sparkling on the stem. Then, with a smile, he raised his eyes and glanced around. A few eyes darted to Sir Edward, but they returned at once to him, intent and intrigued.

'Then,' Henry said, 'why am I here? I came because of the silk. I came because, never having heard of it, not knowing such a thing might exist, I was astounded to learn that it did. When I was given a sample of it I could block out the sounds that had been driving me to distraction. I slept for the first time in months. That night, when the rumble of the traffic, the yelps of the beaten dog, the screeches and oaths of the drunkard who battered his wife – when they were silenced, when suddenly, incredibly, I was free to close my eyes in blessed, blessed quiet . . . In my entire life I have never come closer to a miracle.' He drew a breath, and saw that his hand was steady again.

'Noise is the scourge of our age, gentlemen. It is the dark shadow of progress. We mustn't yearn for the days before technology, or become nostalgic for a past that was poor, unhygienic and devoid of modern comforts. But we must not close our eyes – or ears – to the reality, which is that noise is as damaging to our senses as the smoke and stench of bad air, seeping into our homes and poisoning our lives. And the whole world agrees with me. The best nurses – Miss Nightingale among them, I believe – agree that an invalid may die – indeed, *will* die – sooner if they are not protected from disturbance of every kind. And it is not only the infirm who suffer. Every edition of *Punch* seems to include a cartoon in which an organ-grinder causes a traffic accident, frightens a servant into fits, or drives an author into penury. The misery caused by unwelcome sounds is manifold, and horrible – because, gentlemen, it deprives us of our very selves! I would rather not be able to breathe than not be able to think, or sleep, or love – because that is what is at stake.'

He paused. None of this was what he had prepared; he did not know where it had come from, only that he meant every word. 'What man can live whole-heartedly when he is assaulted on every side by clamour – when he is never safe from the demands of any passing street hawker, when there is nowhere to shelter from the malicious rasping of a musician, or the screams of a dying horse? Not to mention the relentless background groan of the city, monstrous and unending . . . An Englishman's mind is his castle, gentlemen, and we are besieged on every side.' Involuntarily he thought of the cress-seller who had yelled her wares outside the window as Madeleine paced across the room, white-faced; but the memory was distant, devoid of its usual power, and it was easy to let his mind slide past it without stopping.

'Sir Edward introduced me as a medical man. That was a kindness; I am no doctor. But I can imagine what it is like to look on a patient with gangrene, knowing that it is within my power to cure them. Noise is that disease, gentlemen, and the Telverton silk is that cure. No one wants it – or rather, no one wants it *yet*, because no one has heard of it. So if no one has heard of it, then for God's sake let us tell them! And as the word spreads, you will see the true power of what Sir Edward has made. Until now, its very magnificence has been its downfall. It is not until it acts upon your own flesh and blood and sense, that you can believe that it is as extraordinary – no, *more* extraordinary than the most fulsome recommendation. No one buys it, *yet*, because no one has experienced it. But once there is a bale in every haberdashery, there will be a curtain in every parlour. Every man, woman and child will be able to escape from the daily thunder of the modern world. Compared to other silks it is expensive, yes. But we are not selling silk, gentlemen, we are selling sanctuary – and at a time when it has never been needed more.'

He had not realised that he was leaning forward, his hands on the table; now he drew back, picked up his wine and swallowed a mouthful. No one else spoke. He took another gulp, and another, until he had drained the glass.

At last Hinshaw said, 'And the echoes? The Telverton malaise?'

Sir Edward laughed. 'The right side of the silk shuts them out,' he said. 'If everyone has the silk, no one need endure the echoes.'

Colcastle laughed too, shoving his chair back and raising his glass. 'He's got you there, Hinshaw, a palpable hit!' he said. 'If you don't like the echoes from your neighbour's silk, buy some yourself. Doubles the sales.'

'Or you might fold the silk over, to ensure that the right side faces outwards in both directions,' Sir Edward said.

'At twice the price,' Hinshaw said. 'When it is too dear already.'

'Nothing but God is perfect, Hinshaw.' There was a snigger from the other end of the table, and Hinshaw raised an eyebrow, but he tilted his head as if he was conceding the point, and did not reply.

'He is quite right,' a thin, elderly man said. 'It is too dear. Who is it, crammed into little jerry-built hutches all on top of one another, with organ-grinders outside? The middle classes! Not us. That's the point. Anyone who might want the silk is too poor to buy it.'

Henry put his hand out; his head was already spinning

from the wine he had drunk. 'I understand why you say that, sir,' he said. 'But – respectfully – I think you are taking too narrow a view. There are grand houses in every city. Is not Buckingham Palace within earshot of the Mall? There are mill owners in Manchester and Nottingham who surely live near to their concerns, and have both the money and inclination to seek respite. And within the biggest, best-run households there are clattering kitchens and squalling children. There are concert halls and theatres, libraries and hospitals. And . . .' He spread his fingers out on the table-cloth, watching the shadows deepen and slough like snakeskin in the candlelight.

'I am not a wealthy man,' he said, in a different tone. 'I am one of your *middle classes*, I suppose. I could not afford many of the things you would take for granted. But . . .' He had to pause, to draw a breath, to wonder for the first time which words to use. He was not sure; he trembled on the edge of falling silent again, but he sensed Sir Edward watching him and went on. 'I would pay it,' he said. 'I think we would all pay it. For our babies to sleep in peace. For our parents, that they can lie gently on their deathbeds. For our wives, that they may go through their confinement softly—' He stopped. The image that he had managed to push away before rose to the forefront of his mind, brighter than the room around him. Madeleine gasped, paused in her pacing to lean against a tall-backed chair, and in his ears the hoarse cress-seller shouted like an old witch, and swore drunkenly at Argyll when he tried to move her on. And then, or later, he could not remember, Madeleine had pressed her hand over her own mouth, to stifle her cries – and he, oh Christ! – he had shuffled from foot to foot, worrying that Argyll would hear her, and said, 'Perhaps if you breathed a little more slowly . . . ?' That had been before the midwife had come, and before they had called the doctor. Yes, it was one thing to shut out the street; but if he could have drawn a curtain across and told her that she could scream as loud as she wanted, abandon all decorum, all self-consciousness, that there was no need to fear that anyone would over-hear . . . He had not thought of that, until now. Would it have helped her? Would it have made the baby come more easily, so that—?

'Yes,' he said thickly, 'I would pay it. I would pay anything.' He pushed himself backwards from the table and stood up, swaying as the world swayed. 'Excuse me, gentlemen,' he said, and stumbled towards the door.

He did not go far. Just down the passage was the door that led out onto the terrace, and he stepped out into a cold clear night, turning his face up to stare at the stars. He meant to return after a few breaths, as though he had simply had an urgent need to empty his bladder; but he was shaking, his head spinning as though he had run miles without stopping, and his shirt was wet with sweat. Slowly his thoughts cleared and he began to shiver.

It was a long time before he mustered himself and pushed the door open; his eyes had adjusted to the darkness so that he was dazzled by the lamp in the corridor. Through the passage that led to the other side of the house – through the Great Hall, and the front door – he heard the departing voices of the guests, and the rumble of carriage wheels. Had they resented his prolonged absence? Had Sir Edward?

He moved towards the drawing room and stood in the doorway. He had expected it to be busy with servants clearing the detritus away, but it was quiet and nearly dark, now that most of the candles had subsided into dead stubs. Sir Edward was at the end of the table, leaning back on two legs of his chair, his hands linked behind his head and his eyes half closed. When he saw Henry, he rocked forward so that the chair legs landed with a thud. He did not speak; he only looked at him with an odd, unreadable expression on his face.

'Forgive me,' Henry said. 'I lost track of time. I only meant—'

Sir Edward raised his hand, cutting him off.

There was a pause. One of the last remaining flames guttered and died. It seemed to leave the room disproportionately darker.

'It is a good thing,' he said, 'that I am not a vain man.'

Henry was too exhausted to think of any defence. He should have known better than to trust that dangerous rush of inspiration; he should have clung to his dull little speech. He said, 'I'm sorry.'

The other man reached out and picked a thread of softened wax from the only candle that was still alight. He folded it into a ribbon, looped it around his third finger and admired his handiwork. Then, finally, he crushed it into a flat disc on the table. He said, 'You are a very clever salesman.'

Henry said, automatically, 'I didn't intend to be.'

Sir Edward gave a huff of amusement. 'Yes, I can believe that.' He beckoned Henry further into the room. 'Sit down, for God's sake, don't loiter in the doorway like a spectre.'

Henry obeyed him. His limbs might have been made of wax, too, numb and softening. One of his feet caught the leg of the table as he stepped forward, and he almost tripped.

'I thought that you had set out, deliberately, to humiliate me,' Sir Edward said, but before Henry could stammer a protest, he held up his hand to quell him. 'I believe my guests thought so too. They liked you for it. As soon as you made them laugh, at my expense . . . well, it was a masterstroke. By the time you got into your swing – rather purple for my taste, but you have a talent for finding a turn of phrase – they were at your mercy. They didn't notice – or rather, by then they didn't mind – that you turned out to be on my side, after all.'

'You must believe that I had no intention of—'

'As I say, I'm not a proud man. I can endure mockery, if it persuades one or two of them to cough up a few pounds. And they will, I think. Colcastle asked me as he left what rate of interest I thought was reasonable . . .' He picked up his glass and raised it in Henry's direction. 'It was well played.'

Henry felt warmth spread down from the top of his head, melting the wax in his bones, bringing sensation back into his legs. He said, shakily, 'All I did was to tell the truth.'

Sir Edward threw his head back to laugh. 'Yes,' he said, 'quite. Very good. That was what convinced them.'

Henry was not sure whether he was the butt of the joke, but he did not care. 'I hope that you are satisfied, sir,' he said, trying so hard to control his voice that he found himself using the stiff courtesy that he used to talk to cantankerous customers. 'You said it was a test; I hope I have passed.'

'Oh, yes,' Sir Edward said. 'Yes, you have certainly passed the test. With flying colours, I should say.' He tugged at his necktie until it came undone, and dropped it like a dark snake beside the candelabrum with its single wavering flame. He ran his fingers through his hair. For a moment, in the treacherous light, he might have been the same age as Henry; and Henry felt a strange rush of something that was not only admiration and relief. Then he lowered his hands.

'And so . . . what now? What shall I do with you now?'

Henry did not answer.

'Come, come. You are looking at me as though you are

entirely in my power. But you have your own ideas, don't you? I said you are clever, and you are – and not only because you convinced them to invest in my factory. They thought you were speaking to them. But – correct me if I am wrong – I think you were speaking to me. Weren't you?'

'Naturally, I could hardly have excluded—'

'*We*, you said. *We* are not selling silk, *we* are selling sanctuary. If no one has heard of the silk, then let us tell them – *us* . . .'

'It was a manner of speaking. Forgive me any presumption—'

'I suppose I thought you might be useful with the investors,' Sir Edward said, as if he had not heard Henry's interjection. 'A quick word or two in the old men's ears, like a shop-boy, persuading them to cough up. But it seems you have ambitions beyond that.' He tapped the table with a fingernail. 'I am not a halfwit, Latimer. We have placed advertisements for the silk in all the papers, and I expect every draper's shop in the country has had our trade catalogue. It is all very well to say that we should tell people, but as you point out, it has not worked so far, after ten years. So if *we*' – he placed a slight, sardonic emphasis on the pronoun – 'want to tell the world about it, how would you suggest we proceed?'

Henry hesitated. That sly, electric thrill was running through him again, the sense that whatever he said would be exactly right. He laced his fingers together on the table and said, 'May I speak freely?'

'Tell the truth and shame the Devil.'

'It isn't only a question of telling people that it exists and how much it costs. Your trade catalogue is worse than useless – that cheap cover, those lists of prices and awful cramped drawings, and nowhere a hint of artistry or care . . .' He met the other man's eyes levelly, ignoring his frown. 'You told me to tell the truth, sir. Why would someone glance at it twice? Unless they have the silk in their hands, they won't understand, and so naturally they won't want it. You must make them want to see it and touch it. You could send out samples with—'

'At ten guineas a yard?'

'Well then,' said Henry, 'you must *tell* them how extraordinary it is. I don't mean testimonials, or descriptions – although those are not a bad thing – but with . . . With the story of the Greek spiders, brought here against all the odds by an English hero – glittering threads spun in ancient Mediterranean glades – the factory that weaves a marvel out of a cobweb, like a fairy tale – and the silk itself that is somewhere between silver and alabaster and ivory, with a scent like flowers fallen to earth . . .'

'With poetry, you mean.'

Unsure whether he was being ridiculed, he said simply, 'Yes.'

Sir Edward opened his mouth. But as he drew breath, the last candle failed; abruptly they were plunged into darkness. 'Damn it. Come into the hall – here,' he said, and taking hold of Henry's sleeve he piloted him towards the dimly lit doorway. It seemed to take an age, and they stumbled against each other as they emerged into the passage, so that Henry caught the scent of eau de cologne and felt the warmth of the older man's breath. In the stronger light Sir Edward let go of him, but he did not move away. 'You must do it,' he said. 'If you think we must tell the world, you must show me how you think it should be done. Stay here for a while, and have a go at the catalogue for me.'

Henry said, a little hoarsely, 'For how long?'

'As long as it takes. Who knows? If you go on being useful,' Sir Edward said with a glint, 'perhaps forever.'

Henry dragged a hand over his face. It felt alien against his palm, as if someone had put a mask on him without his knowledge, or taken one away. The prize, he thought. This was the prize. *Forever* . . .

'Come on, Latimer. What do you say? You know you did your best to put the idea into my head. If poetry is what is needed, then by God you shall write some poetry. Don't you want to stay? I thought you did.'

'*Want* to? Oh yes,' he said, almost choking. 'But Mr Argyll—'

'Oh, to hell with that. I'll square it with him.'

He imagined Argyll's face, full of disbelief that someone should want *him*, Henry; as if Henry was worth something, and not just a bothersome son-in-law who must be patronised and provided for, a fellow sufferer in the dreary aftermath of death. He imagined the work he could do on the catalogue and the silk – the lovely, mysterious silk, with its whispers and enticing echoes – the days and nights he would spend in this expensive house, the days and nights here, as this man's guest – *friend* . . .

Sir Edward watched him. 'It's all right, then?' he said at last.

Henry nodded, and laughed, although he could not have said what exactly was funny. Only that it was absurd to be offered everything at once, a whole new life, so rich, so exactly what he would have dreamed of.

'Splendid. Now . . .' Sir Edward yawned and touched Henry briefly on the shoulder. 'I'm off to bed. Good night.'

'Good night,' Henry said.

'Oh,' Sir Edward said, and paused in the doorway. 'I was waving this at Colcastle earlier. You may as well have it back. For inspiration.' He held out a square of silk – the very square of silk, it seemed, that he had given to Henry the first time they had met. It glimmered in the shadows, and when Henry reached out to take hold of it, a murmur came and went in his ears, just on the edge of audibility.

Then there were footsteps, and Henry was alone. He held the silk to his chest, and he could have sworn that it pulsed against his fingers. Admiration, he thought, admiration and gratitude . . . That was all. That rush of mysterious yearning that he had felt, seeing the candlelight slide across Sir Edward's face – that had been nothing but admiration and gratitude. What else could it be? A new life. A gift. He was still drunk. Yes, that was it. But abruptly his heart was so light that it felt as though it had come loose, painlessly, from his chest, so that when he shook himself and hurried towards the stairs, he left it behind.

Six

A few days later Henry disembarked into the factory yard and caught his breath. After the insulated peace of the Clarence the noise made him stagger and reach out wildly to steady himself, gasping; but it was exhilarating, too, it shook him to his core so that he wanted to throw back his head and yell, knowing he would hardly hear his own voice. Such noise, such grating, bone-grinding, heart-shattering noise! Noise that blurred every outline, every certainty, even gravity . . . But as he forced himself to yawn, the deafening pressure in his ears eased. After a moment he could think clearly again, and although the cacophony still went on, relentless, he found he had enough presence of mind to turn slowly and look about him.

He had seen the factory from the streets beyond, but he had not grasped the scale, the spectacle of it. It towered above him, a mass of stone and silvery windows, the chimney so close to the high vault of heaven that he could not see where the column of smoke ended and the clouds began. He almost laughed at the monumental audacity of it, the grandeur: to think that such a thing had been built by human hands, and not divine . . . Industry, technology, capitalism – all were entirely the wrong words, when what this inspired was terror and wonder, when every nerve in his body thrummed at the consciousness of power. It was sublime, as a thunderbolt was sublime.

He did not know how long he would have stood there, marvelling, if Worsley had not sauntered towards him, his hands in his pockets.

'Latimer, isn't it? Good morning.' He said it flatly, as if it was too much trouble even to get Henry's name wrong. 'Come to inspect?'

Henry caught himself as his hand went to his pocket. He was not a schoolboy, obliged to produce his exeat. The note on his breakfast tray had said nothing but, *If you wish to visit the factory, the carriage will leave at nine. Worsley will meet you there. E.* But it had given him a peculiar, private pleasure – he had laid his thumb over the initial and pressed, as though it were soft wax, and he had wrapped it in his square of Telverton silk before he pocketed it. Now he said merely, 'Sir Edward suggested I should visit.'

'All right,' Worsley said, rolling his eyes. 'What do you want to see?'

'I don't know,' Henry said. 'Everything, I suppose.'

Worsley walked away without a backwards glance. Henry followed him, fumbling for the propelling pencil and ivory *aide-mémoire* he had brought with him, ready to make a note of his impressions.

They entered the building and hurried down an echoing corridor. Men rushed past, some workers in sweaty shirts, others obviously clerks with high collars and ink-stained fingers. 'Offices,' Worsley said, over his shoulder, 'left, Mr Riley, right, tallymen and accounts. Remind me, what is your area of – ahem – expertise? Selling ear trumpets?'

'Your employer has asked me to . . .' Henry hesitated. It was difficult to explain exactly what he had been asked to do; he could hardly say to Worsley that he had been hired as a poet. In any case, Worsley was not listening; by now he was several yards ahead, and did not pause until he reached the bottom of a spiral stairwell.

'We'll start at the top, it's quieter up there.' The staircase wound up past narrow windows like arrow-slits: up and up, until the sweat sprang out on Henry's forehead. When they finally came to the top, the thump and hum of the machines was dulled by distance. 'This is our drawing-out room,' Worsley said, and pushed open a door.

It was hot and dim. They were high up, close to the roof, and the only windows were at the far end of the space; it took Henry's eyes a moment to adjust to the twilight. Then he could make out star-shaped frames turning slowly on spindles, and children scurrying between them. Worsley put his hand out to prevent him looking more closely. 'Don't. We try not to disturb them more than we have to,' he said. At his voice, a couple of the children looked round, wide-eyed. Then they carried on hurrying from machine to machine. One child was swapping a new frame onto the mechanism; another was replacing the box that stood beside the wheel. Their small hands were deft, reverential; in the tremulous quiet they might have been diminutive acolytes tending to unseen gods. 'It's a delicate process,' Worsley added. 'They need gentle handling – the heat, the dark, the quiet . . .'

At first Henry had assumed that Worsley meant the children, but now it was clear that he hadn't. 'They . . . ?'

'The spiders.' Worsley gestured at the machines. 'Each reeling box holds two dozen of them, held in guillotines. One of the reelers will draw out the silk from the spinnerets and lay them onto the swift – the frame – and then set it turning, which keeps the silk flowing until the spiders are empty. Then the frame of thread is sent down to the next floor for throwing, and the used spiders go back to the spider house.' He pointed into the shadows. 'That boy there, you see? That's one of the runners. They bring up new spiders and collect spent ones. Other runners take down the frames and bring up empty ones. That way we can keep it going all day, without a break. Look, there – three rows down, can you see? She's drawing out the silk.' He pointed. A little girl was holding a thin wand, moving it slowly through the air: in the murk it was impossible to see the thread, and more than anything it reminded Henry of a conductor guiding an orchestra through the slowest of adagios. 'They touch the end of the wand to the spinnerets – tickle them, we call it – and then pull, very gently, to ease out the silk. It's a skilful job,' Worsley said. 'We find girls are more adept at it. The same with filling the reeling boxes – but you'll see that, later, when we go down to the spider house. Now – you see? Once the threads have been laid onto the swift, it can be set turning again.' They stood for a few moments, watching the frames turn. As well as the creaks and grinding of the machines, there was an uncanny sibilance in the air, like faint rain, or whispering; Henry imagined it coming from the spiders, the silk hissing out of their abdomens. 'You can examine them properly in the spider house. Hold one, if you like. But we've seen enough here, I think. Let's go down.'

As they descended the staircase again, Worsley said, 'I don't know what you said to him, but don't think you've taken me in, too.'

'I beg your pardon?'

Worsley shot him a look of utter dislike. 'Sir Edward trusts me,' he said. 'I've been working for him for years. I was one of the first people he employed when his father died.'

'But I hear that he is not making any profit,' Henry said, with more assurance than he felt. 'Perhaps that's why he—'

Worsley swung round, blotches spreading across his face like a rash. 'You keep your nose out. If you disappoint him, you'll regret it.'

'I'm not trying to get in your way. He has asked me to – well, to evangelise a little, that's all—'

'Christ! He's losing his nerve,' Worsley said. 'Clutching at anything that comes his way. But we don't need you. All he needs to do is wait. If he changes tack now . . .'

'I am not suggesting he changes tack. Only that he tells the world what the silk is. He cannot sell it if no one knows about it.'

There was a silence; albeit one that was full of the grinding of machinery. Worsley regarded him with narrowed eyes. Then, at last, he shrugged and continued down the stairs. The noise increased. 'Throwing machines,' he said, pausing on the bottom step. 'With ordinary silk, the thread has to be cleaned, but not Telverton silk. So we go straight to throwing and doubling. That turns single strands into thread with a twist, so that we can use it in the looms. Not that they're looms, strictly speaking, they're warp-knitting machines, but most of the people round here wouldn't know the difference. *Do* forgive me if I'm patronising you.'

Worsley opened the door and stood aside to let Henry look past him into the hall. Daylight streamed in through the high windows onto rows of machines, full of bobbins of gleaming silk. The action of the mechanisms was too fast to follow, and in spite of the busyness and noise the effect was almost one of stasis: like simmering oil, Henry thought, fiercely trembling.

Worsley let the door close again, led him down two flights of steps, and showed him the doubling hall. To Henry's eyes it looked almost the same as the throwing hall above, with the same windows and endless clattering machines, and the same din beating ceaselessly at his eardrums. He could not bear it – and yet he could have watched it forever: the threads that shone, the light that glimmered and pulsed, the machines that danced and never tired. It was only when Worsley grasped his arm that he realised he had been utterly absorbed.

'For God's sake, come on – what's the matter with you?'

He began to retort that he was perfectly all right, but Worsley had already gone down the stairs ahead of him. With an effort he tore himself away from the doorway and followed.

When they came to the ground floor Worsley strode off, waving at an internal window without slowing down. 'The tool-shop,' he said. 'We have a foundry, too, on the other side of the building. It's an enormous enterprise to keep the machines going, as you might imagine.' As he passed the tool-shop, Henry caught a glimpse of huge wheels and thrumming belts that stretched down from the ceiling. Then they stepped out into a narrow, coal-blackened yard. The noise was louder here, with a low drone that came and went in waves.

'Now,' Worsley said, 'I'll show you the weaving shed, and then we'll pay a visit to the spider house.' He had a glint in his eye that Henry couldn't read. 'Oh, it almost slipped my mind. Here.' He held something out, and for a second Henry thought he was offering him a tin of Numms. 'Wax for your ears,' he said. 'You mustn't go in here without it.' He plugged his ears and gestured to Henry to do the same. The wax muffled the higher notes, but it couldn't silence the tooth-shaking hum that underlaid them. His heart had started to beat uncomfortably hard.

Worsley pointed at the door, and his lips made the shape of 'Ready?' He had a glint in his eyes, like a child anticipating a treat. Then he pushed it open, and beckoned Henry into the shed.

It was like falling into a whirlpool: the noise met over his head, submerged him, dragged at every nerve until he thought he must fly apart at the force of it. It had been loud in the throwing and doubling halls, but this was different – this had a visceral, ravenous power, blanking out everything in his head except the urge to flee. He staggered. It was impossible to speak, or even to think; it was only his fierce refusal to concede defeat that kept him from falling to his knees. He snatched a shallow breath and slowly the room came into focus. He saw rows of looms – or whatever the machines were – the needles driving back and forth, mechanisms rising and falling, and men working them; he saw silk glimmering on the loom-beds and jerking on bobbins. A few feet away from them, two workers were gesturing, pointing and flicking their fingers, making fists and striking the air as though they were playing a strange version of odd and even; one of them frowned and bent forward to squint at a swinging lever. When they saw Worsley they melted away, lowering their heads as though they didn't want to be recognised. Then, with a shock, Henry saw a little pale hand emerge from underneath the nearest loom, clutching a tiny handful of silk shreds. He took an automatic step backwards. Of course, children would be the only ones small enough to crawl under the machines and collect the waste . . . He watched as the child emerged, hunched and grimy, wearing a sort of cap and apron that meant it was impossible to know whether it was a boy or a girl. It looked gaunter and greyer than the children in the drawing-out shed, with a fixed, unseeing gaze. It scuttled to the waste bin and then dropped to all fours and began to crawl under the next row of looms.

He blinked cold sweat out of his eyes. The muscles in his legs shook and feverish shivers ran up his spine. The racket was overwhelming – he hardly knew what was real and what was not—

There was a grip on his arm, dragging him round. He stumbled. The world slid sideways, threatening to give way – the echoes rose, malign and merciless—

Then, in sudden, blessed relief, they were outside again, and the door shut behind them, cutting off the noise. He was himself again – a little queasy and weak, but himself – and Worsley was looking at him with a smirk. He said something, and then pointed at Henry's ears. Of course, the wax . . . He fumbled to take it out.

'As you noticed,' Worsley said, 'it has a significant effect. Ordinary looms are noisy enough, but the silk causes such turbulence, it's really quite extraordinary. Only takes a couple of weeks before the men are as deaf as posts. That's why they use signs – did you see? Like monkeys.' He laughed.

'Yes,' Henry said, 'I saw.' His voice was hoarse.

'That's if the echoes haven't driven them to hang themselves first,' he added, and snorted. 'That was a joke, Latimer – the echoes don't exist, it's hysterical nonsense. Did you see the great wheel at the end of the room? That's driven by the main engine, and the ropes transfer power to the machines. Originally this mill was water-driven, and we still use some water power, but now it's mostly steam. The boiler house is on the other side of the coal store,' he added, and glanced up at the chimney that towered over them.

'Yes,' Henry said again. His mind still felt leaden. 'And the child,' he said, 'the children?'

'In the weaving shed we use children from the workhouse. Now, I could show you the boiler room, but I don't imagine that will be particularly relevant to your work. Shall we go to the spider house?' As he led Henry round the side of the building and along the canal, he added, 'There are different rules for children, you know, in silk mills – the work being easier than in cotton mills, generally, and children's fingers more able to do the delicate tasks.'

There had been nothing delicate about the child collecting the waste from underneath the looms – nor anything child-like, except its size. He said, 'And they . . . do they lose their hearing, too, like the men?'

Worsley shot him a look, and his smug, proprietorial air hardened. 'Those children are lucky,' he said. 'They have food and lodging, and the parish is very grateful to us for employing them.'

'Of course.' Henry leant on the wall and looked over the canal at the trembling reflections of brick and weed and sky. The fog was clearing; after the fury of the weaving shed, he could breathe again, think again. He wiped the sweat from his face, and felt a breeze run through his hair. Surely the child's hand had been plumper, the skin pinker, the face more intelligent than he remembered. It had been a child that was fortunate to be paid a fair wage, a child that was well fed and lodged.

Behind him, Worsley said, 'Are you ill? If industry makes you feel queasy, perhaps you had better tell Sir Edward—'

'What I tell him is my business.' He had not meant to speak so sharply, but he was not displeased by the way Worsley drew back and stared at him for a moment. He drew out his *aide-mémoire* again and wrote *benefits of industry* – and then, remembering the intent faces of the investors at dinner, *a net* – no – *a silken web to lift even the lowliest child in Telverton out of the gutter*. Yes, that was it; that was the proper way to think of it.

'The spider house, then. Coming?'

'Yes.' He slid his pencil and tablets into his pocket, and followed Worsley towards the low, dark-shingled building in front of them.

'Before we go in,' Worsley said, 'I must ask you to be careful. These spiders are very valuable, and very difficult to breed. After the wildfires in Greece they may be the last specimens of their kind. They never, ever leave this building, except in a reeling box. Workers who try to smuggle them out are always caught and punished, severely.'

'Are you suggesting that I might want to steal one?'

'Of course I am. They are priceless. Sir Edward might trust you, but I don't. We've had thieves before, turning up here, trying to sneak them away, hiding egg sacs in their boots, and so on.' He opened the door a little way, and Henry heard a faint resonance, a shiver in the air like the note of an Aeolian harp. A trickle of excitement ran down his spine. They went through a little ante-room, where a man with a truncheon threw his newspaper to one side and got to his feet, giving Worsley a hurried nod. Then they stepped into a long, low-ceilinged space that was dim and warm and still.

At first it reminded Henry of the drawing-out attic – the same tepid air and shadows – but then his eyes grew accustomed to the dusk, and he saw that he was wrong. The attic had been a place of meticulous order; this was more like a cave, a maze of glass, a mirage . . . Glass tanks were set in rows that ran the whole length of the room, with grey-clad women moving among them, and two or three children crouched in front of boxes at the far end. But in the half-light it was hard to make out the edges of the vivaria; instead, the silvery webs inside glinted in anarchic palaces and pavilions, swags and nets and intricate criss-crossings . . . The shimmer of the silk played tricks on Henry's eyes, blurring his sense of distance and perspective, like a hall of mirrors – and every mirror had its own voice, murmuring. He tried to identify the sound of his breathing, but it was lost in the fog of whispers and echoes from every corner of every tank.

'Each tank has one spider in it,' Worsley said. The words were only just comprehensible, as though they came through water. 'We lost nearly a whole generation by putting them in together. They eat one another, you see. After mating we have to get the males out immediately.'

Henry said, 'May I . . . ?' He gestured to the nearest tank.

'You can look. Don't talk too loudly or knock on the glass.'

He bent towards it until his face was hardly a hand's breadth from the glass. His reflection wavered, suspended in the darkness among the shining threads. At eye-level, the strands were spaced wide apart, taut and so fine they were only visible here and there; but in the lower corner of the tank the silk was thicker, pale and semi-lucent, like the inside of a shell. He watched. Nothing moved, but he had the impression of something looking back at him: an intelligence that was ancient, and alien. The hissing wavered and recommenced, with a hitch in it like laughter. He said, 'Do they make that noise?'

'What noise?' Worsley frowned. 'Oh, the turbulence. No, that's us, and the silk.'

So the sounds were only heartbeats and air, transformed. He bent his head again. This time his gaze landed on a clump of something caught in the cobweb on the far side of the tank. Sharp corners and blackish clumps protruded from the dense silk; he could make out flaps of withered skin, a desiccated piece of fur, a claw. He recoiled.

'Look out!'

He'd nearly reeled into another tank. He said, 'I'm sorry,' and steadied himself, carefully, his palm flat against the glass. He'd imagined the spiders among twisted olive branches and pendulous vines – not in bare tanks, with carcasses left hanging in the webs . . . But there was a shifting beauty in the planes of glass and cobweb, the glittering eyes watching from every corner, the dark remains of death scattered amongst the silver and pearl. The holy of holies, the innermost sanctuary, perilous to mortals . . . He shook his head, trying to compose himself, but the world was elusive as mist, slipping away when he tried to look at it directly. Was it the echoes, this sense of intoxication, of wonderment – or something else, something almost divine?

'Mr Worsley,' a woman said, approaching them. With a shock Henry saw that it was the woman he had seen weeping in the street, the day he'd arrived in Telverton. But she did not acknowledge Henry, or even glance at him. 'Excuse me, sir. My name is Mercy Harman.'

'What?'

'I am Mercy Harman. I wrote a letter to Sir Edward. Please . . .'

Worsley frowned. 'What could you possibly have to say to him? Get back to your work.'

'I'm sorry, sir, but please – please will you speak to him? Mention my letter. I am desperate for his answer.' Another woman gestured covertly at her through a blurred wall of glass and silk, but she went on, 'Please, sir. Please. I am asking humbly. But my son – he isn't right, since he had to work in the weaving shed—'

'And why was that? Because he was in the workhouse, I assume?'

'Please, sir. It wasn't his fault.' Her voice, already blurred by the silk and that strange drunken accent, quavered.

'I do not deal with correspondence. I am no one's secretary. And if I *were*, it would not be your place to speak to me so impertinently. Now *get back to work*, or you will find yourself on the streets again and your son back in the workhouse. Count yourself lucky you have a job.'

Her hands knotted together in her apron, twisting it into a rope; then, with a rush of breath, her shoulders dropped and her arms fell to her sides. She bowed her head. 'Yes, sir.' She shuffled back towards the tank she had been tending.

'Worsley,' Henry started, but he did not know what he wanted to say. If he tried to intercede, would Sir Edward hear of it, and think he had spoken out of turn?

'Actually . . .' Worsley clicked his fingers. 'Hey. Yes, you – Harman, did you say? – get that spider out, will you? You can show it to this gentleman.'

Mercy fumbled in the tank. 'No,' Henry said, 'thank you, there is no need . . .' Her reflection in the glass might have been another woman, any woman; and just as he thought so, he heard – or imagined he heard – a different, a beloved voice, saying his name. He blinked. Of course it was nothing; only the inconstant whisper of the webs.

She brought out her hand, the fingers curled loosely over the palm, and started towards him. 'No,' he said again, raising his voice, 'I have no desire—' But he broke off and stared into the silvery nave between the rows of tanks, the clustered webs that seemed to hang like banks of fog, blocking out the light. There were women moving quietly among them. None of them was looking in his direction, but he'd heard someone calling. He took a faltering step, not knowing where he wanted to go, only that he'd heard and he had to obey. He said, 'Yes . . . ?'

'Sir? Shall I . . . ?'

'Stand still, Latimer. Where are you off to? Yes, Harman, pass it over – carefully, now . . .'

But he raised a hand, distracted; if only they would be quiet and let him listen . . . '*Yes*,' he said again, 'I'm here . . .' And at the far end, beyond the other women and the children, in amongst the shimmering silk and the treacherous light, he saw her. Only a glimpse, but enough – her profile, the angle of her chin, her hair . . .

'Madeleine,' he said, '*Madeleine?*'

'What the devil are you talking about?' Worsley said. 'Do you want to see a specimen, or don't you? Never mind, Harman, put it back. I say—'

'She was calling me,' Henry said. 'I saw her, over there . . .' He took another step, his knees trembling, a sudden thunder throbbing in his ears. 'It can't be, but . . .'

'Oh, damn it all,' Worsley said. 'Give me a hand here. Yes, you and you, hop to it, can't you see he'll break a tank—'

Henry felt the floor ripple. He looked down; darkness flickered around his shoes, sparkling, sending black sparks flying up towards his face. For a moment all he felt was wonder. Any moment now the veils around him would tear apart, and the world beyond them appear: a world of infinite space and stars, and unimaginable depth and dark. The spiders were the gatekeepers, they spun the doorway into it, and in the blazing dark Madeleine beckoned, yes – or love, anyway, redemption, no more death—

He sank to the floor, using the last dregs of his consciousness in an effort not to crash sideways into the tanks; then the darkness boiled up, and he was submerged.

Part III

Kratos, September 182—

Perhaps I am disloyal to be content, while James sinks further and further into dejection. He curses Gritney and the phantom spiders, refusing to make any plans either to go on or to return home, and I fear he has developed a fondness for the rough resinous wine that one of the men from the village is happy to sell him. But for the last few weeks I have felt myself at home here, engaged in the small daily tasks of procuring food, cleaning our clothes and bartering for small luxuries, and when I have had time to spare I have accompanied Hira in her errands, carrying baskets and water for her like a shadow-slave, glad to be there even though she never thanks me. Most of all I treasure the moments before dawn, when I walk to the shore and find her there, alone, perhaps waiting for me, perhaps not. Then she is like another woman, she will ask questions and tell me stories, and sometimes we have laughed like children; and best of all she will lead me into the water and set me upon my knees in the swaying swell, or hold me as I teeter on my toes in the deeper water, breathing with me until I have mastered my fear and can feel the strength of the sea cradling me. Oh, how I love it, how I dream of it, awake and asleep! I have not told James. He would not understand, my joy in it would be like salt rubbed on his rawness. I do not know if I am being selfish; but surely a wife has a duty to equip herself to support her husband, and surely I am more use to him as I am than sharing his despondency and being likewise good for nothing? Oh, I should strike that out! Thank goodness that he will never read these pages – nor anyone else, indeed. Nonetheless I must remain disciplined, and not stray into unseemly candour. Come, Sophia, be glad you will have no harsher reader than your own future self – and, God willing, if there are ever any children—

I repeat – and underline, discipline; and begin again, since in any case that is not why I took up my pen after such a long silence.

I had thought, until a few days ago, that after all, the island was no more mysterious than any other. But the day before yesterday – was it? No, the day before that – I went down to the beach very early and Hira was not there. I knew I was unreasonable to be disappointed, for she has no obligation to meet me there every day; but when I had waited for nigh on an hour I walked back through the village and found that it was peculiarly quiet. No women were at work in the little patches of garden or spreading linen to bleach in the sun. No one was drawing water at the well. The only people I saw were children, tending fish smoking over a fire; and when I asked them with wide gestures what had happened, they only stared at me, and made no effort to mime an answer. I hurried back to James, and spent the day tidying our little house and gathering flowers to brighten the corner where he sits staring at his books; but whenever I paused outside to listen, I heard no voices or movement, not even the clanging of pots or the slosh of water. The uncanny stillness continued, as though some spell had been cast over the village: for two whole days and nights I did not see Hira, nor any other woman, and I began to be afraid. I do not know exactly what I dreaded: that they had taken refuge ahead of some enormous tempest, or that the village had been raided by pirates? Neither explanation suited exactly, since the children and the few old men I encountered were stolid, neither grief-stricken nor fearful: but they did not or could not tell me the solution to the mystery. And the silence, oh! the silence that hung over the place . . . It was as if the very sea had lowered its voice.

Then, last night, I heard drums. At first I thought it was thunder, and jolted out of sleep sweating and terrified, sure that the anticipated storm had come and we should be washed away. But it was too constant, too rhythmic, with a deep pulse that set my skin tingling. It was coming from inland, beyond the pine forests. When I tiptoed to the window I could see no light, no movement, only the wide spread of stars against the dark slopes. Somehow I knew that Hira was there, at the heart of it, whatever it was; and the thought kept me there until I was stiff and shivering, yearning to be with her and at the same time a little glad I was not. At last I crept back into bed, but in my absence James had spread his limbs like a starfish, leaving the narrowest margin for me, and I did not fall asleep again.

Just before dawn there were footsteps outside. I had not known I was listening, but as soon as I heard them I slid from the bed, caught up my clothes and shoes and slipped out into the chill morning dusk. I took the path down to the sea, and at last, when I emerged onto the pale sand, I saw Hira, as I had known I should. She did not look at me, but she did not show any surprise as I sat down next to her. For a long time we merely watched the sea, and the sky grew light and the water reflected it, and then Hira turned and smiled at me.

I burst out, 'Where have you been? I was scared – I thought—'

'In the sacred place. Do you remember the old woman who lived in the hut at the edge of the cliff, with her grandsons? She is dead.'

'I didn't know – I am sorry to hear it. When?'

'Yesterday.'

'But then – you weren't here. Do you leave, when someone is about to die? Surely—'

She laughed. 'No, foolish one! We took her to the sacred place. It is easier there. Kinder. She died slowly, but as she should, in the place where the gods are. The temple of the spinners . . . Oh, I am too weary to explain this to you now.'

'You took her away from her house, to die?'

'Yes.' She raised her eyebrows at me, with another glint of mockery. 'And she was glad of it. Just as Misia will be glad to go, when it is time for her child to come. It is not a bad place or a good place; it is a place for – for unknotting, for whatever must be. Birth and death, and sometimes other things, in-between things. We all know this, and we go to watch over one another, knowing that one day it will be our turn.'

'And the drums?' I said. 'I heard drumming.'

'After she had gone, we . . .' She shrugged, in the way she does when she does not know the word. She lay back on the sand and closed her eyes.

'Mourned?' I said, but she did not answer. I could not imagine a deathbed up there, in the forests. *The temple of the spinners.* Would it be like the ruins we had seen, near Athens? Or the little Orthodox churches that we had visited, with their dim, jewelled-gold interiors? A place to die and be born – to be unknotted . . . I said, 'Will you take me there?'

Her eyes opened, and met mine.

'Not while someone is dying, I don't mean that, but the place – I should so much like to see the place.'

She held my gaze for a fraction of a second. 'You?'

I started to say, 'Please . . .'

'No. No, how could I?' She began to laugh. 'You, the maggot-woman? No, of course I cannot, how could you think I could?'

'The *maggot-woman*?' I repeated, and I felt humiliation sweep over me. I had thought she accepted me – or at least that she did not despise me . . . 'What difference does it make if my complexion is paler than yours? James cannot abide a sunburnt woman—'

'No,' she said, shaking her head, still laughing. 'No, I do not mean that. You have not yet hatched.'

'I do not understand you at all.' I said it with great dignity, but she did not seem to notice; she subsided back onto the sand with a smile, as though she were still amused by some childish drollery.

There was a silence. The sun had risen behind the island, and the sea glittered on the horizon, although we were still in shadow. Through the salt wind I thought I could smell the daylight, acid and floral as a lemon. I looked down at my hand, which was lying on the sand, only a thumb's length from Hira's. 'Shall we go into the sea?' I said. 'For my lesson?'

'Not now,' she said, and closed her eyes again. 'I am tired.'

'I must go soon,' I said.

'Then go.'

But I did not go. I sat quite still, trying not to betray how disconsolate I felt – how hateful and ashamed and wounded – for I had missed her so, and thought I was more to her than a mere chore. Now I knew she did not care a jot for me, after all – indeed, I might as well not have been there, for after a moment she rolled over, pillowed her head upon her hands, and seemed to slide easily into a slumber. The dark *himation* slipped from her head and her hair shone where it fell across her face. She was so different from James, who snores and flings himself about in his sleep: she was like a rock, an animal, a cup that was exactly full, neither empty nor overflowing. Oh, I cannot explain it! She was so entirely herself, there between the earth and the sky, while the sun climbed and the sea murmured. I dug my fingers into the sand and clenched my fist, as though I could anchor myself there beside her, forever.

Gradually my emotion passed, and I found I was listening to the waves as though to music. There was no melody, only rhythm, deep as the pulse an infant might hear in the womb, but threaded through the deepest notes was something else. I thought I heard a voice calling my name – a child's voice, fragile, unknown, beloved . . . Or is that only my fancy now, as I screw up my face and bite my pen in the effort to recollect *precisely*? I must be strictly truthful, or what is the purpose of this record? So let me say that I heard . . . *something*, or thought I heard something, and as I scrambled to my knees and stared about me, for a fraction of a second it was clear: the heart-rending cry of someone I knew, certain and impossible as a dream. Then it slipped away, swallowed again by the swell.

I sank back onto my knees, breathless. Hira sighed and shifted. There was a jewel caught in her hair – no, a comb, I thought, fine and filigreed, with glints of wire and a central boss of enamel – and then, to my horror, I saw it crawl.

It was a spider. I must confess that my first impulse was to flinch. It was quite awful to see its legs creep so delicately over Hira's hair, until it found its way to her temple and across her cheek. How could she lie there, unwaking, while it crossed the line of her lips? I steeled myself to sweep it away. But before I could reach out it scuttled further into the folds of her *himation*, and Hira turned her head away, her eyelids fluttering.

Relieved of the obligation to touch the creature, I drew back and regarded it, while my hammering heart slowed; and somewhat to my surprise I found that it was worthy of my attention. It was not very much larger than the spiders I have seen in England, but it was much more beautiful: the abdomen was marbled in black and red like a Dutch endpaper, the legs darkly translucent and dabbed with crimson. It was very still; if I had been more whimsical I might have imagined that it was graciously allowing my scrutiny.

A few tiny gleaming threads caught the light, stretched across Hira's mouth. A web, or the beginnings of one. As she exhaled, the strands trembled, with an infinitesimal glimmer, and I heard it again, that elusive lovely call.

I looked wildly over my shoulder and saw no one. When my eyes returned to the spider, it had moved. Now it had climbed to Hira's shoulder, and behind it trailed another trace of silver. I felt an absurd compulsion to lean towards it, closer to that shimmering near-nothing. I yearned to listen forever, in a dream like an opium-eater, until I died of hunger and thirst . . .

Perhaps I was a fool; for it was only then that I realised that the specimen must be none other than the famous *Pseudonephila* that James had so longed to see. In a rush I remembered the last time we had stayed in Athens, and Broderick Jones's ridicule, his insistence that the species was a myth invented to explain the hallucinations of drunken sailors. 'Gritney was a mooncalf,' he said then, 'addled by too much laudanum and poetry. It is a wild-goose chase, Ashmore – you might as well go looking for the Land of Cockaigne.' But the stories were no less than the truth, for here was a spider as real as my own flesh, and a web that sang to me with a siren voice. Where James had failed, I had succeeded – or rather, I had been fortunate, favoured by whichever God had enticed the spider to crawl into Hira's *himation*. I gazed at it, struck dumb by incredulity and triumph.

But it was no good. I had not found its habitat; it was some freak of chance that had made it a stowaway, and soon, no doubt, it would steal away into the shadows. If I ran for James, I guessed I should never find it again. I might, indeed, have asked Hira where it had come from. But I could not bear it if she lied, or shrugged, or pretended she did not understand the question – and she would, I know she would have done! If it had come from the sacred place, which she had refused to show me . . .

I kept my eyes upon the spider, hardly daring to blink. Hira was still asleep, utterly at peace, utterly distant from me. She would not know, or care.

I drew the *himation* off my own head, and with hands that were steadier than I expected I laid it gently around the spider, gathering it at the sides to make a sort of pouch. Hira did not move, but when I glanced at her I hesitated, and it was only the thought of James's approval that gave me the strength to clamber to my feet and hurry away, conscious at every step of my precious cargo.

I had not considered what I should do with the creature when I arrived at our house, and it almost escaped as I set it on the floor, before I had the wit to put an empty pot over it. In the split second before it was hidden from view it seemed to regard me with a baleful, reproachful stare – which of course is ludicrous, since it is not possessed of features which allow any variations in expression. I hesitated, but it would have been unkind to James (and foolish, when I had screwed my courage up to carry it in my own hands) not to allow him the opportunity to examine it.

When I opened the door to our room, James opened his eyes with a start. He clapped his sweat-wrinkled Bible shut and got to his feet, already exclaiming, 'Sophia! Your clothes are dirty, and there is a cobweb in your hair – I did not think you would abuse your liberty so—' but I dared to interrupt him, and as soon as he comprehended what I meant he forgot the drift of his criticisms and pushed past me, eager to see the spider for himself. At first he did not believe that it was indeed a *sireine* (and he cannot be blamed for that, since it had not had time or space to spin the silk that distinguishes it); but at last excitement overtook him and he waved me away. 'I shall want peace and quiet,' he said. 'Entire quiet, please – you had better go outside, even your footsteps would disturb me,' and then he turned his back so decisively I felt as though I had ceased to exist. I was determined, however, not to feel it as a snub: what mother, seeing her child launch himself delightedly on a toy she has provided for him, does not rejoice? I quashed my vainglorious desire to be thanked, and absented myself as he had asked.

And this evening, although he did not dine with me and still, indeed, has not come to bed, he passed me as I sat on the veranda and gave me his old crooked smile, the one that he would give to Jesus Christ should he ever look on Him face to face. It goes to my soul like brandy, that smile. He said, 'Ah, Sophia, my beauty of cloudless climes and starry skies,' and blew me a kiss; and I am happier than I have been for some while, and I shut my eyes and find that it is easy to turn my prayers to his – our – God, and drive away the memory of this morning, and Hira's sleeping face, and how I crept away with the spider like a thief.

James did not come to bed last night, and I was afraid this morning lest I should find him ill or angry or both. It is so rare these days that a moment of gladness lasts; for a long time, I have only seen those brief moments of softness drowned in strong drink, and then lost upon the morrow when he wakes with a sore head. So I crept from my bed as silently as I might, thinking to find a cup of water and a plate of fruit to lay beside him, in case he woke with any appetite. But as soon as the wood creaked under my bare feet I heard answering footsteps, and he was there in the doorway, dishevelled but smiling. 'Sophy,' he said, 'it is the morning already! I have only just seen how pale the lamp is in the daylight. Come, come,' and he took my arm and pulled me into the room at the front of the house. 'You see here?' he said. 'The spider has spun me a web. I think I have tamed her,' he added, laughing. 'She and I have been in conversation all night – oh, Sophy, I forgot my evening prayers!'

'I am sure that her Creator will take it as a compliment,' I said, daring my luck.

He shook his head at my frivolity, but still smiled. 'And her silk,' he said, 'her silk is a marvel. To think that I have found the first verifiable specimen of the *Pseudonephila sireine*! Damn those simpletons in the village, I suppose they have no conception of what is on their very doorstep . . . It will make my name – my fortune! My brother cannot dismiss me now. I might as well have found a mermaid or a unicorn.' (I suppose, as he had been working all night, it had slipped his mind that it had been I who had found the spider; not that it matters.) He piloted me towards the far end of the room, where there was indeed a web, a yard or so wide, strung across the doorway to the veranda. 'Now,' he said, 'sing.'

I thought his exhortation was addressed to the spider until he shook me, not unkindly, and repeated, 'Sophia, sing! I have been whispering and orating and humming all night, and my vocal apparatus is exhausted. Anything will do.'

I glanced at him, bewildered, but I had the impression that his gaiety rested upon a very narrow edge, and I did not care to test his patience; and so I began to sing the old air, 'Early One Morning'. But I found myself catching my breath and coming to a halt, for the room seemed to shift around me, sliding a little as though it bent towards my voice. I began again hastily, anxious to please James, but he laughed and raised his hand in a gesture of satisfaction.

'You hear it too!' he exclaimed. 'It is a siren voice indeed, is it not? Do you feel that the room has elongated and constricted unpredictably, and that you yourself are precipitously drawn towards the centre of the web?'

'Yes,' I said. There was no need to search for my own words: his were a perfect summary of the sensation.

'Yes! Exactly,' he said, and bent to the floor, gathering up pen and commonplace-book to make a note. 'Oh, I shall write the finest essay on this phenomenon! Broderick Jones will be sick with envy.' But as he stood up straight he staggered, and I saw for the first time how the long night had left the marks of exhaustion upon his face. I caught hold of him, and for once he did not push me away but submitted meekly to my aid. 'Thank you, Sophy,' he said. 'It leaves one rather light-headed.'

'You must eat,' I said, 'and sleep. You have been too hard on yourself, my dear.'

I shrank a little as I said it, anticipating a sharp retort; but he nodded. Then he clutched at me. 'But Sophy – you must watch her. I will prepare a case for her when I am rested, but if she escapes—'

'Yes, my love.'

'No, no! How dare you humour me, like a child? Stay here, and watch her! You must not move from this spot. If she tries to return to the forest, you must catch her – she is mine now, you understand, *mine*. I may never find another one. You promise, Sophy? Not a muscle, whatever happens.'

I nodded. At last, searching my face with his eyes, he nodded too, and sighed such a breath that the room whispered around him like a gathering storm. He let go of me and slipped through the doorway to our bedroom. A few moments later I heard his clothes drop to the floor, and his body onto the palliasse of our bed.

I drew a stool into the centre of the room and settled on it. But even though I made no sound, I found myself glancing continually over my shoulder, convinced that I was not alone; and at last I drew the stool back until my shoulder blades rested against the wall. The spider began to refresh its web, with intricate criss-crossings of the centre whorl. At first I thought I should not be able to bear the tedium of waiting while James slept – not knowing how long I should be obliged to remain in that room, like a prisoner; but after what might have been half or three quarters of an hour I found that my attention ceased its flitting and buzzing and grew still. I thought of the great basilica of Vézelay, and its Roman arches; of the painted church of home, with its peeling saints and their long quiet faces, their hands raised in blessing; and of the sea breaking upon the shore while Hira slept.

And it seemed to me that we made a kind of pact, the spider and I: that I should watch over it, and in return it should continue to please James, and thus to please me.

Kratos, September 182—

Until now I have not had either the will or the opportunity to write: James has been (I may write it here) a tyrant, ordering me to leave him alone during the day and to stay quite still at night; once, when any reasonable husband would have been lying beside me asleep, he came in upon me when I was using the pot and stood in the moonlight like an avenging angel, complaining that my piss rang out like church bells, and how could he hope to work in such a din? For the last few days I have been unwelcome in my own house. Because the spider has strung its web across the door to the veranda, I have been obliged to enter the house on hands and knees, like some heathen pilgrim, while James hissed through his teeth and exhorted me not to endanger some crucial thread. Then he would return to his commonplace-book and the crude percussive instruments he had constructed, while I crept humbly to bed. To be quite frank I was beginning to chafe under this treatment, and to wonder how long I might stand it, and how on earth I should proceed when my sufferance was expended. But the Almighty never sends us a trial we cannot endure, and on (I think) the third day I returned, just before sunset, to find James in the garden, gazing around him with the sweet amazement of a child awoken from a dream. He called, 'Sophy!' and held out his hand to me. 'I have written a comprehensive account of the spider and its characteristics,' he said, before I had set foot upon the veranda, 'and you shall be the first to read it – I shall dedicate my discovery to you. Or perhaps you might prefer me to explain in ways more suited to the feminine mind. Come, let me demonstrate my experiments, you shall hear it all with your own ears and I will anatomise the results for you.'

'How clever you are,' I said, and he led me to the doorway where the spider hung, hardly visible now that the sun had dipped behind the trees. And it is true; he *is* clever. I hesitate to set out here what he told me, for I know my inferior understanding may mangle it, and his essay will tell the world much

133

better than I can. But it is a useful exercise for one's own comprehension, and I know that my future reader will pardon me for inaccuracies – whoever you are, my dear, I know you will be kind – so let me attempt to summarise his lesson.

It is James's belief that the spiders prey on bats, which navigate by a song inaudible to human ears. I was surprised to hear that, but James rolled his eyes and said he should soon lay open phenomena which would strain my credulity even more; and he told me with some relish of many experiments which confirm it, when bats have had their eyeballs cut out and their ears burnt away. 'Now you might think,' he said, 'that the *sireine*'s web works on the same principle as any other: that its prey merely blunders into it, and there thrashes against the sticky threads until it is weakened enough to be wrapped in silk and sucked dry. But the ingenuity of the Almighty goes far beyond such reliance on chance. The web entices the bats towards it, through a masterly feat of deception.' Here, if I remember correctly, he took up a pen and used it as a pointer, approaching the web and lowering his voice so that the room should not resonate too distractingly. 'Now, Sophy, the effect of *sonation* is created by an impetus that starts a vacillation within an elastic medium. That is' – he saw, I suspect, the inability of my female intellect to follow his words – 'when something strikes something else, it makes a wave. Imagine a splash which begins a ripple in a tank of water: there are peaks and troughs, moving points where there is either *more* fluid or *less*. When the wave reaches the ear, *audition* occurs as the organ perceives the rapid changing of density.' He paused, to ascertain whether I had understood so far; which, I think, I had. 'Now, here is the point,' he went on, turning aside momentarily from the web to gesture. 'Imagine another splash at the other end of the tank which sets up another ripple, so that the two meet in the middle. What happens? It depends, does it not, on the timing and position of the second splash? Either the waves meet, and, their rhythms coinciding, amplify each other – so that the peaks are higher and the troughs deeper – or they are opposed to each other, so that both peaks and troughs are flattened, and the waters are calmed. If they are *exactly* opposed to each other, then what results is a surface like a mirror, as though neither splash has occurred: that is, silence.'

'I think I begin to grasp it,' I said.

'See here,' he said, and swung back to the cobweb. 'Such a singular, a stupendous mechanism for entrapment! I cannot tell how the threads are composed, but my hypothesis is that the outer rim of the web – here, you see – is sensitive to vibration, so that every tiny breath is transmitted inwards, towards the centre. Then here, where the web is densest, there is a kind of miracle. The silk reflects the sound outwards, but the reflection is not a mere, mindless reproduction – for that, of course, would not account for the differences in time, direction and distance. Instead it is as though, sensing a lock, it creates a key – or an intaglio to a cameo, if you like; it moulds the air like wax under the impress of a seal. Do I make myself clear? Whether this is due to the configuration of the strands, or only to the infinitesimal properties of the silk, I am not yet sure; I wonder whether there is some axis of reflection within every strand, combined with material that has peculiarly resonant properties. What is extraordinary is the way it must physically embody a complex formula where "x" is transformed to its corresponding "y". I have never seen such perfect evidence that God is an enthusiast of algebra.'

'Indeed,' I said. I am not a particular devotee of algebra myself, but I suppose if God invented mosquitoes and leprosy, He would not be ashamed of any branch of mathematics.

'And that is not all, Sophy! For so far, however wonderful,

what I have described is a matter of physics – a machine, if you like, where one part responds to another, producing an acoustic result. I believe that what the bats *hear* is an absence at the heart of the web, a mere nothing – as though the web were a ring surrounding a clear path. But that on its own would not be enough; the chance of a bat choosing that particular direction would be no higher than any other route through the obstacles presented to it. I contend – I am almost certain – that there is another element to the spiders' entrapment. The web not only disorientates the bat, it attracts it. Have you ever seen a cat mazed by catnip, or a chicken hypnotised by a line drawn in chalk? Gritney said that the bats fly straight towards the *sireine*'s web as though it calls to them: into the very densest weaving of silk, the most lethal place of all. That is not explained by any auditory phenomenon alone; that speaks to me of a different kind of lure.'

'You mean,' I said, thinking of the voice I had heard, 'that there is a kind of music, beyond the limits of our own hearing, but perhaps still in the air – a celestial music – and they hear it, and love it?'

He grimaced. 'I wish you would attend to what I am saying, Sophy, and not depart on your own flights of fancy. I am not talking about music.'

'I only meant – like the sirens – perhaps that is why they are called *sireine*—'

'Gritney may have named them, but he never had the wit to capture one! Who has been studying this specimen, you or I? Or should I give you this,' he said, offering me the pen with heavy irony, 'and allow *you* to educate *me*?'

'I am very sorry,' I said.

'Quite,' he said, somewhat mollified. 'There is much that remains to be elucidated, and I am glad of it, for it will all provide material for my essays. I do not pretend to have answered every question after only four days of study.' He began to gnaw his thumbnail, his gaze returning to the doorway, even though in the dusk I did not think he could see the web or its chatelaine. 'Music,' he said, 'yes, perhaps there is something in that idea, for it acts upon the soul through the senses – even in us it can inspire divine madness, ecstasy or despair . . .'

I said nothing, not wanting to recall his attention. But at last he looked again in my direction. 'My darling,' he said, 'my own dear Sophy.'

I did not want to vex him; but I could not conceal the tears that rose in my eyes to hear him speak so tenderly. 'Yes, James.'

'You are so kind,' he said, 'so womanly, so loving. And I am an old bear, sometimes, amn't I?'

'No,' I said, 'no, you are passionate, that is all.'

'Go to bed,' he said, 'but do not extinguish the lamp. I must put my spider somewhere safe, and then I shall come to you.'

I said nothing; I could not have borne it if he had changed his mind. It had been so long since he had slept beside me, let alone embraced me as a husband should embrace his wife, and I was half choked by hope and desire. I kissed his hand, and obeyed.

I heard him catch the spider with a grunt of triumph; then he did as he had said, and came to bed.

Kratos, November 182—

I have not dared to take up my pen again until now. I still tremble, writing these words, as if the very action of it might do or undo some spell. But I think – I am nearly sure – I hope, that by God's infinite love, through the intercession of Jesus Christ, in answer to my endless, hopeless prayers— Oh, Sophia, *write* it!

I think I have conceived James's child.

Seven

The Silk depicted in these pages is spun by Spiders from the myth-
ical vistas of the Ancient World, and made into a material finer,
lighter and airier than that of the mulberry-worm. It has the
glimmer of opal, the shimmer of pearl, and the sheen of silver; and
it encloses the listener within a silence so perfect . . . Henry's pen
paused above the paper, while with his left hand he flicked
over a page of a thesaurus. He crossed out 'shimmer' and
wrote 'lustre' above it. But he could not think of a good
way to finish the sentence, and he raised his head again
and stared into the hearth, where the fire had subsided to
a few glowing embers. Apart from the dying firelight and
the lamp beside the desk, the library was dark and still:
there was only soft shadow, and glints of gold from the
spines of books and the ornate ceiling, and the quiet patter
of rain on the window.

He ran his hand over his eyes, which were sore and gritty.
In the days since his visit to the factory he had thrown
himself into his work on the catalogue; he had written and
sketched for hours on end, pacing the room when he could
not think of the perfect phrase, editing and re-editing his
foreword until he knew it almost by heart, pausing only to
imagine Sir Edward's reaction. He had worked late into the

nights, putting off the moment when he retired to bed; even in his sleep he had dreamt of words, picking them one by one out of billowing webs to find that they came alive and writhed in his hands.

A silence so perfect . . . But inspiration had run dry. His gaze drifted to the picture that hung in the alcove. The woman's dark eyes stared back at him, as if she had something she wanted to say.

The door opened. 'Latimer,' Sir Edward's voice said, with a hitch of laughter, 'you gave me a shock. Working late, aren't you?'

Henry swung round, pushing the chair back and getting to his feet in one movement. 'I hope you don't mind,' he said, 'I have mostly been working in my room, but I came down to consult—'

'Don't be absurd, my dear chap.' As he came into the circle of lamplight Henry saw that Sir Edward was flushed, a little dishevelled, and his collar was open at the base of his throat. He looked down at Henry's papers. 'What's this?'

'I thought the catalogue should have a kind of foreword – a note to the customers, explaining—'

'Ah yes. Poetry. Good, good.'

'It's not quite finished, but if you would like to read it, sir . . .' Henry held it up. Suddenly his breath did not quite reach the depths of his lungs.

'No need, not now.' Sir Edward turned away; but instead of leaving the room, he crossed to the window and drew aside the curtain to stare at his own reflection.

Henry nodded. In silence he laid down the paper, picked up his pen again, and bent his head over it.

'Come, come. Don't sulk. I am sure it will do very well, and when I am sober I will give it all my attention. Is your work coming along nicely?'

Henry could not help smiling at that, although he could not have said why. 'I hope so. But I have done more than you asked for. It is not only a new version of the old catalogue. It is entirely different.'

'Yes?'

'The words are important, of course. And the engravings must be well drawn, and the covers luxurious, and I suggest a frontispiece of the spiders in their natural habitat, to evoke the far-flung glamour of the island. But I have divided it into rooms. Every section should start with a picture of a graceful, fashionable interior – and then there should follow the items, beautifully delineated, with plenty of space around them.'

'Hmm,' Sir Edward said, on the edge of a yawn. 'But extra pages mean extra expense, and—'

'Your previous catalogue advertised nothing but draperies,' Henry said, unable to stop himself interrupting. 'Endless draperies, which – forgive me – were almost identical on every page, and poorly rendered to boot. But here . . .' He rummaged through his papers for the sketches he had made. 'This is the nursery. We will have a canopy for a cradle, with lace or ribbons, a whole page of different trimmings; curtains for windows and doors, patterned with motifs suitable for infants; a uniform for a nurse, so that she can move about the room entirely silently, without disturbing the child as it sleeps. We have a child-sized cap – padded, if desired – to protect sensitive ears from the noise of traffic. We have a christening robe, which will ensure that the solemnity of baptism is not interrupted by any inappropriate noises which might emanate from under an infant's skirts.' He paused for breath, and found he was on his feet. 'Every room in the house has its own need for quiet and privacy. Not only the nursery and the sickroom, but the study, the parlour, the bedroom, the water closet.'

Sir Edward walked over to the desk. He plucked the pages from Henry, and held them closer to the light.

'That is the mourning section,' Henry said. 'If we are looking for a market for silence, we must not overlook death. Imagine,' he went on, 'if every pall and covering were made not of black velvet but of silence itself. And the houses of the bereaved, hung with drapes – the widow's weeds, her veil . . . No one dares to baulk at the expense of a funeral.' In his mind's eye he saw Madeleine laid out, the black-clad visitors, the draped mirror, the waxy white lilies gleaming in the half-light from the curtained windows. The voices had seemed loud in the stillness of the house; the murmurs of conversation had threatened to turn his stomach. But now, in this rich, gilded room with this extraordinary man, it seemed a long time ago: he could look at it and think, dispassionately, that of course he would have bought yards of silk, of course he would have paid any price, of course anyone would. 'Love,' he said, 'is a great stimulus to expenditure.'

Sir Edward raised an amused eyebrow. He turned another page. 'Handkerchiefs,' he said, 'veils, corsets – yes, I suppose no one wants creaking whalebone at a burial – livery for carriages, muffles for horses' hooves, gowns for the hired mutes, gloves – what purpose would the gloves serve?'

'None,' Henry said, 'but they would complement the rest of the ensemble perfectly.'

This time Sir Edward's laughter was long and unguarded. 'I see,' he said finally, and flipped through the last few pages of writing. 'And this . . . ?'

Henry did not need to read the words. *For uses of the silk as yet unthought-of and undreamt, we offer our services in development and construction of any article: meekly admitting that there are mysteries as yet undiscovered, and awaiting with anticipation the inventions and requirements of our clientele.* He said, 'The last section is a bit of a gallimaufry – confessionals, consulting rooms, solitary-confinement cells, hooded straitjackets, train carriages and so on. But I thought it wise to offer to make anything else they could think of. I thought I might write to Marshall & Snelgrove,' he added, 'offering to send them examples. And,' he went on quickly, remembering the shop-girl's snub, 'I wondered if perhaps you might want to set up a small showroom, here in Telverton.'

'Hmmm.'

'And there is another thing,' Henry said, with a sense of recklessness that was not entirely unpleasant. 'There is no glamour in "Telverton" – the word, I mean, not the place. Telverton evokes nothing but a factory town. I think you should call it "arain" silk. It is an old word for spider, from French. It has more charm, I think.'

'More poetry, you mean. Arain . . . it is rather pretty. Like a girl's name.'

Henry looked up at him, but Sir Edward did not meet his gaze; he only put down the papers and reached out, absently, to lay his hand on Henry's shoulder. Henry froze, his heart thumping; he did not dare to move, he wanted that thought-less, preoccupied touch to continue forever.

The older man strode to the sofa and perched upon the arm of it. He turned back to face Henry. 'Tell me,' he said, 'what you want. Truly.'

There was a pause, while in spite of the darkness, the blood rose and tingled in Henry's cheeks. 'I beg your pardon,' he said, 'I don't exactly—'

'A poet, a young romantic, a visionary. You are remark-able, Latimer. And yet you work in a little shop in London for a dour old Scotchman.'

He bit his lip; it was not fair to describe Argyll that way, and yet it was not unfair, either. He stammered, 'I scribbled verses, that's all. I would blush to read them now.'

'But no longer?'

A memory came to him, lit by a flame guttering in an icy room: himself hunched at his desk, and in his trembling hands a letter he had received from his old professor: *My dear Latimer, I think that your efforts suggest a great deal of promise* . . . Triumph, even as the ink in his inkwell froze over. He had felt the same elation these last days, finding the right word. 'No,' he said. 'I stopped, after I married.'

'Ah.'

'It wasn't Madeleine's fault. I mean, naturally . . . I had been living very frugally, you see. I had a modest income, and if I eked it out I could stay in my garret – well, a little better than a garret, I suppose, but I could not have kept a family there. And then quite soon we were going to have a child. We were happy.'

'A child? My dear chap, I did not realise I had taken you away from your—'

'No,' he said, too sharply; but it was too late to soften it, or take it back. 'No,' he said again, more slowly, 'she is dead too. She died. Madeleine gave birth to her and then . . .'

He should not have said it aloud: all at once he saw the bundle in the midwife's arms that he should have asked to hold once at least, just once! He had been numb with shock. He had refused to look away from Madeleine's absent, peaceful face, or let go of her hand until they prised it out of his grip – but he should never have let them take the little one away before he had even . . . But he should have been relieved not to hear a baby cry, because what could he have done? A man, without feminine instincts, without breasts or soft hands or melodious voice, with nothing but a fierce ache of protectiveness and grief, which would have been worse than useless if that tiny – if it, if *she* had been there, crying . . . 'She died,' he said again. 'Both of them died.'

'I am sorry,' Sir Edward said.

'No,' he said, 'no, it was for the best, I could not have . . .' He heard what he'd said, and a sort of roar rose and fell in his ears. 'I mean – that is—'

'I understand.'

Perhaps he only meant that he knew what Henry had been trying to say. But their eyes met and Henry had a lurching sensation in his chest like a lungful of air when he'd been drowning. *Take heart.*

Sir Edward watched him, composed, still, attentive – as though suddenly he were sober, while Henry's head spun. 'Love,' he said, very softly. 'That is precious beyond all price. I know what it is to lose a wife, for everything you hold dear to be destroyed all at once . . . It has lost its sting now; but it takes time, Latimer.'

Henry cleared his throat sharply. 'Time,' he said. 'Yes.'

'Trust me. It will become easier.'

'I hope so.'

Sir Edward stood up and approached the desk. 'Love,' he said again, as if to himself. He reached out, took hold of Henry's hand and eased the pen out of his grip. He set it to one side, without taking his eyes from Henry's face. 'And now,' he said, 'you have another chance. You can begin again, here. With your poetry. With the silk. With me.'

For a moment Henry saw the library as if through a veil, the dim gold lights blurred by a pale glimmer, a faint whisper in his ears. He said, hardly breathing, 'Yes.'

Silence. Suddenly Sir Edward drew back. 'Come,' he said, 'I will look over your work properly tomorrow. I have never given you the grand tour of Cathermute House – let me show it to you in all its glory. It has a peculiar romance at night, like something out of Mrs Radcliffe – one expects to come across plotting villains and imprisoned princesses.'

Blindly, Henry followed him out into the passage. And as they passed through room after room – while his host pointed out the painted walls, staircases and ornate ceilings and medieval panelling, ceramics and *objets d'art*, engravings and tapestries and clocks – his gratitude grew, until it tightened his throat and pricked behind his eyes. He could not believe it, but it was true: he was beginning again.

He had never ventured into the Great Hall by night, and he felt a thrill as he descended the stone stairs and stood in front of the huge dark hearth. The room was drenched in silver; the rain had stopped and the moon had risen, and it blazed through the high windows and threw the lamp into insignificance. Above them, the minstrels' gallery was full of shadows as solid as its carved screen; the long table and chairs in front of the windows were an altar flanked by thrones. The ceiling met in a high vault, where the dark thickened to absolute blackness.

Sir Edward put the lamp down on the table. After a moment, without explanation, he extinguished it. They stood still in the fragile, enchanted stillness.

There was a face at the far end of the room, beyond the pillars that stood beside the staircase. A tingle of shock went down Henry's spine, and he took a half-step backwards. Sir Edward laughed softly. 'It looks best by moonlight, I think,' he said.

The face stayed perfectly immobile, white and small, the eyes and mouth dark. It was picked out in pearly grey, and it seemed to hover in the shadows, disembodied, gazing not at Henry but past him, unblinking. Then belatedly he real-ised that it was a painting, turned to *trompe l'oeil* by the unearthly light. As he moved towards it he made out the rest of the picture: a rocky, wooded glade, full of shadows and hanging leaves, and a stretch of glassy water. The face was that of a young woman peering from between the boughs of a weeping willow, which partly concealed her body, although leaning close to the canvas Henry could make out her slender shoulders and the creamy curve of one breast and thigh. A pale hand held the branches away from her face so that she could stare outwards. And her expression . . .

'If only she could speak,' Sir Edward said.

Henry raised his hand and let it pause an inch from the canvas, as if it had met a pane of glass. In the foreground – the object of the woman's gaze – a young man knelt over the still pool, looking down at his reflection. His hair curled over his forehead and temples, and water dripped from his hand as though he had paused, mid-drink, struck by his own beauty. It would, Henry thought, have caught anyone off guard, when they saw it for the first time. 'Yes,' he said. 'She's beautiful.' Although it was the sort of beauty that made one flinch; feeling her vulnerability, he wanted to draw a curtain across her half of the painting, so that he could look at the rest without guilt.

'Poor Echo. I wonder sometimes what it would feel like, to be condemned to say what you never wanted to say, while the most important thing of all is beyond your reach.' There was a pause that felt as though something unspoken was hanging in the air like invisible fruit, left unplucked. Henry looked sideways, but the moonlight was spilling over Sir Edward's shoulder, glittering in the ends of his hair and casting his face into shadow.

'Yes,' Henry said again. He could almost have believed that the canvas was a sheet of gauze, nothing but a curtain dividing them from the world of gods and nymphs and metamorphoses. They could step forward together, through the fabric, into that half-glimpsed forest glade, and there . . . But he could not imagine what waited there. 'Poor Echo,' he repeated, because he could not put the other thing into words.

'I had these paintings commissioned when I decided that the silk would make my fortune. My wife thought it hubris.'

Henry dragged his attention back to reality. 'To be great one must dare great things.'

'Ha! Yes. And the factory— But you visited it, didn't you? I have not asked you what you made of it.'

'It was magnificent – it *is* magnificent.' He blinked away the memory of the looms and their cacophony. 'The scale of it, the pure force of the machines, and the beauty of the silk . . . It made me think of Burke's essay on the Sublime.'

'Worsley reported that you found it rather overwhelming.'

Henry could guess exactly what Worsley had said. 'I must apologise if I inconvenienced him. I assure you it will not happen again.'

'Don't be foolish. I know the silk has more effect on some people than others, and no one really knows why. You are sensitive to it and he isn't, that's all.'

'I am sure that as I grow accustomed to it—'

'How prickly you are! Suppose what you are apologising for is precisely the reason I asked you to stay. You have a susceptibility, an affinity – call it what you will. But I do not think it is a weakness. You understand the magic of the silk in a way that Worsley does not and cannot. And as well as that you are intelligent, ambitious and charming. If I were to choose a man to stand at my right hand . . .'

Henry wished, suddenly, that the lamp was still burning; he would have given anything to see the other man's face more clearly. He said nothing.

'If I had married earlier, and had a son,' Sir Edward said, reaching out in the darkness to touch the painted face of Narcissus with one finger, 'he might have been your age. A young man, just setting out, just starting to learn who he is . . . But I will never have a son of my own, now. I do not hold out very much hope that Philomel will marry, and if she does I do not imagine my son-in-law will be competent to run a business. I have less time left than I care to dwell on, and when I grow old . . .'

'You will surely find someone you can trust,' Henry said, in a low voice.

Sir Edward turned to face him. He chuckled, and the sound seemed to come from everywhere and nowhere, as though the shadows echoed his amusement. 'You blockhead,' he said. 'What I am trying to say is that, if I am not very much mistaken, I already have.'

Eight

Henry did not see Sir Edward again for some time. But he had no leisure to be lonely when there was an artist to be chosen, and engravings to be commissioned, and a printer to be found, and instructions to be written; there was the design for the cover, and the foreword, and the letters that should accompany the catalogue when it was finally printed. The days passed in a blur of activity, and when they ended he fell into his bed exhausted and satisfied. He could not remember the last time he had worked so hard, and felt so perfectly in control of his own destiny; it was a heady, exciting, intoxicating feeling. He hardly even had time to think of Madeleine.

But a few weeks later he received another note from Sir Edward, a note that was mysterious in its brevity, saying only *Meet me outside the Angel, Tuesday at 5 o'clock*. That day he had business in Exeter, but he conducted it swiftly and arrived in Telverton with plenty of time to spare; to pass the long minutes before his rendezvous he sauntered towards the factory. When he came to the bridge he paused, his hands in his pockets.

Opposite him, on the other side of the canal, were the ruins of a castle. Willows overhung the banks, bending towards their reflections, and behind them the sunlight caught the corner of the castle's old chapel. As he gazed, he saw a child in white emerge into the green space between the hillocks and tumbledown walls, the ribbons on her hat fluttering. He leant forward. Just then she turned; she was too far away for him to see her face, but he recognised her from the swift energy of her gestures – and yes, now Miss Fielding was coming after her, tightening her bonnet strings against the strengthening breeze. She signed something, and Philomel skipped into the shadow of the chapel.

He had half an hour before he was due to meet Sir Edward, so he hurried across the bridge and along the side-street that led to the ruins. Through the pattern of the ragged chapel window he glimpsed Philomel's pale dress as she turned in impatient circles; she was humming loudly, and for a second he tried to identify the tune before he realised that of course there was none. He looked around for Miss Fielding.

She was standing with another woman, in the shadow of a broken-down staircase that led nowhere. Miss Fielding was staring at the ground, biting her lip, listening; the other woman turned, raising her hands a little, and cried, 'But you must! What is the good of you being in his household, if you cannot—'

It was Mercy Harman. Close to, her resemblance to Miss Fielding was striking: the same wide mouth, the same eyes, the same shape of the face, only hers was gaunt and shadowed, marked with pain.

'Enough!' Miss Fielding said. 'I'm sorry, but I can't. I care about—'

'Yes, yes! About Philomel, who is hardly in need of such loyalty. What about *my* child?'

'If I could help him, I would. But I *can* help Philomel.'

'Oh!' Mercy flung up her hands. 'Damn you, Ruth, I am desperate, I cannot bear it . . .'

Miss Fielding did not move to comfort the other woman. 'I know,' she said. Then, as she saw Henry, her expression changed. 'Mercy—'

'If you will not help me, there is no more to be said. I shall find my own way.' She gave Miss Fielding a last look from narrowed eyes and hurried away. If she recognised Henry as she passed him, she made no sign. He stood still, watching her until she was obscured by the gatehouse walls; then he looked at Miss Fielding, and raised his hand in greeting.

'Mr Latimer,' she said, drawing herself up. 'I gather from the servants that you have been asked to stay a little longer at Cathermute. I must congratulate you on the change in your fortunes.'

'Good day, Miss Fielding,' he said, ignoring the stiffness of her voice. 'I saw you from the bridge. I hope it is not bad manners to impose my company on you.'

She shrugged. 'This is a public place.'

'Her name is Mercy Harman, is it not?' he said, and had the satisfaction of seeing her blink. 'She works in the spider house. Is she your sister?'

Her jaw clenched; then, with a sudden gesture of resignation, she shook her head. 'My cousin,' she said. 'I would say *there but for the grace of God*, except that if God can wreak such injustice I do not think *grace* is the right word.'

'Is she sick? I saw her crying, the day I arrived.'

'Since there is nothing to be done, let us change the subject,' she said shortly. 'I must return to Philomel, she will be wondering where I have got to. Come.' As she moved away, and he followed in her wake, she gave him a softer look over her shoulder. 'What brings you into town, Mr Latimer?'

'I was visiting an artist in Exeter to commission some new drawings for the catalogue,' he said, hurrying after her. 'And you?'

'We have been at Philomel's dancing lesson.' They paused in the chapel doorway. Philomel emerged, skipping from foot to foot, and waved to Henry. He waved back. 'She is always very jolly, afterwards. It is her favourite thing. She is making great strides with the polka. She has a very good sense of rhythm, for her age; she can sense the vibrations, you know.'

'And she is not – that is, the other children are not unkind?'

'She has private lessons. Her father insisted. He did not want her to be an object of curiosity or pity.' Her eyes followed Philomel as she darted away to gather wild flowers from the base of an old wall, and after a moment she set off after her. 'That is his right, of course. Perhaps if he ever sees her dance, he will see that he has no need to fear.'

'I'm sure he will,' Henry said.

'To be quite honest I let her stay in town longer than was necessary. She loves it here, you see. To see other children on the street, using fingerspeak – that is what she likes best.'

Henry felt the rhythm of his steps falter. He had not thought about it before: how it might be for a child – a clever, curious child, like Philomel – to see others talking in her language; how it might feel as though the world were spread out in front of her like a map in primary colours.

Miss Fielding paused and turned to wait for him. 'She is not allowed to talk to them, of course. You must not mention it to Sir Edward. But there is no harm in my letting her stand for a little while to watch them . . .' She glanced at him, and nodded, as if his lack of objection had reassured her. 'You see, the factory has only been making the spider silk for ten years, and that was when the workers began to lose their hearing entirely. So it is mostly the children who speak fingerspeak as I and Philomel speak it, with rules and grammar. The adults who have gone deaf have not the same facility. There is a great difference between fingerspeak and pantomime, you know; if you ask Philomel some abstract question she can answer perfectly well – for her age, anyway. You must not think that we are merely playing charades. But for those who have not mastered it . . . Some of them can read and write, but not all. For those who cannot, their ability to communicate is shrunken. Like an atrophied limb, if you like: they may limp along, but they can never run, or dance. If Philomel is forbidden to use fingerspeak, she will be the same—' She stopped, and bit her lip. 'But I digress.'

Henry said, frowning, 'Did you invent fingerspeak, then?'

She laughed. 'No! I was taught it – or I learnt it, rather, as I learnt English.' She paused, looking at him with new warmth. 'My father's favourite sister went deaf when she was very young. She was taught Mr Braidwood's language of signs. Then my father learnt it from her, and I learnt it from both of them. But there is a Telverton dialect now, thanks to the children; my aunt often complains that a Londoner would not understand them . . .' She looked past Henry's shoulder and pointed with a reproving look at the green lichen dust on Philomel's dress. Philomel giggled and ran up to thrust a wilting bunch of dandelions into her hand. Miss Fielding gestured thanks as the child swerved away, darting now towards the willow tree that overhung the canal. 'My father was the schoolmaster. I might have gone into service when I was old enough, but when the factory was converted and the children began to go deaf he asked me to take the lowest form. That was where Sir Edward found me – or rather his agent. He did not visit me in person; I was not important enough for that.'

There was a silence. She looked down at her bunch of weeds, but instead of throwing them away she laid them carefully on a tree stump, as though someone else might want them. Philomel was stripping leaves from a willow branch. She bent it into a pale circle and put it on her head like a wreath. Miss Fielding signed something to her, and the girl gave a delighted hiccup of laughter.

Henry said, 'How do you say "Philomel" – in fingerspeak?'

'I hardly ever need to. But when I do, it is like this.' She clasped her hands, drawing them towards her heart. A bird, he thought, captured and sheltered in her bosom.

He copied her, and she smiled. 'More or less.' But after a moment her eyes went back to follow Philomel; as if, beside the child, Henry was of no importance. 'My aunt was angry with me, you know. For presuming to give her a name in fingerspeak. She told me I was not Philomel's mother, and I had no right. I told her I loved Philomel more than anyone else, and who would name her in her own language, if not I?'

Philomel scampered back to them, her pale circlet sliding over one eye, and Miss Fielding took her hand. 'Perhaps,' she added, to Henry, 'if you are interested, you might like to meet my aunt before you leave. She can speak for herself, you know – if I interpret, she can tell you much better than I can what it is like—'

'No need.' She frowned, and he added, almost believing it, 'Or maybe when the catalogue is done, and I am not working so hard.'

'Will you not go home when the catalogue is finished?'

'No,' he said, and laughed at her expression. 'I hope to be of use to Sir Edward even after that. Who knows how long for? Which— Oh, that reminds me . . .' He drew out his watch. 'I am supposed to be meeting him in ten minutes, near the Angel. He wants to show me something.'

'I see.' She glanced down at the little girl, who was gesturing a question, and replied with more signs. 'I am telling her what you said,' she added to Henry. 'It is only polite.' After a moment she added, 'She should like to see her father. I suppose you would not object if we walk with you? He is so rarely at home.'

'No, of course not . . .' But she had already swept past him, pulling Philomel after her.

The Clarence was waiting at the corner; as Henry approached, the door swung open and Sir Edward leant out and called, 'Latimer, hop in. Oh – and Miss Fielding, an unexpected pleasure.' He hesitated, then clambered onto the pavement, holding out his hand to Philomel as if she were a puppy. 'And you, little one. How are you?'

'How – do – oo – do,' Philomel said, and beamed.

'Yes, yes,' he said. 'Quite right. Well, Latimer, I have something to show you. The agent came up trumps, and – well, it's a surprise. Come. And . . .' He hesitated, looking down at Philomel's delighted face. 'I suppose, as no one but us will be there, you might come too. Then you can ride back in the carriage afterwards. Would that be suitable, Miss Fielding?'

'If you think so, sir.'

'Good, good. Come on, then.'

Obediently Henry climbed into the carriage. 'Where are we going?'

'You'll see.' A moment later they were all settled, the door was closed, and they were rolling along in the hushed twilight of the Clarence, while pale shadows came and went on the gauze-covered windows. Sir Edward's eyes danced, and his hair had been ruffled by the wind; he looked almost as young and eager as Philomel. When Henry began to ask another question, he held up his hand to cut him off.

At last the carriage rolled to a halt. Sir Edward pulled down the silk with one finger, squinting through the gap. 'Here we are,' he said. 'Clovelly Street.' He threw the door open, jumped out and held out his hand to Henry. 'Hurry up.' He did not wait for Miss Fielding and Philomel to disembark, but took hold of Henry's arm and drew him along the pavement.

They were in a wide, quiet crescent. The houses were large, built in buttery stone, with porticoed doors and tall windows; railings separated the areas from the pavement, so that each façade was set back from the road in an easy extravagance of space. Henry let himself be piloted to the house on the corner, like a child.

'Close your eyes.'

Henry laughed. But although Sir Edward was smiling, he was serious; and at last Henry put his hands over his face, and after the click of a lock and the creak of a door he felt warm hands on his shoulders, pushing him forward. He almost stumbled, and the grip tightened, holding him upright. 'Can I . . . ?'

'Yes.'

He opened his eyes, blinking. They were standing in a dim, enormous hall. A marble staircase reared gracefully up and over his head, and tall doorways led off from every side.

'The house is called "Sub Rosa". There's a plaque over the door. Appropriate, isn't it? The rose being the symbol of silence.'

Henry looked around, taking in the Classical proportions, the shadows and smoothness, but his gaze was drawn back to Sir Edward's face. They stared at each other. The older man's eyes were still shining with that mysterious merriment.

'Do you like it?'

'Yes, naturally, but—'

'Would it do as a showroom?'

There was a pause. At last Henry stammered, 'I – I'm not sure I understand . . .'

'You said you wanted a showroom. Have you changed your mind?'

'Do you mean—? Forgive me, I—'

'Oh,' Sir Edward said, with a mock-languid sigh. 'Oh, I see, you had in mind something like your father-in-law's shop. One meagre little room, full of glass cases. Is that right?'

'I had not exactly—'

'But that is not your life any more, Latimer. You are not working for a penny-pinching old thread-paper like Argyll. Now you have the whole world at your feet.' He stepped back and threw his arms out. 'So, tell me. Will it do?'

Henry could not speak. Surely this was a dream, or a misunderstanding; he could not be offering him this whole house, this wonderful, echoing, gracious house . . . But Sir Edward, laughing aloud now, took his arm and began to steer him from doorway to doorway, and then up the stairs; he was talking, but his words did not penetrate the fog of Henry's joy and incredulity, he could not do anything but stare at the vistas that opened in front of him. There were rooms, and more rooms; high ceilings, bordered by ornate friezes, white on white; floors that were bare and soft with dust, marble mantelpieces with foliage and cherubs, a ball-room hung with shrouded chandeliers.

Slowly his sense of reality began to return. 'It must not look like a museum,' Sir Edward was saying, 'it will simply be like walking into the quietest, most luxurious dwelling in Telverton. You must fit it out room by room, to advertise every conceivable article. The drawing room, the music room, the nursery – and I thought perhaps a parlour laid out as though for a death, sombre but not theatrical, black-bordered drapes, a pall, serenity and so on. Downstairs we might have a dining room to serve tea. I wonder if we could pay an organ-grinder to loiter outside, so that we may pull the curtains and demonstrate . . .' He halted on the landing so that Henry almost walked into him. 'But I am blathering on and on, and you haven't even said whether you like it. Tell me, my dear fellow, is it suitable?'

Henry faltered. 'Won't it be – awfully expensive?'

'Pish, what does that signify, if it has the desired effect?' Then he added, with a strange note in his voice, 'I thought it would please you.'

'Please me? Oh,' Henry said, exhaling helplessly, 'yes, yes, of course it pleases me . . .' He could see it: silk in every room, clinging and billowing like woven silver, filtering the light that passed through the draped windows, adding subtlety and softness to every surface – pearly, rich, rare . . .

'I am glad to hear it.'

'I am quite at a loss, sir, I – I cannot thank you enough.'

'Any thanks at all would be a good start.'

'Thank you,' he said, 'thank you – I—'

'I am only teasing. Your face says it for you.' Sir Edward reached out and brushed his knuckles against Henry's cheek. Henry's face flared as hot as if it had been scalded, and every particle of his body thrilled, electric, glowing.

Sir Edward hesitated, as if he would add something, but instead he moved past Henry through the next door. The room beyond was the ballroom, and tall windows ran the length of it. The fine day had dulled to a cloudy evening:

outside, a single line of clear sky blazed gold and amber between streaks of red. Henry halted in the doorway, taking in the jewelled light on the polished floor; then, on a sudden careless impulse, he danced forward and spun on his heels, pretending it was his, all his. Then it broke in on him that it was not pretence; it *was* his, or as good as. The realisation made him stop dead, and his feet skidded; he flailed, undignified, and Sir Edward lunged forward, catching his hand to stop him falling. 'What is it?'

He did not care how foolish he looked. 'A ball,' he said, 'we must have a ball here – a gala opening – the occasion of the year . . .'

'My dear fellow, whatever you want . . .'

You have the whole world at your feet. Was it true? Anything he wanted? Surely . . . The vivid evening light shone on Sir Edward's face, turning him to gold. Henry held on to his hand, unwilling to let go, on the edge of tears, almost, with happiness; and in a pure, overwhelming, impossible flash it came to him that what he wanted was Sir Edward Ashmore-Percy himself. He froze, his heart thundering.

Sir Edward did not move either. He watched Henry, a smile playing at the corners of his mouth. The sun dipped, emerging from its veil of cloud, and its splendour overflowed the sky behind him.

Nine

Sir Edward did not accompany them back to Cathermute House. Philomel fell asleep, her face pressed against Miss Fielding's shoulder; Miss Fielding sat with her eyes resting upon the covered window, as though she could see past the silk and the darkness, discouraging conversation. Not that Henry was inclined to speak. His head was spinning, his heart drumming: he could not forget the moment when Sir Edward had taken hold of him, and he had thought . . . felt . . .

It was impossible. It was madness. He had never considered such a thing – not beyond the trivial depravity that there had been at school, universal yet unmentionable. He had desired Madeleine – of course he had, there had been a child to prove it – but it had not been like this, not this compelling hunger that filled him with joy and desperation. He could not believe that it had not – *did* not show on his face. Had Sir Edward seen it? He had not moved away, not until . . . If Miss Fielding and Philomel had not stepped into the ballroom behind them, and the little girl launched herself into a polka with a squeal of pleasure – what would have happened then? Nothing, he told himself, nothing. But . . .

He shut his eyes, and saw the sunset.

He was betraying the memory of Madeleine – and worse, the future they had hoped to have, and their daughter. It was less than a year, since . . . Impossible. Obscene. But it did not feel obscene; it felt – *right*. If this was a new life – a new world – then how could it be wrong, to fall in love? Even with a man – another man . . . It was so new, so marvellous, all of it! He would have rejoiced merely to live in a world that had Sir Edward in it, but more, everything else too, it was a profligacy of riches, of delights! The silk, the factory – oh yes, the house, the house that would be a cave of secrets and luxury, glimmering, enticing, the house that he would make, himself . . . all that, and this man, finally a life that he wanted, finally – *love*.

You can begin again, with me.

But what did it mean? What would it mean? To be lovers, to be – to be able to touch him, possess and be possessed, Henry did not even know, could only imagine – but yes, he could imagine, he *could*—

He felt Miss Fielding glance at him, and away. He drew his hand across his face, and for the rest of the journey he recited poems in his head, determined not to let himself think.

He had work to do when he got back to Cathermute, more work than ever now; but he could not concentrate. When he got back to his room he rang the bell for a brandy – 'A bottle, in fact, to save you coming back' – and as he drank it he stared unseeing at the fire in the grate. He knew that he should have been afraid, and ashamed, to realise such a thing about himself, such a dangerous, alien, sinful thing . . . but Sir Edward had not moved away. And that meant – oh, what did it mean? What, *what*?

Whatever he felt, he could not act upon it. In the first

place, gross indecency was against the law – *gross indecency* seemed such an absurd phrase for what he wanted – but never mind that, do not think of that now, it *was* illegal, even if . . . No. He could not deny the wave of desire that had swept over him then and still tingled, deep in his belly and groin; but neither would he allow it to rule his better judgement. It was enough, it was wonderful, this exhilarating rush of happiness, to be alone in front of the fire remembering that touch. To live under the same roof as Sir Edward; to be able to see him, to do his bidding and do it well . . . It would be ungrateful to ask for more. He had never felt like this, not even after Madeleine accepted his proposal, not after she told him they were going to have a baby—

He drained the last drops from his glass, and poured another. That life was behind him: in front of him was Sir Edward, the house, the silk . . . The house – Sub Rosa – the biggest gift he had ever had. A gift he must prove himself worthy of. So much money would pass through his hands! And it would take weeks – long weeks, busy weeks, while he checked off lists and paid bills and visited showrooms and God knew what else. It was on altogether a different scale from the new catalogue. And then, with the gala opening, even more work, more responsibility, more, more . . .

He let his head fall back. The warmth and the alcohol were making him sleepy. Oh, but he could see it; through the wavering haze of brandy and firelight, he could see the ballroom – full, glittering with dresses and jewels, shining faces lit by the dazzle of chandeliers, all wide-eyed glances and admiration. There might be two string quartets, at either end, with nothing but a single silk curtain between them: and then, at a nod, the veil would be whisked aside, and the music would burst into sudden *fortissimo* . . . It would be extraordinary: the talk of the town, the envy of those not invited. Sir Edward would agree. He would agree to everything. *Whatever you want . . .*

Begin again, with me . . .

There was a knock at the door. He floundered upright, and his cheek peeled away from the leather of the chair with an unsavoury tearing noise. He had been so lost in his reverie that for a moment he did not know where he was. He looked around blankly at the little room, taking in the shabby bedstead and the faded prints as though he had never seen them before. As he said, automatically, 'Yes, come in,' he felt the residue of drool on his cheek stretch and crackle. He scrubbed at his face with his shirt-cuff.

It was Miss Fielding. She hesitated. 'I did not mean to disturb you.'

'No,' he said, automatically, 'no, you are not disturbing me, not at all. What is it? Would you like to sit down?'

'I – yes, perhaps,' she said, and took the upright wooden chair beside the desk.

There was a pause. The fire had burnt low, and he leant forward and jabbed at it with the poker. He succeeded in rousing only a brief glow and a shower of sparks. The embers' bright underbellies rapidly faded to grey. He began to say, 'I am sorry—'

'I hope that you will forgive—' Miss Fielding started, at the same time. She stopped and drew breath, before she began again. 'No, Mr Latimer, it is for me to apologise. I probably should not be here so late, and now that I *am* here, I am going to speak out of turn.'

He glanced at her, sudden unease churning in the pit of his stomach. She had come into the ballroom with Philomel just as – just after Sir Edward had caught his hand. There had been nothing to see, nothing that would have betrayed him. Had there? He poured himself more brandy with an expansive splash, as if to underline his mastery of the situation. 'I'm all ears.'

She nodded; and nodded again, as though to delay the moment of speech. He had never seen her so hesitant. He drank his brandy, and waited.

'Go home,' she said.

There was a silence. The fire rustled in the grate.

The unease was stronger now, closer to fear. He said, 'I beg your pardon.'

'You should go home,' she said. 'Go back to London. To your—'

'I do not have any family in London.'

She did not flinch. 'To your life, I was going to say.'

He wanted to retort that he did not have a life in London, either, but it would have sounded childish. 'I'm afraid I don't understand,' he said. 'There is no reason for me to leave. Quite the contrary.'

He thought she repressed a grimace; in any case she looked into the hearth and seemed to think for a moment before she replied. 'You are angry with me,' she said, 'and I don't blame you. How impertinent I am, to suggest you cut short your career here! What can I possibly know – I, plucked from poverty to be governess to a deaf-mute child?'

'None of that had crossed—'

'You have no reason to trust me, I know. But you must, Mr Latimer. Please. There is nothing good for you here.'

He stared at her. 'You saw the house,' he said at last. 'It is spectacular. Sir Edward trusts me. He has spoken of my future prospects, as if . . . It is my chance – my chance to make my name, and my fortune. Not to mention the progress of science – the silk – the benefits to mankind.'

'I know,' she said.

'Then why – why on earth would I give up? Are you genuinely suggesting that I should simply return to London? Now? To abandon Sir Edward just when he has begun to rely on me?' His voice cracked a little as he said *Edward*.

She did not move, or speak; only looked at him as though he would be able to work out the sum for himself if she did not help.

'I thought you understood how important . . .' But his breath came too short to finish the sentence, and he turned aside to make sure that she could not see his face. What had she seen? Nothing but two men, in the blaze of a spring sunset, laughing . . . How dare she make him cringe at the thought – make him ashamed, when there had been nothing shameful about it? What business was it of hers, anyway? But he must not be angry with her, he must not let her think that he had anything to hide. 'But why?' he said. 'Why should I go? You must not fear for Philomel, my work is entirely unrelated to her – and I shall not tell her father that you persist in the fingerspeak.'

'Oh! It is not that – let us forget that.'

'Well, then, *what*?' He had said it without thinking. He ploughed on, afraid to let her answer. 'You have always wanted me to leave. Ever since I got here you have tried to make me concede defeat! You have tried to warn me away.'

'And you have not listened,' she said, with a sudden edge in her voice that made him bite back the rest of his sentence. 'I should have told you again, more clearly – again and again, until at last you heeded me.'

'*Told* me?' he repeated.

She winced. 'It is my fault, Mr Latimer, I have been a coward. I have thought – wished – hoped that I should not have to speak. But after today . . .'

A last spurt of bravado made him say, 'What happened today?'

'I overheard a little of what Sir Edward said. I suppose you think I was wrong to listen,' she added, with a flash of defiance, 'after he had been kind enough to invite Philomel – and it was so empty and old, so beautiful, it felt as though we had stepped into another world. But . . .'

He clenched his jaw. It was coming now.

'That is it, I suppose. It *was* another world. And all of his grand schemes . . . It is for your sake that I beg you to go. Or rather . . .' She shook her head, grimacing. 'Oh, I am explaining this so badly – forgive me!' A moment's silence; then she said, with a gesture of defeat, 'It is the silk.'

He waited, thinking he had misheard; then, when no more was forthcoming, he gave a huff of resentful bewilderment.

She straightened in her chair as though he had cracked a whip. 'It is wrong, Mr Latimer. I cannot express it any more simply than that. The silk – is – *wrong*.'

He drew in his breath, light-headed with relief. She was not accusing him, she had simply got some kind of bee in her bonnet . . . 'Of course it is not,' he said. 'It is a marvel. You must not cavil at the new, simply because it is unfamiliar. All the advances of our age seemed magical, once. Think of the telegraph, photography, lucifer matches, laudanum . . . Surely you can see its possibilities?'

'Oh, no one can hear you speak about it for five minutes without seeing its possibilities,' she said. 'That is exactly my point! The silk is bewitching, I grant you, but it is dangerous.'

'I suppose you are referring to accidents at the factory, but I don't imagine there are any more there than—'

She struck her hand sharply on the arm of the chair. 'The accidents?' she said. 'Do you mean the accidents, or do you mean the destroyed children? Mercy's son, rendered an idiot? The suicides, the druggards, the wife-beaters and murderers? The misery for which Telverton has become a byword? Ha! Do you see how the silk has acted upon you already? Would you have dismissed those so easily, a month ago?'

'Mercy's son?' He frowned, trying to recall what Mercy had said to Worsley that day when he had visited the factory, just before he fainted. She had been writing to Sir Edward – yes, that was it, her son had been in the workhouse. 'He worked in the weaving shed,' he said slowly, trying to piece the fragments together. 'And she thinks—'

'It made him – ill. Worse than ill. He is an idiot now.'

'You mean that the noise damaged his hearing?'

'No! Come, Mr Latimer, I of all people know the difference between a deaf child and an idiot one. It would break your heart to see him. The noise damaged his mind.'

'But . . . surely that is not . . . the men who work in there are perfectly all right. Accidents happen in every factory – Sir Edward would not allow—'

She shook her head, as though he had said something very stupid. 'I am talking about the silk itself, not the factory, although God knows that is bad enough. Do you really understand what it is, and what it can do?'

'Yes, I do. Perfectly. He has explained—'

'Oh!' She threw up her hands, and drew a deep breath before she went on. 'The way you speak . . . I can see why he wants you. You are very clever at making your enthusiasm seem rational. But the silk has enchanted you.'

'Hardly,' he said, forcing a chuckle.

'Yes, it has. And I do not mean that metaphorically. It sings to you, and you are enthralled. You tell yourself it is a simple equation, a matter of algebra: that on one side you may have silence, and on the other a little unnatural noise, causing some small disruption of the aural nerve, and that is it. Two sides, predictable. A discovery that will prove both beneficial and profitable. A gift of God, in fact, laid out ready for the taking. But what if you are playing with something you do not truly comprehend?' She looked up at him. 'The silk is a mystery. It is arrogance to think that you can manage it, like a machine; it has more power than you realise.'

'I am not so naïve as not to understand that every advance has a price.'

'Not a price. A curse.' She paused; but she did not retract the word. 'The spiders were brought here, to England, by great injustice, by a man who despised them and thought he had a right to take whatever he pleased. Where they came from, they were revered and treated gently; here they are kept in boxes without light or air, and their webs are stolen . . . I know the silk is not sentient – but sometimes I almost wonder if it can be angry. It did that man no good, and it has done Sir Edward no good, and it has brought great harm to everyone else who has come close to it.' She faltered, as if she heard the absurdity of her words; but nonetheless he could see that she believed them. 'I thought the factory was doomed,' she said. 'Everyone did. A vanity project, which would crumble when the Ashmore-Percy money ran out. The silk would rot in the warehouse, too expensive for anyone to buy; the looms would be converted back to lace. And the cloud over Telverton would lift. But now I am afraid that you will succeed beyond your wildest dreams. And then . . .'

'And then . . . ?' he said.

'Oh, I do not have your gift for eloquence,' she said, spreading her hands sharply. He had the sense that the gesture meant something blunter in fingerspeak: something like *I give up*. 'I cannot say, exactly.'

'Then you will forgive me if I do not understand, exactly.' He meant the mockery to be gentle, but it made her wince. There was a silence. The fire was almost extinguished, and the room was cold.

She stood up. She looked tired. He wished he had been kinder. The night before Madeleine's pains began, he had spoken harshly to her; he could never undo that. 'Please be assured that I will consider your words carefully,' he said. 'I hold you in very great regard.'

She gave him a crooked half-smile; then, abruptly, she held out her hand to him. 'Come,' she said.

'What?'

'It is my turn to show you something. *Come.*'

He hesitated. She took up a lamp, opened the door and stood in the doorway, waiting. He got stiffly to his feet and followed her.

She led him out into the corridor, commanded him to wait, and a moment later re-emerged from the night nursery at the far end, holding something in her other hand. Then, passing very close to him, she bent to unlock the door opposite the schoolroom, and stood aside to let him past.

He stepped inside, and caught his breath.

He had never wondered about the rooms on this side, opposite the schoolroom; he had assumed they were Miss Fielding's own rooms, or the nursemaid's. But they were not: he knew that immediately from the dead silence within, the unnaturally perfect silence that could only mean that the walls and windows were lined with arain silk. Around him the room was a gaping void to his ears, even as his eyes began to penetrate the darkness. He was right: where the lamplight played on the walls they gleamed, lustrous, as though they ran with water. He said, 'What is this?'

She set the lamp down on a table. The circle of light

illuminated a pile of boxes and trunks against the wall. 'These were Lady Cecilia's rooms,' she said. 'Philomel's mother, that is. And how she must have suffered . . . But it doesn't signify . . . it is not what I wanted you to see.' She threw open a trunk, made a low whistling sound between her teeth, and sank onto her knees to peer more closely at its contents. Her profile was silhouetted against the lamp, her eyelashes glinting.

Suddenly the moon appeared, dazzling and haloed behind a veiled window. He started forward. Miss Fielding did not look up; she shuffled sideways, raising old volumes to peer at them before she set them aside. Closer to, he could see that the panels of arain silk across the window were doubled: absorbing sound, but keeping it inside, too. He looked around, now able to make out the rest of the room in the moonlight. There were the trunks and boxes – the baggage from a long journey, perhaps – where Miss Fielding was kneeling; a wooden chair with a splintered strut against the wall; a few wisps of rotten silk below the window; and in the corner, a blue glass bottle with a broken neck. Laudanum. It brought to mind the splinters he had found in his own room, as though someone had used it often, and had a habit of smashing the bottles . . .

In the wall on his left was another door. He walked towards it, expecting at every moment that Miss Fielding would call him back. But she only muttered, 'Oh, where is it?' and ignored him.

He stepped through. It was a larger room with a row of windows, all, again, veiled in nacreous, dusty silk. It was entirely empty; the walls were bare, the grate plain and swept clean. In front of him, on the wall opposite the windows, were three patches of colour, painted directly onto the pale-washed plaster. Although they were bleached by the moonlight, he guessed that the first was a silvery blue-green, the next the ochreous, rusty tones of Devon earth and stone, and the last brighter, picked out in purple and white. They meant nothing, and yet he had the sense that if only he could focus properly the significance would come to him, as though they were a triptych in a pagan temple. In the scarlet of the central painting – painting! But what else could he call them? – was the body of a spider, caught and embalmed in a crust of colour.

As he recoiled, he saw another door opposite him, open at exactly the same angle, as if he were in a maze. But beyond it was the last room. It was much smaller, but furnished, after a fashion: there was a narrow iron bedstead with a stained mattress, and another chair against the wall. The window was veiled, as the others were, but a ragged sliver of moonlit sky showed through a rent at the corner. It gave the impression of a cell, long abandoned. There was a flaccid bit of fabric hanging from the head of the bed, which still bore the traces of being knotted. Someone had been tied to—

No. It might be for a birth. The midwife had put a strip of hessian on their bed, for Madeleine to pull on – had said that it would help, when it came to bearing down. Yes – the stain on the mattress – blood, blood on the floor—

He turned on his heel, striding blindly back the way he had come until he stumbled to a halt in the first room. As he entered, Miss Fielding was kneeling among a mess of old books, pulling clothes from a wooden trunk. She drew out a creased muslin gown, then a mangy velvet dress with a high waist and a ruffle at the collar. 'I suppose the trunk was brought here when Sir Edward's great-uncle died. Since Lady Cecilia was— Since these rooms have been empty, the servants are up and down the stairs all the time with boxes and old furniture . . .' Suddenly she held up a slim, water-warped account-book. 'Here it is! I should have guessed I'd put it back where I found it.' She passed it to him.

It smelt of mildew. 'What is it?'

'A diary,' she said.

'Lady Cecilia's diary? You can hardly expect me to peruse the private papers of—'

'No. Not hers. Sophia Ashmore's. No doubt no one thought it was important, after she died. I believe I am the only person to have read it. But it will tell you more about the silk. It will show you what I cannot say. And then you will believe me, and go home.'

'I am not sure I have time—'

'You must,' she said. She sat back on her heels and looked up at him. 'Unless you are afraid of what you might find there.'

Suddenly he was so tired that all he wanted was to stumble into his bedroom, fall upon his bed, and lose consciousness. He was sick of the uncanny silence of the room, and Miss Fielding's demanding eyes. If he had not answered when she'd knocked, he might still have been dreaming, staring into the sunset-blaze of the fire.

He said, 'Very well,' and stumbled out into the passage. The flimsy book in his hand felt so heavy that he might have been carrying a woman's body, and not merely her life.

Part IV

Kratos, November 182—

Who is reading this? Who will ever read this? It is not for posterity: the interested historian will read James's account, which will be erudite and masculine and therefore worth the reading. It is not for James himself. It is not for my friends, for I no longer have any – unless you count Hira, who cannot read. It is not for my children, for they do not exist.

Is it for God? Is God reading this?

Well then, if You are reading, may You damn Yourself to hell.

I should not have written that; but if God can read my writing, He can read my heart – and if He can read my heart, He will know that it is fear, not sorrow, that makes me want to scratch it out. So let it stand. One more sin, that is all; one more smirch of grime upon my soul, which must surely be thick with dirt already. I suppose the Devil might grow a garden there, if he wished.

I am feverish. I know that because I am cold, while my sweat wrinkles the page; and because Hira – a moment, while I put my pen to one side – yes, Hira has just held a cup of bitter tea to my mouth, and tipped it until I was forced to drink to the dregs. I do not think she approves of my scribbling, but she sits back and folds her arms, saying nothing. And I must – I must get it down, I must put it into words, although

I do not know why. I began to write: a voice crying in the wilderness . . . but that is blasphemy. Another sin. And I am not a prophet, I do not prepare the way for anything.

A voice crying. Yes, that was how it began.

I had been sleeping well; living well, indeed, like a jellyfish on the sea, full of light, drifting here and there in the current. James was absorbed in his correspondence and his study of the spider, and I enjoyed his inattention; it left me free to wander and dream and rest, to glut myself with fruit when I pleased and to fast when I did not. For the first time I believed that I knew best, for myself and my secret, beloved burden. I did not even tell Hira, although once when we were undressing to swim I saw her look at the new blue veins upon my breasts, and smile. I was not sick, but sometimes I would feel my guts roil, as they did when I first met James, and before my wedding, and before we set out for Greece. Then I would get up and pace, until I could settle again; it was the loveliest restlessness I have ever felt. I thought myself in Elysium.

I was a fool, I suppose.

It was – I count upon my fingers, looking back – oh, only yesterday, I think! Night. I was asleep, in the warm salty tide of sleep which has swallowed me every night. When I was wrenched from it, I felt the shock run through my body, from jaw to knees, leaving me breathless. For an instant I was wet and chilly in spite of the hot summer night: paralysed and rigid, staring up at the muslin that drapes our bed. Then, slowly, the motion returned to my hands and limbs and I sat upright, trying to regain my calm. But I could not tell what had roused me. It had not been a nightmare – or rather, I could not recall any nightmare; it had not been James, who protested drowsily and dragged the coverlet back onto his own shoulders. But I was trembling, and there was a strange liquid sensation around my bowels and bladder. The moon was full, and there was enough light to see that there was no one in the room but James and I, and that nothing out of the ordinary crept across the floor or watched at the window. And yet . . .

I slid carefully – for I did not want to disturb James – out from the bed. When my feet met the floor it seemed to slide back and forth. I did not know what to do. My only certainty was that I should not wake James. I hesitated. If I had got back into the bed, and lain still . . . but I could not. I had the idea, I think, that I might walk into the village and find Hira, although I could not have said why. I was not exactly frightened; instead I had the sensation of a mysterious imperative, an order that I might not disobey.

Then it came again: a voice, crying. I knew then that it had been the same sound that had plucked me into wakefulness and left me stinging; but beyond that, I could not formulate any coherent thought, I only stood still and endured. It might have ripped my heart out of my breast, that sound; I wished it would, so that I would not have to go on hearing it. It was a hook that tore through me and a noose that choked me back, and so I staggered, unable either to move towards it or retreat. I do not know how long it continued before there was respite. When I had regained my self-command I was pressed against the wall, although I did not remember crossing the room.

I could see through the open door into the other end of the house, where James had been conducting his experiments. Near the window something shimmered and flashed like lightning in a bag; there was a dark shape in the centre of it, the silhouette of broken wings. I cannot describe the horror of it.

179

The bed rustled, and James sat up, pulling the muslin aside. The innocent familiarity of the noise almost made me weep. He said, 'What are you doing?'

I shook my head. He pushed his hair away from his face, frowning at me; I could tell that in a moment he would berate me for my speechlessness, but I could not master myself. 'What is the matter?' he said. 'Why did you wake me?'

I do not know what I would have said. But in the silence it came again: a shriek that seemed to fill my eyes and mouth, a scream of such misery and outrage − of pain − that James recoiled as though he had been struck. He said, 'What is that? Oh, Sophia, for heaven's sake, stand up − you are not the heroine of a Gothic novel.' I know he was alarmed; that was why he spoke so roughly. He leapt from the bed and cast about for his slippers, but he, too, was shaking.

I should have been grateful for his bravery, but somehow I wished he had remained unconscious. He strode towards the sound − it had dipped, now, to a terrible bubbling croon − and as he passed through the doorway he caught up the length of wood that he keeps there to batter the scorpions to death.

I followed him, with such effort that it was as though I walked through some viscous liquid. He darted forward and the scream rang out again − we cowered, covering our ears − and then, in the brief pause, he straightened, peered into the mess of bright and dark that hung across the window, and laughed.

'Extraordinary!' he said. 'Look, Sophy, my love − am I the first Englishman to lay eyes upon this? See, my spider has escaped her prison somehow, and there is a bird in her web . . .'

I dared not sink to the floor, for fear of his disapproval. I said, 'It is a bird . . . only a bird . . .' but my throat was dry, and my head spinning.

'What a noise! Quite eerie. Like a harpy.' He laughed; but

when the bird screeched again he could not maintain his levity, and we both shrank away. It was jerking and convulsing in its silken trap, and its voice was like a child's – an infant's, abandoned, tortured, alone . . .

I felt something inside me overflow, like a cup. I thought that I had soiled myself.

'I know the species, and the cry – it must be the web, not the bird, that creates that eldritch tone,' James said. 'I must make notes, this is a fascinating development. Fetch me my memorandum book, and a lamp, will you?'

I tried to turn. But there was liquid pouring out of me, and onto the floor. I could not cover it with my foot, there was too much – the map of an alien country spreading in front of my eyes, an archipelago splashing into existence on the floor. I wondered if I might find some pretext to sit down, so that James would not notice the stains in the moonlight. Or if I might faint, becomingly; and as if in answer, the corners of the room began to blacken and whirl unnaturally, and my blood sang in my head.

James said, 'Hurry, Sophia. This is giving me a headache.' He winced, while the bird's screech scraped inside me, scouring the hollows of my bones. 'Damn it, I shall have to kill it. But I suppose I may recreate something similar. I expect that boy – Aktion, is it? – can trap something like it . . . Sophy, my book, please!'

'Yes,' I said, or rather I heard myself say it, without knowing how the sound arrived at my own ears. I was not sure now which thrumming note came from the bird, and which was inside my skull.

James swung his makeshift weapon into the web. It was strange, how in spite of the other noise I distinctly heard the silk tear. There was a cacophony of clapping wings and cries, a confusion of crashing and the hard reverberation of wood against wood. I felt every impact go through me, like phosphorescence flickering in the dark. Then it was over. I felt an absurd gratitude for the silence – the imperfect, insect-riven silence of a Mediterranean night. Then the corners of blackness swept up and met above my head like a sheet of velvet, and I knew it was too late.

It was not, after all, a very becoming faint. When I opened my eyes James was cursing quietly, batting away the moths from the lamp that rested on the floor beside me. He said, 'What is this mess on the floor?' and held blood-tarred fingertips to the light, squinting at them. 'Ugh,' he said, and wiped his hand on the floor. 'Do you not have rags, for your courses?'

I said, 'Please, will you send for Hira? I think I am sick.'

'You are an Englishwoman, Sophy, it is not befitting—'

'It is a woman's sickness, James.'

He sat back, biting his lip. I suppose he was flinching from the thought of a real doctor, a man, examining his wife, for at last he said, 'Very well. We will get you to bed, and I will ask her to come. Although I expect a good sleep will put you right.'

'I can get up,' I said, for I found that I could, quite easily. I was in no pain; in fact I felt nothing, except a great desire to sleep. I did not need to look down at the stains. I had felt the blood run out of me, easily, thin as milk, and I knew how much there had been. I walked quite steadily back to bed, and allowed James to help me lie down. I did not ask him to find me a clean gown. I closed my eyes and heard him leave.

I do not know how James found Hira, but when I opened my eyes it was light, and he was leading her into our bedroom. She said to him, 'Go,' and he glanced at me and withdrew.

I wanted to say, 'You see? He loves me,' but abruptly I knew I could not speak without weeping. She laid her palm on my forehead, and although she was only testing for fever I felt the tears rise and slide from the corners of my eyes.

'He said you had a bad . . .' She made a gesture like water falling from her hands. 'The moon-blood – yes?'

'I am with child,' I said, and saw her bite her lip. 'It has not come out of me,' I said, 'I am still – it is still there, it clings on, it is a strong little thing. I would know if it had slipped, would I not?'

She took my hand. 'Perhaps,' she said. 'We will wait and see. How long . . . ?'

'A few weeks,' I said. 'It is very small. But I know it will live – it must live.'

She nodded. I thought, then, that she was agreeing. 'Let me look at you.'

'No, please, I cannot bear it,' I said, and then, because she sat back, quiet-faced, and did not insist, 'Very well.'

She washed her hands in warm water before she touched me, and she was very gentle. I thought of the doctor who'd visited my aunt Elizabeth in her confinement, who, she told me, had traces of dried blood around his fingernails before he laid a hand on her, and I was glad I had stopped James sending for a man from Theotokos. But when she had finished washing her hands again, she said nothing; and then I was angry. Surely she could feel if the child was still in place? She sat down, and read my face, and sighed.

'I do not know your words,' she said. 'Not for this. The pocket that holds the baby is not unstitched. It may hold, or it may not. For the moment you have stopped bleeding.'

'It will,' I said. 'It *will* hold.'

'There is often blood, like that. It does not always mean that the baby is lost. But—'

'Thank you,' I said, and gasped as though I had been drowning. I expected her to get up to leave, but she did not.

'What is it?' I said. 'What are you waiting for? It is still there, isn't it? The danger is past.'

'I am in no hurry,' she said. 'No one else is ill today. It is pleasant here.'

I laid my hands across my belly and shut my eyes. I could not remember the last time I lay idle, while another sat beside me: it made me think of my childhood. I had always been glad when I was ill enough to claim my mother's attention, and not Lucy; I remember the envy I felt when Lucy lay dying, and then the shame. I never told anyone of that, not even James (who would have condemned me without pity, and rightly) but in that moment I had the impression that Hira would listen if I told her, and shrug, and see nothing in it but the natural hunger of a child to be cherished. And *this* child, I thought, *this* child will never lie awake wondering if its mother wanted it at all. This child will live in the unwavering sunshine of ardent love, and run strong and vigorous along stone paths, barefoot – and when she needs the respite of coolth and shadows, James will be there with his stern principles and his discipline. She will be born in this land, and she will thrive. I felt more tears leak from my eyes. Please, I said, to the God who made the spiders, please . . .

I heard Hira yawn. Then she began to hum quietly. The song was not exactly melodious, but it had a repetitive softness like running water.

She stopped, abruptly; repeated a phrase, as though she were awaiting an answer; and then the stool scraped on the floor as she stood up. By the time I had opened my eyes she had disappeared through the doorway. I heard her footsteps crossing the outer room. She sucked in her breath as though she had been struck.

I rolled over and raised my head, listening. There was a faint crackle like ripping seams; then the small chink of china, and then I thought she padded across the room, and away. She did not return. For a long time I thought she had left, in spite of her words, and gone back to the village. I lay down again, and now I refused to weep, I set my teeth and tried to swallow the ache in my throat. I was not alone. I had my child.

I had almost drifted to sleep when I heard her footsteps returning, and a single defiant crash of breaking pottery. I could not tell what had happened until James cried, 'How dare you? You ignorant savage, you have killed it.'

'No,' she said. 'It is you who are ignorant. You keep one of our sisters in a prison, and make her spin inside your house? You are arrogant and stupid. Do you think you are her master?'

'I have no idea what you mean,' James said, and I could hear that he was so incredulous at her insolence that for the moment he kept his anger at bay. 'In that bowl there was a splendid example of the *Pseudonephila sireine*, discovered by my wife. I am studying it. If you have hurt it there will be consequences for you. It is worth a great deal – indeed, it is priceless, the only known specimen—' I heard him scrabble on the floor, and the sharp whisper of fragments as he searched through them.

'I have returned her to the forest. That is where they live. It is not for you to bring them into your house.'

The frenetic sifting stopped. 'I shall do what I damn well please, and not be told by a slip of a peasant girl—'

'No, you will *not*,' she said, and I trembled at the silence that followed her voice. 'You will listen to me, Mister God-is-a-man-like-me, because this land is my land and not yours. You are like a baby, reaching for every snake and scorpion that you see, because you do not understand that some things are venomous.'

'No *Pseudonephilim* are dangerous to humans,' James said;

185

I think he was trying to scoff, but there was a quiver in his voice. 'I am not afraid of a little nip from their jaws, in the interests of science.'

'Still, you will not understand!' she said. 'Oh, you men, your religions are all the same. You ask for stories of the old gods, and look down your white nose at us as though we believed them all, and think yourself superior – and yet you take what you want, as they did.'

'How dare you? I am a Christian. I hope that my life is an example—'

'Oh yes,' she said. 'You are an example of your kind. You show that fine words do not stand in the way of imprisonment and theft.'

'Get out,' James said. 'This is my house. Get out, before I lay hands on you.'

'I am here because you asked me to look after your wife. Is your vanity more important?'

James drew a long, righteous breath. 'She asked for you, and I was prepared to indulge her whim. But it is obvious that there was nothing gravely amiss, only some little disorder of the matrices. And you – you will never be allowed under this roof again. I thank God you have exposed the darkness of your heart to me, before you had time to poison my wife's mind against all that is good and true.'

Hira hissed through her teeth. 'Then go and comfort her yourself,' she said. 'And never, never bring one of the sisters inside – never, you hear? It is madness. To think that you may have killed your child with the spider's song, and yet you still will not hear—'

'My child? What child? Have you no shame? You stand here, in my house, and lie to my teeth – come—'

I heard, to my horror, the sounds of a struggle: James's grunt as he pushed at her, and the thud of Hira's feet as she twisted away. I hauled myself upright and clambered off the bed, but I lost my balance and was obliged to clutch at the wall. I croaked out James's name. I thought Hira answered, but I could not make it out past James's yell of pain and outrage, and the frenzied scrabble of sandal soles on the floor.

He hit her. It made a flat, sharp noise like a drumskin breaking.

I staggered to the door where I could see them. 'James,' I said again, with a dry mouth.

Hira brought up her knee into his groin. His knees landed on the floor with a thump. He bent over as though he were a Mussulman, praying. Hira's eye was red, and beginning to swell. I thought, what have I done?

I said, 'Please . . .' not knowing what I asked for. Hira looked at me; James did not.

Then the pains started.

The agony did not last long. Not as long, certainly, as the throes of childbirth. I was going to write *deliverance* – but I was delivered of something. It was something that was not yet recognisable: a fragment of offal with the insubstantial smoothness of liver, a deep clotted red; and attached to it, a little length of meaty string, and a rigid, bloody-silver bulb, like a brined shallot. It was the length of the smallest segment of my smallest finger: a nothing, a trifle, a piece of flesh that passed out of me more easily than some *merde* has done. And once it had dropped into the chamber pot, along with a few pink drips of fluid and blood, the pains stopped, quite pat and polite, not needing to insist now that their duty had been accomplished and my womb was neat and empty.

Hira bent over the pot, touching the thing gently with her brown fingers. Then she nodded, washed her hands, and passed me a cloth so that I might rinse myself. When I was clean she put her arm about my shoulders and helped me back onto the bed. She lifted a cup to my lips and told me to drink. I obeyed her; I could not think of any reason to resist. I lay quite still, in the numb ease that comes after the cessation of one kind of pain and before the onset of another.

'It is over now, I think,' she said.

I nodded.

'You will sleep.' She sighed, and patted the cover into place around me; it is the first time I have known her make an extraneous gesture, and I wish I had found solace in it. 'Has this happened to you before?'

I shook my head, and the oozing tears began again, running coldly into my ears. I stared up at the muslin canopy, watching it waver and steady, waver and steady, as the water rose and spilt. Hira filled the cup and set it on the stool beside me. Then she stooped for the pot and lifted it in her arms.

'What are you doing?'

'I will take this to be burnt.'

'No,' I said, and clutched at her arms, 'no, you must not, no, please—'

She frowned. 'What will you do with it?'

'I do not know,' I said, and the truth of it choked me. 'But it is my baby – you cannot burn her as if she is rubbish, she is—'

'It is not a baby,' Hira said, without unkindness. 'A seed is not a tree.'

'Then it is the seed of my baby, that is enough for me. At least it should be my hand, not yours, that—' But I could not get enough air to go on speaking. I held on to Hira's wrist, digging my nails into her skin, and wept. I felt her sink onto the stool. She cradled the pot on her lap and waited for my sobs to subside.

'Very well,' she said, when I was quiet enough to hear her voice. 'I will leave it here, for now. I will come back. At sunset we will bury it.'

I nodded. I took the pot from her and put my arms around it. A hysterical woman, tear- and blood-stained, embracing a stinking chamber pot . . . But I did not think, then, of what a picture I made. I rested my face against the cool lid, glad that I did not have to let go yet.

When Hira came back, the sun was dipping. The handle of the chamber pot had left a dent like a bruise in my forehead; I felt it tingle and smart as I raised my face. She sat down – she smelt of something aromatic, like rosemary – and held out a folded cloth to me. 'Here,' she said, 'it is a gift.'

I did not take it. My arms were sore, but I would not loosen my hold until I had to. She unfolded it, more and more, until I would have been surprised at how fine and large it was, if I had cared. It gleamed uncannily in the shadows, as oily-smooth as still water. A *himation* of some silken stuff, lovelier than anything I had seen her wear.

'We will put the little one in it, so that she may lie quietly,' she said.

'I do not want it,' I said. 'I would rather she have my night-gown.' I would rather she had my body, but I could not give her that.

'No,' Hira said. 'Take it.' She pushed it towards me. 'Do you hear? On this side, it turns the world's voice back on itself, so that all who hear are afraid. It will keep the animals away.' Now that she said so, I thought I could identify a tremulous breath in my ears, echoing and distorting her words. It raised the hairs on my arms. I considered how quickly a pair of claws would dig, and jaws would snap up that little dangling bead of meat and pulp, and did not reply. Hira turned the fabric over so that it lay across her hands, shimmering. The miasmic whisper was extinguished. Now she said, 'Do you hear the silence? Inside, no noise will disturb her, nothing will wake her. She will sleep quietly.'

I slid my hand over it. There was no sound, no friction of skin over threads; I might have been a ghost.

'We lay our dead in this cloth,' she said. 'It is made from the webs of spiders. Spiders like the one your husband kept — but we will not speak of that. It is not for the living. It would make you sick after a while if you wore it; the mind does not like the way it changes sounds, like a reflection in disturbed water. But the dead . . . it protects and keeps them, until the dust takes them back to itself.'

I thought of my child drying to nothing under a thin layer of dirt, until she could be lifted by the wind and blown through the pines to the sea, cradled like an infanta in the richest silk I had ever seen. Without speaking I let Hira ease the pot out of my grasp and lift the contents gently into the centre of the cloth. She held it open so that I could press my fingers to my lips and lay the kiss on top. Then, with great gravity — as though it *were* a baby, in spite of what she had said — she folded it into a soft bundle, and laid it in my arms. 'I will go and prepare a place for her,' she said. 'It will not take long.'

'You must tell James,' I said, as she disappeared. 'She was his child too.'

I was not sure whether she had heard, until she returned: and then I saw that James was behind her, stormy-browed, refusing to meet my eyes. She said, 'It is ready,' and helped me out of the bed, kneeling to slip my shoes onto my feet while James glared over my shoulder at nothing. But she did not take my arm to lead me out of the house, past the low stone walls where the hibiscus and oleanders grow, to the margin of the pines; instead she walked ahead, and James was forced to take my hand when I held it out to him with a beseeching look.

He glanced at the bundle that I carried pressed to my breast. 'What is that?'

'Hira gave me a *himation* for a shroud,' I said. 'It will keep the animals away.'

'Oh, pagan superstition,' he said. 'She'll ask you for money later, you mark my words. A piece of rag would do just as well.'

'No, James. Listen.' I lifted it towards his ears, although I would not let him take it from me. 'Do you hear?'

He paused, and rubbed a fold of it between his fingers. 'Why, it is extraordinary!' he said, and the pettishness left his voice and face. 'What is it? Where does it come from?'

'It is from the spiders,' I told him, and saw from his countenance that he had suspected as much.

'The *sireine*? Yes, of course,' he said, before I had time to answer. 'Oh, the cunning liars, so they do know of the spiders! More than know . . . This is what Gritney hinted at. I have heard of spider silk being woven, but this, the sound it makes . . . it keeps the scavengers away, does it? Hmm.'

'And on the other side there is silence,' I said. 'Deep, unbreakable silence, so that the dead may sleep as soundly as – as the dead should.'

I was certain that he would ask me, soon, how long I had been expecting our child, and how I was bearing the loss; but he nodded and said, 'Unfold it a moment, will you?' without showing any sign that any amongst the sleeping dead was dear to him. I turned over a loose corner of fabric, and he bent towards it and scringed his eyes with the effort of attention.

'Here,' Hira called, from the shadows where the trees grew tall. Where she stood there was a shallow scrape in the dry earth, not more than a hand's breadth in depth; I suppose that means they set great store by the silk and its power to repulse scavengers.

She held out her hands to me. As I went to meet her each step took more and more of my strength, until I felt as though my lifeblood were seeping out through my soles; but at the last, when I would have given up and knelt upon the ground to lament, James took my hand and said, 'Come, Sophy, take heart, my dear.' His unlooked-for kindness bore me up until I could bend and set down my bundle in the little stony furrow at Hira's feet.

'Will you say a prayer, James?' I asked.

'But that is— Very well,' he said, with a foul look at Hira, and launched into a collect that included a prayer for the king and those about to be ordained, although it said nothing of children yet to be baptised. But it was something to hear holy words spoken, as though the grave were indeed a grave, and its contents beloved of God.

Hira kept her eyes downcast. When James said, and I echoed, 'Amen,' she looked at me and nodded, as though something were concluded. Then she took up the shovel she had used, and began to push the mound of loose dirt over the silvery folds of cloth. When it was covered, she brushed her hands against her skirt and turned on her heel to leave without a backward glance.

I could not speak. I crouched and placed my hands on the grave, palms down, pressing as though I might feel the shape of my child under the layer of soil.

'We must leave something here,' James said, 'or we will not be able to find it again.' He plucked a spray of leaves from the nearest shrub and drove it into the earth, where a headstone would have been. 'Now come inside, Sophy, I am being eaten alive by mosquitoes.'

I think if he had not thought to mark the grave, I would have resisted; but I thought of the grief (or it might have been his love for me) that had prompted it, and could not bear to vex him. If I had been alone, I would have bid her sleep well, and dream sweetly; but James was tugging my arm, and I resolved to return when I awoke in the morning, to pour out all that I had not been able to say. There was no need for haste; she was quiet now, and patient, since time no longer had any meaning for her.

I slept fitfully, tossed back and forth between waking and dreaming, but at last it was a nightmare that flung me onto the shore of the real world, and left me open-eyed and shivering. I suppose I was already hectic with fever. I did not dare shut my eyes, for I could still see the lingering last scene of my dream: a hunched, ravenous beast that scratched away at a new grave. I strained my ears for the sound of its claws, but all I heard was the incessant cicadas, and the far breath of wind through the pines, and James moving in the outer room. I should have been comforted; but finally I got to my feet and blundered to the window. I could not go back to sleep until I was sure.

I could not see the little mound in the darkness below the trees, but nothing moved, there was no slavering shape, no teeth or eyes.

In the outer room I heard the trickle of water, and suddenly I was possessed by a great thirst. The cup beside the bed was dry; I wrapped myself in a sheet against the chill (although the chill emanated from inside, not outside, my flesh) and went to the doorway.

James was bent over a basin, rinsing out a shirt in a pool of lamplight. I was grateful to him for doing it himself: in that moment I think I loved him as much as I ever have, as he bent over the menial task, his hair falling over his face. In spite of my thirst I did not want to interrupt him.

He lifted the dripping shirt from the water, rubbed at it with the cake of soap, and startled as though I had caught him in some misdemeanour. 'Sophy!' he said. 'You have barely slept an hour.'

'I wanted a cup of water.'

He went to the shelf, took down a cup and filled it for me. 'Go back to bed.'

I drank deep, and held the cup out for more. This time he huffed a little, and after he had given me the full cup he took hold of my shoulders and steered me towards the doorway. I stumbled under the weight of his hands, and felt sick. 'Let me sit down,' I said, 'I will not disturb you, I promise.'

'I am working, Sophy,' he said.

'I will be quiet,' I said. But I think it was not my pleading but my weakness that defeated him, for he caught me when I staggered and pressed me ungently onto a stool. He glanced back at the wet shirt that lay gleaming on the table, beside his open memorandum book and his magnifying glass, and bit his lip.

It had no sleeves, that shirt; nor collar, nor yoke, nor seams. I had been mistaken. It was not a shirt, but a *himation*. Even under the suds and the clinging smears of soil it was so lustrous it seemed to be emitting light. The water pooled and ran in its folds like *essence d'Orient*. There was only one place at the centre where a few reddish streaks dulled its shine, and I could see that James's efforts had already softened those stains, and that soon they would come out with the other dirt.

The cup of water I was holding tilted and spilt. I fumbled to right it. I did not want to look at James's face, and yet I found I must.

James made a brief, casual motion of his hand. 'Yes, indeed, that fabric is quite unique,' he said, and I knew from his tone that he anticipated an intemperate reaction and was determined to remain rational in the face of it. 'You know, my dear, it is extremely felicitous that it has come into my possession.'

'You dug up the grave,' I said, or think I said; perhaps I did not say it aloud.

'It was a crime to bury such a thing before I had a chance to examine it – and for what? I do not believe that you were even with child, Sophy; you simply had a few untoward lumps in your menses. Oh, it is tiresome how incapable you are of turning your attention to anything outside yourself! Here you may see one of the most miraculous objects you have ever encountered, and you sit gaping at me like a moonstruck Jeremiah.'

I said, 'And the – the thing we buried?' I did not want to provoke him, but I could not say *lumps*, even though she could not hear me.

He grimaced with impatience. 'There was nothing there,' he said. 'From all the fuss you made, I anticipated a homunculus, albeit a small one. But there was not a speck or a jot of anything human.'

'And what happened – to the – the—?'

'The bits of carrion I threw aside, I suppose. I cannot remember. Really, Sophy, I am weary of your foolishness. Will you be keeping your monthly rags, henceforth? Will I be obliged to genuflect to your filth, like a Papist?'

I did not answer. I walked past him to the window, and I saw a flicker of incredulity in his eyes, because I did not heed his outrage or beg for his forbearance. The remains of my child had been consumed or carried away. I stared out into the silvered night, and a wave of cold swept up from my feet so that I might have been looking upon a hoar frost, and not that fierce pagan moonlight.

Then I turned and left him alone; and he could not find fault with that, because I was obeying him.

Ten

Henry raised his head. He had heard the familiar striking of the Cathermute clocks – that loudest chime lagging behind the others, as though it were further west and determined not to let anyone forget it. The sky was shining inexorably through a gap in the curtains. He had spent the whole night at his desk, reading. He dragged his hands back and forth across his face but it did nothing to ease his discomfort. His eyes stung.

He shut the journal on its last, half-blank page, and got up. He could not think clearly. His mind whirled, his stomach churning with emotions he could not name. Yesterday's sunset, Sir Edward's hand in his. Then Miss Fielding's level stare, the silent rooms dripping with silk, the barred windows – and the journal – the island, the sea, the women . . . Why couldn't Miss Fielding mind her own business? He did not have time to think about some long-dead woman, even if she had discovered the spiders, even if what she wrote about the silk made him wonder, uneasily . . .

It will tell you more about the silk. It will show you what I cannot say. And then you will believe me, and go home.

And Mercy's boy, turned into an idiot. The rooms with barred windows, covered with silk – Lady Cecilia's rooms.

197

Sir Edward had never mentioned . . . Suicides, druggards, murderers. *A curse.* Henry grimaced, strode to the window and back, trying to clear his head. It was not true. It could not be—

There was the sound of whistling, and footsteps mounting the stairs. It was unmistakeably Sir Edward. Henry halted, his breath coming short. Suddenly he was conscious that he was dishevelled, unshaven, in his shirtsleeves, and that no doubt he still smelt of strong drink. Even so, when his host knocked and opened the door, he felt a surge of the same incredulous joy he had felt the day before. But it might have been years ago, not hours, that he had felt it; and it had a bitter after-taste, tainted by what he had seen and heard and read since.

'Latimer! Ah, good, I hoped you'd be awake.'

'Yes,' he said, 'come in,' although the other man was already striding past him to the window and pulling the curtains open. It was a glorious morning.

Sir Edward flung himself into the chair and looked up at him. 'I couldn't wait,' he said. 'After yesterday. We must get to work. So tell me what you need. More money, I expect, you always do. No, don't look like that, I'm only ragging you, I want the best of everything, no expense spared.'

Henry tried to smile. 'Yes,' he said.

'Good. I thought Midsummer's Eve for the grand opening. What about it? Does it give you enough time?'

'I – yes, I expect so.'

'What is it? I don't begrudge the money, truly.'

'I am just a little seedy this morning.'

The silence went on. 'I thought,' Sir Edward said at last, 'that you liked the house. I hoped you would. But if—'

'I do,' Henry said, 'I do, I am overwhelmed by your generosity, I . . .' He stopped. He could not bear to be thought ungrateful, but his voice would not obey him.

A beat of silence. Then Sir Edward got to his feet. 'Very well,' he said, 'I see I have disturbed you. Excuse me.' He brushed a speck of dust from his trousers and stepped past Henry, to the door.

'No,' Henry said, just managing not to paw at his sleeve, 'no, please – you've been so kind. I am only . . . please—' He stammered, again, to a stop.

Sir Edward gave him a long look; then, at last, he took Henry's arm, pushed him into the nearest chair, and crouched down so that he was looking up into Henry's face. 'Something is wrong,' he said. 'Tell me. Is it the house? Is it too much? I . . .' He hesitated. 'I know that sometimes I am too anxious to please my friends.'

'The house is magnificent.'

'Then . . . ?' A flicker crossed his face. 'Perhaps,' he said slowly, 'perhaps, if yesterday – in the heat of my enthusiasm—'

'No,' Henry burst out, 'of course not, there is nothing you could do to – no, last night, after I returned here, I discovered— That is . . .' He made an effort to compose himself. 'Last night Miss Fielding came to see me. She is concerned about the silk.' Sir Edward raised his eyebrows. Before he could speak, Henry ploughed on, 'I don't mean that it matters very much what she thinks – it is superstition, I believe – but she said things, she took me into the rooms next door, where your— Lady Cecilia lived . . .' He knotted his fingers together, searching for the right words.

'I see.'

'She gave me the diary of the woman who brought the spiders home. Your great-aunt, I suppose. And she told me that the silk was dangerous. Evil. That there have been accidents at the factory. Children hurt.'

Sir Edward drew back a little. Then he stood up and

walked to the window, turning his back. 'There are always accidents,' he said, quietly.

'I know that. Indeed, I—'

'You will not find a single factory in the world that does not take its toll in human suffering. And those who pay the price are sometimes those we would most wish to protect. It is heart-breaking. And by God I wish it were not so.'

'I did not mean to suggest—'

'I think every day of what I want the factory to be. A beacon for Telverton, a place where we weave not only silk but prosperity and hope. When it is successful I will build schools, housing, hospitals – I will pay ten times, a hundred times over for every accident. And still, yes, still I will stagger under the burden of knowing there were women and children who suffered to make it so.'

Henry stared at the floor. 'I know,' he said.

'My dear fellow, I am not rebuking you for asking. It does you credit.'

'Yes. Thank you, sir.'

Another, longer silence.

'Ah,' Sir Edward said, and now his voice was so low Henry could hardly hear him. 'It isn't that at all, is it? You saw Cecilia's rooms for the first time. And no doubt the servants have told you some slanderous version—'

'No one has told me anything,' Henry blurted out. 'I would not be so impertinent as to listen, if they did.'

'It seemed obscene, didn't it? A suite of rooms, all lined with silk, bars over the windows. You asked yourself, why was she kept secret, a prisoner there, so that no one could hear her screams? What kind of man would do that to his wife? What vile, revengeful villain . . .' Sir Edward broke off and turned away. His body was very still; only one hand was clenching and unclenching as if in time with his heart.

'Cecilia was no prisoner,' he said at last, his voice harsher than Henry had ever heard it. 'Not the way you imagine. She was . . . dangerous. To Phil, to— Never mind. She was mad. No one told you that? No, I suppose not, if you didn't ask. She had an accident, when she was expecting Philomel. She lost her hearing. She had been a musician, and she could not bear it. She would scream until her throat bled, trying to make a sound she could hear. She would attack anyone who came near her – the doctors, or the maid, or me.' He swallowed. 'And then, after Philomel was born, she grew worse. We had to keep them apart. It was like a night-mare, I prayed I would wake up, I used to pray that one day she would simply – be herself again, as she had been. But she was gone, the woman I married was gone, and in her place was a kind of fiend.'

Henry's throat ached. He said, 'I am so sorry.'

'Yes. Yes, thank you. It doesn't hurt as much as it did,' he added, with a little grimace, like a schoolboy after a beating. 'It is a difficult thing to speak of. Mostly I don't care what people hear, or what they think of me – but you, I can't stand to let *you* think . . .'

'No,' Henry said, stumbling to his feet so that the chair scraped noisily on the floor, 'there was no need, forgive me, I should have known – I did know, of course – that you would never have—'

'Hush. There's no need. But will you trust me, now?'

'Of course,' Henry said. He was trembling with the effort it took not to reach out.

'Good,' Sir Edward said, and for a moment Henry saw the blaze of a sunset superimposed on the shabby little room. He swung away, with an oddly determined lightness, and glanced down at the diary that was open on the desk. 'This is it, is it? My great-aunt's journal?'

'Yes.' Henry copied the other man's tone of voice, with an effort. 'Miss Fielding thought I would find it enlightening.'

'Did she? It's a damned cheek for her to go rummaging in the family papers, I must say.' He picked up the little volume to scrutinise it. 'And was it? Enlightening, I mean?'

'Not – particularly,' Henry said. 'Miss Fielding thought it might give people strange ideas about the silk.'

'Oh?'

'The islanders seem to have used it for religious purposes. I don't think we'll want to do that, will we? I can't see the Archbishop of Canterbury being in favour.' He was pleased that Sir Edward laughed. 'Anyway, most of it is just a record of her life. There are some places which are rather – unsuitable.'

'Hmmm. Well, I'm glad we've rescued poor Great-Aunt Sophy from oblivion. Or from Miss Fielding's clutches, should I say?' He slid the book into his pocket. 'You don't mind if I borrow it, do you?'

'It is yours, Sir Edward.'

'Yes, of course.' The older man hesitated. 'Well, thank you, Henry. For telling me about it.'

Henry nodded. He felt as though he had never heard his name spoken aloud before. *Henry.* Would he ever dare to say, *Edward*? The thought made heat sweep up and down his body: it was more intimate, somehow, than the wordless imaginings of the evening before, when he had closed his eyes and thought of skin against skin, teeth on flesh, hands— He shifted sharply from foot to foot, jerking his mind away, but when he looked up he saw that Sir Edward was watching him. Helplessly he stared back, unmanned. He had never felt like this, not even when he was courting Madeleine.

Sir Edward smiled. 'I must go. I'm seeing Worsley after breakfast.'

'Yes.'

'Just one thing,' he said, turning back in the doorway. 'This room – I had no idea it was in such a bad state. I'll tell the servants to move you to the one next to mine. Does that suit you?'

Henry could not exactly identify what he felt; it was a delicious kind of queasiness, a sense of travelling at high speed, of falling without fear. He said, 'Of course. Thank y—'

But Sir Edward was gone, striding from the room without waiting for an answer, as if he did not want Henry to see his face.

Later that day Henry took the carriage into Telverton, to see Sub Rosa again; then he went to the printers, and the tailor, and had dinner at a chop-house near the mill leat. But he hardly knew what he was doing, or saying, or tasting. There was a bubble of happiness in his chest – or rather, growing from his chest and swelling until he was floating in it, buoyed up and drifting.

When he arrived back at Cathermute it was late afternoon. He walked through the Great Hall, and stopped. Miss Fielding was standing alone in front of the triptych of paintings; not, as he would have been, absorbed by *Echo and Narcissus* but by the panel next to it. This one was full of rich reds and ochres, earth and sand; under a setting sun, a maiden in a white dress was offering something to a half-naked man in crimson drapery. Behind them, a solid slab of stone opened on a thick line of darkness. The artist's skill somehow managed to evoke a stifling, treacherous quality to that deep black, as though unseen teeth and claws lurked out of sight. It was

Theseus and Ariadne, of course. Henry's gaze moved across systematically, paying attention to the folds of Theseus's cloak, the evening breeze that seemed to lift Ariadne's sleeve, the glint of a bronze anklet, until they lighted on the skein of thread that she was proffering to Theseus.

It glowed. It was round and smooth, painted with a nacreous sheen that was at odds with the realism of the other textures – indeed, it stood out, so that he was surprised he had not noticed it at once, first of all. It was only because he knew the myth that he could see it was a ball of thread, or meant to be; it was not like a skein at all, it was more like a pearl, lustrous, enormous, unlikely. Why had the artist painted it so oddly – so deliberately oddly? Then he noticed that, only just visible, a tiny spider hung from Ariadne's finger, and he understood. The clew was spider silk. He glanced sideways, at the third canvas, where a young woman was showing a tapestry to a pale, crowned goddess: Arachne and Athene. Echoes, and threads, and spiders. Sir Edward must have commissioned them as a sly allusion to his hopes of success. He had chosen the artist well, Henry thought, with a prick of jealousy.

Miss Fielding glanced at him briefly, then turned her gaze back to the painting as though they were strangers in an art gallery. 'Poor Ariadne,' she said. 'To betray everything, and then be betrayed in her turn.'

'She should have known better,' Henry said.

'Ah,' she said, with a quick, short laugh, 'but the stories you men tell us . . .'

Henry didn't reply. He could not imagine telling anyone a story, or not in the way she meant.

'I take it you were too busy, after all, to read Sophia Ashmore's diary.'

'I read it last night.'

'Oh,' she said.

'It was very interesting. Thank you.'

'Did you understand why I gave it to you? The things she says about the silk—'

'Don't worry,' he said. 'I don't think there is any danger. Sir Edward assured me that it would all be all right.'

She swung round, staring at him, a frown line between her brows. 'Sir Edward?'

He wanted to laugh; not at her, but at how little she knew. 'Yes,' he said, 'it's all right, everything is all right. And he has told the servants to move me into the room beside his.'

He did not wait for her answer; he could not wait to see the new room, and he was so full of happiness he could not stand still any longer.

He halted on the threshold of a large, gilt and green bedroom. Although the sun had dipped behind the house, the window was so high and wide that the whole space seemed full of light. A maid was bending over a monumental chest of drawers; as she took the pile of garments from another girl's arms she said, 'Is that the lot? You didn't forget anyth— Oh, I'm sorry, sir.'

He looked round. The bed was large, as heavily carved as a rood screen, and spread with an embroidered coverlet; the fireplace was imposing, and the grate twice the size of the one in the bedroom he had left behind; the walls were painted, not papered, and an intricate pattern of gold leaves wove tendrils across the chimney breast and approached the window as though it threatened to creep over the panes. There was an ornate, straight-backed chair in the corner, made of gilded wood with Gothic ornaments and pinnacles. The effect was somehow medieval, gracious and a little oppressive: like the house itself.

'The bell's there, sir,' the maid said, nodding towards it,

'if you need anything.' Was he imagining it, or was her tone more deferential than it would have been yesterday?

Both maids bobbed a curtsey and left him alone, his head spinning, a little breathless. They had not lit the lamps, and the changing light lent a dim softness to every surface, as though the room were painted on satin. He had not expected— Well, he did not know what he had expected, but not this, he would never have dared to hope for this. This was a room for a guest – a member of the family, a son . . .

There was a knock; then, before he had time to answer, the door opened. It was Sir Edward, dressed for dinner, the air around him fragrant with cologne. 'I cannot linger,' he said, 'I am to dine in town, but I wanted to ask if you'll come with me to see the Quakers next week. They are considering arain silk for their Meeting House, and I should like to pour a little honey in their ears. They are a prickly lot, but they pay their bills on time.'

For a split second Henry could not speak; Sir Edward had appeared too suddenly, too pat, as though he had been summoned by Henry's own thoughts. With an effort he said, 'Of course.'

'And let me have an update on the catalogue as soon as you can. I liked the roughs of the gloves and veils, but there are too many. And I've told Worsley you can have whatever you want. He didn't like it – you'd think he was signing the cheques himself.'

Henry laughed.

'Anyway, I'll let you get settled in. How do you like the room?'

'It is wonderful, quite wonderful – thank you.'

'I am delighted to hear it.'

'You are kinder than I deserve.'

'Let me be the judge of that.' There was a silence. Sir Edward looked at him, faintly quizzical. There was nothing unkind in his expression, but Henry could not stay where he was, exposed, afraid of betraying himself. He swung away and walked to the window, cracking his shin on the rung of the gilded chair as he passed. He caught himself on the windowsill and tried not to swear.

In the last few minutes the afternoon had tipped into evening. Outside, the lights of Telverton were beginning to twinkle in the valley under a haze of blue smoke.

There was the rustle of clothing and footsteps moving towards him, and the lemon and wood scent of cologne. He did not turn. His cheek was tingling where Sir Edward had touched it, as though it had been a moment and not a day ago. He stood quite rigid, unable to think, and even when Sir Edward took hold of his shoulder he did not look round.

'Henry,' he said, so low it was almost a whisper, 'can I trust you?'

'Of course.'

Sir Edward made a noise a little like a laugh; but it was not a laugh, or not really. 'Look at me, for God's sake, won't you?'

Henry obeyed. With a shock, as he turned, he found their faces only a few inches apart, a hand's breadth between their eyes and lips.

'I am counting on you. You're my man, aren't you?'

'Yes.'

'You promise?'

He felt as though he were dissolving, like a pearl in wine; soon he would be reduced to a mere streak of iridescence in the dim air. 'Yes,' he said, 'I promise, of course I promise.' He hardly knew what he was saying, but it didn't matter.

Sir Edward's hand tightened until it was painful; then he

dropped it, and nodded, and stepped backwards. They stared at each other, with nothing but twilight separating them.

Sir Edward said, 'I must go.'

'Yes.'

There was no more leave-taking. There was no need for it, Henry thought, as the door closed, leaving him alone. Everything had been said, everything understood. He thought: he knows, he knows and it's all right, it's only a matter of time.

He dropped into the gilded chair. A moment later, without knowing exactly why, he fumbled in his pocket for the square of silk that Sir Edward had given him – so long ago! – in Argyll's shop. He stretched it between his hands, listening to the hole it made in the world, the absence that begged to be filled. Then he turned it over and closed his eyes. The echoes of his own breath and pulse rose around him: whispering, enticing, promising.

Eleven

In the weeks that followed, Sir Edward was at home very little, having business in London that had to be accomplished before the gala. At first Henry had struggled to conceal his disappointment, but as time went on he found a curious relief in his host's absence. On the rare occasions when he caught a glimpse of him, Henry's heart leapt, and his stomach tightened; their conversations over dinner left him breathless; and when they finally retired to bed, the other man's footsteps in the room next door would stop him sleeping. He had never known, before, how unsettling – how uncomfortable, indeed – hope could be. During the day he could almost forget it; but at night it felt like a shard that had split off from his breastbone, and there was no position that did not leave its sharp edges digging into him. He had never known how soft his innards were, how much air he was obliged to draw into his lungs, how thin his skin was. He lay awake, listening to the silence after Sir Edward had gone to bed, and had to remember to breathe.

All this made it hard to work; and he had to work, or he would fail. There would be time later for midnight meanderings through the moonlit rooms, for lingering together over brandy and cigars, for jokes imparted through a mere wordless flick of the eyes . . . Time, later, for everything he could imagine – everything he dared to imagine. So he almost welcomed the inevitable departure, the quenching of a flame, the breaking of a spell: he was himself again, and content to work, and wait. Everything he did was for the silk, for the factory, for Sir Edward; it was a promise. And he was as happy, probably, as he had ever been.

But it was a vertiginous, forward-tilting sort of happiness. He could not stop to savour it, for every moment flung him on to the next in a joyous, urgent rush. There was so much to do, and so little time. In the morning, when he got up, he would often find notes to himself, scribbled half unconsciously: *Price list. Embroidery motif for bridal veil – spiders? Holm oak leaves, vines?* Or, *Flowers!* Sometimes he would waver on the edge of panic. To think that all this – the gala, the catalogue, the investments, the Ashmore-Percy fortune, the future of the silk itself – rested upon his shoulders: his, Henry Latimer's, a mere aurist, not even a poet . . . What had possessed him to attempt it all? What would happen if he failed?

But he would not fail. The world had tipped in his favour, so that gravity itself was on his side. Every step, every leap and every effort carried him further than the ordinary laws of physics would have dictated. It was luck, but not mere luck. The artist and the printer reached an uneasy truce, just in time, and the first proofs of the catalogue came out with hardly an error; when the block-cutter went off sick, his apprentice, through some miracle, made an exquisite job of the front cover; the harp-maker from Cardiff professed himself perfectly ready to visit the West Country, for a price; the head gardener at Cathermute announced resentfully that in fact the roses *would* be profusely in bloom by midsummer. The invitations were sent out, weeks in advance, after three long days of making and checking lists, supervising the factory clerks (whose copperplate handwriting was better than Henry's own), and cajoling Sir Edward through the drudgery of addressing those of particular importance himself. And Sub Rosa . . .

Ah, Sub Rosa! In Henry's fitful dreams, it grew towers and attics and staircases, courtyards and great halls of pillars open to the skies like the Acropolis. He wandered through it like a heroine in a fairy tale, struck by the doors on every side, big and small, of horn and ivory, ebony and jet, amazed that he had never noticed them before; and somewhere, he knew, there was a locked chamber, and he must not approach it, he must turn aside now and return to the entrance hall, where there was work to do . . . In reality it was more prosaic, curtained and furnished like the house it was; but nonetheless there *was* a kind of bewitchment in its high, hushed rooms. It was nearly ready now, awaiting only the last touches, the *lampshades?* or *embroidered slippers?* or *silk lilies!* of his nocturnal musings. It was utterly transformed, so that he felt a distinct surge of pride when he walked through the front door – letting himself in with his latchkey, and indulging (just for a second) the childish fantasy that this was indeed *his* house . . . He often sat at the desk in the study, although he did not have the leisure to dally there long; he stepped into the hushed and glimmering bathroom to inhale the scent of violet soap, and make believe that the tap for hot water was real and not sham; he stood beside the canopied bed, listening to his own intimate breath. When at last the catalogues arrived he set them out himself in the dining room, so that each small table had its own dark leather tome, glinting with the fruit and filigree of the artist's design.

The only places in which he took no pleasure were the mourning parlour and the nursery. Not that he avoided them – but they were, like the rest of the house, nearly finished, and he had trained himself to glance round, assessing the details of what needed to be done with a purely professional eye. He had no wish, in those rooms, to pretend that he was the head of the household. He was glad that he had decided against a wax effigy; for the same reason, he spoke more sharply than he should have done to the woman who sewed the drapes for the bassinet, when she suggested a life-sized doll to go in it.

But he was too busy to think very much about Madeleine, or the past – or even Argyll, whose dry, dutiful letters had never ceased to come, and were now piled up on one end of Henry's mantelpiece. At the other end was a thicker wodge of letters from Henry's cousin in the North Country. Recently he had lost the desire even to open those; a few days ago, after he had forced himself to skim the most recent, he had written: *Kind though you are, I do not think I shall be at liberty to visit you for some time, and cannot predict whether it will be months or years before the opportunity arises. I have important work to do here, and must not allow other concerns to distract me* . . . He paused, and a drop of ink rolled from his nib onto the paper. He added, *I hope to send more money as soon as I may.* His cousin would certainly be offended. But that did not matter: Henry had no time to occupy himself with all that. There was too much work to be done. When the reply came, he hardly noticed; he only paused for a moment before he slipped it unopened into his suitcase, piled the others on top and shut the lid.

The time slipped by, faster and faster, and as if to echo his mood, the glorious weather held, a premature summer that strengthened the smells from the gutter and baked the ruts in the roads as hard as stone. At first he did not dare to hope that it would last until Midsummer's Eve; but slowly, as the day grew closer, he thought – no, believed – no, *knew* that it would. Everything was on his side, even the sun itself.

A fortnight, ten days, a week. Sub Rosa was nearly, very nearly finished, apart from the final touches, and the catalogue was to be delivered the next day – and suddenly, as he emerged one morning into the sunlight of Clovelly Street, it came to him that for an hour or so there was nothing he might usefully do. He was so unaccustomed to the sensation that he laughed. Then, with a wonderful feeling of playing truant, he set off towards the Angel to have a drink.

He was crossing the bridge, pausing to look down into the water, savouring the luxury of leisure time, when something in the corner of his eye made him turn. Was that Sir Edward, sauntering round the corner? He called out, but already a hansom had hidden him from view, and by the time Henry had ducked sideways to follow, the man was nowhere to be seen. He hesitated, ignoring the yell of the cabbie, and then set off down Leat Street towards the factory. Yes, there he was, disappearing through the factory gates – yes, his familiar walk, his hands in his pockets, his hat a little askew.

Henry hurried after him. He could invent some excuse, some pleasantry, anything. All he wanted was a few seconds, a smile and a look: that would be enough, that would turn the rest of the day into something wonderful, like a diary entry underlined in gold. He ducked through the gates, caught a glimpse of movement by the canal wall, and jogged round the corner in pursuit. Here he was forced to halt and wait for a workman to stagger past with a piece of machinery in his arms; when at last he reached the little yard behind the spider house, there was no one to be seen. The space in front of him lay very quiet and still in the sunshine. To his right, there was a long, low hut running along beside the canal, with curtained windows. There was no hint of movement or noise from inside, but he thought, staring at it, that perhaps he had heard a door close just before the workman stepped into his path.

He looked around. There was no way of telling what the hut was, and he did not remember Worsley pointing it out to him the day he'd first visited the factory. Perhaps the simplest thing was to knock: but then he would need a pretext, and an apology at the ready.

''Scuse me, sir.'

He looked around, then down. A small, grimy boy was glaring up at him, a large box clasped to his chest.

'Forgive me,' Henry said automatically, and stepped out of the way. The boy adjusted his grip on the box and set off carefully towards the main building. On impulse Henry called after him, 'Wait,' and the boy turned, very slowly, to stare at him. 'What is that building? Is it an office of some kind?'

'Not going in there,' the boy said, 'I'm going up to the attic with these.' He raised the box a little, with preternatural slowness; Henry realised that it was a reeling box full of spiders, and he was forbidden to jolt them.

'I'm not telling you to go in,' Henry said, patiently, 'but what is it? What happens there?'

The boy scraped one foot in the dry dust until a cloud rose up to his ankle. 'Mr Worsley's room, that is,' he said at last. 'His lab-ror-a-tory. Been busy lately.'

'Yes, I imagine he has.'

'They orders extra rats. And puppies. My sister says there was monkeys delivered one day but she's a liar.'

'Puppies? For Mr Worsley?'

'They come out funny. Like the echoes, only worse – different – I dunno. Funny. If they come out at all. One fell out the sack and Maisie took it home, only it wouldn't eat or drink, just lay and looked up at her till it died.'

Henry frowned. 'I don't understand,' he said. 'You mean Mr Worsley has live animals delivered? What on earth for? You are surely not suggesting any—'

'No,' the boy said, turning away, 'no, I don't know, never mind, I have to go. Sir.'

Henry called out, to his back, 'Did you see Sir Edward going in – just a moment ago?' but the boy did not show any sign that he had heard, and an instant later he had disappeared into the main building.

Nothing moved behind the curtained windows; the silence fell again on the little yard, and nothing broke it. He must have imagined that door closing. There was no reason to believe that Sir Edward was inside. After all, here at the heart of the echoes, it was entirely possible that his ears had played a trick on him. He had become accustomed to the malaise, he hardly noticed it at all now – but the silk was all around him, out of sight behind every wall, and every sound was as untrustworthy as a will-o'-the-wisp.

And Worsley . . . Henry's head was beginning to ache in the sun. When the gala was over, and he had a chance to speak to Sir Edward, he would make sure that Worsley was dismissed. That would put an end, thank God, to whatever he was up to in there with— But surely the child was making it up! Teasing him, Henry, because he looked so well dressed and out of place, and because he had said, 'Forgive me,' to a little scamp half his size. Yes. He drew a sigh of relief, feeling foolish. Of course there was nothing sinister behind those veiled windows. It was probably some kind of store room. In any case, he was sure now that he would not find anyone worth finding. He adjusted his hat and turned to leave.

There was a commotion behind him – a woman's voice, and around it, a ghost chorus of whispers, voices that were human and inhuman and halfway between . . . He spun round. Two women stumbled out of the spider house, one wrenching herself away from the other. Behind them, he caught sight of the glittering tanks, and heard the voices whirl and echo from every side. *Madeleine* – no, no, of course not—

'I heard him! I heard his voice – how he used to be – calling me, I must go to him—'

'Mercy,' the smaller woman said, 'calm yourself. Listen to me. *Listen.*'

'If he is calling me, I must go, I *must go* . . .'

There was a struggle. Henry did not see exactly what happened, but Mercy slumped to the ground, her knees bent, and began to cry.

The other woman looked down at her. 'Come, girl,' she said, 'you know full well it's the webs. If he were calling you you'd not hear it. Would you?' She sighed. 'Now. You go home. I shall cover for you. Don't argue. You get some sleep. Not at your mam's, mind – don't go and see him, that'll upset you more, and he doesn't know whether you're there or not, right? If he was calling for you, your mam would tell you – she'd come running, wouldn't she? Because he's never going to say anything. So you go off home, and you forget this. And tomorrow you come back here and you stuff your ears with wax if you have to. You listening to me, Mercy?'

Mercy was still weeping, but slowly she grew quiet. At last she took the older woman's hand, and got to her feet.

'Good girl. Now, I'm going back in. You sneak out. Don't let anyone see you.' The woman patted her shoulder and went back into the spider house. There was another murmur, a pang of yearning and sweetness, before both doors shut.

Mercy looked round. Henry drew back into the shadow of the doorway – but too late. 'You,' she said, a little thickly. 'What are you doing here?'

'I was looking for Sir Edward.'

She nodded. Her face was blotched and red. She wiped her nose on the inside of her wrist. 'Friend of yours, is he?'

'I suppose so.' There was a pause. He cleared his throat. 'I am very sorry to hear—'

'You wanted to help me,' she said, suddenly. 'You offered to help me. Do you remember?'

'Naturally,' Henry said. 'Would that I could.'

'But you can,' she said, 'you can, please, wait—' Suddenly she fumbled in her bodice and held out a greying packet of papers. 'Here, sir,' she said. 'You see? I have a letter from the doctor, and from the vicar, and from a man from London, who visited Joe and said – they have all said, sir, that it is because of the looms, and that he will never be well again. I paid them to come, sir, it was not charity; they are educated men and I pawned my Sunday dress so that they would write it down for me. Joe is my son, sir. He was in the work-house, I tried and tried and I got this position in the spider house so I could take him back, but they'd put him to work in the weaving shed.'

'Yes. Yes, I knew that – Miss Fielding told me a little of your story. It is very sad.'

'But he will not answer my letters, sir. Sir Edward, I mean.'

'He is a very busy man. I expect he will get round to it soon – things have been rather hectic, recently, we are planning to—'

'You must give these letters into his hands yourself, and

say – say you know I am telling the truth, and make sure he reads them. Perhaps if he sees that other men, other educated men, think I am not a madwoman . . . Please, sir. I am desperate, and he must help me.'

There was a pause. She stared at him, her eyes wide and ringed with red. 'I think,' Henry said, 'I think he knows – and cares, cares deeply. I think he cannot bear the thought that anyone has suffered—'

'*He* cannot bear it? He has not lost his son, his only . . .' She made a quick, repressed motion with the papers. 'He will not answer my letters! I have proof here of what they did. And my son will never be right. If you had a child, sir, like my Joe—'

'Very well,' he said, too sharply. She could not know, after all, that he had once had a daughter. He took the dog-eared packet from her hand. 'But you are unfair to Sir Edward, Miss Harman. He is a good man.'

'You mean—'

'I am sure he will wish to help. But in return you must stop telling everyone that it is his fault. It isn't, you know. Every factory has accidents.'

She nodded, slowly. 'I don't care what I say,' she said, 'if he'll help me. Help Joe.'

'Good,' Henry said, although it did not exactly feel like a victory.

'Thank you, sir.' She dipped her head to him and hurried away.

He pushed the bundle of papers – still warmish and greasy from her skin – into his pocket. He had saddled himself with an unpleasant task, and gained nothing; somehow the shine had come off the afternoon, and he could not quite recapture it. The factory was a grimy, unpleasant, noisy place. Worsley was welcome to it. He resolved that he would not come here in future, unless it was strictly necessary – no, his place was at Sub Rosa, and when Sub Rosa was finished, it would be at Cathermute with Sir Edward.

He turned and strode back towards the factory gates, while the hostile sun beat down and his head ached harder than ever.

Henry did not see Sir Edward after all, either that evening or the following day, as he dined out late and left early again the next morning. Henry did not even pass him in the corridor. At night he lay with his eyes open, listening for any breath or sound from the room next door; and the smallest rustle of bedclothes or footsteps made him feel as peculiarly ashamed and stirred as if he were crouching on the floor to look through the keyhole. If only Sir Edward would knock – if only . . . But he did not; and at last Henry drifted into an uneasy sleep.

But on Sunday morning there drifted through the open window the unmistakeable baritone strains of 'The Seeds of Love'. Henry did not realise he had frozen until he felt water soaking into his sleeve; then he finished swiftly, cast his razor aside and hurried to dress for church. It was ridiculous to feel such happiness. And when he walked into the church, blinking in the blaze of stained-glass colours, how laughable – and wonderful – it was to see the back of Sir Edward's head, so familiar and unfamiliar, so like and unlike the visions Henry had conjured in the dark!

The service passed in a dream, even the sermon. When it was over, Henry followed the rest of the congregation out into the churchyard and stood waiting, his back against a yew tree. At last Sir Edward emerged, deep in conversation with one or two men whom Henry recognised from dinners at Cathermute House, but as he looked around he saw Henry and broke off. 'Latimer,' Sir Edward called, striding towards him, 'how are you? Shall we take a turn about the church-yard?'

One of the men had followed him. 'Yes, sir,' he said, 'it is all very well your promising, but with the shortage of labour and the extra work—'

'Yes, well, you will discover more at the proper time,' Sir Edward said, waving him away. 'It's nothing,' he added, to Henry, 'only my business affairs refusing to observe the Sabbath. How the devil are you? I have been away from home so much recently you're practically a stranger.'

'Quite all right,' Henry said, and laughed without knowing why.

'Come on, before that old mosquito has another go at me. Sting, sting, sting, he can't help himself. Thank God I have you.' He steered Henry down a little slope towards the far end of the churchyard, where a lonely angel wept in the shadow of a tall oak, and a clump of bushes cast a froth of blossom over the stone wall. A blackbird was pouring out a remarkable torrent of melody. 'That's better. Ah, look, they're leaving. How quiet it is, listen . . .'

For a moment neither man moved. Faint voices called goodbyes, and carriage wheels rumbled along the road on the other side of the lych-gate; then, at last, there was nothing but the blackbird, endlessly repeating its fragment of song.

'I sometimes think,' Sir Edward said, 'that nothing is quite as lovely as an English country churchyard – especially on a day like this. Heavens, this weather – look at the colour of the sky! Let's pray it holds for the party.' He moved away and paused in the shadow of the church tower, staring through a gap in the trees down into the valley. Today, as it was Sunday, there was no plume of smoke above the factory chimney, only the faintest lingering haze.

Henry joined him there, shoulder to shoulder. There was only a finger's width of sunlit air between them.

Finally Sir Edward shook his head as if a fly was buzzing in his ears. He said, without looking round, 'It is all ready, is it?'

There was no need to ask what he meant. 'It will be.'

'I can set my mind entirely at rest?'

'Yes.'

'Hmm.' He smiled; but his face was gaunter than Henry remembered, and there was a red tracery of blood vessels at the corners of his eyes. 'In a year's time, we shall stand here and reminisce, I suppose. About how my fortune was made. About how the bills piled up, but we held our nerve – hey?'

'Yes.'

'Yes. Good. Well, it is certainly the talk of the town. Not a single invitation declined so far. Orders for the silk are up already, so that's something.' His eyes slid back to the factory.

Henry nodded. He wished it were not there. He did not want to be reminded of it, not on this blue-gold day, with a sky as bright as enamel and a breeze that ran caressing fingers through his hair; not now, standing beside this man for the first time in days. He only wanted to think about Sub Rosa, and the gala, and – most of all – what would happen afterwards, when it had been a triumph . . . But he could not push away the memory of Mercy's tear-swollen eyes; and involuntarily his hand went to his pocket, touching the greasy packet of papers through the cloth. He had promised . . . He glanced sideways. They might not be alone again for a long time, and surely there could not be a better

moment than this one, in the Christian peace of the churchyard. He drew a deep breath and said, 'I went to the factory
on Friday. I thought perhaps I saw you, but I must have
been mistaken.'

'Were you there? I must have missed you by a hair. I
popped in to see Worsley.'

'I . . .' Henry said, and cleared his throat, 'I saw a woman
in great distress. One of the spider-house girls. She told me
that – that her son was ill, because he had worked in the
weaving house.'

'Oh?'

'She asked me—'

'For God's sake!' Sir Edward spun round, his hand raised
as if to defend himself. 'Do I not have enough to think
about? Some woman whining – heavens, it probably isn't
even true – and what am I supposed to do about it, some
workhouse brat, some little inbred by-blow, what the hell
am *I*—?' He stopped, and passed his hand over his forehead.
'I'm sorry,' he said, in a different tone. 'I have been working
so hard . . . I didn't mean to shout at you. You know how
I feel about the accidents. They haunt me. But I thought
that you – *you* understood, at least.'

'Indeed I do,' Henry said. 'I know how much they grieve
you. That is why—'

'Yes. I thought we had been over all that. Unless you
think I didn't mean it? Or that I was only brushing you off?
No, you can say it, if you want. If you think I am simply
another unscrupulous adventurer, tell me so, to my teeth.'

'No,' Henry said. 'I only—'

'You said you were my man. You promised. I thought—'
Sir Edward stopped. His face was tense with fatigue and
pain, as though Henry had struck him – as though an equal,
a friend, had struck him.

Henry stared at him for a second; a second that seemed to last for ten breaths, or twenty. He had not known he had such a capacity to hurt; mixed into his guilt and pity was a strange triumph, a perverse joy that this man cared so much what he said or thought. With an impulse that shook him like a bolt of electricity, he took hold of Sir Edward's shoulders. 'I'm sorry,' he said, 'forgive me, you know how much I admire you. I didn't mean to suggest that you had done anything shameful.'

They looked at each other, in silence. 'No. No, I know you didn't. It is my fault,' Sir Edward said at last. 'No . . . It was unforgivable to speak to you like that. I know you are on my side. You are, aren't you? Only sometimes I feel surrounded by those who think the worst of me, who want me to fail.'

'I am at your side, sir. I shall be at your side for as long as you want me.' He said it on a single breath, without pausing; but even when it was said, he did not want to take it back. Sir Edward glanced down, as though he had only just noticed that Henry had caught hold of him; then he looked back into Henry's face, and slowly his smile reached his eyes.

Suddenly, a long, fluting chord was carried on a gust of breeze: inside the church someone was playing the organ. They both looked round, stepping apart. The notes split apart, repeated, broadened into many-voiced harmony. It was not the same player who had accompanied the hymns, and the difference made Henry's scalp tingle. 'Who is playing?' he said.

'A boy from the village, I believe. The vicar lets him practise.'

'It's wonderful.'

'Not bad, is he?' Sir Edward said. 'Might have to sack the organist.' The sound washed towards them like water.

The sun danced, caught in the ancient dark branches of the yew.

Henry took a step towards the porch. He could just see, blazing through the dark archway, the vivid robes of a stained-glass saint; and the music rose even higher, running up and down the octaves. It had a reckless, childish passion, like Philomel throwing herself into a game. He paused on the doorsill, steadying himself against the stone upright. He sensed Sir Edward at his back; he did not need to turn and look, it was as if every sense extended further than it ought, behind him and to every side, out into the sparkling, sonorous air.

The music stopped, midway through a bar. A moment later it began again, pared to a single phrase that repeated and repeated. It ran down Henry's spine like a touch, striking the same nerves over and over. His throat constricted as though he were trying not to be sick; but what he was resisting was something else, something purer. He bent his head and drew a long breath, staring at the floor.

'What's the matter? Too hot? Here . . .' Sir Edward took hold of his free arm.

Henry turned. The music ran through his head, swaying, lifting him. 'No,' he said. 'I have never told you what it has meant to me, sir, to be given this chance . . .' The words spilt out of him, entirely sincere, and wrong. 'That is, I am in your debt—'

'My dear fellow, there is no need—'

'No – please – I must speak – I must tell you . . .' He did not know exactly what he was going to say. If he could only let the sunshine and music speak through him; if only this perfect moment would translate into perfect meaning, into eloquence beyond the mere movement of lungs and tongue and lips . . .

Sir Edward waited. Henry stepped wordlessly towards him.

There were footsteps, the rustle of a skirt, the squeaky chuckle of a child, the click of small boots skipping over stone – a clear voice, 'Sir Edward – good morning – and Mr Latimer . . .'

He reeled aside. For an instant all he saw was the emerald dazzle of the sun on the grass, as though his eyes had forgotten how to focus. He heard the older man say, 'Ah, Miss Fielding, Philomel. I had no idea you were inside.'

'We came in to say a prayer, and when the music began we stayed to listen. Philomel enjoyed it.'

'Oh? But—'

'She loves to sit very close, and feel the air vibrating. She says that her body sings even though her voice cannot.'

'How quaint. Well, as long as she does not make herself conspicuous.'

'No one saw us, sir.'

'Good, good.'

Henry drew his hand across his forehead, trying to compose himself. 'Good morning, Miss Fielding,' he said. 'Good morning, Philomel.' From the child's wide-eyed wariness, he guessed she had been warned to keep her hands linked behind her back, so that she did not forget herself and sign in front of her father.

'Well, I must go back,' Sir Edward said, suddenly brisk. 'I rode down, so I cannot offer you a lift. I shall see you tomorrow, Latimer, before I go back to London— Ah, no, perhaps not. Anyway, make sure you put the speech for the gala on my desk soon, won't you? I have a devil of a job learning things by heart.'

Henry said, 'Yes, of course. I—'

But the other man had turned away, and only gave a

jaunty backwards wave as he sauntered towards the lych-gate. Henry raised his own hand, stupidly, in answer; he felt a tug in his ring finger as though a thread connected it to his heart.

Miss Fielding was watching him. She looked away to sign to Philomel, and added, to Henry, 'If you will excuse us . . . Philomel has an early luncheon on Sundays.'

He was not sure if her voice was cold, or merely neutral. 'It is good to see you both,' he said. 'Philomel looks very well.'

'She is.'

'And you?'

'I, too, am quite well.'

'I have not had a chance to speak to you for weeks. I wish – I hope that when the gala is over, I can visit you in the schoolroom.'

'I cannot prevent you from doing anything you choose.' She said it levelly, as if she was daring him to quibble. 'Good morning, Mr Latimer.' She set off down the path, turning to beckon to Philomel when she lingered to peer curiously at the yew berries.

'I suppose,' he said, raising his voice, 'that you despise me for staying. After everything you said to me.'

'What? Oh, that. It was weeks ago. I hardly remember what I said.' She signed again to Philomel, more sharply. 'Really, Mr Latimer, it is your business what you do.'

He bit his lip. Clearly, in fact, she still bore a grudge; and abruptly he had no patience with her, he did not see why he should apologise when he had done nothing wrong. What did he care, really, if she did not like him? He was Sir Edward's man; no one else mattered. He gave Philomel a brief, warm smile – it was not her fault – and strode past them both, under the lych-gate and on to the road. Then, as he came out into the sunlight, some impulse made him turn. 'Here,' he said, digging in his pocket. 'Give these back to your cousin. I cannot do anything with them.'

'What?'

'Tell her I tried. But it is nothing to do with Sir Edward. And he has enough to think about, with the grand opening and the investors. She must let him alone, do you hear? She should be grateful to have work. Tell her that if I hear from her again, she may not even have that.'

Miss Fielding turned the packet over in her fingers, frowning. At last she said, 'You mean Mercy?'

'If she needs help, tell her to ask the Quakers. I gather they fall upon any opportunity to meddle in other people's affairs.'

She held his gaze. Then, without answering him, she put the papers into her reticule and held out her hand to Philomel. This time the child came straight to her, and they walked away together, their shadows moving ahead of them down the road.

Henry swayed forwards, with a sudden impulse to run after them. But what was there to say? He had been hard, perhaps – but he had only been thinking of his duty. He bent his head and stared at the ground for a long time, unseeing. His mind whirled with the factory, and the silk; and the gala, and the high rooms of Sub Rosa, with their gleaming lustrous drapes, their silence and echoes; and Sir Edward. If only Miss Fielding had not interrupted them, again . . .

When at last he raised his head, there was no one to be seen. The organ had stopped playing, and the only sound was the breeze rustling the trees and dancing through the grass. He tilted his face back to the clear blue sky, inhaling the scents of dry earth and pollen, and began to walk. It was not until he passed the gatehouse and was walking up the drive to Cathermute that he found he was pressing the back of his hand against his mouth, as if there were a thorn under his skin that he could not dislodge.

Twelve

The weather did not break. It held, just; and when Midsummer Day dawned cooler than the previous days, with a haze over the sky that did not quite burn off, Henry was glad. In the early summer heat he had worried that the banks of candles, once lit, would turn even the tall, cool rooms of Sub Rosa into a Turkish bath. The flowers, too, would benefit from a more seasonable temperature: the vases and bowls of roses, beautifully interlaced with sprigs and fronds, would almost certainly last the evening. Already, as the final day slid by and he paced from room to room, the air was full of their scent. Soon the perfume would be drowned in cologne and pomade, powder and perspiration, but for now it was like waiting in a garden – waiting and waiting until his heart would burst . . .

At school, he had once helped build a stage set for . . . he could not remember now whether it had been *Troilus and Cressida* or *Iphigenia in Aulis*; in any case it had been a mock pavilion, badly built by schoolboys, with walls that rippled and shuddered whenever an actor crossed the stage. But by chance on the day of the performance he had found himself in the auditorium alone, and in the expectant silence, the smell of dust and old excitement, he had seen the unmistakable glamour that clung to the wobbling structure of canvas and wood. This was the same sensation, only more – more enchanting, and more terrifying. In a few hours it would be the scene of a great spectacle, the making of Sir Edward's fortune and his own: the most important evening of his life.

Not that he was alone now. No such luck, he thought, as the Cathermute maids swerved out of his way, their arms full of dusters and mops, squeaking with laughter once he had gone past; it was as busy as a dress rehearsal, with voices calling from floor to floor. The kitchen was full of women, and the door swung back and forth endlessly, letting gouts of noise flow out and fill the passages. There was the chinking of porcelain, the thuds of furniture being rearranged, and the frantic scratch of hard brushes on the marble as the footprints of the last deliverymen were scrubbed away; and all of it was punctuated by yells and laughter, calls and commands, until he thought that if the house had not been full of arain silk his eardrums might have burst. And he was doing no good at all, standing in the hallway watching other people dart back and forth, so full of purpose that they hardly gave him a second glance. One maid, hurrying out of the cloakroom with a smudge on her nose, almost knocked him over. At last he could not bear it any more, and retreated up the stairs.

He found himself in the gallery, where he could stride up and down unobserved. The floor had been polished that morning, and the veiled afternoon sun glowed softly on the wooden boards. It had the dignified quiet of a much larger space – the hall of a museum, or the nave of a cathedral – but as he moved through it he could not help faltering, as if there were someone beside him, moving out of sight as he looked round. It was his own breath, echoing back to him from the exhibits: the ghostly susurrus as he passed the harp, the just-too-lingering murmur from the curtained confessional, the dead silence of the empty-eyed scold's muffler. The bridal gown stood in the bay of the window, a glimmering confection of lace and gauze, a falling deluge of roses. He had wondered, uncomfortably, whether something simpler would have been more effective, but now that it was in place, unshrouded, he could see that its extravagance added to the effect, as though some natural phenomenon of blossom or sea-spray had been bewitched into stillness. In the bay of the other window, with its back turned, there was a dark figure: the hooded assassin's cloak of black wool, double-lined with arain silk, which promised absolute silence and discretion. He had thought to make a playful contrast between the two. Now, looking at the two faceless shapes, they made him shiver; but not without a certain pleasurable *frisson*, and a consciousness that their effect was very striking.

He consulted his watch, and his stomach turned over. He could not remember the last time he had eaten, although it must have been more recent than the last time he slept. It would not be long now. In an hour there would be carriages outside and people coming up the stairs, bustling, chattering, pointing . . . The candles should be lit by then. The food would be laid out, the salads and shapes of blancmange and the two enormous tongues, sliced and tied together with ribbons. The string quartet would have arrived, uncased their instruments, tuned up. Sir Edward would be looking over the notes of his speech, or scribbling last-minute prompts on his cuff, pacing back and forth in nervous impatience. And he, Henry . . . His gorge rose again, harder. His work would be over; he would be powerless to change anything. And in a rush the enormity of his terror caught hold of him. This had cost more money than he could reckon up, more

231

money than he would ever possess in his life. If it was not a success . . .

He lifted the curtain that hung across the nearest window, brought it to his face and inhaled the scent of it. Then, on impulse, he wrapped it around himself, closing his eyes, so that he heard nothing and saw nothing, and for what might have been seconds or minutes he tricked himself into not existing.

When he opened his eyes, he was no longer afraid. The house was magnificent: it spoke for itself. He let the curtain fall across the window and took a deep breath, smiling.

Some half an hour later he emerged from the tiny box room at the top of the house where he had changed his clothes, and descended the stairs. Below him, the noise of the party rose in a liquid bubble of voices and music. But each separate sound was softened by the silk that covered almost every surface: the effect was magical, vivid and insubstantial, as though a coloured plate in a book had come to life.

It was not yet dark outside, and the sky was a profound, fragile blue, shining through the curtains at the tops of the windows; below, where the candlelight fell on the silk, the shimmer of the flames overlaid it with gold. The roses, overflowing the niches and banisters in profuse garlands, were the same shifting colour as the fabric; the marble floor reflected every gleam, as though deep lights moved within the stone. And through every doorway he could glimpse the rich, lustrous sweep of more silk, draped or taut, embroidered or smooth as water. A palace of cobwebs, he thought, spun from nothing, an enchantment. But where was Sir Edward?

There was a tide of people pressing and swirling through the hall, bunching outside the cloakroom, calling to acquaintances

over one another's heads, divided here and there by determined currents of boisterous young men or dowagers with
sharp elbows. But in spite of the obstruction every face was
laughing or at least good-humoured, and already he could
make out fragments of conversation coming from the doorway
of the dining room. 'Have you seen . . . ?' one woman said,
and another broke in with, 'This stuff on the tables – heavens,
they have put it absolutely everywhere . . .' Henry stood
aside to let a knot of silver-clad maidens pass him, hurrying
to escape their chaperones. It was extraordinary how their
silk dresses gave them an air of exotic mystery, like nymphs.
He knew that it was simply because their attire muffled the
natural vibrations of the flesh beneath, but he found himself
staring after them, bewitched. They might have been walking
on water, clad in cloud . . .

The front door let in the sound of more carriages, more
footsteps and voices. So many people! He could well believe
that no one had declined an invitation; there must have
been more people here than had been invited. Surely the
whole population of the town was here – or everyone who
mattered – and men from further away, too, sleek London
bankers with gold repeaters and dour gentlemen with the
flat accents of the North. He even saw Hinshaw, in his old-
fashioned clothes, looking about him with impassive curiosity.
A trio of women stood close to him, draped with silk *à la
Grecque*. Their tailor was a clever man, Henry thought,
showing the silk off to its best advantage. Might the Regency
line flourish anew, due solely to a fad for arain silk?

A maid went past with a tray of champagne, and he
caught up a glass and drank deeply from it. But he did
not have time to linger; he wanted to find Sir Edward
before it was time for his speech. He hurried up the stairs
and into the gallery. It was a very gratifying scene. In front

of him, a dignified matron ran her hand along the strings of the harp, amid much shuddering and giggling from her ringleted daughters; two married couples fluttered and exclaimed at the array of drums, one of them crying, 'Oh! I can feel it in my teeth!'; a bearded man was peering thoughtfully at the soldier's tent that was pitched in the centre of the room. On Henry's left, near the doorway, the mayor was deep in conversation with three young ladies, who gazed up at him with parodically attentive faces. 'It means "under the rose",' he said, with a self-important cough, 'which is a Latin phrase meaning "in secrecy". I believe it was built by one of our less respectable prime ministers, for his—' He stopped as his wife turned away from a pair of ballet slippers with a raised eyebrow. 'That is – excuse me, my dears, I entirely forgot to whom I was— Built for a female . . . a friend of the family . . .

Further away, the bearded man gave the tent pole a tug, sighed, and moved on to stare at the caped straitjacket and gag. 'Ha,' he said, quite loudly, and another, thinner, younger man stopped staring at a panel of lace to look round. 'Did you see this?'

'Yes,' the younger man said. 'Rather unpleasant, I thought.'

'Oh, I don't know. More humane than some of the things I've seen. And I expect the other patients would be glad of it. They're appallingly noisy places, asylums.'

'I couldn't say.'

'No, well.' They exchanged a glance. 'I wonder if Ashmore-Percy is selling them to Ronford House. Or donating them, for a discount.'

'Well, the advertisements did say the silk would be all the rage among the aristocracy.' The younger man laughed, caught Henry's eye, and gave him a long, hostile stare. 'Good evening.'

'Excuse me,' Henry said. 'I did not mean to eavesdrop—'

'Good,' the older man said. 'Come on, Fred, I must get some more of that mediocre champagne before it goes flat. Heavens, it's hot in here.'

'It's the damn candles,' Fred said, tailing obediently after him. 'We'll be lucky if the house doesn't go up. Remind me not to get more than a few metres from a door.' As they stepped out of the gallery they were laughing again. Henry did not understand what he had overheard, but the tone of their sneering had been unmistakable, and he wished he had spoken out more strongly in his employer's defence. He waited in the bay of the window, beside the faceless bride, until he was sure they would have gone.

As he ascended the stairs, he heard a clock strike: in a quarter of an hour the footmen would summon the crowds into the ballroom. He stopped in front of the principal bedroom. He had left the door open, with only a silken rope strung across at waist height; now it was closed.

He raised his hand to knock, but before his knuckles touched the wood it was jerked wide and he found himself face to face with Worsley. 'Latimer! What are you doing loitering out here? Get out of my way, will you?' He pushed past, without replacing the unstrung rope. In the room beyond, Sir Edward had been pacing, the notes of his speech in one hand; but now he paused mid-step, smiled, and called out, 'Come in, if you want. I've just sent Worsley for a glass of brandy. I'm as nervous as a kitten.'

Henry entered the room and shut the door. With the door closed, the supernatural hush was almost oppressive; the candle flames were the only thing that moved, so that everything else – the curtains, the silvery undyed-silk rug, the tea-gown dropped across a chair as if it was still warm from a woman's body, the canopied bed – might have been made of alabaster or mother-of-pearl.

Sir Edward pushed the wodge of paper into his pocket and began to bounce on his toes. 'Well. So here we are, finally. Pleased, are you?'

'If you are.'

'I will be, once I've got this damned speech out of the way.' He grinned, a little too broadly. 'It'll be worth it.'

'Would you like to go through it? I could—'

'No, no need, Worsley put me through my paces.'

It did not matter. Henry had been the one to write the speech, and once the gala was over there would be time to address the question of Worsley. He could not bring himself to care about anything, except this moment: this room, with the silk on every side and Sir Edward opposite him, smiling. He thought that he could hear, under the thud of his own pulse, an answering murmur.

'What is it? Are you afraid that I shall let the side down?'

'Of course not.' It was like being drunk. Perhaps he *was* a little drunk, already, from the hastily bolted glass of champagne and the heat. 'You will be magnificent.'

'Thank you. I'll do my best.' Sir Edward tilted his head with a grin, half mockery and half – what? Henry stared back, dazzled, trying to decipher the look in the other man's eyes: and then, although he had not exactly named it to himself, another voice in his mind said, *now.*

Suddenly the room was uncomfortably warm. Henry found himself stumbling to the window and drawing the curtain aside in a kind of panic, afraid of something he could not name. Or perhaps it was not fear, but something else, something just as urgent and visceral, something that threatened to be stronger than he was. He had to resist it; if he betrayed himself . . . Fresh air swept across his face, cooling the sweat on his forehead, ruffling his hair. As the draught moved through the room the candles dipped; he had the impression that reality itself had flickered for a moment, as though it were composed only of ideas and light.

'Oh, Lord, what's the matter? I'm the one who has to give a speech. You don't have anything to worry about.'

'I suppose,' Henry said, with some difficulty, 'I am tired, that's all.'

'Yes. Yes, of course. Quite right. You've been working hard, I expect.'

'Harder than I have ever worked in my life.'

'And the place looks splendid—'

He turned. 'For you,' he said. 'I did it all for you.'

Sir Edward blinked. 'Well – good,' he said. 'Yes, I am very pleased, as I said—'

'I have thought of nothing else . . .' He did not know whether he meant Sub Rosa or Sir Edward. 'I have hardly slept. When I did, I dreamt of – of this, of the silk, of you—' A scalding wave washed over him. He leant towards the window, thirsty for another waft of cool air, any physical sensation that might make him feel solid again.

'Have you been drinking, Latimer?'

'No,' he said. 'Or rather, a little – one glass.'

'Steady, steady – you had better sit down.'

'It is just a reaction, that's all – forgive me—'

'For heaven's sake, sit *down*.' Sir Edward took hold of him, untenderly. 'Here. Move your feet, won't you, that's right! Now sit, take a deep breath. You've gone quite pale – you're not going to be sick, are you? I dare say I could find some smelling salts somewhere.'

Now he was half lying on the bed, the curtains falling around him in shimmering veils, the voice above him coming

and going as the breeze stirred the fabric. On the bed . . .
He did not dare to follow the train of thought; he shut his
eyes briefly, fighting to control himself. 'I am not ill,' he
said. 'I haven't eaten much today – or yesterday, or . . . it
doesn't matter. Give me a second and I will be perfectly all
right.'

'Stay there.' Sir Edward relaxed his grip, and warily – as
if he were ready to wrestle Henry back onto the pillows,
should he resist – withdrew a little. 'Shall I send for a glass
of water?'

'No. Thank you.'

'There, your colour is returning. Don't get up yet.'

'I never thought, when I ordered this bed, that I should
be the one to lie on it.' He should not have said that.

Sir Edward smiled, but something else came and went
behind his eyes. He said, 'That reminds me. I have a surprise
for you. A good one, I hope.'

Henry felt his stomach lurch a little: like the moment,
he thought, when a boat entered the open water. 'What is
it?'

'I have commissioned a painting of you.' There was a
silence. Sir Edward laughed. 'You look appalled. Don't you
want to be immortalised in oils?'

'Me? Why?'

'Why do you think?' That spark again in his eyes.

Henry swallowed. 'I don't—'

'He's going to paint you as Harpocrates – the god of silence,
you know. Reclining among veils of silk and wreaths of
roses, half asleep, your hair tousled. We might hang you
above the hearth in the drawing room here, instead of that
looking glass. Or beside *Echo and Narcissus*, I haven't decided
yet.'

There was a silence: too long, too full. 'I thought

Harpocrates was a child,' Henry said, a little hoarsely. 'In the encyclopaedia in the library he is a child.'

'Why not a young man, instead? Poetic licence. Here . . .' He plucked a rose from the nearest vase and tossed it into Henry's lap. 'Your emblem.'

'Do I have a choice?'

'Do you want one?'

Henry took up the flower and worked his finger into the centre of it, feeling the fleshy parting of the petals around his fingernail. He was conscious that the older man was still smiling at him with that not-quite-malicious gleam; and his whole body was trembling – too hot, too full, threatening to betray him. 'I don't think I would be a very good sitter,' he said. 'I greatly admire the artist who painted the pictures at Cathermute, but my features could hardly live up to Narcissus or Theseus—'

'Not him,' Sir Edward said, shortly. 'I believe he is dead, anyway.'

'I'm glad.' He hardly knew what he was saying; he had a sense of vertigo, of being suspended by threads that were snapping one by one.

'You know you are quite destroying that flower, you ungrateful scoundrel.'

He looked down. It was true: torn petals lay like curled scraps of ivory upon his dark suit. He brushed them away with an unsteady hand. 'If anyone should be painted as a god,' he said, 'it is you.' It should have been a joke, but it was not.

'Oh?' Sir Edward raised his eyebrows. 'Bearded, with a thunderbolt? Or rising from the waves, with a triton and a crown of seaweed?'

If he had answered immediately, he might have saved himself. But for a moment he could not speak; and in the pause, the last strand broke. There was endless nothingness beneath him – endless space, endless speed as he fell – and no way back. Very low, very deliberately, he said: 'Just as you are.'

Sir Edward did not move, but his expression changed: as though, until this moment, he had seen only a meaningless pattern of shadows where now he saw Henry's face.

There was a silence. Henry had thought that he had become an amateur of silence, in all its timbres and guises; but this had an unfamiliar completeness, an aching quality that was both expectancy and ending. He could not breathe, but he did not need to breathe. He had seen Sir Edward understand. For this eternal instant, it was enough.

'Ah,' Sir Edward said, so softly it was like a note of music.

'I love you.'

'I see that.'

No more words came to him, nor any sense that more were needed. He had no hopes, no fears, he could not conceive of time continuing beyond this, beyond the man watching him, entirely serious, entirely attentive.

Then, with a suddenness that winded him, all the cogs and shafts of his body jolted screeching back into motion. His head filled with an appalled, appalling cacophony: dear God, what had he said, what had possessed him? 'Forgive me,' he stammered, although he could hardly hear himself through the din of his own shock. All this time he had dreamt – imagined – a moment like this, and now he had done it, he had stepped into his own foolish trap. He should have waited, he should never have, never . . . Oh, to be able to think! 'Forgive me – such impertinence – I didn't mean—'

'Oh yes, you did.' Sir Edward shook his head, his eyes alight. 'It is too late to try to take it back now.'

'I am sorry – truly—'

But he did not have time to finish, even had he known what he intended to say; for Sir Edward had leant forward, taken Henry's face in his hands, and kissed him.

It lasted a second, perhaps, or less. It was not lingering, or sentimental; it had none of the tentative fluttering and hesitance of the first kisses between himself and Madeleine, it was no elusive butterfly-soft brush of lips but the planting of one male mouth firmly against the other, with an easy assumption of mastery and possession. It told him that he had not been deceiving himself; but it told him, too, that he had not deceived Sir Edward, that his desire had been as clear as a line of print on a white page. It might, indeed, have been humiliating – if Henry had not wanted it to endure forever, if it had not made every nerve in his body thrum with a note too high to bear. If it had continued . . . There was enough time, just, to feel the exact press of unfamiliar flesh against his, a trace of hot breath and moisture, the hard grasp of fingers along his jawline; and at the same moment he wondered what was going to happen, felt his whole body brace and thrill to the uncertainty, the knowledge that he was on the brink of something he had never experienced, the stuff of speculation and yearning and fantasy.

Then a bell rang, faint as the peals of another world, and Sir Edward stood up.

The door opened. The clangour intensified. Then Worsley stepped over the threshold, and as he shut the door behind him the bells were muted again, soft but clearly audible through the thick uncurtained wood. His gaze slid over Henry as though he was not there. 'Your brandy, sir,' he said, holding out a glass. 'And that is the signal for them all to move into the ballroom. Are you ready?'

241

'I will be. Give me that.' Sir Edward gulped half the glass, and drew a steadying breath. 'That's better. I had almost forgotten my nerves; Latimer has been distracting me admirably.'

'When you are ready, sir.'

'Here,' Sir Edward said, holding out the brandy glass to Henry, 'you may as well finish this. I expect you need it as much as I do.'

'Thank you,' Henry said. He was amazed to hear how clearly he managed to speak, how neatly the vowels and consonants worked together, as though he were in perfect control of himself.

'Well then, wish me luck.' But he did not wait for Henry to reply; and a moment later he had disappeared into the corridor, with Worsley tight on his heels.

Henry shut his eyes. With his free hand he held on very tightly to the bedpost, squeezing and squeezing until the wood was damp against his palm. Then he put the rim of the glass to his lips, touching where Sir Edward's mouth had touched, and drank.

A few minutes later he followed the last of the guests into the ballroom. On a dais at one end, ringed with candelabras, in front of an arras of silk, the string quartet was playing the overture to an operetta. As he entered, a footman in the doorway gave a long nod to another, who made a gesture to the quartet. They drew swiftly to a flourishing crescendo and lowered their bows. The ordinary rustles and murmurs of the assembly were swallowed by the curtains across the windows; from the silence that fell, they might have been in a theatre at the climax of a drama.

Sir Edward stepped into view upon the dais, and bowed. 'Ladies and gentlemen,' he said, 'thank you for coming to my party.' There was a ripple of jovial amusement; a few young men at the back cheered. 'You are all most welcome. I hope you have all had the chance to wander through the rooms here. To those of you who have seen the silk before, it will come as no surprise that it is extraordinary; to those of you who have not, I hope you will stay as long as you wish, to admire, and marvel . . .'

He was delivering his lines with as much conviction as any actor. Henry stared at him, his mind whirling: how did he have the presence of mind to gesture and smile at the right moments, after what had happened? Surely he felt as Henry did – luminous, blazing, full of incredulity that no one could *see* how every particle of him had been transformed? He bit his lip, afraid he would burst into a joyous shout. How marvellous it was. They were the only people in the room – in all of Telverton – in all the world – who knew what had passed between them. What a joke – what a huge and sacred joke! It was impossible, wondrous, intoxicating – beyond words . . .

'The fortune of the factory,' the object of his reverie was saying now, 'is the fortune of Telverton – *your* fortune, ladies and gentlemen . . .'

He wanted to watch him forever, but just then Sir Edward's impersonal, amicable gaze slid in his direction, and he did not dare to meet it. If he should give himself away . . . Instead he turned his eyes sideways, hardly moving his head, so self-conscious that he thought even that tiny gesture might somehow betray his feelings. But no one recoiled, or caught their breath; indeed, no one gave him a second glance.

He caught sight of Miss Fielding in the corner, against the wall, behind two tall, dandyish men in embroidered waistcoats. Her face was turned to the small stage, so that he could only make out the side of her head and her hair. He had not known she was invited, but he knew her from her height and the shape of her cheek. What would she say, if she knew that *that* had happened? For a moment he longed to tell her. Oh, to throw caution to the wind, to speak it aloud, to boast . . . He thought she felt his stare, like a cloud passing over the sun; but instead of turning to see who was looking, she shifted sideways, keeping her gaze directed towards the dais, fumbling with a reticule that hung from her wrist.

'. . . magic,' Sir Edward was saying. 'But that is not all. Silence is the root of sleep, of rest and of health. But it is only the beginning. The opportunities it affords are even greater than our achievements so far. What you have seen here is nothing, compared to our ambitions for the future.'

Distantly, behind the glittering veil of his euphoria, Henry felt a shadow of confusion. He looked back at the dais. Behind his master, Worsley was surveying the crowd with a puffed-out chest. 'Currently,' Sir Edward went on, 'in my laboratory, we are hatching miracles. *Miracles!'*

These were not Henry's words. From the way Worsley was smirking, it was obvious who had inserted them.

'What we hope to make, ladies and gentlemen, is an instrument that produces, not notes, but emotions. You have heard how the silk affects our ears. But that is not the only organ it touches. It sets the heartstrings resonating, and penetrates the soul itself.'

The audience was listening with expressions of congenial interest; they did not seem to wonder what these fine phrases meant. Why should they? They had seen the advertisements proclaiming marvels, and this was no different, no more or less significant. It was only Henry who stood still, his finger-nails digging into his palms, trying to decipher the look on Sir Edward's face. *The soul itself . . .*

'Gentlemen,' Sir Edward said, ' – and, ladies, you must forgive me, for I am now addressing potential investors – what I will be offering, very soon, is a solution to every human ill. To every disharmony and disquiet of the psyche, and to every social misfortune that follows from it. To hysteria, and discontent, and disobedience. To poverty, since if everyone knows his place there need be no deprivation, either of the mind or the body. To—'

Henry did not understand. This was utterly new.

'An end to industrial strikes, to divorce, to every crime of insubordination and arrogance – yes! Ladies and gentlemen, I am promising you a new world, where the human mind will at last be in tune with its surroundings – eliminating every discord, every false note . . .' Sir Edward spread his arms as if to invite applause, and the audience obliged, with a good-humoured lack of passion. Here and there men were muttering to one another, or thoughtfully stroking their whiskers. 'Thank you. I am glad to see that you share my enthusiasm – and this will change all our lives, I promise you that. It will . . .' But he stopped, frowning sideways at a disturbance in the knot of people closest to him: a woman had fainted, Henry thought, until two men jumped aside, and a portly widow staggered and cried out. A tall figure pushed past her and stepped into the open space in front of Sir Edward. It was Miss Fielding.

No. It was Mercy Harman. How could he have mistaken her? Now he could see that her resemblance to her cousin was superficial: he had been deceived by her figure and the shape of her face. She was well dressed, but the gown did not fit her, and she wore no jewellery, nor gloves on her raw red hands. What was she doing here? Had she forged an invitation, or bribed another guest? And why, *why* would she come here?

'Madness,' she said, in her low, blurred, hoarse voice, and Sir Edward blinked.

'I beg your pardon, madam,' he said. 'As you see, I am currently—'

'*Madness*,' she repeated, more loudly, and there was a faint incredulous giggle from one of the young ladies. '*That* is what you are offering – madness, and misery, and death! Worse than death. You are not a good man – he is not a good man!' she cried, turning to the onlookers. 'He pretends he is, but the factory is an abomination, a curse upon the town! He is heartless. What he sells is malice, murder – sin.'

While she spoke the whole room had been frozen; now, belatedly, one of the footmen started forward, his arms outstretched.

'Despair,' she murmured, with a sudden sickening intimacy, as if for a lover's ears. 'Horror. You have blood on your hands – the blood of an innocent – blood, *blood* . . .'

Sir Edward said, 'Who the deuce are—?'

She flung herself at him. It might have been an embrace – one arm caught his neck, her cheek pressed close to his – except for the guttural sound that came from her throat, and Sir Edward's grunt of pain as he staggered backwards under her weight. Her other hand was hidden in the swirling silk of her skirts; then she pulled back as though to look into Sir Edward's eyes, and swung her fist into the narrow space between them. Something caught the light – a streak of reflected gold – and then Sir Edward twisted and gasped and dropped at her feet. The thud of his knees on the floor was half swallowed by the silk draperies: in the dead silence the flimsy noise seemed implausible, like a badly judged stage effect.

Then – but no, it could not have been in that order, Henry could not have heard the sound before the sight met his eyes – then, or before, it did not matter – then he saw the red stains upon Sir Edward's shirt front, and the air turned to stone in his lungs.

Mercy turned. She might have been the heroine of a Greek tragedy: her hands and arms and the pearl lustre of her dress were drenched in scarlet, and a few finger-marks of the same colour stood out upon her temple like a sparse garland. Against the tissue-paper pallor of her skin her eyes blazed, circled with dark, extraordinarily beautiful in her ruined face.

The girlish voice that had giggled, a few seconds before, screamed. The footman leapt forward again, as if reminded of his duty; another woman wailed, sagged against the wall and slid to the ground in a billow of skirts; more voices rose, Worsley dashed to Sir Edward, calling for help; and Mercy flew, straight as an arrow, towards the door. The crowd parted in front of her, leaving a clear path.

It did not dawn on Henry that he was in her way until she was within arm's reach. He had not meant to block her exit; but he could not move. Behind her, the footman was fighting ineffectively against the current of people, as a man shouted, 'Help, here, my daughter!' and a group of women pushed forward to peer at the swooning girl. 'Let me through, I am a doctor,' another man called. He shoved past a sobbing matron, who dropped a vial of smelling salts and began to shriek.

Over Mercy's shoulder, Henry saw the doctor attain the dais at last, and bend over Sir Edward. Worsley was dead white, and swearing. Was that movement, behind them? A twitch of a blood-stained hand? Please God, Sir Edward was alive . . .

Then Mercy stumbled into his arms, and the noise of the room seemed to recede. He had not reached for her; she had taken hold of him and was breathing in gasps, shaking as though she were at the centre of a maelstrom. She was on the edge of collapse. They stared at each other. The smears of blood across her forehead gleamed against her skin, and he could smell the thick metallic stench of it; and yet what he read in her eyes was not guilt but accusation. It burned into him like acid. He stood perfectly still, breathless, waiting for the thrust of a blade into his chest, wishing it were over and done.

Then she pushed him away. He stepped backwards, unresisting. His arms fell heavily to his sides. She spun past him, suddenly light on her feet, as if by some impossible alchemy she had drawn his strength out of him for her own use. He heard her breath as she ran down the stairs, and the belated, bewildered grunts of the footmen as she slipped past them out into the street.

'Latimer – stop her! Good God, man, what are you *doing*? You damned idiot, you let her go!'

He looked round. Sir Edward was striding towards him. His dripping cuff sprayed blood as he raised his arm, and a woman recoiled, gasping and wiping frantically at her face. 'You *had* her – right there. What were you doing to let her past?'

'You're alive,' Henry said, 'oh, thank God—'

'Of course I'm alive, damn you! Pig's blood, that's all it is, she burst a bladder of it on my chest, the mad bitch. When I lay my hands on her—'

'I thought you were—'

'Winded me, that's all. Go *after* her – yes, you, don't stand there gawping, halfwit – what are you waiting for?' He snapped his fingers furiously at a footman, and a few coins of red spattered across the floor. The footman gabbled an apology and obeyed.

Then he returned his gaze to Henry. 'You fucking fool,' he said, low and venomous. He slammed his hand into Henry's chest, knocking him out of the way. Henry stumbled backwards. No one offered an arm to steady him. He bowed his head and stared at the crimson handprint Sir Edward had left over his heart.

Thirteen

Once, when Henry was a boy, there had been a spring storm so violent it felled the oak outside his uncle's house. He had been very small – it must have been only a few years after his parents' deaths – and he had slept through the noise without being roused; but when he did wake, in the early morning, he had heard the utter silence outside and known that something was wrong. The wind had died, but no birds sang, no animals rustled, no wheels creaked along the distant road. He had crept to the window and raised the curtain with a tentative finger; and although he gasped to see the enormous tree across the lawn, its desperate roots grasping at emptiness, he was relieved, because he had been afraid of something else, something worse.

There was the same quiet now, when he opened his eyes. He did not know where he was. The shapes in front of his eyes were dim and grey, as insubstantial as smoke, lit only by two rectangles of faint bleak daylight; there were pale slopes and curves looming on every side, gigantic and impossibly distant, like a landscape glimpsed through mist. It was only when he raised his hand that the perspective corrected itself. Now he could see he was in a room – a spectral room, full of furniture that was not quite solid, all of it wavering a little as if in a draught – a nursery, with a low nursing chair, a bassinet with a sweeping canopy, and a row of diminutive shirts hanging as if to air in front of the unlit grate. He stayed very still. He had never imagined what it would be like to be a ghost, but now he knew it would be this: an existence in a world of treacherous fog, believing oneself to be the only reality. Any moment now he would see a silent nursemaid glide past his eyes and lift an infant from the crib.

The horror of it made him sit up, and his head knocked sharply against the door behind him. That, at least, was solid. And the noise he had made – an undignified grunt of pain – was muffled but reassuring, vibrating in his skull and ears as it should have done, more or less. But then, where was he? He rubbed his eyes and blinked: yes, that was better, the edges of everything were clearer. He was sitting on the floor, like a child; that was why everything was so strange and high.

And he was cold. He glanced down and saw bare skin: he was shirtless, wrapped in some diaphanous stuff that had slipped to one side. He clutched at it, bewildered. What—?

On the floor, a few feet away, lay a stained bundle of cloth. It had dried to a brownish carmine colour, stiffened into folds like some obscene flower. A high ringing began in his ears. Blood, it was blood. Madeleine's blood, or the baby's – it had poured out of her, on and on, unstoppable, and he had watched, frozen, until his determination to be unmoved had slipped into desperate hope, into prayers, and then into creeping, inexorable wretchedness and guilt. He should have called a doctor when she begged him to; he should have listened to her – oh, God, he should never have married her, never touched her, it was his fault that she was dead – and the child, the little girl, who had slipped out motionless and blue—

He dragged himself into a crouch and staggered to his feet. He was not thinking, or thinking only that he wanted to get out of this place, to find somewhere else to rest, away from the blood, the place where she had died—

The length of silk fell from his body and tangled around his ankles. He dragged himself free and kicked it aside; and then, as he braced himself against the wall to heave a deep breath, he remembered at last where and when and who he was. Madeleine was dead, yes, but long dead, dead far away. That was his own shirt, stained with pig's blood, which he had removed the night before in disgust, and then wrapped himself in a piece of drapery to keep warm. And the room he was in was not the barren, dusty nursery in London, but its counterpart in Sub Rosa, which had never been meant to accommodate a real child.

Slowly the memory of the previous night returned to him. A few images stood out clearly, like tableaux: Mercy with the face of a ruined divinity, the crowd agape, Sir Edward drenched in blood – and stinking, Henry remembered now how he had stunk like a gutted pig . . . He could remember, too, the shimmering drapery that had hung over the bed, the fleshy ivory of scattered rose petals, the shocking euphoria of the older man's mouth against his own; but that was tainted by what had come after. He had felt such perfect happiness. He had felt a new life stretching before him, a new shining kingdom of desire and secrecy and triumph. And then Mercy had destroyed it, as utterly and cleanly as an avenging goddess. He tried to tell himself that at least the silk would be the talk of the town – there would be more publicity than he could have dreamt of . . . But now when people spoke of it, it would be as a pretext for gossip and prurient speculation. Now *arain* would be always in the same sentence as *madness* and *sin* and *despair*. And Sir Edward— But he did not want to think about Sir Edward.

How the guests had enjoyed it! They had left quickly, the women clinging to their husbands' arms. More than one young lady had paused at the head of the stairs to catch the banister and stagger in a half-swoon. They did not swoon entirely, of course, since that would have endangered their lives and coiffures; just enough to fall into the supportive embrace of a young man. The doctor, cheated of the prestige of reviving their host from a real injury, had taken it upon himself to shepherd the crowd away from the ballroom, as if it were not blood upon the floor but vitriol that might eat away the soles of their feet. The local men had lingered only to smirk behind their moustaches and gulp a final glass of champagne; and the businessmen from Exeter and London and Manchester had been the first to leave, disappearing so quickly they might never have been there at all. Only Hinshaw, one of the last to leave, had paused to look into Henry's eyes, and said, 'If thou need'st help . . .'

His kindness had been more humiliating than the others' indifference. Henry had turned aside without a word, snatched a half-empty bottle of champagne, and climbed the stairs away from the voices and bustle. Had it been only that modest quantity of champagne? It was a blur, compounded by his sleepless nights and empty stomach; it might have been one bottle, or several . . . All he remembered was drinking, gasping for breath, and drinking again, until the liquid coursed past his collar and down his chest.

He had not known, or minded, where he was going. He could hardly recall the configuration of the rooms; he thought for a while he was in the Sub Rosa of his dreams, where endless doors had opened off every passage and staircase, like a maze. He went upwards for longer than seemed possible. No one had remembered to replace the candles on the upper floor. The last of them were guttering as he turned the corner of the staircase, stepped into the nearest room and shut the door.

His head was spinning. Over and over he felt Sir Edward's hand in the middle of his chest, pushing him backwards. The sensation was so strong that he looked down at his shirt. It was filthy with blood; there was the mark of Sir Edward's splayed fingers, but around it there were clotted streaks and spatters which must have come from wrestling with Mercy – and below, a thick, encrusted patch where she had leant against him, as close as a lover. It reeked. He reeked. And yet what came out of a pig, he thought, was so like what came out of a human being – the abattoir floor, in the end, so like the mess of any other death—

He ripped the clothes from his upper body and flung them to the floor. Then, because his bare skin prickled at the exposure, he dragged a length of silk from the nearest chair and wrapped it about his shoulders. The nightlight fluttered in the draught.

He sat down on the floor, pulling the silk tight. As it covered his chest it changed the resonance of his heartbeat, but he was trembling so much he did not care. He felt too sick to close his eyes; and anyway, he did not want to fall asleep, he was afraid of his dreams. He fixed his eyes on the light, and braced himself for the oncoming hours as if they were a storm.

*

The next morning – dull, chilly, overcast, a half-morning in shades of grey and silver – he trudged back to Cathermute House, aching and unshaven. As he crossed the Great Hall he almost tripped over a maid who was scrubbing the floor. She shuffled out of his way, her head lowered, as if she did not dare to look up; but as he reached the far end of the room the back of his neck prickled. He glanced back. She was staring after him, slack-mouthed.

His bedroom door, like the front door, was open. An older, softer-faced maid was moving back and forth in front of the window, with piles of folded linen. He said, 'Leave that, will you? Just put it anywhere.' Then when she paused and stared at him, her arms full, he added, 'Bring me breakfast. And in half an hour I should like a bath.'

She said, without setting down the linen, 'Certainly, sir. But—'

'An early lunch, then, if there's nothing left of breakfast.' His suitcase was laid open on the coverlet, half full of his things. 'What are you doing?'

She did not answer.

'You're packing for me,' he said. 'What for? Who told you to do that?'

'I'm sorry, sir, it's almost done.'

'No, that's all right, but . . .' He rubbed his forehead. Perhaps he was being sent to Exeter, or London, or Manchester – perhaps there had been an investor unable to attend the gala, who wanted to speak to him in person – perhaps—

She wavered, dropped the pile of shirts into the case and hesitated, glancing at the open drawer on the other side of the room. 'Would you like me to come back later?'

'Yes.' It must be some kind of mistake.

She glanced up at him through her eyelashes, and something in her expression made his stomach swirl and dip. 'Ring for me when you want me to finish, sir,' she said, then bobbed a curtsey and ducked towards the door. But there she paused to look up at him, and bit her lip. 'Sir . . .'

'Yes?'

She hesitated. 'There is a note for you. It might explain . . .'

Perhaps she pointed, but Henry had already seen it: a paper square on the mantel. As he crossed the room to retrieve it, the door closed with a soft click. *Mr Latimer*, it said on the envelope, and inside:

I have no more need of your services. Hence your presence is no longer required at Cathermute House. I remain, cordialy yours, Sir Edward Ashmore-Percy.

He sat down beside the window. His hands were steady, his breath slow. He stared at the bed, and at his suitcase lying open.

Sir Edward must have written it early that morning. Or late last night. It might have been the first thing he did when he got in; or the second – he must have washed first, since there were no smudges of blood on the neat white envelope.

He read it again. This time he noticed the spelling mistake. *Cordialy yours*, he thought. He clutched at the words for a moment before they gave way, flimsy as a stitch. It was a form of words, no more. Sir Edward was neither cordial, nor his. If only the thanks were heartfelt – if only there were a hint of friendliness or regret, however trifling, however pitiable – Henry would have held on to that; he could have forgiven anything, if some note of affection had crept in. He would have been grateful. But the note was as cold as if they were mere acquaintances, even enemies. As if Sir Edward despised him – or as if, Henry thought, with a lurch of pure horror, he blamed him not only for Mercy's escape but for her attack. Could he possibly know that Henry had turned Mercy away? Oh, those letters! If only he had passed them on, if only he had been braver . . . But surely Sir Edward would understand, would know that if Henry had realised the danger— No, he thought desperately, no, Sir Edward must know that he had only acted for the best – Henry had *said*, for God's sake, he had said *I love you*—

He could not bear to finish that thought. But when he wrenched his eyes away from the letter they fell again on his half-packed suitcase. He saw too that his dusty cases of auricles had been ranged against the wall, as if ready to be carried away. He imagined the footmen ejecting him. If he lingered they would be only too ready to usher him through the corridor and down the stairs. The maids would look on curiously, whispering behind their hands. He would be left standing beside his baggage at the lodge, alone, helpless, humiliated.

He must see Sir Edward as soon as possible.

He hurried out into the corridor. But as he descended the stairs, slipping through the soft-edged patches of stained-glass colour on the landing, he grew conscious of the quietness of the house. The scrubbing of the hall floor had ceased. An older maid was dusting the furniture along the passage, but her small movements only drew attention to the lack of any other sound. Sir Edward was a noisy man; even when he was only reading or writing letters he hummed and grunted and kicked his feet against his chair, endlessly restless. Henry knew, before he knocked on the study door, that it was hopeless.

He had avoided the maid's eyes, resolutely, as he passed; but now he knew she had paused in her work and was watching him. No one answered from within the study. He knocked again, and again, which was absurd, since if Sir

Edward had been inside, he would have been growing impatient at the continued disturbance.

'He's out,' the maid said, finally.

'So I gather.' He turned, and she gave him a small, insolent smile. 'When will he be back?'

'No idea. Sir.'

'Where is he? The factory?'

'Don't know that either.'

'No,' he said. 'I suppose you don't.'

She went back to her work. Finally she finished the last curlicue of the cabinet and moved away.

What could he do? Not wait here forever. He rubbed his forehead, trying to think. A letter – not explaining himself, for he could not think how he could do that in writing, but begging— requesting an interview. He darted into the library, and reached for a pen and paper. *Dear Sir Edward . . .* He wanted to say, *I meant everything I said to you; you must not cast me away, I beg you.* Instead, after a second's thought, he wrote, *Thank you for your note. I would be grateful if I might claim a few minutes of your leisure, before I depart for London.* He resisted the impulse to add anything else: a calculating part of him suggested that it was better to be brief. *Yours—*

He could not bring himself to write a polite form, *yours most sincerely,* or *your obedient servant,* although both were true. He hesitated; then, not knowing what else to do, he simply added a full stop and his full name. Folding the paper over, he slipped into the corridor and slid it under the door of the study.

He was still holding the pen. He hurried back into the library to replace it – as if, he thought, he would be accused of stealing. Absurd. He let it fall on the desk, and drew a deep breath. Opposite him James Ashmore and his wife watched him from the alcove. He turned away, as if they were real observers, as if they could see his desperation.

Now. Now, what? He could not simply wait. He could not . . .

And if, at the end of all the waiting, Sir Edward did not change his mind—

He put his hands over his face. He remembered the morning of Madeleine's death when he had left the room, at last, because the maid had told him that Argyll was downstairs. He had got up from his chair and walked away from that appalling silence. He had paused to listen, straining his ears, for the sound of a baby crying. He had heard nothing. And then, like a child himself, he had slipped down onto his knees. He had thought then that he would never have the strength to get back to his feet.

Now he told himself that it was not the same. It was not death. It was not his own flesh and blood, carried out of reach. And if, yes, it was because he had made a foolish mistake, then at least it had been because of love, not a failure of love. At least, *this* time—

There was a hand on his shoulder. His heart jumped, but he already knew from the shape of the fingers, and the faint indefinable scent, who it was. A day ago he would not have minded that touch, he would have smiled and pitied her. Now he hated it, because she was not Sir Edward. He looked up. 'Miss Fielding,' he said, and could not think of any more words.

Behind her, Philomel was twisting one leg around the other, regarding him with frank interest. Miss Fielding caught her eye and signed, with a swift, reassuring sweep of her hand. He envied them their wordless understanding; he envied them everything else, too.

'What is wrong with you?' she asked.

'I am perfectly all right.'

'I rather doubt that,' she said. 'Are you ill?'

'No.'

'I am not a very good ministering angel, but if I can ring for anyth—'

'No!'

She stepped back, raising her hands, and he drew a deep breath. 'No,' he said again, more calmly this time. 'Thank you, but really, there's no need. In any case, I'm not sure whether the maids would – that is, I am meant to be . . .' He stopped.

'What?'

'I am no longer Sir Edward's guest,' he said. He turned away from her to hide his face, and found that he was staring at the picture of Sophia Ashmore. Her dark eyes looked back at him, judging him, as though he should always have known better than to hope.

Part V

Kratos, April 182—

Today I swam alone. I did not care if I drowned, but I knew I should not. I was part of the sea, I could have floated forever and the current would have borne me home. When at last I came dripping out of the waves, Hira was sitting on the sand, watching me with an expression I could not identify. I spattered her with water and she smiled, but that curious, observing look did not quite leave her face.

When I had dressed she said, 'Here,' and held out a pot. 'This is for you. Eat a fingertip's worth, the first twelve mornings after you bleed.'

I removed the lid. It was a green paste, thick with an acrid scent: some herb, pounded and mixed with oil. 'What does it do?'

'It will help a child-seed root itself.'

'Thank you.'

Hira nodded. I have never told her how much I long for another child; we have never spoken of the one who was lost. I suppose there has been no need.

I dipped a finger into it and touched my tongue to the stuff. But as I nearly gagged on its bitterness, Hira caught my hand. 'No!' she said. 'Only for the first twelve days after your blood starts. And only a fingertip's worth, no more. Do not be tempted to think that more will work better. You understand? It is important. No more than I have said. Unless . . .' She hesitated, and let go of my hand, and shrugged.

'Unless what?'

'Unless you decide that – after all . . .' She stopped, her eyes on mine, as though she expected me to understand perfectly what she meant; then, like a teacher with a disappointing pupil, she sighed. 'Unless you change your mind. About the baby.'

'You mean . . . ?' But she did not answer me. I stared at her. I had heard of women who confected abortifacients, but I had never imagined that any of them might bear a face like Hira's. 'You are speaking of an atrocity,' I said, hoarsely. 'After what happened to my child, you think that I could *choose—*'

'I am only telling you that you might choose it, if you wished.' Her gaze slid past mine, upwards and eastwards; and although you cannot see the village from the beach, I knew suddenly that she was looking towards the house where James and I live. For a moment I felt my breath come short: how dare she condemn him, I thought, she had no right to pry into our private affairs. What was it to her if he was less of a husband than—? But before I could complete the thought, some other sense told me that she was not thinking of James, but of old Montague Gritney.

I do not know how I knew it. I suppose it must have been her expression, or the way she held herself. I saw her then as I had never seen her. I had gathered crumbs of the story, here and there, and knew she had been an orphan – a little drudge for all the matrons of the village – when Gritney took her into his house, and that she must have been thirteen or fourteen when he died. But I had never thought – never speculated . . . I thought I understood then why the women here treat her as they do: they fear her, I think, they are grateful for her help and her knowledge, but there is something that makes them avert their eyes.

Oh, I can hardly bear to remember! Hira – who has never shown weakness, who has always looked as though she pitied *me* . . . Whatever that unloved child was forced to do, she deserved pity, not censure. I wanted to take hold of the little girl's hand and lead her home, and I knew it was too late.

I put my arms around her. For a heartbeat she was rigid, and I cursed my own ineptitude; then she laid her head on my shoulder. I thought at first that she was humouring me, and was laughing inwardly at my needless attempt to console her. But when at last I began to draw away, she hesitated before she let me go.

Kratos, last week of May, I believe, 182—

My courses came while I was in the village, helping Hira with a child who had burnt himself. I crouched beside her to hold the pot of ointment and the soft cloth, and when I stood up I felt the blood run down my leg and soak into my skirt. She said nothing then, and I turned aside as soon as I could to staunch the flow with a rag. But afterwards, as we were walking to the hut at the far end, where Misia lives, she said, 'The leaves do not work for you, then.'

'I do not know,' I said.

'They are powerful,' she said. 'If they do not work, we should try something else.'

'I cannot tell if they work,' I said. 'I may as well go on with them. Unless you are possessed of something that will enable me to conceive without James's intervention.'

I thought that she was going to reply, but she only glanced at me, biting her lip, and we walked on in silence.

Kratos, June 182—

This evening, while I was undressing, James came and sat upon the bed, clutching his memorandum book. I felt my heart begin to beat faster at his proximity: it was too soon after my courses, but it was not impossible, if nature were kind enough to stretch a point . . .

'I have exhausted my study of the silk in its knitted form,' he said, flourishing the book under my nose as though I might wish to peruse his diagrams. 'It is knitted, you see, not woven, and it must be the shape of the knots and the asymmetry of the construction that create the effect. But now I must have another spider. If I am to write something truly profound, I must connect the two phenomena. I must show the world that I am a natural philosopher, not a mere – empiric.'

I did not know the word, but it did not matter, for he was not expecting an answer.

'You must procure me another specimen,' he said, and turned his gaze on me. 'As many as possible, in fact. I have plans to— Well, never mind that, we will talk that over another time. I must have some spiders.'

'I do not know where I should find them, James,' I said. 'It was the merest chance, last time. It was only because it had crawled onto Hira's shoulder—'

'Well, you must ask her where she'd been, then. And don't let her lie to you. I know what they're like, they're as sly as anything, these ignorant peasants. And stupid, wilfully stupid. What do they know of research, and scholarship? Make her tell you. Bribe her, if you must.'

'I do not own anything she would want.'

'Nonsense. Offer her your wedding ring, that's gold.'

I kept my voice low and steady. 'She forbade us to touch the spiders – don't you remember? She said—'

'Damn it all, Sophy, will you help me or won't you?' He leapt to his feet; his fists were clenched. 'How dare you sit there, sweet as milk, denying me? You are as bad as she is – worse, since you should know better. Don't think I have not noticed how much time you spend with her – she is an infidel, a Jezebel—'

'She is no such thing!'

I had raised my voice. James glared at me, white with fury.

At last he bent and collected his memorandum book. 'Let me say this,' he said at last, 'so that you may be in no doubt. I can neither love nor desire a wife who is so devoid of proper feeling. I have said nothing of your unwomanly forwardness – ah, you may well blush – but now I will speak quite plainly. Do not think that you may entice me into your bed until you have remembered your duty. Why should I give you a child when you give nothing in return? Good Lord, I see you flinch at the very idea of chastity. What have you become? Turn your eyes inward, Sophia, and see how rotten you are.'

I said, choking, 'Many men would want an heir.'

'Many men would want a whore. I am not one of them.'

There was silence. I knew that it would enrage him if I wept, but I could not stop the tears spilling down my cheeks. He watched them fall, and said nothing.

'Very well,' I said, fumbling for my wedding ring. It stuck on my knuckle, and I had to dig my nails into my finger to get it free. It seemed an age before I held it out. 'Take it. You may use it to bribe Hira, if you wish.'

He plucked it from my palm. Then he turned towards the window, and flung it out. There was the briefest spark of moon- or starlight glinting in an arc as it fell; then it was extinguished, somewhere on the ground beneath the trees. Then he caught up the lamp, strode out of the room, and left me in the dark.

I wept all night, lying still and silent, as though there were some broken pipe inside me that would not stop leaking. But today I walked alone into the forest, further and faster than I have ever done before, and my left hand felt so light I trailed it along every branch that I passed.

Kratos, July, or August, I think

I am so tired I can hardly see; but I must set this down, for it is like a dream, already beginning to slip away. I will set it down, and then I will sleep. Come, Sophy. It is such a small task, is it not? So small and so easy, compared to the other travails of creation . . . But I do not trust myself to find the words; what I have seen was so marvellous and so real.

No matter. I will attempt it.

I awoke gently, easily, as though it were the morning and not the night; as though, indeed, it was some internal command that had roused me, and not some external sound. When I opened my eyes there was a figure beside our bed, and yet I was not afraid – I pushed myself up on my hands and stared through the darkness to make out who it was. It was a woman – a girl, but I did not recognise her. A soft, unfamiliar voice said, 'Hira – says – come,' with the childish emphasis of a lesson learnt by rote.

I did not question her; I had been waiting, expectant, ever since Hira and Misia left a few days ago. I followed the unknown girl, and although she did not speak I knew where we were going, and why. We climbed a steep, rocky path, and although it was long I did not mind, I could have walked on in the dark forever, knowing that Hira had sent for me.

As we reached the backbone of the hill, and came upon a

clearing, the moon – which had been dodging and bobbing behind the trees – seemed to spring into the sky and hang there like a tarnished mirror, so large that I could see every pit and imperfection. In front of us an arch of stone stood blackly against the shimmer of the heavens. Through it I saw a scatter of flames, and a grove of tall oaks, and the hunched shapes of women sitting on the ground . . . but at first I could not identify the sheen of silver light that lay beyond their silhouettes. The back of my neck prickled, and the hairs on my arms rose, and I paused mid-step. The girl took my hand, pulling me forwards, and I was obliged to wrench my gaze away so that I did not stumble. Then she pushed me firmly to the ground. I caught my breath, and looked about me.

We sat – all the women of the village, I think – in a clearing, large enough to accommodate half a dozen evergreen oaks. Opposite us, beyond a far scatter of untended lamps, there rose shining translucent sails and domes that were neither ice, nor alabaster, nor quicksilver, nor any other substantial thing that I might name. Here, only ten or twenty yards from where we sat, a pavilion stood a little taller than the height of a man: its roof was a spiral, its walls curved, the shape turning inwards to a point as though a gargantuan nautilus shell had been polished almost to transparency. Behind it, another mass of the same stuff rose higher; its glimmering walls met in a point like the upturned hull of a ship, and above that long keel-spine lay the great sparkling sweep of the galaxy. I could not tell what it was, or what purpose it might serve. But after a little I saw the walls bend and dip in the breeze, and understood that they were made of fabric – and then (how James would mock me for my slowness!) it broke upon me that they were constructed of the silk of the *sireine*, as strong as steel and soft as oil. Great tents, then – but from the way the thin shrubs grew around them, and tall stone pillars stood at their corners, I could see that they were not moved, nor made to be moved: they were there for every season, set carefully to be in harmony with the sky and the spheres.

I frowned at the thought: rooms that were made of the same stuff as shrouds . . . But there were no horrid whispers nor half-heard warnings hissing upon my ears; there was only the deep, sacred silence of a shrine, strong enough to hold the murmurs of the seated assembly without being broken. It seemed to me that I could breathe more deeply there than I ever had before, as though I had boarded a craft which could bear me through any storm without foundering.

On the other side of the clearing a woman laughed, with a note that ended in the sudden check of her breath. She got to her feet, and from the enormous swell of her belly I knew it to be Misia. Beside her − my heart leapt absurdly − was Hira, and together they walked in a circle for the length of a dozen breaths, and then came back to the cluster of lamps and sat again. A gust of breeze carried the scents of raspberry-leaf tea and goat's milk. We waited, and the stars wheeled slowly above us, and dawn came; and Misia paced and rested and groaned, her voice growing harsher. At last she cried out: and the women who had been sitting on the ground moved out of her way like a parting sea, so that Hira could lead her across the clearing to the entrance of the nearer shrine. Through the opalescent silk I saw Misia lean into Hira's arms − not embracing, but bracing, as though in anticipation of a high wind.

'Soon,' a woman beside me said, 'soon. Watch.'

There was not much to see: only Misia braced against Hira, breathing shallowly now, her eyes open but blank. Gently Hira prised Misia's hands away from her shoulders and placed them upon the central upright pole of the tent, so that she could bend unburdened to squint between Misia's legs. With a shock of – what? Terror, I think, and hope, and utter disbelief in spite of the long hours of waiting – I saw that she had made a cup of her hands, ready to receive the child; and then, at last, as the woman beside me gripped my hand and my eyes stung with the fixity of my stare – at last, at last . . .

Then, from nowhere, there were three people in the tent where there had been two: an impossible arithmetic that made me gasp and grin, and the other women with me, while the baby's wail rose in confusion and outrage. For a moment we sat petrified; then a great sigh spread over the clearing, and an older woman came hurrying past with water and cloths. Now all was busyness, the entrance panel of the tent was thrown back and the others entered, mopping and dabbing and wrapping and carrying out all the small, messy offices that were required – but all in glowing silence, while Misia's baby protested at its bright, dry, gaping new world. A little while later I caught a glimpse of a greyish meaty bag slithering into a bucket on the end of a cord. Hira knelt over it, dabbling with her fingers out of sight, and then nodded as if satisfied. Then the old woman took hold of Misia's arm and spoke to her gently. They had let her keep the infant in her arms, already nuzzling at the nipple; and when all was clean, Hira bound a length of cloth around her chest with the baby in it, so that it was curled between her breasts, flesh to flesh. Then they led her out of the tent. She blinked in the low morning sunshine and brought her hand to cup the infant's head, as if to protect it, or to assure herself that she was not dreaming.

A kind of swift levity leapt across the space like flames taking hold: there was laughter, a raucous voice raised, and a shout of some lewd congratulation that made Misia giggle helplessly until she winced. Hira grinned and called back a retort that raised even more laughter.

271

Until that moment I had felt myself an unlikely part of their sorory; but as the hilarity grew, and I was the only one who could not even smile, since I did not comprehend the joke, I recalled that I was not only a woman but an Englishwoman – and so not, after all, one of them. Perhaps they would have celebrated with the same frankness if I were to travail among them. But I should never know; there would be no birth for me, and no infant.

No one was looking at me. I approached the tabernacle, which stood empty; the stone floor had been swept, but still bore traces of stains and footprints. Was this also the place where they came to die? I stood on the threshold, and the hairs on my arms stood up, a strange shudder running through me, a mixture of yearning and fear.

'No further,' Hira said, and her hand closed about my upper arm. 'Not for you, not now.'

I turned to her. She had washed her hands, but there was a smear of dark red across her breastbone; it ought to have made me recoil, but I wanted to put my mouth to it and lick it away. I felt heat sweep up from my feet, and sweat break out over my scalp.

I said, 'It is sacred, isn't it?' and for a moment I did not know exactly whether I was speaking of the tabernacle or of something else, the mark on her skin or her hand touching my arm.

'Yes,' she said, 'it is sacred.' But as I trembled, as though on the brink of some other revelation, she looked past me to the hanging veils of silk. 'It is older than those stories your husband cares so much to hear; and truer. It does not take the pain away, you understand. But she puts herself into the hands of another, and she does not fear. She has no mind of her own. There is only her body, which knows its task, and the other, who keeps her safe.' She sighed, and drew her hand across her face; I noticed then how drawn she was, and how dark the skin under her eyes. 'It is a hard thing to do, to stand inside the' – here she used a word that was not English, something like *histra* or *mistra* – 'and not forget all that makes us human. You must hold your mind steady so that the other may put hers to one side.' She gave me a wry smile. 'It is hard to explain, even in our own tongue.'

'You mean a sort of . . . mesmerism?' Of course she did not know the word, and I cast about for a better phrase. 'I have heard of animal magnetism – James had an enthusiasm for it – he said there were men who might make an experimental subject obey without question.'

Hira narrowed her eyes. 'The obedience is to nature,' she said. 'We speak the commands of the body, that is all. What must be done for a child to be born. The time to wait, the time to push, the time to breathe. More would be – an abomination.'

'I think I understand,' I said, afraid that I had insulted her; but she nodded without rancour. I think she is as immune to vanity as anyone I have ever met. 'And is it – safe?'

'No,' she said, with a wondering look. 'Birth is not safe. It is painful, and dangerous, and many women die. That is how things are. But it is better not to be afraid. That is what is sacred: not the birth, for that is sacred everywhere.'

'The silk,' I said, 'is it the silk that works such a miracle?' But I knew already that it must be. Some trick of the vibrations in the aether – the attraction or repulsion . . . Here it was not woven in the same way as the shroud: it was thinner, more like lace, and it had let voices pass through. And its purpose . . . How James would startle and drag his hands through his hair, how his eyes would widen and his mouth water at such a discovery! How he would grin, how he would harass his acquaintances at the Royal Society, how he would petition them for money to buy spiders and pregnant women, to test his hypotheses! I thrust away the thought of him, to stare once more at the silken tabernacle. 'It is a different stuff from the grave-cloth,' I said. 'It is nearly transparent, and the weave shines like moiré. It must be some effect of the space between the threads — the irregularity, perhaps — or is it the shape of the tent, that spiral?' It came to me that I had heard James speak of the eternal line and the *spira mirabilis,* and was racking my brains as to how I might express those ideas to Hira: then, hard upon that impulse, I discerned in a flash that I was just like the men I despised, the scholars who would pluck every iridescent *how* and *wherefore* from a beetle and leave it flightless in the dirt. Why should it matter to me? It was as it was, that was all; that was enough.

Sacred. I know James would be angry with me for that word, but it was true, for all that. I was in the presence of God — of Hira's gods. I could feel them in the silence within the tent. They were not, in spite of what James might say, the gods of Homer and Ovid. The gods of the old myths are childish, violent, all too human. Here, on this island, they have clung to something deeper: mysterious, alien and kind. Kinder even than— I was about to write, *my* God. But He is not my God any more; let James keep Him, if he wills. If I have a God, She is the one who can stand as steady as a tree, holding another's pain so that a child may be born.

I put my hands on my flat belly, and told myself that I was glad not to have to dread the pangs of childbirth; but I could not hold back my tears any more, and I moved my hands to my face and wandered blindly into the edge of the forest, until I found a private place to drop to my knees and weep.

After a long time Hira came. She did not attempt to comfort

me. She sat beside me, her hands loose and crossed in her lap, her eyes on the fragments of sky that shone through the trees, and waited. When I was a child, and ran away to cry, I always hoped that someone would come searching for me. How odd it is, that the first time my wish was granted should be in the vivid heat of a Mediterranean island, and the searcher an impassive peasant woman who still bore the smear of another woman's blood.

'Come,' she said, eventually. 'You have given this enough. Now . . .' She gestured as though she took something from me and buried it in the earth.

'I cannot—'

'Yes, you can.'

'I will never have another child.'

She shook her head, watching me, half smiling. Then she reached out and brushed a tear from my cheek with her fingertip. Although her hands were clean I thought I caught the scent of something earthy, like flowers trodden into soil. 'You will never drown in too much love,' she said. 'It is like water, it finds somewhere to go.'

I bowed my head, shocked by the hunger that sung through me, afraid that somehow I would betray myself. But she did not move, and after a minute I said, 'Why did you tell me to come? I am not one of you. Before, when I asked if I might see the sacred place, you laughed.'

She shifted a little, and the dry leaves beneath her rustled. She reached out and took my hand. She tilted it back and forth, and I saw how there was still the ghost of a ring on my finger. 'You are not a maggot any longer,' she said.

I did not comprehend what she meant. At first I thought it was mockery. But when I met her eyes, her expression was — oh! I do not know how to describe it. It was as she might have looked at one of the women in the old myths: as though

Bridget Collins

I had been transformed into a tree, a bird, a constellation of blazing stars ... If I had seen it anywhere else I might have thought it was admiration, and pity, and a kind of pride. But I did not think, after what I had seen that morning, that she had any reason to look at me so; not when she was the one who had welcomed a new life into her cupped palms. She had caught the future, borne on a rush of blood. *She* was the marvel, not I. And yet ...

She smiled, straight into my eyes. For a moment it was as though I was touching not the woman she was, but the abandoned little girl she had been; and I thought that, after all, I could love her and lead her home, I could heal the wounds she had suffered. My heart jolted with a kind of joy I had thought I should never feel again. But the moment was brief: brief as a heartbeat or a gasp. Then I saw plainly that she was herself, perfectly here and now, just as I was myself and not the child who had cried and longed to be coddled. And we were women, not rivers or flowers or pillars of stone – no, we were flesh and skin, bodies, human bodies, female bodies, and I could hardly bear it. I thought that if I moved I should spill out and never gather myself again.

She stood up, her hand still tight on mine. 'Come.'

'Where? It is finished, isn't it? Misia's baby—'

'No, it is not finished. Come with me.' She led me back into the clearing. I did not know what she had seen in my eyes; I did not know what had been there to see.

Misia was asleep, her froglet baby beside her, its fists curled under its chin, and an old woman sat at her side, knitting upon needles so fine they were hardly discernible. It was later than I had realised. The sun had passed overhead, and the other women were on their feet, clearing away cups and bowls.

Hira took me to the nearest bucket and wiped my face with

a dampened corner of her own *himation*. She put her hands on my cheeks and turned my face to the light, until she was sure it was clean. Then she said, 'Go,' and pointed.

She was indicating the tent that stood behind the coiled-shell tabernacle: the greater roof, like the upturned hull of a ship. It glimmered blue, reflecting the sky like the stillest water. It had thicker veils — or perhaps it stood at a different angle to the light — for it was only as translucent as opal or milk-crystal, and the figures within were faceless shadows. It sent a shiver over me, of fear, or anticipation. 'Go,' she repeated, and pushed me. 'You have been here, with us. You have every right.'

'And what shall I do there?'

'Whatever you will.'

'Not without you,' I said.

She took my other hand. I felt as naked as I had on my wedding night; more naked, since there was that band of bare skin around my finger, skin that had not been touched since before I was married. I thought there was a nerve there that led right to my heart. 'Do not be foolish,' she said. 'Go.'

'Hira,' I said, my voice unsteady, 'not without you.'

She looked at me with the lovely bronze-mask stillness that I had noticed the first time I ever saw her, in the light of the setting sun. Then she leant towards me, and pressed her mouth against mine.

I staggered. I felt as though I would never breathe again, and I did not mind.

She smiled; and it was the smile of a love that did not care for limits, a love as strong and sure as a rope.

'I must wash,' she said. 'I will join you. Trust me. Go.'

The pavilion was not, as I had thought, a single chamber: rather, it was a maze, a labyrinth of silk and stone, so echoing and shimmering that I lost my way before I had taken a step. There were wider spaces, curves and cells that led on one from another. Here and there a few women sat on the floor and smiled or offered me water as I passed. I suppose they knew the intricate leadings, the criss-crossing passages, as blood knows the secret spaces of the body. There were voices, singing. Melodies rose like flotsam and subsided again into silence. Strange harmonies ebbed and flowed like the swell of the sea in deep caves, or the prayer-calls of the towers of Atlantis, carried to the shallows ... A lullaby for Misia's child, I thought; or a hymn of thanksgiving to the gods that had watched over her. I closed my eyes and wandered blind, listening, trailing my hand along the silken walls. I was not afraid of being lost, since I knew Hira would find me.

It is not quite clear in my memory; it is obscured by the glimmering mirages, the shadows and reflections that wavered everywhere I looked. Yes, she found me – Hira found me – and I had no need to think, or speak. It was a ritual that my body knew, although I did not. I do remember her mouth, her hands, her eyes; and I remember how she murmured my name, and how hers stuck in my throat. I remember, too, the last thought that came to me, before the waves of silver met over my head. I had imagined that I was the one who might lead Hira home: but as we trembled together, exchanging breaths, I knew that we had found our home days ago, weeks ago, the evening I climbed the path and saw her there in the sunset.

Then, as the tide of voices rose, the drums began. I do not think I was asleep – perhaps I was more awake than I have ever been in my life – but I do not remember how they started, only that they surrounded us like thunder and their rhythm transformed the world. The space around me trembled, liquid and heavy. Hira's mouth tasted of the sea. I felt as hollow and light as fish-bones. As the drums went on, the space inside me grew; I thought I might unravel like a skein of ink in water. Whirling currents of silver flowed through the most intimate places of my body. They connected me to the sky, the forest, the silk and the spiders that spun it . . . To Hira, to Misia and her baby, and further too, further out past our house, and James, and the sea, all the way to England, to my sister and my mother, past death itself – until everything, every edge was blurred, every distance shrank to nothing, and my heart was a vessel that held the whole world, and the next. I was infinitely capacious; I overflowed. I had room within me for another child, for many more children, my grandchildren and their children, as though I could feel the seeds of ten generations clustered in my pelvis like pearl beads.

We danced, I think. We danced and sang, and we rode through eternity on the back of a single night. After Hira I think I remember others' hands on me, a tremendous force, the taste of salt and blood; and gentleness, too, and the deaf and blinding dazzle of exaltation.

I know that if I tried to describe it to him James would stare, appalled, and call it a bacchanalia. Perhaps he is right. It was something divine, at least, something that possessed us and left us both victor and vanquished; something that I would call ecstasy.

Three days later

Was it a drug? I can almost believe it, except that I did not eat or drink anything that was offered to me. If there were such a thing as a love philtre – and, if there were, if it were not a draught but a woven thing, a device made of threads and seams – a web, indeed – then I would swear that what I feel now must be the effect of it. The compulsion, the desire, the heat in my veins, the hook in my heart – for I never, not even with James, I never dreamed that it might be like this, that my whole being should yearn and yearn for another until I cannot remember my own name! If I were a scholar I should scoff at the paltry effects of the spider silk on the human ear and instead anatomise my own tremblings, my own tears, my own urge to put my hand into the lamp-flame merely to distract myself. I cannot even compose this without pausing to pace back and forth, and now that I sit down again I can think of no more words but oh, oh, oh!

I have not seen her. I have not had time to see her, for James has occupied my every waking moment. It is unbearable, but for once he is not deliberately cruel; in fact he is trying to please me. As I walked back through the forest I thought I heard a footstep, and dreaded lest he had followed me – but he is not the kind of man who would meet betrayal with kindness, or make shift to woo me back to him if he thought me in the wrong. And he has been kind, oh, so kind . . . When I arrived home I washed as quickly as I could, and tidied myself with shaking hands, ready to pretend I had only been walking in the woods – and indeed I did not know exactly how long I had been gone – but he did not catechise me, not at all. He took my hands, and before I could comprehend I felt a ring sliding onto my finger, and he said, 'I found it for you, my love,' and when I looked down there was my old band of gold, a little dusty, and that other, ghostly ring was trapped forever underneath. 'I have been a bad husband,' he said. 'You must forgive me, sweetling, we will begin again.' And then he began to tell me how our meagre belongings should be packed away to protect them from the damps of winter, and I have not been able to sway him from the scheme — although our belongings survived last winter quite easily, and it was hardly worse than a February in Sussex — and he insists that we labour side by side like Adam and Eve. Once Hira came to the edge of our garden, but James called me at that very moment, and caught my wrist when I hesitated. He even collects the food and drink from the village, because he says I have been his servant too long; and I smile and thank him and want to scream. Oh, to touch Hira's hand — to feel, again, that I have come home . . .

Patience, oh, patience! Once James's present fervour has burnt out, there will be time. We will go back to how it was. I will be able to walk with her into the village, to help her with her ministrations, to slip out at dawn to swim beside her, without James throwing a possessive arm across me to keep me near. She is constant; I would know, through my skin, if she stopped loving me. She will be waiting.

And it must be finished soon. He has enlisted the help of a few glowering peasants — for the work, he says, that I am too delicate to carry out — and stays up late into the night planning the systematic removal of our most precious boxes to Theotokos, where there are thicker walls and sturdier roofs. I slave at his side, and go to bed so exhausted that I do not even wish he had resumed an interest in my body—

Ha! As if on cue, he arrived at my elbow, with a question regarding which box I would prefer my books to go in. But when I began to get up, he patted my shoulder and told me I must finish my diary, he would not be one of those husbands who come between their wives and their amusements. To demonstrate his goodwill he brought me a cup of rather pungent tea, and stayed until I had swallowed a few mouthfuls.

Oh, I miss her! I want to write her name over and over.

Some nights I have heard the spiders calling in my dreams; and Misia's baby, crying out, in that first wrenching affront of light and air.

I will go back soon, and when I do, I will speak to the gods there. I will ask them what I must do, and they will tell me.

Fourteen

Henry stood quite still, staring up at the portrait of Sophia Ashmore and her husband. Behind him he sensed Miss Fielding gesturing to Philomel, who huffed and withdrew. There was no other sound until her footsteps had reached the top of the staircase and scuffed reluctantly away into the east wing. Then Miss Fielding shut the library door. He thought that she would sit down, but instead she walked to the bookshelf and ran her hand over the gold-tooled spines. 'Your work is finished, I suppose,' she said.

He did not answer. She looked over her shoulder and seemed about to speak; then, instead, turned to face him and tilted her head to the side as if she wanted to sketch him. If it was a tactic to make him break the silence, it was successful. He said, 'No. Not finished.'

'But he has had enough of you.'

He pressed his hands together, trying to keep calm. But the seed of anger grew and grew – good God, the look on her face, as though he were some kind of specimen! – until he could hardly breathe. 'No,' he said, his voice trembling a little, 'no, it is not that.'

'Then—'

'He was attacked at the gala – your cousin, your damnable, crazy cousin—'

'I did not know her intent.'

'But you heard what happened?' He did not wait for an answer: of course she had heard. 'She made a scene – she called Sir Edward a murderer, a peddler of despair and madness, in front of everyone – flung pig's blood about like a lunatic! That's what they'll talk about now. Not the silk. Not whether they should invest, or how lovely it is, how glamorous. No! The only subject on their lips will be Mercy, and her accusations. She has ruined everything.'

'I am sorry that all your work was in vain.'

'Oh, you are, are you?' She flinched, and he was pleased. 'Forgive me if I find that hard to believe. On the contrary – you may congratulate yourself, since now you have achieved what you wanted.'

'I do not see what I have done wrong. I gave her back her letters, as you told me. It is not my fault that she was desperate, when her last hope was gone. As for the gala, I do not know how she got hold of an invitation. I did not receive one myself.'

He ground his heel into the rug as if, with enough effort, he could crush the rose woven into the pattern.

She went on, in a low, steady voice, 'You are unjust. I care only for Philomel. She is all, she is everything to me. As for Sir Edward . . . I do not see why he would blame you. I promise you, if you have done something to offend him, it is not that. He has grown tired, or vindictive, or bored – or you have somehow outlived your usefulness.'

Henry flinched; and in spite of himself, he plucked at his shirt front as though he could still feel the bloody handprint there. If it was not Miss Fielding's fault, then it was his own: his useless, idiotic stillness when any normal man would

have taken hold of Mercy and yelled for a policeman . . .
You fucking fool. He burst out, 'He has given me my marching
orders, and that is what you have always wanted, isn't it?
I shall go back to London, and you can keep Sir Edward
and Philomel all to yourself. There'll be no foolish stranger
to pity you. You must be delighted.'

'Pity me?' For an instant he saw something leap in her
eyes, a flash of emotion too swift to be identified – even,
he thought, even if he had cared . . . Then she gave him a
long look. 'You are right,' she said, 'I will be delighted not
to be the recipient of a stranger's pity.'

'I should never have let myself believe that we were
friends,' Henry said, 'I should never have trusted you. Since
the day I arrived you have been doing your best to get rid
of me.'

'You seem to imagine that I have a great deal more power
than I do.'

'Don't deny it,' he said, enraged suddenly by her steadfast
gaze. 'You have always resented me – you were afraid I
should make Philomel hear, and then you would not be
needed any more.'

'That is entirely—'

'You tried to persuade me to leave almost the first day
you met me – then, when that did not work, you tried to
shame me, you tried to drive a wedge between Sir Edward
and me. You gave me that abominable diary, which you
had no right to touch – as though a dead woman's scrib-
blings were anything to do with me, or the factory!' He
could not bear to look at Miss Fielding any longer. But as
he swung round he caught sight of the picture in the alcove,
and flinched: as though Sophia Ashmore were in the room,
listening. Her eyes were wide with reproach. Certainly she
had been impulsive, intemperate, injudicious – but what

had she done, really, to deserve such misery? To be exiled from the one place where she had found love . . . He knew, now, what that was like. For the first time he noticed how her hand lay across the top of her abdomen, the fingers spread in a gesture that was both protective and afraid: as though, he thought, it was the last precious thing left to her. He did not want to feel sorry for her – it was utterly unwelcome – and yet with sudden clarity he remembered putting his own hand against Madeleine's belly, and the extraordinary thump and slide of small alien limbs against his palm. He had jerked away, as if he had been stung. If he had known that he would never even hold his daughter, he would have held on; he would have clung to Madeleine's flesh and its longed-for burden as Sophia Ashmore clung to hers.

But she had no right to stare at him like that, in such despair – not when she had her husband, and the baby . . . He held up his hand, stupidly, to block her painted gaze. 'It is not the same,' he said aloud. 'She was not alone.'

'What?' Miss Fielding said.

He grimaced. 'Nothing.' He could not remember what he had been saying, before.

'Philomel? She is perfectly—'

'No! Sophia Ashmore. She should have known better than to betray her husband, to let herself be seduced by the peasants and their silk – and she should have been thankful to come home; she had her child, at least.' He stopped. In the corner of his eye Miss Fielding had made some sharp, half-quelled movement. 'What?'

'There was no child.'

He turned to stare at her. 'You must not say so,' he said. 'How dare you say so? Even if it died – I suppose what you mean is that they both died – but a dead child is still a child.'

286

'No. She died, certainly. But she died of a cancer. There was no child.'

He stammered, 'But in her diary – and look at her, for God's sake—'

'She was mistaken. If you do not believe me, ask anyone in the village. The thing she thought was a baby grew and grew, long past the span of a pregnancy, until it killed her.'

He swallowed. There was no reason not to believe it. And it was no worse than Madeleine's death: to die from a child, or die from a disease, what difference did it make? How absurd to be affected by the absence of a child – someone else's child – a child who had never existed. *I put one hand on my belly and willed the child to quicken, but she is obstinate, she waits for something, some voice that she has not yet heard.* That child had never quickened.

'I suppose it was better,' Henry said, hoarsely, 'or there would have been arguments over the spiders. If there had been someone else to inherit, not only Sir Edward . . .'

Miss Fielding drew in her breath, as if to say something; but the moment passed. And the silence that followed brought Henry back to himself, as if speaking Sir Edward's name had broken a spell: what did he care, really, for a woman he had never met, and her barrenness? All he cared about was Sir Edward, who had offered him a new life, whom he loved . . .

He said, 'I must talk to him before I go. He—'

'Don't.' She said it without hesitation, with entire authority. She might as well, he thought, have had her governess's pointer in her hand. 'Just leave, Mr Latimer. Trust me. Shake the dust off your feet and be grateful—'

'Grateful that he has sent me away? No. You don't understand, there is still work to be done – more work than ever.' He could not stand the expression on her face; he did not

287

want her sympathy. 'At the very least I must explain to him. I must know that he forgives me.'

'Forgives *you*? I thought you said you had done nothing?'

'If he blamed me I could not bear it.' He was in danger of betraying himself, but he could not hold back. 'I owe him everything. I have never met anyone like him. He is . . .' He wanted to say *wonderful, extraordinary, breathtaking*. 'He is a kind man, a decent man, he would never do anything mean or cowardly. There must have been a misunderstanding – he must have a good reason to send me away.'

He was expecting her to interrupt, but she waited – ostentatiously, he thought – for him to finish before she sighed and leant back against the bookshelves. She said, at last, 'You don't know him very well, do you?'

'Ha! Better than you,' he said, and bit his tongue. One indiscretion now would ruin everything – wreck it all beyond repair – but if only she knew, if only he could throw it in her face that Sir Edward had kissed him . . . 'He talks to me as an equal; you are only a governess.'

'I have lived in this house for years. *You* are only a visitor, Mr Latimer.'

'You are a woman,' he went on, 'a *servant*—'

'As are you! You surely do not imagine yourself something more?'

He stared at her, and to his fury he found that he could not answer.

'He is not a decent man,' she said, and although her voice was low, it was hard. 'He will use you or play with you, for as long as you are useful or amusing. You are not the first, you know. The artist who— But never mind that. You are labouring under a misapprehension if you think he deserves any loyalty. Nor does he care for your friendship, or your finer feelings, or anything except himself.'

Henry stumbled to the door. 'I will not listen to this. I do not wish to know why you are so intent on pouring this poison—'

'I stay for Philomel,' she said, and in spite of himself he paused. She was very upright, her cheeks very red. It was hard not to believe in her sincerity. 'If it weren't for her . . . I wish he had never chosen me. Mercy should never have attacked him, but I understand why she did. He is despicable. He *does* have blood on his hands. And worse.'

'Oh, come now! Every factory has accidents—'

'Not like this. The children – my God, the *children*, Mr Latimer . . .' She turned her face sharply away from him.

'We have been over this before,' he said. She was wrong – she was sentimental – she did not understand . . . He added, in a voice he did not recognise as his own, 'And there is no need to blaspheme.'

'Children deafened by machinery – worse, their minds ground away by the endless noise – *that* is the blasphemy! But of course it has nothing to do with him. His hands are as clean as the driven snow. Whose fault *is* it, then?'

'It is a regrettable reality of industry.' *And by God*, Sir Edward murmured in his memory, *I wish it were not so.* But now the words rang hollow.

'*Children*,' she repeated, 'they are children! Have you no heart? Do you absolve every criminal, every murderer so easily? Or is it merely that you are in thrall—'

'How dare you?' he cried, the last thread of endurance snapping. 'How dare you call him a criminal, when he has done nothing but good for Telverton, for you, for Philomel? You are under his very roof. Have you no propriety at all?'

He had taken a step or two towards her; he had not meant to raise his hand – had certainly had no intention of striking her – but she gave a tiny involuntary shudder, as though bracing herself to withstand a blow. It shocked him as much as it did her. They froze, staring at each other.

'Do you know,' Miss Fielding said after a moment, her voice trembling, 'why Philomel is deaf?'

'What?' He took a long breath, forcing his arms to his sides. His confusion took the edge off his anger. 'No. I imagined some illness in infancy.'

'She was born that way – although of course they could not be entirely sure until she was a little older.' She paused, as though inviting a question. He did not speak. 'It happened when she was in her mother's womb. But it was not an illness, Mr Latimer.'

'Then—'

'I suppose you know what happened to Lady Ashmore-Percy. A version of it, anyway.'

'Yes, indeed,' he said, 'Sir Edward told me himself. It was a tragedy. Will you stoop to use his wife's death against him?'

She held his gaze; and although he did his best, he was the first to look away. At last she said, 'It might have been better if you had asked someone else. Then at least you would know that she is alive.'

Alive.

He heard again Sir Edward's voice: *I know what it is to lose a wife.*

'She lives at Ronford House, near Exeter,' Miss Fielding continued. 'A madhouse. A pleasant, light, airy one, I gather, newly built – with a billiard table for the gentlemen patients, although that would hardly make a difference to her. She has been there for years.'

'Does Philomel . . . ?' It was not what he had meant to say.

'Philomel is too young to comprehend.'

There was a pause. He knew what she was waiting for him to ask. With a sense of defeat, he said, 'Very well, then. What has it to do with Philomel's deafness?'

Miss Fielding walked to the window and looked out at the park. 'When this house was built, the architect argued with Sir Edward,' she said. 'About money, at first. He had grand ideas, and kept having new ones. He demanded more and more, and Sir Edward resented it, which was not unreasonable, I suppose. They began to dislike each other. And at the same time . . . Cecilia Ashmore-Percy was a very beautiful woman.' She gave him a quick sideways glance, expressionless. 'I only saw her once, myself, when she gave out prizes at the school in Telverton. She sang to us – she was an accomplished musician – and I still remember how lovely she was, and her voice . . . She had spirit, and brains, and talent. Perhaps it was inevitable that men would think she was untrustworthy.'

'You mean . . . ?'

'By the time the house was finished she was expecting a child. There were rumours that Sir Edward did not believe it was his. And then . . .' She chewed her lip. 'She was locked into the weaving shed, at night. There was— They called it an accident. But somehow the machines were set running. The noise—'

'I've heard it.'

'Then you can imagine. Except . . .' She shook her head. 'To be locked in the dark, for hours, alone, with that . . .'

He tensed his shoulders, trying not to shudder. He had been overwhelmed after a few minutes. She would have panicked; she would have beat at the door, begging to be let out, unable to hear her own voice. *For hours.*

'When they found her, the next morning, she was stupefied. They brought her home and waited for her to wake up. When she did, she had lost her hearing.'

291

'Yes. And that sent her mad. Sir Edward told me that. What does it matter how it happened? What you've told me is hardly—'

'She went mad because she was kept imprisoned, and after Phil was born they would not let her see her, and she was entirely friendless. Because they drugged her and beat her when she did not obey. *Not* because she was deaf, although that must have been terrible; because she was speechless, and abused, and alone, and her baby had been taken away. And—' She hesitated. 'And because the silk ate away at her mind, I think. Living like that, with it on every side . . . In the end she could not tell what was real and what was not.'

He tried not to think of restraints tied to a bed, or smashed laudanum bottles, or a woman shrieking for her child. He said, 'The weaving house – it must have been an accident. What else could it have been?'

'It was lucky for Philomel that she so favours Sir Edward. At first he would not even look at her. But she has nothing of her mother in her face at all, and when he saw how like him she was – when he knew she was his daughter – he could not do enough for her. Perhaps he feels guilty.'

'Is it your suggestion that—?'

'I am suggesting nothing,' she said. But she added, after a moment, 'Only that someone must have set the engine going, to power the looms.'

'But this . . . If it is true, why did you not tell me before?' But in a flash he knew. It was only now that she could speak the truth – now that Sir Edward had dismissed him, and he did not matter . . . Hardly knowing what he said, he cried, 'You are blackening the reputation of my friend, an admirable businessman and a devoted father. I take it you have no evidence at all to support your insinuations?'

She said nothing. He went on, hoping to see her concede a point – any point! – 'If you have only seen Lady Ashmore-Percy once, how can you know that Philomel does not take after her?'

'She sat for one of the paintings in the Great Hall. The architect was an artist too, and he painted them before . . . You must have seen it.'

'You mean Echo,' Henry said. 'Then she *was* beautiful.'

'No. Arachne.'

He had never looked closely at *Arachne and Athena*, the last panel, in the shadow of the staircase; he had always lingered in front of the other two. He could not now recall it.

'It's strange,' Miss Fielding said, 'but when I think of her it isn't Arachne who comes first to my mind. It's Marsyas. The musician flayed alive at the whim of a god.'

There was a silence. Henry turned and left the room without another word.

The study door, glimpsed along the far passage, was still closed. Henry felt sick. But there was nothing but rumour to suggest— No, he would not dignify it with a moment's consideration. It was true that Sir Edward had lied about his wife – or was it? Henry could not be quite sure whether Sir Edward had only jumped to the wrong conclusion. But either way, he knew better than anyone that grief could make you swerve aside from the truth. If anything, Henry thought, it was proof that he mourned as sincerely for his wife's madness as he would have for her death, and that was surely to his credit. As for the accident – of course it had been an accident, only malicious gossip would suggest otherwise . . .

Slowly he crossed the Great Hall to the pictures. Sir Edward had wanted to hang him there, with the others. *Among veils of silk and wreaths of roses, half asleep, your hair tousled . . .*

Perhaps, still, one day . . . The god of silence, the youthful son of Aphrodite: with his face, his body, immortalised forever for Sir Edward to look at.

But another impulse drew him onwards, past the silver-aqueous blue and green of *Echo and Narcissus*, and then the ochre and scarlet of *Theseus and Ariadne*. Beyond it, in shadow, was the last panel. While Echo was picked out in moonlight, and Ariadne blushed in the dying light of the sunset, the two figures of Athene and Arachne were flattened by the stark glare of noon. Under a pitiless sun, they faced each other: and yes, Arachne was beautiful. He had imagined Cecilia soft-faced and feminine, but her likeness was tall, with long eyes and sharp cheekbones, a face that blazed defiance and a consciousness of her own worth. Athene, graceful and fair-haired, was almost overshadowed – or would have been, were it not for her expression. There was a mixture of bruised pride and complacent dominion in the goddess's grey eyes; and her hand, at her side, was poised to bring down the transformation. In a split second she would trap the mortal woman in a shrivelled eight-legged body and a web of her own making. He drew back. It was not a pleasant painting. And yet when he looked back at *Echo and Narcissus*, that appeared weak in comparison. The moonlight had lost its spell; the faces were conventional. Narcissus was contemptible, Echo merely pretty. And Theseus was over-muscled and thuggish, while Ariadne was gullible, deceived. It was only a reaction to a morning of shocks and distress; and yet he could not shift the sensation that the others were wishful fictions, while this one told the truth.

He did not wish to look any more. But the banks of colour – blue-green-silver, crimson-gold-earth, bleached-pale-and-purple – reminded him of something. He frowned, scrabbling for the recollection. When it came, it made him flinch as though he had been jabbed with a needle. The positions, the size, the precise shades and disposition of the pigments . . . They were the same as the panels of splashed paint he had seen in the deserted rooms in the east wing: the rooms that Miss Fielding had shown him, in which Cecilia Ashmore-Percy had been shut up – where she had given birth, and spat blood, and finally gone mad . . . And where, by the kindness of her captors, she had apparently been allowed to make her own versions of those myths, without faces or figures or names.

When he left Cathermute House the sky had grown darker, the morning's haze solidifying into lowering storm-clouds. Perhaps he could have asked for the carriage to take him into Telverton, but he could not bear to wait. He hurried down the road, breaking into a sweat in spite of the growing chill in the air. Sir Edward would be at the factory – or at least someone there would know where he was . . . As he descended into the town, the pressure built in his ears; his heart stuttered, *a test, a test, a test.*

When he came to the factory a few murmuring men turned to stare at him, their expressions unreadable, but no one accosted him. Riley's office was dark and locked. Very well, then, he would try the laboratory; surely sooner or later he would run across someone who knew where Sir Edward could be found. At the very least, he would ask them to convey a message. He ducked into the little alley between the spider house and the canal.

The door of the laboratory opened. A grey-headed man came out, removing his spectacles as he stepped into the yard, sweeping his other hand across his eyes. For a second Henry thought he might be vomiting, but there was no sound, and when at last he turned round there was no gleam of moisture around his mouth.

The laboratory door opened again: this time it was Worsley who came out, flicking soapy water off his hands. 'Compose yourself, Gower, don't be grotesque—' He stopped. He said to Henry, 'What are you doing here?'

'Is Sir Edward in there?'

'No, of course not. What do you want?'

'Where is he?'

'How should I know? I am not his secretary.'

'I need to see him.'

'Do you?' Worsley raised his eyebrows. 'And do you imagine he will want to see you?'

'Well then – would you give him a message? Ask him – tell him I will be staying at the Angel,' Henry stammered, cursing himself. He should have turned on his heel and left as soon as he saw Worsley. He looked at the other man – Gower – and said, 'Please, if you know where he is . . . There has been a misunderstanding.'

'No misunderstanding,' Worsley said, stepping forward. 'He has had enough of you, that is all.'

'I had nothing to do with Mercy— with the woman who attacked him at the ball. Nothing at all. If he thinks—'

'Oh, Lord, that? Hardly. It was embarrassing, certainly, that you let her slip through your grasp like that. I can't say that he was pleased. But that is nothing, really. We'll find her.' He added, to the other man, 'If you've finished puking—'

'Wait,' Henry said. 'Then – tell me, what have I done? I have worked so hard, I have given him everything.'

Worsley gave a bark of laughter. 'Your *work*?' he said. 'Flattery and extravagance. Carneying the investors and spending Sir Edward's brass. He might as well have hired a whore.'

The blood rushed to Henry's face, stinging, as though he

had been slapped. 'You are jealous,' he said. 'You know that it is I, not you, who has brought arain silk into the regard of the public, and that Sir Edward's success will be due to me and my efforts.'

'Stuff and nonsense! If it weren't for our experiments, he would be facing bankruptcy – yes,' he added, with a mocking emphasis, 'due to *you and your efforts*. Your wheedling, foolish, self-important little efforts, which have utterly drained his purse. No need to pride yourself on those, my friend. I've been telling him all along that you'd pour out his lifeblood if it suited you, and last night he admitted I was right. And do you know who will save his fortune? Me. My discoveries. So run along now, and be grateful he doesn't bill you for all the money you've pissed into the gutter.'

He could not think; Worsley's accusations were unjust – they were, they must be! – and yet he could not put forward a counter-case, or even a question.

The other man, Gower, was dabbing his forehead with a trembling hand. Henry saw his eyes slide to the laboratory, as a chastised child would look at a whip, and something leapt in the depths of his mind, making a connection he could not name. He said, slowly, 'Your discoveries?'

'Yes. Weren't you listening last night?' Worsley grinned.

Sir Edward had said, *In my laboratory, we are hatching miracles* . . . But what else? Some talk of an instrument, Henry thought, a panacea, a solution to every human misery. Nothing that might make Gower look as he did . . .

Puppies . . . *They come out funny. If they come out at all.*

'Ah,' Worsley said, rocking back on his heels with cheerful malice, 'but I have been unfair to you, haven't I? You *have* helped him. Some of his success *will* be due to you and your efforts. Not directly, I'm afraid – but without you, I would never have got so far. Well, no hard feelings – why don't you come in and see what we've been working on?'

'I don't know what you mean.'

'That journal you dug up. It was invaluable. So you *did* do something to earn your keep.'

He shook his head, but when Worsley took hold of him and steered him towards the laboratory he did not resist. The factory noise was grinding into his bones. *Without you . . .* He stumbled past Gower and through the open door.

The laboratory was a neat, clean room, full of greyish light from the veiled windows; there was a bare, scrubbed workbench, chairs, presses against the walls, a blackboard. The door at the far end was closed. Worsley leant against the wall, his hands in his pockets, watching him; Gower hovered in the doorway, and after a moment he muttered, 'Mr Worsley . . .'

'I see no great advances,' Henry said.

Worsley smiled. 'Would you like to see the inner sanctum?' He did not wait for Henry to answer before he opened the far door and beckoned. A kind of bitterness drifted into the air, like an acrid hint of smoke. Henry felt a jolt of curiosity and repugnance. He followed Worsley to the doorway, and looked in.

Here, too, the windows were covered with silk, and the light that filtered through was soft and blanched. Above him, hanging down to the height of his head, was an insubstantial glinting spiral of silk. It reminded him of a monstrous seashell, worn to translucency by the waves. He stared up at it.

'Aha,' Worsley said. 'My lovely little invention. Worsley's daughter, I call it, although Gower calls it a ghost cage. What a marvel it is! What it creates is not the silence of the ears: it is deeper than that. It is the silence of the soul. And without you stumbling on that diary, we might never have realised.'

He had not stumbled upon it. He had been given it, so that he might learn what damage the silk could do. And then he had passed it straight into Sir Edward's hands, so that he might be reassured, and absolved.

'Do you remember the birthing tent? This is something like that. She was quite clever, in some ways, she noticed the shape and the golden ratio – although we had to work out the weave for ourselves, by trial and error.'

'Would you like to experience it? Step onto the mark.' Worsley reached for a rope and the bell dropped. Automatically Henry ducked forward to avoid being hit by the rim; he found himself standing on a scuffed chalk cross. Around it there were scratches on the flagstones, and a mess of mottled dark stains. One was like a handprint, half the size of his own. For an instant he began to wonder what that meant. Then the rim met the ground, and he was standing in a sort of curved inner cone, made of rings of . . . some kind of wire, he thought. Pearly fabric was strung across it, making odd chambers; he could have put his fingers into them. But he could not move his arms. He could not move anything except his gaze. His tongue felt like a gag.

He was not . . . he could not . . . He was conscious, somehow, of a greyness in his brain, of a feeling of heaviness, as though he were made of clay; and his thoughts, which should have leapt and darted, could only flounder opaquely. Not that he could have described it to himself: there was no place for words to form. Even the smallest impulse to name what he felt was quenched, swallowed, dragged under. Not clay, quicksand. He ached. He knew that. And yet it was not part of him, it was simply how the world was. Had it always been like this? He could not struggle, he could only endure. He heard Worsley say, 'Stand on one leg,' and the command was like a helping hand, lifting a fraction of the burden: the weight of being himself was a little alleviated as he raised one sole from the flagstones and stood obediently, trying to keep his balance. After a while he became aware that his ankle hurt, and his clenched toes, too, but he accepted it as necessary.

'Take off your jacket.'

It was difficult, since he was still standing on one leg, but it was important to do his best. It was not that he wanted to please Worsley; merely that Worsley's orders seemed exactly that, the only order in a chaos of mud. They were not friendly; they did not speak of human connection; but they were a rope that might keep him from being sucked under. When he had taken off his jacket (which dropped from his fingers as though they were incapable of grasping, now that they had completed this particular task) he waited for more. He did not hope, or desire, more instructions. But they were the only part of this new landscape that made sense. Worsley said, 'And your necktie, please.'

'Mr Worsley, I don't think—'

'Shut up, Gower. Latimer, make a noose. That's right.'

He looked down. He did not think he knew how. He could not remember. But his hands knew. They moved, twisting the fabric through itself, forming a slip-knot. He did not wonder what it was for.

'Good. Tie it to the top ring. Tightly. Don't worry, it's sturdier than it looks. Yes, that'll do. Now, put the loop around your neck. Under your chin.'

He obeyed. The touch of the necktie against his skin reminded him of something, or rather made some flicker, some trapped bubble tremble under the layer of deadening bog. He let his arms drop to his sides. His hands felt like gloves full of mud.

'Now,' Worsley said, 'I am proposing to pull this handle, which will raise the hoop above your head. I take it you have no objections. You may answer me.'

'I cannot think of any.'

'No. Although it may be uncomfortable. Your death.'

Henry understood, of course. He understood that if Worsley raised the hoop, he would find himself strangled on the end of his own necktie. And he did not disbelieve Worsley, when he said he would do it. But any fear he might have felt was buried too deep – was, somehow, over-sludged too thickly. If any emotion did ripple a perceptible tentacle, just beneath the surface, it was relief. He said, 'I suppose it may.'

'Then . . .' Worsley took in a breath, and jerked on the rope.

There was a shout of, 'Mr Worsley!' There was a tightening – a black cloud boiling, a pressure around his jaw and windpipe, a sickening sway – he was up on his toes, suspended by his throat . . . And then it subsided, and he was on the floor. Someone reached underneath the lowest hoop and cut the tie with a pair of scissors. Then the cage rose, glimmering, and reality flooded in. Henry lay still, his face against the stone floor, as though he had washed up on some strange shore.

Fifteen

He sat at the bench with a glass of water in his hands, tilting it, watching the liquid obey its laws no matter what he did. Gower was clearing his throat over and over, as if he had a blockage he could not quite cough up; Worsley was standing with his hands in his pockets, half turned away, looking out over the canal. Henry sipped the water. It tasted of metal. His larynx hurt when he swallowed.

Worsley said, 'Rather impressive, don't you think?'

'Of course it was only – he was only making a point, you were perfectly safe,' Gower said.

'I'll concede it was a little theatrical, Mr Latimer, but I did so want you to appreciate all the possibilities. To be the object of an experiment gives you a real comprehension, much more than someone else expounding on their findings. Don't you think? Your elaborately furnished house is really only the same thing, isn't it?'

Gower said, 'Are you all right, Mr Latimer? It can take a little while to come back to yourself. Drink your water, that's right.'

'It's very concentrated, the effect, in that apparatus,' Worsley went on. 'It's very good for demonstrations. Less so, for wider applications – you couldn't keep someone under that thing for very long – but we're working on that. And it serves its purpose. It has even come in useful, once or twice—'

'In theory,' Gower said. 'We can see its *theoretical* usefulness.'

'But the principle . . . Oh yes. And we have you to thank for the principle, Mr Latimer. Or rather Sophia Ashmore, and her pagan friends.' He nodded, as though to acknowledge praise, although Henry had not spoken. 'Yes. Good God, man, you've been barking up the wrong tree, with silent this and silent that – cots for infants, for heaven's sake, when we've invented *this*! You know what is worth most, in this world, Latimer? *Submission*. Find a way to sell submission – to make other men into willing slaves – and you will be a wealthy man. Well. *I* shall be a rich man. And so will Sir Edward.'

But submission, Henry thought, was the wrong word. What he had felt was more an erasure of self: a silence that had left him not without a voice, but without anything to say.

'Now, you will probably think – and you'd be right – that unquestioning, indiscriminate obedience is of limited use. Imagine what would have happened, back there, if Gower had started to give you orders too!' He sniggered. 'But imagine this, instead: an army of workers who never argue. Who never strike, who never ask for more, who are content.' Perhaps Henry had moved, because Worsley raised a hand. 'No, really – they will be content. Or as near to it as such people can be. They will work in the factory as they have always done, but when they return home, any little complaints, any inappropriate yearnings, will be smoothed away. No political leanings, no problematic discussions, no *sedition*. No bloody lending libraries, and no evening classes, because once they're indoors, it'll be the factory bell that summons them out again.' He smoothed his hair down at the back of his head, like a preening bird. 'It sounds like a castle in the air, doesn't it? But it will be reality, very soon. Our model housing will show the world what can be done. And so cheaply, considering! Yes, arain silk is expensive, by weight – but only a few strands, cunningly constructed, can do it – a few threads in the walls, set apart by exactly the right amount of space – it's precision that's needed, attention to detail, and then . . . oh, I have been inside a room that has already been finished, and it is astounding. So subtle one can hardly feel it, and yet unmistakable when one knows that it's there.' He paused. Henry thought he would say more, but he only stared into the middle distance for a moment before he continued. 'Sir Edward wondered – knowing, of course, how contrary the workers are in this damned town – whether they might decline, if rumours started to circulate. But the way they live now – how could they? The men might try, but their wives will wear them down. Spacious, light, sturdily built – gas and water laid on, roofs that you can trust, walls that are not running with damp. Even if they knew . . .' He shrugged. 'And in the worst case, there are always the Irish.'

There was a vibration in Henry's bones: a long, low thunder that he could not identify at once. He turned his head, stiffly, and saw the sliding shadows of rain on the silk-blinded windows. It was darker, suddenly. The hut trembled and thrummed as water hammered against the walls and roof.

Gower walked his fingers over the bench, back and forth. He said, staring at them, 'The houses will really be very nice.'

'No more strikes,' Worsley said. 'Everything running as it should. Yes, I think we can congratulate ourselves. Every factory owner in England will want to use the silk, once they see how it transforms our workers. That should be enough to make us millionaires.' He gave a satisfied nod, staring into the middle distance; then a slow smile spread over his face, as if he had seen an old friend. 'But that is only the beginning. Ah, Latimer, it should have been obvious. We should not have needed the journal of an hysteric to make us think of it. The world is divided into predators and prey, do you not agree? It is only a question of deciding who is which . . .' He made a weary gesture, sighed, 'Oh, be still, Gower, I am not talking about Darwinism, only reality!' then he looked back at Henry. 'Imagine,' he said, 'if the order was established, once and for all. In every country, in every town, in every street, in every house. Those who are prey will feel no pain. They will fall easily, softly, into their fate – no suffering, no fight, no tiresome resistance. Servants will serve. Children will obey. Women will lie down and give themselves, and never say a word. Men like you . . .' He paused, deliberately, as if he were teasing out a long thread, seeing how long it would stretch. 'Well, who knows? Perhaps men like you – parasites, I mean – will die out naturally.'

Gower cleared his throat. 'The experiments on . . . on animals,' he said, 'weren't . . . I mean, that was only inci-dental. We weren't trying to hurt them. No one will ever use the silk for that. Not now. What we've invented elimi-nates any need for – that sort of thing. It's much better this way, you see.'

There was another silence. A trickle of rainwater seeped under the door. 'I suppose,' Worsley said at last, with a sort of snort, 'that you are sitting there feeling hard done by. But you mustn't flatter yourself. Blocking out organ-grinders, or helping old biddies to sleep, or preventing a lady's digestion from distracting her companions . . . it is so trivial. A nice money-spinner, but that's all. Who *cares* if the baby wakes? Insane asylums and Quaker meetings and concert halls – women's business!' He shot a malicious smile at Gower. 'When it can do *this* . . . Just you wait. Sir Edward won't just be a millionaire. He'll be the most powerful man in England.'

'And there may be other uses, too,' Gower said. 'If the other things in the diary are true. Surgical chambers. Religious buildings. It will be a – a blessing to mankind.'

'The details are all secret, of course,' Worsley said, 'in spite of the announcement yesterday. You are honour-bound not to mention it. Not that we have competitors – the spiders are ours, and we have no intention of letting anyone else get their hands on them – but we will be announcing our new products in our own way, at our own pace.'

The rain went on hammering on the roof. The scent of water on bone-dry earth blew in on a chilly draught from the window.

Henry heard himself say, 'And Sir Edward knows of all of this? He knew what you were doing, all along?'

'Naturally he did. He employs us, does he not?'

Henry stood up, picked up his hat, and opened the door. A gust of rain hit his face as the noise rushed into his ears. It was falling so heavily the air seemed to be full of glass rods, drilling down, splintering on the standing water. His feet and ankles would be wet the moment he stepped out, and the rest of him would be drenched within a few seconds. But after all it did not matter, it did not seem real, there was still a kind of numbness under his skin. Worsley said, 'We won't see you again, I hope.'

He did not answer. He stepped into the yard, and cold flooded into his shoes and socks, climbing up his trousers so they clung to his calves. The ground had been baked hard

306

by the long weeks of heat: now the water stood on the surface without soaking in, already a hand's breadth deep. He walked, picking up his feet like a wading bird, towards the alley that led back to the main yard. The noise was so thick it was as though he had gone deaf: he could perceive no individual sounds, only a featureless, dizzying roar. But as he stepped into the alley he looked back. Gower was splashing after him, careless of his own wet feet. As he approached, Henry caught a few not-quite-overwhelmed syllables; then Gower was close enough to make himself heard above the storm and the machines. 'You mustn't think,' he said, 'you were in any real danger. You weren't, I promise.'

Henry stared at him. The rain was driving under his hat. When he blinked, water trickled off his eyelashes and down his cheeks, and it took a heartbeat before he could see clearly again.

'Even had he wanted to, I would not have allowed it,' Gower said. 'Please believe me. I would not have let him . . . kill you.'

Henry felt again the necktie under his chin, and saw the black clouds waiting to engulf him. He said nothing.

Gower chewed his lip, squirming a little, his spectacles spattered and the hair on his bare head beaten down by the rain. He said, 'It isn't our fault, you know. It isn't. We are not bad men. It is men like Ashmore-Percy. The ones in control. We cannot stand up to them. No one can.'

Henry turned and trudged through the rising flood, his head lowered, without replying.

He crossed the threshold of the Angel like a survivor of a shipwreck: wet to the skin, and so chilled that he could hardly turn the handle of the door. He went to the bar and asked for brandy, mumbling through cold lips. Water crawled like lice over his scalp and down his face. The publican put a glass in front of him and he drank, hardly tasting it.

'Christ, I need a drink,' someone said behind him, with a grim sort of laugh. 'This damned weather. Haven't seen it this bad for years. Factory side of town it'll be nosebleeds and headaches tonight, and suicides tomorrow.'

'It's not the suicides I'm worried about,' another man said, 'it's the river. This rain, after the spring we've had . . . It'll be coming down off the moors in torrents.'

'Ah, well. I expect it'll stop,' the first voice said. 'Glad I don't live on Leat Street, though.'

'They'll be putting sandbags down in Sharland's Court, I bet.'

Henry set his glass down. 'A room,' he said, and a maid showed him up a narrow staircase and into a dingy bedroom. He did not take off his wet clothes; he got into the bed as he was, and buried his face in the limp pillow, shivering as though his bones would break. He did not want to think, or feel. But he could not keep it at bay forever.

Sir Edward. Sir Edward, whom he loved. Whom he *had* – no, still loved, oh God, yes, still loved. That kiss, how could he forget that kiss, when he had dreamed of it for so long? Nor could he regret it. Or rather, if he had the choice to do it again or turn away – to take back what he had said . . . No, he would not. *I love you.* He would say it again. He would do it all again. He would do anything . . .

No. It was too late.

He did not want to believe that Sir Edward knew of the ghost cage. Surely he could not have known of the obscene experiments, the catatonic puppies, the child's handprint on the floor of the laboratory. No, it was impossible. He was a decent man, full of humanity and generosity – he had said, *take heart*; he had been kind, he was kind . . .

308

But he must have known. Of course he had. Worsley had said as much. And the speech at Sub Rosa . . . *An end to every crime of insubordination.* Was that what he had meant?

Henry pushed his face deeper into the pillow, but it was no good. Miss Fielding had been right. If he had listened to her, instead of letting his own desires deafen him – his desires, and his ambition . . . The silk was an atrocity. He knew that now, and nothing else could ever be the same again: even the memory of Sir Edward's mouth against his. He saw again the silk-covered windows of the east wing, and the little-old-man child who had crawled under the looms. No one would ever help it. No one cared.

He could not lie still, after that. He got to his feet and stumbled to the window, wanting to distract himself. It was later than he had realised, and the light was failing. The rain was still falling in sheets, pattering on the window pane so thickly he could hardly make out the buildings opposite. In spite of his efforts he thought of the women at the mill, sending their children to nurses who fed them syrup of opium to keep them quiet; he thought of Mercy's boy, driven out of his mind by the noise of the machines; he thought of Philomel, deafened in the womb by an accident that had not been an accident.

In the room below, a raised voice cut through the hubbub of the public bar, followed by a mess of scraping chairs and footsteps. He peered through the window to see several men spill out into the street and hurry away down Silver Street, their heads lowered against the pouring rain. Another figure darted off in the other direction. It had fallen oddly quiet in the bar below.

After a moment he rang the bell. When the maid appeared he said, 'What is happening?' and when she looked blank he nodded at the window. 'Where did they go?'

'Oh,' she said. 'Yes. Urgent call for men. They're putting up barriers on Percy Street in case it floods. The silk warehouses.'

'What about the factory?'

'What about it?'

'Is that in any danger? The mill leat—'

'No. You ever seen in there? The leat's got brick walls the height of a man. The water couldn't get that high. Anyway, the Tell never floods as bad as the Exe.'

'All right. Thank you,' he said, and she left, shutting the door after her. What was he going to do? The question had been hanging in the air for as long as he'd been in this room, with the damp and the smell of wet wool; it was only now that he acknowledged it, and he couldn't think of an answer. Well – go home. What else? Back to London. Back to Argyll. Back to the silent house and Madeleine dead and no child—

He was halfway across the room before he decided. Before he knew what he was doing he had stepped out of the door, banged the door behind him and was running down the stairs. He dived through the bar and out into the rain. The cold water stung his face; either it was icy cold, close to sleet, or he was feverish. He hunched his shoulders and battled through it, while the wind blew soaking gusts into his coat and drove drips down his collar.

He had not formulated a plan, but he knew where he was going. He could not rest anywhere else . . . He had not known what he was hoping for, until he'd asked whether the mill leat might flood: and then the leap of his heart, the flash of exhilaration, had told him. For that split second he had felt a savage joy at the prospect of destruction – the same that had crackled like fire when he imagined the bales of silk in the warehouses floating from their shelves and losing their glimmer in polluted water. He

crossed the bridge and turned towards the factory gates –
which were closed, of course. It was dark now, and the
lanterns on their posts were dim and wavering, the glass
streaming. He looked through the wrought-iron bars. He
could not see any other light.

He shut his eyes. He could feel the echoes washing over
him, carried like the pounding of the rain on the wind. It
was like being drunk: the world slid away and resettled,
again and again. How had he ever enjoyed the sensation?
He grabbed for the gate, pulled himself up in a slippery
scramble until he was straddling the topmost curlicue –
appalled at both his lack of agility and his own daring – and
dropped painfully down on the other side, ankle-deep into
a puddle. It had happened so quickly he could not quite
believe he had meant to do it: but here he was.

He paused for a moment, but the same sense of unreality
cushioned him. He was not really here; he was not really
trespassing on Sir Edward's property; he was not really
intending any harm . . . No one could see him. He was
invisible in the wet rushing dark. He splashed a little way
forward into the wide expanse of the yard, and with every
step he grew more certain that no one would challenge him.
The nightwatchmen, the repairmen who worked overnight,
the rat-catcher – or whoever, he thought, conscious of how
little he knew, after all, of the factory's workings, whoever
might ordinarily be here – had all been summoned to protect
the warehouse. He was alone.

Nonetheless some instinct made him keep to the deepest
patches of darkness as he skirted the yard and slid into the
alley that led to the laboratory. His feet were so cold they
had begun to go numb, and the noise echoed as though he
was in a tunnel, coming from every side. He started to
wonder if somehow he had lost his bearings. But just as the

panic threatened to master him, he came out into the smaller yard. He waded forward – the water here was up to his knees – and understood why he had been so disorientated: the quiet flow of the leat had been transformed into a thundering torrent, so loud it caught in his throat and made his ears ache. There was no word for the cacophony, the growling wail, the suck and swirl and crunch. He put his hands up to block it out. With the sound deadened, he knew it was only the flood, carrying debris down from the moors. But abruptly he was afraid that the echoes would overwhelm him, and he struggled through the dragging water to the door of the laboratory.

Of course he would not be able to get in. But even as he cursed himself for his stupid optimism, the handle gave and the door moved a little: hindered from swinging freely by the standing water, but enough to tell him that it had been left unlocked. With a new desperation he pulled at it until he could squeeze through the gap. He staggered over the threshold, tripped and careered wildly across the room. His legs thudded into the workbench. A second later, when the pain had lessened, he saw that he had caught his foot on a sandbag in the doorway. He shut the door and sagged against it, breathing hard.

There was a strange peace in the little room. With the silk over the windows, the sound of the storm was vastly diminished; there was the stillness of a repressed sigh – or of a deathbed, the pause after a breath when another might come, or might not. There was a candle on the bench, lit and flickering. Next to it was a half-packed box of bottles and two others full of tools and books. On the top of the latter pile was Sophia Ashmore's diary. The lowest shelves had been cleared, and a cupboard door was hanging open. But whoever had been here was not here any longer. He

could see through the far door: that room, too, was un-
occupied. He had blundered in here, but he had been lucky.

And now he should take advantage of his good fortune
– if that was what it was . . . He rummaged in the box of
tools until he found a knife and a hammer. There was
something alien about the sight of his hands holding them,
like a drawing in the *Illustrated London News*. He was not the
sort of man who committed criminal damage. He carried
them carefully into the far room, and took a deep breath.

The only light was what spilt through the doorway. He
looked up: the skirt-bell glimmered above him, its edges
melting into the shadows. The ghost cage, Gower had called
it. He hesitated, still staring up: more than anything he
wanted to see Worsley trapped on his knees, gibbering,
begging . . . No. He was not Worsley. He did not want
revenge, he wanted . . .

But he was not sure what he wanted; and he did not
have the time to think about it. He reached for the rope
that was looped around the fastening on the wall and
unlooped it, too hastily, so that it fouled the fastening and
had to be rewound. At last he lowered it to the floor. But
now it seemed so flimsy – so simultaneously anodyne and
risqué, like a woman's petticoats in a closet – that he could
hardly trust his memory. He almost knelt down and tipped
up the lowest hoop, ready to crawl under it again, just to
be sure . . . Then his eye caught the gouges and stains on
the floor, and he recoiled. Did the thing have some seductive
power? Did it call to its victims? Or was it just that he was
light-headed and a bloody fool? Dear Christ, if he had stooped
under – and been held there, deprived of thought, of voli-
tion, until Worsley returned tomorrow morning . . . He
reached for the knife.

It was quick work. The knife was sharp and the threads

were taut: they might be stronger than they looked but still, he thought, they were cobwebs. He cut round the tiers one by one, enjoying the flick of parting silk against the blade. The hoops fell to the floor. In the end he did not need the hammer; his feet and body weight were enough to splinter the light wood into pieces.

Once it was done, it seemed a trivial victory. He nudged the fragments with his foot; he thought, now that the silk was no longer strung in its precise parallels, that he could hear it whisper. Its power to command was destroyed, but it would be easy to make another. He had stamped on a few days' work – weeks', at most – and it was probably not even Worsley who would undertake the task. Any man, given the blueprint and the right tools, could do it. The bell was made of so little: silk and wood and knowledge. Now that it was invented, Henry was powerless to uninvent it. And Worsley had said that he had already been in a room with silk in the walls.

He looked up. Had he heard something? Or seen . . . ? Surely he had seen something pass over the silk across the window – a paler dark, an eddy in the storm. He swung round, leaving the broken cage where it was. If he was caught here . . . He flung himself through the doorway. His mind ran ahead to what Worsley would do – the dawning delight in his eyes as he realised that Henry was at his mercy—

No one was in the laboratory. No one was at the window. But he did not wait. It might have been Worsley, or it might not, and he dared not take the chance. He paused only to catch up Sophia Ashmore's battered blank-book as he passed, tucking it under his shirt, and then threw himself out into the rain as though it were a raging sea. It took his breath away as he plunged through it. He did not take the alley back to the main yard; without thinking he chose the narrower, roundabout path that led along the canal and past the spider house. The noise rose as he came closer to the swollen mill leat. It was like being submerged: sharp sounds broke against his ears, flattened and half swallowed, impossible to decipher. He thought he heard the cry of a child. And then—

Madeleine. It wasn't. No. But he jerked round, unable to stop himself from following the sound of her voice. She had called him by name. Or at least . . . He wiped his sleeve across his face, trying to hold on to reality. It was common to hear human voices in the wind; here, with the storm and the flood, so close to the silk, naturally the phenomenon would be at its height . . . There was no baby drowning in the canal. There was no ghost, no reproach – no *Henry, please, save her, please!* But still he said, 'Yes. I'm here, I'm here,' and turned in a circle, searching. Oh God. She was not real – but he could not walk on as if he had not heard, he could not leave—

He saw her.

She was slipping into the spider house. She was hardly more than a ripple in the downpour, a space where rain was not falling.

He followed her. He thought he was calling, 'Madeleine, Madeleine,' although he could not hear his own voice. If there had been a child struggling in the waters of the canal, it had been sucked under, it was beyond help by now. He staggered through the door of the spider house, and the diary slipped to the floor as he reached out for her.

The door swung shut behind him, muffling the noise. The little antechamber was dim, but the stove was lit and there was enough of a glow from the coals to make out her face. He had never, really, believed that it was Madeleine; and so it was astonishing how the grief caught him round the throat, how he wanted to fold to the ground and close his eyes.

It was not Madeleine, of course. It was Mercy.

She was hunching one shoulder. He just had time to wonder whether it was some new injury, then she swung the arm towards him, and he saw that she was holding a heavy iron bar. He ducked away, knocked into the night-watchman's chair and crashed to the ground. His head caught the corner of a table and white stars flashed across his vision. He had pulled the chair over as he fell, and he held it in front of him like a shield, scrabbling backwards out of range. He must have looked risible: an undignified parody of a lion-tamer, fending off a single slender woman. He said, 'Wait – I mean you no harm . . .' Not that he was in any position to harm her, scuffling through the dust on his haunches. 'Please don't hit me with that—'

'What are you doing here?'

'Please – will you put that down? Please. I am alone – I do not wish to hurt you. I let you go, did I not, after the ball? *Please.*'

Her grip on the bar did not loosen; but very slowly she lowered it to her side.

'Thank you,' he said, and cautiously got to his feet, setting the chair back in its place. 'I saw you and – well, I mistook you for someone else. I am sorry if I startled you.' His voice sounded unexpectedly matter-of-fact, as if they were acquaintances who had met on a street, in broad daylight.

She was staring at him with narrowed eyes. She said, 'You're *his* friend. You took my letters and you never showed them to him, did you? Or did you look at them together and laugh? You don't care – you could have helped me, helped Joe . . .'

'No . . . well . . . I did not exactly put them into his hands, but—'

She came at him again. He tried to fend her off, twisting her wrist against the elbow, harder than he meant to. The bar clanged to the floor.

'Let go of me! *Let – go*—' She threw herself backwards. He released her, shocked at the terror in her face, as though he were the assailant. She cowered against the wall, and he saw how thin she was, how translucent her skin, how fragile her bones. She was tensed as if to endure some outrage at his hands. She said, 'I will kill myself before you can drag me ten paces.' She drew a bottle from her pocket and snatched out the cork. 'Opium and arsenic,' she said. 'Once I've swallowed this, you'll have no more power over me.'

He froze, not moving his eyes from her face. 'It's all right,' he said, 'I am not Sir Edward's friend. He has sacked me. There is no need to drink that. I promise.'

'Then why are you here?'

'I came to destroy something, in the laboratory.' He was so intent on her hand, holding the lethal bottle, that he hardly paid attention to what he said; he only cared that with every steady word it sank a little further away from her mouth. 'They have made a – a horrible thing, in part because of something I did. And I could not bear to think of it, so I came to break it into pieces.'

There was a silence. He willed her to put the cork back into the bottle. She said, 'You are trying to trick me.'

'No. How can I prove it?'

She stared at him. 'I am going to smash the tanks and kill the spiders.'

There was a silence.

'Give me back the bar,' she said.

He stooped and took it up. As smoothly as he could he

put it on the table and stepped back. 'Where is the night-watchman?' he said. 'I thought he was not allowed to leave his post?'

'If what you say is true, you had better go before he comes back.'

Henry glanced at the table. Beside the bar was a news-paper, a little crumpled, as if it had been thrown down in a hurry, and a pipe that still oozed smoke. He thought he could see a shred of steam rising from the tea in the enamel mug. How had she persuaded the man to leave it? 'You bribed him.'

'No! We—' She stopped short, biting her lip. So she had an accomplice; that made sense. He imagined some kind of diversion – a child knocking at the door, begging for help, a man staging an accident, or a mysterious light, crossing the yard . . . That was better, anyway, than beating the watchman's brains out with that iron bar. 'It doesn't matter,' she said. 'Now leave me alone. I don't have long. I won't tell anyone that you were here.'

Did she trust him? Or was it only that she did not care, as long as he did not stand in her way? As soon as it was done, would she raise the bottle to her lips again, and drink?

He crossed the room to the opposite door, the door that led to the spiders. She shrank back against the wall as he passed, but he did not look at her. He opened the door and stared into the glassy murk, his stomach churning. He had forgotten the sound: that elusive whisper, unique among all the noises of the factory and effects of the silk. Even now, against the background of the storm, it was unmis-takable.

There was a footstep behind him. But the vibration seemed to come from the wrong direction, and in the corner of his eye – in the nearest tank, as though the panes were half mirror, half dim, bottomless lake – he glimpsed the swirl of a floating face, dark eyes and nacreous lips . . . When he looked straight at it, there was nothing. Or rather, there were the indistinct threads and sails of a cobweb, glimmering in the shadows, and Mercy's reflection. She was at his shoulder. She said, 'Stand aside.' Her voice called resonances, shimmering, from every wall of glass: and for a moment he had the impression of an endless corridor, like the infinite multiplication of two looking glasses, silvery and moonlit. And at the far end – yes – there was a figure, both like and unlike himself, a man cloaked in shadow. He clutched at the doorframe. Only an illusion, only his own reflection. But if he stepped closer, he might see that dark-clad man smile at him. He might see, with a shock, that the face was not his own, but older, assured, mocking; and even though he knew it would be a phantasm, an emana-tion of his own desires, there was nothing he wanted more. He wanted to chase after him, and lose himself in that impossible maze. He told himself that it was only the silk and the glass; it was only the spiders' trickery, acting on him, disorientating him, as though he were their prey, as Worsley had said . . . But it was so clear, so heart-wrenching. And perhaps he *was* their natural prey, for more than anything he wanted to succumb to it. If he allowed Mercy to break open the vivaria, he would never see that ghost again.

And everything else that came from the silk . . . It came to him, in a rush, what it would mean if the spiders were destroyed. The factory – Telverton – the whole Ashmore-Percy fortune – everything would be laid waste. If he had been caught breaking into the laboratory he was almost sure he could have prevaricated. This – no, this was different. This would be a crime of the highest degree; this might mean public shame, imprisonment, hard labour. Never to return home – his name to be dragged through the mud, despised . . . It was not too late to turn back. He might go to find the nightwatchman; Mercy would be apprehended, the factory saved; and perhaps his service would be rewarded. He might win back Sir Edward's confidence – and with it everything else, everything he had lost . . .

He stared into the translucent depths of glass and darkness, his throat tight. He could see, now, that what resembled a man's face was a particular merging of webs and shade, and if he moved to left or right it would resolve itself into its component parts.

Mercy pushed past him. He did not prevent her. He turned away, back into the antechamber, and bent for the poker that stood beside the stove. Behind him, he heard the first jolting smash of metal and glass, and felt the roots of his teeth sting at the impact. The sound came again, and this time he heard not only the splinter of the tank breaking but an eerie thrum, as the vibration swept through the building and every thread and particle of silk and wood and glass answered in its own voice; it made him think of church bells ringing in drowned villages. But it was only audible for a split second: the next moment there was another crash, and glass pattered to the floor, and he stepped into the spider house with a poker in his hand, already swinging it towards the nearest tank.

It was not joy. It was not madness, either. But it was close to both: so close that he was utterly lost to himself as he swiped and thrashed in a frenzy of exertion. Glass broke around him like flying storm-waters: it sprayed, it threw stinging splinters into his face, it glittered and sang. And

the silk ripped and shredded and tore, turning to grimy rags
on the end of his poker. The spiders' staircases, their ivory
palaces, their lustrous castles in the air: he beat them all
into clinging shreds, gasping with satisfaction. It was a sort
of carnage of veils and lace – except that there was broken
glass everywhere, blood smeared on the handle of his poker,
and all the time the *noise* of it, the relentless sickening notes
buzzing in his bones, the hum that made it hard to breathe.
Tank after tank was reduced to jagged diamonds and dust.
On the other side of the room, Mercy flung her bar against
the last intact panes, fierce and methodical; he swung
sharply away as a larger shard flew towards him, and felt
it cut his cheek. He stumbled into a wide sheet of web,
strong enough to catch his ankle. Beyond it was another
sweep of silk, reaching to the ceiling of the tank like the
drapes of a child's bassinet; he drove his poker into it, and
slashed at it again and again, until the airy curtain collapsed,
no longer resembling anything but a cobweb. Underneath
was a dark, scabrous knot. He recoiled. He had hardly seen
the spiders: only glimpses of scuttling things that made him
shudder, and a tickle of something on his face that made
him grab convulsively at it, only to find a wet lock of his
own hair, dripping. But now he paused, staring at the clod
of blackness. Was it a spider, or the desiccated carcass of a
bat or a rat? He kicked a fragment of glass towards it, and
it stalked sideways. But it retained a kind of dignity: a long-
legged, careful presence of mind, as though it was older
and wiser than any flailing human. *Will you walk into my
parlour? Said the spider to the fly* . . . And he raised the poker
to shoulder height and brought it down, with every ounce
of his strength.

But there was no need to kill them all. He remembered
Worsley saying, *They eat one another, you see.* It was enough

to break the tanks open, and stir them into action; then they would finish the job themselves. He wiped the sweat from his forehead and let his arm drop, surveying the wreckage. The spider house was a landscape of shattered glass, the last corners webbed with cracks, the silk in grimy swags or curled in grey clumps on the floor. A few black spiders were scattered among the glittering dust, curled over and motionless; a few more moved, like tiny dark hands, inching out of corners. It was done. Now it was left to them to complete the final act.

But Mercy had not stopped. She was crouching now, bringing her iron bar down, over and over, in the same place. Below it, on the ground, the glass was ground to a streak of powder, as white and fine as chalk. It made him think of the rat he had seen in the cage, turning endlessly back and forth. He said, 'Mercy . . .' She did not hear. He set his poker down and walked towards her. Closer to, he could make out a dark smear with a few splayed filaments where the abdomen of a spider had been pounded into nothing. He jerked his gaze away, afraid he might see a many-eyed head, intact and staring at him. The bar went on falling, automatic as a machine.

'Mercy!' He grabbed her arm, harder than he meant to; she struggled, snarled, rocked sideways on her haunches, fell. The bar clanged to the floor. For an instant she was clawing at him, and her hand caught the cut on his face in a blaze of pain. He only just had the self-control to pull away instead of striking back at her. 'For God's sake!' Then at last she was still.

Perhaps one of them would have broken that fragile silence. But before he could draw breath – before the right words could come – a faint swinging light spilt from the antechamber. It caught on every fractured surface, raising glints and sparks the colour of flame. He turned. Nothing was visible in the doorway but the bright circle of a storm lantern, with a cluster of shadows behind it.

He heard a man choke in shock, and master himself; and then, a little overlapping, there was Worsley's voice saying, with icy equilibrium, 'Latimer, is that you?'

Sixteen

It felt as though sticky threads had settled across Henry's face, gumming his mouth shut, covering his nose so that he couldn't get enough air. He tried to wipe them away with the back of his hand, but the sensation persisted. No one else moved – neither Mercy, nor the two patches of shadow behind the inscrutable lamp – and the only sound was the dying patter of the rain on the roof. Slowly he managed to peel his lips apart, but there was no way out, now. He had been caught in the act, and there was nothing he could say or do to avert disaster.

Then Mercy scrabbled for something in her skirts, and he forgot everything but the knowledge that she had a bottle of poison, to be taken in case of capture. He dived for her hands and wrenched them apart. 'No, no, you mustn't,' he said, and something fell to the floor. He didn't have time to look, she was resisting him, flinging herself from side to side, beginning to sob, and it was as much as he could do to keep hold of her. Agony blazed in his knee but he ignored it. 'Help me, Worsley!' All that mattered was that she should not find the little bottle – that she should not be allowed to—

'Help him,' Worsley said, and then, louder, 'Help him! For heaven's sake . . .'

The nightwatchman crunched through the debris, reached down and pulled Mercy to her feet, knocking Henry aside. Mercy shrieked and battered at him – perhaps she was trying to grab the bar that lay beside his feet – but he shook her, hard, so that her teeth clacked, and she quietened.

Henry said, 'Please don't hurt—'

'Shut up,' Worsley said, and then, to the nightwatchman, 'Get her out. Tie her up.' He jerked his thumb over his shoulder and stood aside from the door. The other man steered Mercy forwards. She took a few steps, reeling and defeated; then a last flare of defiance rose in her face and she jerked to a halt, turned her head towards Henry, and spat.

Worsley did not speak again until the nightwatchman had manoeuvred Mercy through the doorway, grunting. Then there were the faint sounds of wooden chair legs grating, and the clatter of a box opening, and the flick of a rope. Worsley stepped forward and drew his shoe through the broken glass until he uncovered a tuft of pale cobweb. Then he lowered himself onto his haunches, put the storm lantern down beside his hip, and stared around. He swore a vicious oath, almost under his breath. Then he looked at Henry. 'How utterly useless you are,' he said, with weary contempt.

Henry got to his feet. In struggling with Mercy he had knelt on a shard of glass; a wide wet patch was blooming through his trousers over his kneecap, and it hurt to straighten his leg. He tried to summon some words of defiance, but his mind was blank.

'Come on,' Worsley said, getting to his feet.

Henry stared at him. 'What—?' Then, with a slow swirl in his gut – as though a current had reversed direction – he understood. Worsley had seen Henry pulling the iron bar out of Mercy's grip, as though he were stopping her. Henry had dropped the poker by then. And he had called for help, and she had spat at him, for his betrayal. It must have looked as though he had been trying to protect the spiders – as though he still hoped to redeem himself to Sir Edward.

Worsley was already hurrying out into the antechamber. Stiffly, Henry lurched after him, past the nightwatchman stoking the stove on the other side of the room; past Mercy, tied to the chair, her eyes closed. 'Don't take your gaze off her,' Worsley said to the watchman. 'She may look like no trouble but she's a mad bitch, she'll get away if she can. Latimer, stop dawdling.' He flung the door open and strode outside. Henry hesitated; Mercy's face was as immobile as a sleeping child's. Could he save her? He must. Somehow. Perhaps if he played along, pretended, then . . . At least he might buy himself some time to think, to find a way . . . He followed Worsley out into the open air.

The rain had stopped. The clouds had frayed into scraps and remnants, and a full moon seemed to race between them. The light was furiously bright, dimming Worsley's lantern to an ember. The effect was disconcerting, as if they had emerged into a different world. Although the clouds were moving swiftly, at ground level the air was still. Henry had grown so accustomed to the hiss of the rain that in spite of the thunder of the canal, he had the impression of a great, almost impossible quiet, as though his own heart had ceased.

Worsley crossed the stripe of shadow cast by the chimney and hurried down the narrow alley between the corner of the spider house and the main building. He came to the door and unlocked it. 'This way.'

They had come to the base of one of the spiral staircases. Moonlight spilt through the windows on the half-landing above. But they did not climb the stairs; instead Worsley led the way into a dark corridor, raising his lantern as he went.

He fumbled for another key and opened another door. Then he was searching for something with one hand, while the light threw crazy slices of shadow over the shelves. It was a small room, or perhaps a large cupboard; boxes fell to the floor, and Worsley stooped and emptied their contents out, pushing the boxes towards Henry. 'Here,' he said, 'take these,' and went on stripping the shelves. Things pattered and clinked around his feet – nails, or fastenings, or bobbins, Henry thought. Worsley bent and gathered up the boxes.

'What are you—?'

'For the spiders, you fool. They'll eat one another. We need to save as many as we can.' Worsley stood up, cradling more boxes between his elbow and one hand, the lantern bobbing in the other. 'If we don't save enough to breed from . . .' He shoved Henry, hard, in the ribs.

Henry stumbled obediently in the same direction. He must play along. Even if it meant saving the spiders – if he had to choose between Mercy and the destruction of the spiders, he must choose Mercy . . . But how could he help her, he thought – *how*? They came out into the moonlight. There was a faint buzz in his skull, dispelling the unearthly silence; he pressed his tongue against his palate, resenting the distraction, wishing he could think more clearly.

'Right,' Worsley said. 'We'll scour the place. Get all the live ones out of the corners. You be careful, you hear me? Damage one and I'll have the hide off you. She must have come here during the storm on purpose so there'd be no one here to help. Once we've saved what we can, I'll throttle her.'

Henry came to a halt. He supposed it was a figure of speech; but he was not sure. He had thought the asylum at Exminster was the worst that might happen to her – but—

'I'd rather kill her now,' Worsley said. 'Sir Edward won't care. One whore more or less, who gives a damn? It's not like the other one, no need to keep up appearances.' He bared his teeth. 'By God I'll work her over, if she's ruined us.'

Henry looked down. His shadow lay thickly at his feet, deformed by his armload of boxes. The distant thrum increased. Oh, God, if he could only *think*! Time, he must have more time . . . He said, staring into the depths of his shadow, 'The other one?'

'What?'

'You said, *the other one*. No need to keep up appearances, like the other one.'

'Did I? It doesn't matter.'

'The other accident,' Henry said, without knowing whether or not it was a question. 'Or the other . . . whore?'

Worsley huffed out his breath, but all he said was, 'Come on, will you?'

'You mean Sir Edward's wife, don't you? Lady Ashmore-Percy.' Henry could not wrench his gaze from the darkness at his feet. He did not need to: without raising his eyes he could see through the brick walls that stood between him and the weaving shed. She had screamed to be let out, while the noise beat in her ears and deafened the child in her womb. 'Was that you? Did you imprison her there? And set the machines going, on purpose?'

'Listen . . .' Worsley cleared his throat. 'We don't have time for this. The boss won't thank you for standing around gossiping when the spiders—'

'You disgust me,' Henry said. Suddenly he found that it was easy to look into the other man's face; and with satisfaction he saw Worsley's jaw drop. 'You are a despicable blackguard – a monster, a coward. I hope you *are* ruined. I hope you find yourself in the gutter.'

One of Worsley's boxes had fallen to the ground, but he

did not stoop for it. 'Oh, *I* am a blackguard, am I? I was acting on Sir Edward's orders.'

'You're a liar.'

'No. No!' he repeated, and laughed. 'Not on this subject, anyway. And you, Latimer, *you* . . . You come crawling to Telverton, trying to insinuate yourself into his good graces. You say whatever he wants – oh yes, you make a fuss of all your finer feelings, but you would do anything to be in my place, wouldn't you? You would cheat and lie and murder for him, as I do. The only difference is that you would lie to yourself as well. You might have thrown in the towel and gone home, but oh no, you stayed for as long as you were welcome. You delivered Mercy to us just now, knowing that she will be locked up, or worse. And you're helping us now. So shut your insolent mouth.' He paused, for a heart-beat. 'And the next time you speak to me like that I will make you into a shrieking lunatic, just like *Lady*' – he put a mocking emphasis on the word – 'Ashmore-Percy.'

Henry shut his eyes. For a moment he heard Gower's voice: *we cannot stand up to them.* And underneath it was that quiver in his bones, like the approach of some unseen wave. He let the boxes slip out of his arms and tumble to the ground.

'Oh, for heaven's sake, let us get to the matter at hand—'

'No,' he said. 'I will not. I cannot.'

'My word, what a time for histrionics! Don't be absurd.'

'I am not going to obey your orders,' he said, and thought that perhaps, after all, it was true. 'Why should I? I would be glad to see you destitute – and Sir Edward, too. Why do you think I'm here?'

'What do you mean?' But he did not have time to answer before Worsley added, with a slow edge in his voice, 'Why *are* you here?'

'I helped Mercy to destroy the spider tanks,' Henry said. And for the duration of the words he believed that he had come for that, and that alone.

'You're her accomplice? But . . .' Worsley shook his head. Now another box slipped out of his grasp, and another; he hardly seemed to notice them falling. Slowly his frown gave way to a different expression: intent, almost serene. 'You helped her,' he echoed, and his voice was as soft as silk. 'You helped her kill the spiders.'

Henry said nothing.

'When I have done with her,' Worsley said, 'I will start work on you.'

Henry had not been afraid for himself, until now. He had only thought of Mercy – and then of Philomel, and Lady Ashmore-Percy, and a righteous flame of anger had eclipsed everything else. It was only now, watching Worsley's expression change, that he realised how foolhardy he had been. He was alone, in the darkness, with a man who took pleasure in pain; if he called out, no one would come to his rescue. He said, trying to make it sound like a command, 'Let us go. You needn't tell Sir Edward that you ever saw us.'

'And why would I do that?'

'If you let us both go, I will never repeat what you've told me. I'll carry it to my grave. Otherwise—'

'You may be closer to your grave than you realise,' Worsley said, and smiled.

'It's one thing to dispose of a woman like that – poor, half mad already; she can be bundled into a madhouse quite easily, no questions asked – but a man of good family, educated, cultured . . . You would encounter difficulties. Inconveniences. Far better to come to an arrangement—'

'Ah,' Worsley said, 'but you have not factored in the pleasure of it.'

There was a silence. That distant rumble tugged at Henry's attention, insistent.

Worsley took a step towards him. He had let go of all but two boxes, and the one in his right hand was crushed out of shape. 'I would enjoy it,' he said. 'You don't understand that, do you? Oh, the look on that bitch's face, just before I shut the door on her – I often close my eyes, to remember it . . . She thought she was better than me. Just like you do. Call me a coward and then beg for your life, will you? I'll tell you what, Latimer – I'll deal with the woman quickly, for your sake. And then I will have such fun with you! Next time you wake up, you'll be in the ghost cage. Shall I make you cut off your own arm? Or your ears? Or cut out your own tongue, maybe? And then leave you to bleed to death? And best of all, there'll be no inconvenience, no difficulty at all, because I won't have laid a finger on you. You're a widower, aren't you? Must have been grief, they'll say, he must have lost his mind. Although I pity your family, when they hear that you mutilated yourself horribly before you put an end to it.'

'No,' Henry said, 'you will not.'

'Is that so? How will you stop me? You think your begging will melt my heart?'

'No,' he said. He wanted to put his fingers in his ears – to block out the distraction of that gathering thunder, real or unreal – but he was too conscious of his shaking hands. 'Because I destroyed the ghost cage, too.'

Worsley blinked. He did not seem to hear the noise; which meant, perhaps, that it was in Henry's head. He said, 'When?'

How long had it been? 'An hour – a little while ago . . . The laboratory door was open. I went inside. I cut the silk apart, and broke the frame.'

Worsley's half-smile had disappeared. He was looking at

Henry as if he could see through him, all the way to the horizon.

A gust of wind swept a cloud away from the moon, and silver blazed across the sky and the wet ground. Henry blinked. And then Worsley was on him, diving through the dazzling black and white of moonlight and shadows. He grabbed Henry's shoulder – tipped him off balance – drew back his arm to punch—

Henry tried to duck. But with a terrible slow clarity he knew he had not moved fast enough. He saw Worsley's fist coming towards him, and could not evade it.

He did not lose consciousness, but his vision blurred as pain slammed into his jaw and ribs. When he was upright again, blinking water out of stinging eyes, his arm was twisted behind his back and he could not extricate himself. At first he sagged, his knees grazing the ground, but a cruel grip jerked him back to his feet. 'Do not struggle,' a voice said, and he did not. Then he was steered past the factory building, and over crunching gravel, while hot breath came and went on the back of his neck. It was as much as he could do to walk: there was no possibility of pulling away, not if he did not want to rip his arm from its socket. He was weak with pain; neither his muscles nor his mind were working properly. They crossed a patch of open ground, and then walls closed on either side. And then—

They were at the door to the weaving shed. He recognised it, without curiosity, the way he might react to a twist in one of Madeleine's magazine stories. The hero, he thought, faces deadly peril . . .

Worsley tightened his grasp on Henry's wrist. With the other hand he fumbled in his pocket for his bunch of keys. They clinked against one another as he inserted one into the lock and turned it.

'Wait a bit, Worsley,' Henry said, 'what about the spiders? Aren't you wasting time?'

'It won't take long.'

'You can't – really, this is—'

'Shut up.' He gave Henry a sharp push, letting go of his arm: and as the blood rushed into the joint, and pain made him deaf and blind, Henry stumbled over the threshold and crashed into the corner of a loom. 'Goodbye, Latimer.'

And with all the belated force of a dam breaking, Henry felt panic flood into him, driving out the fire in his shoulder, fierce as life itself. Worsley was closing the door. He flung himself against it, pushing with all the strength he had.

Worsley gave a dry, breathless chuckle. It only added to the panic: this was how he must have laughed, before; how he must have relished the moment as the door was shut and locked—

But Henry was not a woman heavy with child, and terror gave him a ferocity he had never known. He drove the door open and Worsley staggered back, the note of his laughter turning thin and high-pitched. Henry shouted something – some obscenity – and his voice rang off the brick walls, multiplied in echoes that for once were natural, comprehensible to his mind as well as his ears. Worsley squirmed away. He raised his hands to ward Henry off. 'Come on, my dear chap, you didn't think I would really . . .'

But he had been right to be afraid. And he was still afraid. It crackled and sang through every nerve. It made him want to hit out – to drive Worsley to the ground and bludgeon him until he could never get up again – to strike and hurt until he was sure that he was safe, that he was the only one who could walk away alive. His knees trembled with it. It—

No. It was not fear – or not only fear – that rose through his body, churning his guts. The rumble he'd heard was all around him; he was sure now that it was real. He froze. Worsley's face flickered; then, abruptly, he twisted to follow Henry's gaze.

It grew louder – past thunder, past noise; it made the air shudder, and came up through the ground as though the earth itself was about to split. And then, as it reached its peak, there was a deep jolt that seemed to punch into Henry's abdomen, bypassing his ears. The timbre of the sound changed: now, over the roar, there was a liquid, gurgling note, almost melodic . . .

'Dear God,' Worsley said.

In the moonlight, spreading towards them, was a wave of water. It poured through the gap between the buildings and broke over the ground, flecked with foam; it was so like the sea that Henry expected it to recede, leaving streaks of bubbles, before it was overtaken again. But it did not. It kept on coming, swift and inexorable. There was a shock of cold as it hit Henry's ankles and splashed up his calves. He caught his breath. Then the wave swept past, out of sight, and around them was an expanse of silver water, pocked and wrinkled by eddies. The wall ahead was illuminated in stark moonlight, and he could see the level steadily creeping upwards against the ranks of mortar and brick.

Worsley said, 'Something must have broken down the canal wall.'

Henry could not move. Already it was inching up over his knees. A dull ache throbbed where he had knelt on the shard of glass. Something nudged him under the surface and he flinched and tottered: but it was only a thick branch, pressed against his shin by the flow. He bent and tried to push it away, but it swung back and wedged itself between his legs.

'Help me,' Worsley said, and his voice was high and hoarse. 'Help me – I cannot swim.'

'The spider house,' Henry said. 'Mercy.'

'What of her?' Worsley's face was in a rigid grimace. He started to wade towards the flooded alley, his arms pumping stiffly. 'We mustn't get stuck here – we shall be washed away – I can feel it getting higher . . .'

'She is tied up. She'll be trapped. If it goes on rising—'

'Help me,' he said, almost shrieking. 'Hold on to me, that way neither of us will fall.'

Henry stared at the waters pouring through the narrow gap, spreading into the yard with a deep scalloped edge of scum and detritus. Then he grabbed convulsively for the branch that had caught between his knees: it might help to steady him. Unlike Worsley, he could swim, but he was not sure that it would save him if he lost his footing in that terrible river.

Worsley saw him straighten up with the branch in his hand. 'Latimer, please!' As soon as Henry was within reach he clenched both hands on Henry's arm, with a fierce, convulsive grip.

In spite of his resentment, Henry did not shake him off. Inch by inch they made headway against the battering stream, lifting foot after foot, swaying and breathless with effort. Then at last they were clear of the alley. Ahead of them, moonlight danced and split and glittered, punctuated with dark flotsam; the buildings rose from wavering reflections, transformed into unlikely vessels. The spider-house windows were dark. Henry said, 'Perhaps they have saved themselves – taken the lamp—'

'Don't be stupid. They're probably underwater. We must get to safety.'

'We must find them,' Henry said, and his heart flung itself against his ribs as though it would shatter. 'If there's any chance—'

'Oh, for pity's *sake*!' Worsley tugged his arm. 'As if they matter.'

Henry turned. 'Get yourself to safety if you must,' he said, raising his voice over the rush of water, 'but I have to— Let go of me, let *go*—' He dug the branch into the water, trying to steady himself against Worsley's frantic clutching.

'But I can't *swim*,' Worsley yelped. 'Damn Mercy – help *me*!'

Henry jerked away; and as he reeled, driven sideways by the force of the current, the stick he was holding swung through the air, trailing drops. An impact jolted up through his bones and made his teeth rattle. Suddenly the fingers scrabbling at his wrist let go, leaving a circle of tingling flesh where they had been. There was a cry, beating wings of shadow, a crash of water. He rocked back, blinded by the spray. When he had wiped his face, Worsley was gone. It was impossible; it was like a magic trick, a man vanishing into a hall of mirrors . . . Henry stared about frantically, seeing nothing but splintering moonlight and reflections.

No. Not gone: there, in the water. Henry said, 'Worsley?' but his voice was hardly audible against the noise of the water. That could not be him, face down, drifting already, already nearly out of reach. Henry had not hit him hard enough to— No, surely any moment he would drag himself up, gasp for breath, swear . . . But he did not. The hair on the back of his head spread out like weed.

Henry said again, 'Worsley . . . ?' He should have dived into the treacherous current, sweeping with his hands to find some handhold, the collar of Worsley's jacket, a fistful

of hair . . . The flood was up to his chest. It was too late
– or it would be, if he did not move now, *now* . . .

A grinding, scraping growl rose to a monstrous shout, as
though the whole world were being ripped out of its foun-
dations. He looked up.

Ahead of him, in the moonlight, the spider house was
surrounded by a curling, hump-backed serpent that seemed
to swallow itself, gorging and growing fat before it was rolled
under the surface by another wave. Something else – a wall,
a barrier – had given way. He tried to take a step, but the
pressure swept his foot backwards. He had no more time to
think of Worsley; instead he thought of Mercy, and then of
the broken tanks, the dead spiders . . . Was all that glass carried
in the flood? If he opened the spider-house door, would he
be met by a mass of water studded with shards and splinters?
If, indeed, he could manage to drag the door open at all . . .

He slipped, sank, gulped foul liquid and came back to his
feet in a threshing frenzy. The impossibility of getting to the
spider house flashed into his mind, then was eclipsed by
terror. There was no hope of saving Mercy, any more than
he could have saved Worsley; nor any hope of saving himself.
He was going to die. It was not enough to be able to swim:
the tide would pull him down, batter him with planks and
rocks, drive him into a corner and crush him.

He was facing back the way they had come. Ahead of
him, the main factory building seemed to push through the
torrent like a juggernaut, hammered by surging spray. Soon
the deluge would be at head height – pounding through the
high windows, climbing the stairs . . .

The staircase. Ahead of him he saw the door he and
Worsley had come out of, before the canal wall gave way.
They had been hurrying, with their arms full of boxes; they
had left it open.

He almost choked on hope. But he dared not pause even long enough to acknowledge it. He plunged forward, frantic, scooping his arms through the water and blinking away the foul drops that flecked his face.

Then, somehow, he was grabbing at the upright of the doorway, shocked beyond gratitude to feel the solidity of it. The stairs ahead of him rose from the lapping reflections, slicked with silver. He waded forward until his shoes met the lowest step; then, numbly, he climbed. He reached the half-landing and paused to look down through the narrow window. He braced himself for what he might see, floating, but it was hard to make out anything in the mirror-mess of debris.

Up here, the noise was a little less. He leant on the wall with both hands. He was standing on solid ground now but it seemed to move beneath him.

There was a great creak and rasp, like claws on stone, or a rusty nail, drawing blood . . . Then it broadened, splintered, faded. It was the sound of defeat – of a structure demolished; its last protest, its final dragging shout before it disintegrated. He peered down. Nothing.

Then he saw the landscape tilt, changing before his eyes. He could not take it in, he could only watch, clinging to the windowsill with bruised hands. Things were moving that should not move. He drew a wet sleeve across his eyes, but it was not his senses that were betraying him. Below him there was a shift in the pattern of buildings and flood, a kind of tremor, a creeping . . . The water piled up in skeins, tangled and spun itself into a net around and over the spider house, throwing loops over the roof. The building lurched forwards at a new angle. It inched and crawled, as though it were wounded, trying to escape. And then, rumbling, as the current tore away the shingles and poured through the windows, it collapsed.

It was over more quickly than he would have believed: it was gone, gulped down, leaving nothing but a raft of wood and broken beams like a giant's game of spillikins. He stood, unthinking, unmoving, until the flood had finished with it. Behind him he heard the anodyne lapping of water as it crept up to the next step.

Then he walked, leaning heavily against the wall like an old man, up the next flight of stairs to the next landing. His knee was bleeding. He was chilled to the bone. No one knew he was here. No one would come. He could not find the energy to care. He sat down against the wall, letting the noise resonate through the brick into his skull, and shut his eyes.

Part VI

How long will it be, now? I wait and wait. I must have counted wrong. But if I have, where did this child come from?

I thought there was a part of the ecstasy I did not remember. I thought there must have been another there, a man as well as Hira. I tried to remember another mouth, another pair of hands, another body; and although I could not, I rejoiced to think that my daughter had sprung from that night, conceived in a temple, in a rite of love. I preferred that to thinking that James had asserted himself on my body, after he drugged me . . . But now I count and count, over and over, and either way I cannot make the sum work. Could he have laid hands on me another time, without waking me? Or someone else, since James has disdained my body for months? I shut my eyes and try to remember the men on the voyage. The sailors flinched when I walked past; they said the spiders would bring bad luck, and blamed me for it. I do not think they would have touched me. Nor the other passengers, the young men on grand tours, aspiring to be poets, or the old man travelling to see his cousin in Marseilles. But there must be an answer. I am not hysterical, I know that if it was not a swan, or a shower of gold, or a monstrous bull, it was a man. Somehow my baby was conceived. If that was how – well, I do not care, however it was I would let it be done again, without protest.

It is appalling, to write it; or it should be. If I had any proper feelings left, I would be appalled. But I am not. It would be rank hypocrisy to be appalled, when I would not regret anything that had planted this seed in my belly. I have never felt love like this, not even for James, not even for Hira. If I can feel this fire of devotion, now, before my daughter has drawn her first breath – then what will it be, when she is in my arms? I do not care who fathered her. Let her have many fathers, or none. I am her mother. She is mine. Mine.

I wait. But I can wait. If these months have taught me anything, it is that. I wait and say nothing, and all the time she grows, as if my very silence nourishes her. When she is born . . . Soon. It must be soon. And then . . . Oh, it has been so long! It is so cold here, and so grey, even though it is summer, and I miss Hira so much that sometimes I bite my own hand to stop myself crying out. But there is something to wait for. A new life, mine and my daughter's.

James tells me he is thinking of the future, too. Perhaps he is, in his way. We have been sitting for our portraits. When we are finished, and varnished, and framed, we will hang above the hearth in the drawing room. We will hang there for generations. He says that his sons will admire us, and be grateful – because, after all, the spiders will have made our fortune, and the Ashmores will be rich and famous. He is not talking about this child, since he is as capable of arithmetic as I; so it does not matter that I know – I *know*! – that the child I bear will be a girl. Nor would he believe me if I said that the spiders will not make his fortune. He spends hours hunched in his study, weaving threads together, making notes. He rarely goes out; he looks pasty and ill. So do I – but then, all my force goes into keeping my daughter alive. She takes everything I can give, and I love her for it.

I imagine her asleep in her saltwater bed, like a pearl in an oyster. Soon. Soon.

I will not waste my strength on being afraid. I will need it – for her, for me. Oh, if Hira were only here! Sometimes I wonder what she is doing. I lie in bed and close my eyes. I follow her as she climbs the path from the village, watch her raise her face to the green shade of the holm oaks and smile, alone, content. I smell her sweat, and the sweetness of herbs trodden underfoot. Then I reach out to take her hand, and I feel the miles that separate us. Oh, I want her, here, now! I want her to be at my side when my labour begins. I want her to be the one who catches my daughter, to be the first to touch her, to raise her to my breast. But I will never see her again. And I will not waste my strength on longing, either.

The days repeat. Nothing changes, except that the year advances and my daughter grows. She, too, is saving her strength. I remember Aunt Elizabeth telling me how her children would swim up and down in her womb, and turn somersaults when she ate water-ices. But my baby bides her time; she is quiet, and careful, and when she moves it is only a fluttering of her tiny fingers, so gentle it might be mistaken for a rumbling in my guts. I am glad: the world likes us best when we are docile and silent, and we do not take up more space than necessary. Later I will teach her to be sly, and find her own way without seeming to resist, like water that slips out of a man's cupped hands. She will do everything that I cannot.

Oh, it has been so long! I am tired. I hurt all over, I cannot stop passing water, I cannot eat. But it is precious. I want her to come, and at the same time I do not; because when she is born, she will never be as close to me again.

*

When I went to feed the spiders this morning I found James asleep in the orangery. It was early, colder and greyer than it has any right to be in August, even in England, and my bones ached. I went to the box where the rats squeak and rustle, and slid it open. One has just had a litter. I counted the others: there would be enough without my having to disturb her nest of wriggling pink babies, and I was glad. It was not until I reached for my gloves that I saw James, slumped on the floor with his head resting against the lowest vivarium. There was an empty bottle beside him, and the smell of alcohol rose on his breath.

I set my gloves aside again. It was strange to look down on him, especially in that silver olive-tree-dappled light: he looked young, his hair clinging to his forehead, as abandoned as a little boy. If it had not been for the spiders behind him, I could have forgotten everything that he had done, and loved him again.

I reached out and touched his cheek. But the feel of his flesh – clammy, cool, a little gritty with the morning's stubble – made me draw back, remembering the smoothness of Hira's skin and the liquid heat of her mouth.

He did not wake. The nearest spider twitched a little on its web, and I thought I heard a murmur, as soft as though it were coming from inside my own skull. They are small, the spiders. They are smaller by far than the rats I feed them, and the bats they ate on the island. They do not overpower their prey, but cradle them, let the silk calm them, drink them dry as they dream.

I thought, If I wished I might open the tank, now, while James is asleep.

I thought, He might not wake.

I thought, What would happen, if he did not wake?

346

I imagined the spider creeping forward over his face. If he did not stir, it would go back and forth, slowly, slowly wrapping him in silk, covering mouth and nose and eyes. Slowly it would turn his face into something else, a blind white hood, a chrysalis, a nothing. It would settle under his jaw, find the right place to pierce his skin. If he had not woken yet, he might not wake at all. I might open all the tanks, until there was a spider sucking at every vein. Perhaps he might never wake. There would be justice in that. More than justice.

The spider did not move. It is absurd to suppose that spiders can feel hatred, but they do, I know they do. They want James to pay for what he did; and if he does not pay then their hate will endure, for generations, for as long as it takes. A curse. Please, I thought, if there is a curse, turn it aside from me and my child. If they must claim their debt, let it be through me, at my choosing, let it be James and no one else who pays . . .

Then it was too late. Before I had decided what to do he opened his eyes, and for a moment he smiled.

'Sophia,' he said. 'What are you doing here?' When I hesitated he looked about him and seemed to remember where he was. He clambered to his feet, knocking the bottle over, and glanced at me shamefaced. As if I had not known that he drank! He bent close to the tank and tapped his finger against the glass. Still the spider did not move; but I felt its disappointment, and its fury.

James let his hand fall, and turned back to me. For once – perhaps it was the clear morning light – he seemed to see me, myself. 'Oh, Sophia,' he said, suddenly. He had a look that I had not seen upon his face for a long time; not since before my first child was lost. 'It is not too late,' he said. 'We have come so far. We have so much to forgive, both of us. But we could, if we chose. We loved each other, didn't we?'

I did not speak. I was afraid of the echoes from the webs. I did not want to hear my answer turned into something it was not.

'When your. . .' He paused, and began again, his voice very soft. 'When our son is born we can begin again. Please, Sophy.'

I stared at him. I do not know why he would say such a thing after so long. Only, I had almost been free of him, had almost begun to think that there might be a way . . .

'You must not think that I do not see that you are suffering. I have written to the doctor to come to examine you. I should have sent for him months ago.'

I forced myself to say, 'That is kind, James.'

He nodded. He gave me a smile, which grew strained when I did not return it. 'Yes,' he said, 'well.' And he strode to the rats' box, drew on the gauntlets, and scooped up something that wriggled and chirruped. With his other hand he opened the closest vivarium, and dropped it in. It was the rat with her suckling litter, her tiny pups like the phalanges of a baby's fingers. They tumbled and squirmed on the floor of the tank, while their mother writhed, caught in the web, trying to bite at the threads. The silk magnified her squeak until it was like a needle in my ears.

'Go to bed, Sophy. You must rest. I will look after the spiders from now on.'

'Yes,' I said. I was wearier than I have ever been. I did not look back as I obeyed him.

Soon the doctor will come. He will tell me how long I have to wait, and how it will be, and what I must do, to prepare. He will not be like Hira, but he will help me. I am sure of it.

Soon, soon, soon. And when my child is born, I will find a way to break the spiders' curse, if it exists. I will find a way to be free.

Seventeen

When Henry awoke he was not at Cathermute House, nor the Angel, nor in his house in London. The bedroom he lay in was a pleasant one, bare and restful; although he did not know where he was, it was not entirely unfamiliar, as though it were not the first time he had awoken in it. His head was heavy; he had the sensation that it had hurt, before, but hurt no longer. He pushed himself up on his elbows. The sky outside the window was whitish, with the soft pallor of an overcast summer day, and the trees were heavy with leaves that were past their prime. He started to get out of bed, but the movement tired him, and he lay back. The bed had no hangings, and he could see faint green shadows dancing on the ceiling. They were the brightest thing in the room, apart from his own flesh: everything else was in shades of grey, and his nightshirt was the colour of ivory. There were no pictures on the walls, and no rug on the floor.

The house was quiet. He dozed, and woke again, and this time when he woke a plump matron in a dove-coloured dress was sitting beside his bed, ready to feed him beef tea. She laid her hand on his forehead before she left, and he submitted to it as naturally as if she were his maiden aunt, or his mother. Shadows grew around the bed, and a golden

349

circle sprouted on the ceiling where someone had lit a lamp. Dreams came and went, leaving him with no memory of them but vivid colours and a sense of something left undone.

When he surfaced again he was alone, and thirsty. There was no clock in his room, but it was late. Gingerly he swung his feet down to the floor. He paused in case his head should start to spin, but he felt remarkably steady, and after a few seconds he got to his feet. He looked about for a dressing gown, but could not find one. Instead he dragged the charcoal-coloured blanket from the bed and draped it round his shoulders. Then he crept out into the corridor.

At the top of the stairs he looked down into the darkness below, and saw the gilt outline of a door with light behind it. He descended the stairs, and knocked. 'Come,' a voice said, and he opened the door.

It was Hinshaw, the Quaker. He was reading beside an empty hearth, but as soon as he saw Henry he put his book down and got to his feet, reaching out to take Henry's arm. 'Art thou ailing?' he said.

'No,' Henry said, 'I couldn't sleep, and I wanted a drink of water.'

'I shall fetch it,' Hinshaw said. 'Wilt thou take something to eat?'

'I would love a brandy, if you have it.'

Hinshaw said, with a glint of humour, 'We do not keep strong drink in the house. But I am glad to see thee recovered enough to want it. Sit down.' He moved past Henry into the dark depths of the house.

Henry sat, with the same quiet lack of surprise he had felt earlier. As soon as he had seen the woman in her grey dress, he must have guessed where he was – or perhaps Hinshaw too had come to see him while he lay unconscious . . . He let his head loll against the cushioned settee. It was a more worldly room than the bedroom: quite ordinary, in fact, with walls of books, a desk and chair, and a mirror over the hearth. There was the faint sweetish smell of pipe-tobacco.

A moment later Hinshaw elbowed the door open and came into the room, bearing a tray: Henry's glass of water was accompanied by bread and cheese and dried fruit. 'If this is too indigestible, please do not eat it,' he said, 'or Rachel will have my head.'

'I must thank you,' Henry said.

'No need.'

'I mean – for everything. How long have I been here? You have looked after me, I take it, since . . .' He stopped. He did not know how to describe that night; it seemed impossibly distant, like an event in a novel he might have bought at a railway station.

'Since the flood,' Hinshaw said. 'That was three weeks ago.'

'You have been very kind – and after I was rude to you, when you offered help—'

Hinshaw raised a hand to cut him off. 'Say no more about that. Thou hast been ill. Exhaustion and fever, the doctor said. The cut on thy knee began to mortify, and we were afraid thou might'st lose the leg. But thou wast lucky.'

'Do Quakers believe in luck?'

Hinshaw gave him an amused glance. 'Dost thou mind if I smoke?'

'Not at all.'

'I have many vices,' he said, reaching for a pipe and filling it with deft fingers. 'Thou had'st better not base thy assessment of Friends on me. Better look at Rachel. She is an example, if thou lik'st.'

The charity chafed less, coming from Hinshaw, than it might have done; and with a sense of resignation that was half fatigue, he sat back in his chair, picked up the glass and drank it down. The water was clear and tasted faintly of stone; if all water were as good, he could happily give up brandy. But the thought brought in its wake the memory of that – that *other* water . . . He tried to blink away the image of the swollen canal, and put the empty glass aside, queasy.

Hinshaw was watching him. Now he took a long draw on his pipe, and lifted a hand to wind his fingers through the smoke as if it were a thread. 'I suppose, if thou wast lucky to survive,' he said, acknowledging the word with a faint emphasis, 'thou wast unlucky to have been there in the first place.'

There was a silence. Henry knew, with a kind of dread, that Hinshaw had meant it – tactfully but unmistakably – as a question; and it would be ungrateful indeed not to give his host an answer. He said, carefully, 'I went there to find something of mine that I had left there.'

'Didst thou find it? There was not much in thy pockets.'

'No,' he said. 'No, I . . .' But his throat closed. The vision of the debris-laden flood rose into his mind's eye as inexorably as it had risen in reality: driving everything before it, overwhelming his other senses. He felt again the pressure of it against his chest, the impersonal, irresistible surge that had tried to topple and drown him – saw the fractured reflections, the horrible glitter of moonlight as it whirled and sprayed against walls – heard the roar, the grating howl as the spider house gave way, the splash as Worsley fell sideways. He clenched his fists, trying to exorcise the sensation of that impact jolting all the way up to his shoulder, and Worsley's limp hand slipping off his wrist. He had done nothing wrong – had not meant to do anything wrong – and in any case, he could not have saved Worsley once he had fallen . . . 'I don't remember very much,' Henry said. 'Only the flood, and getting to safety – and the spider house, I saw the spider house being washed away . . .'

Hinshaw nodded. 'They discovered you the next day, almost by chance. There was a body found,' he said, without turning his eyes from the space where the flames would have been. 'Samuel Worsley. One of the factory clerks, I believe. They think he was trying to save the spiders. A brave man.'

'Yes,' Henry said, 'I suppose he must have been.' If he had been going to tell Hinshaw the truth, it would have been then. It was only once the moment had passed that he knew that he would not, that he would take the secret to his deathbed, and that by doing so he was admitting that perhaps, after all, he was not guiltless.

There was a pause. Hinshaw went on smoking, as though he were alone.

'Was anyone else . . . hurt?'

'The nightwatchman is lost. He was probably swept away with the building. Yes, it was a bad business. But we can thank the Almighty that no one else was in the factory.'

'Not luck, then?' Henry said, and had the reward of Hinshaw's half-smile. But in the quiet that followed he thought of Mercy, and the flash of relief and levity died. So her body must have been washed away; her family – her son – would never know how she had perished, or why. Any more than Worsley's family would . . . He said, 'And the factory? Is it still standing?'

'Mostly. The spider house and a few other parts were destroyed, the rest is still there. But the mess . . . Every part of the ground floor is deep in mud and filth, and the machines are clogged with it. If Noah alighted there, he'd go back into the ark and pray for more rain,' Hinshaw said, with only a glint in his eye to suggest that he was joking. 'No, there'll be no work done there for a long time, if ever. Even if the spiders had survived, it would be a lost cause.'

'They're all gone?'

'Oh yes.' Hinshaw sighed and drew his hand through his hair, tugging it unselfconsciously into clumps. 'That's another man who has been unlucky. I say that advisedly, although it would be tempting to ascribe it to the will of God. Sir Edward Ashmore-Percy, I mean.' He glanced at Henry, and away.

Henry swallowed. He said, 'Will he suffer much – financially?'

'He will be absolutely ruined, I should say.' Hinshaw paused, his hand still buried in his hair, and regarded him. 'That surprises thee, I see.'

'Yes,' Henry said; although the impulse that had made him shift against the creaking leather had not been only surprise. He looked down, away from Hinshaw's shrewd gaze.

'The family was wealthy. But the Ashmores' fortune was made by lace, two generations ago. There was a dowry from Sir Edward's wife's family, too, but by all accounts that was gone before she was sent to the asylum.' He said it matter-of-factly. 'No, there are enormous debts. That's common knowledge,' he added, 'not gossip. There were disputes when Cathermute House was built, and unpaid bills. I heard that the architect died in penury. And the factory . . . Well, thou know'st better than anyone that Sir Edward has been desperate for investors for some time. Every day that passes it runs on borrowings, and all he wants is good money to throw after the bad.' He blew a plume of smoke and frowned at it. 'It caused a lot of talk,' he said, 'that he let thee promise so much in his name. I suppose thou did'st not know he did not have it to spend . . . I should have warned thee. I do not like to see men gambling, especially with stakes they cannot afford. It was not thy fault; Sir Edward should have told thee.'

'He said I could have whatever I wanted, to make the silk successful.' But Henry *had* known; or rather, he had chosen not to know.

Hinshaw nodded. 'He is a fool, and a reckless one at that. And the silk . . . No matter how much investment he gets, it will not be a good venture. It is simply too expensive. Those who can afford it, can afford space and air and isolation: those who cannot, cannot. The market is small. And the costs of producing it . . .' He sighed.

Henry bit his lip, wondering if he should confide the secret of Worsley's discoveries to the older man, but before he could decide, Hinshaw got abruptly to his feet and strode to the bookshelf. Although he stood there for a moment, staring at the spines, Henry had the impression that he was not seeing them, that he had moved because he could not stay still.

'I will rejoice from the bottom of my soul if the factory closes,' Hinshaw said, in a new tone. 'I was glad to see it swamped in mud and clogged with rubbish. It is a rotten place, a gangrene . . . It has turned Telverton from an ordinary town into a purgatory full of feeble-minded children and drunkards and suicides. It is not the factory itself I resent,' he said, with obvious effort, 'I am not sentimental – employment is a great good, and we must have mills, we must have industry. It is not even the noise, because all machinery is noisy, and there is always the Telverton fingerspeak. That is a useful thing – a silver lining. To see it flourish the last few years amongst the children – even our own young ones use the signs to talk in Meeting between themselves, when no one is looking.' He smiled, shortly. 'If deafness were all . . . But arain silk is perfidious. Sometimes I think it corrodes the human soul. Its silence is meretricious, and its echoes are a curse.' At last he blinked, adjusted the position of a few books, and stepped back, as if to maintain the illusion that he had only wanted to neaten the shelf.

Henry said, 'But I thought the Quakers were considering it for their— your Meeting House.'

Hinshaw flicked him a glinting look. 'We are considering it still. And I believe the warehouses survived the floods, so the question still stands. But I shall minister against it, and I have no doubt that I will carry the day.' He came back to his seat, picked up his pipe and seemed nonplussed to find it extinguished. He set about lighting it again. 'Even if it were not for the echoes . . . Quaker silence is a different thing entirely. It is a discipline – we wait upon a spirit which may or may not come to us – not an end in itself. Although some of my Friends would probably disagree. The silk is the opposite. It protects thee from unpleasantness, but at a cost to those outside its circle; it is a courtesy enforced, if thou lik'st, and a courtesy enforced is nothing more than tyranny. And it is not worshipful to ensure that no one can ever disturb thy own peace, even if thou feel'st thou canst worship better without the distraction. The imposition of silence on oneself may be a good; the imposition of it on anyone else is always an evil.' He shook his head, with a sudden self-mocking grin. 'But I am maundering,' he said. 'Thou should'st be able to rely on a Friend for brevity, at least. And thou hast come downstairs for the first time in weeks, after a long fever, and all I can do is talk! Let's get thee back to bed.'

Henry let Hinshaw help him to his feet without raising his head: he did not want to see the other man's expression, or expose his own to scrutiny. The stairs seemed endless, but Hinshaw's arm was unwavering, lifting him at the precise moment when he transferred his weight upwards. They rounded the landing and made their halting way along the hall to Henry's room. 'There. Wilt thou have a lamp? Or a candle?'

'No,' Henry said, getting into bed. 'Thank you. I'll go to sleep now.'

'That's right. I'll tell Rachel not to wake thee for thy breakfast. God bless thee and thy dreams.' He turned to leave.

Henry said, 'Hinshaw?'

Hinshaw paused.

'Did Sir Edward call on me, while I was ill? Or leave a card, or a – a note?'

Hinshaw shook his head. 'No. I have no letters for thee.' He added, after a brief look at Henry, 'If it's a matter of money, thou must not worry.'

Henry shut his eyes. 'No,' he said, 'you are very kind, but it isn't money.'

There was a silence. Hinshaw took another breath, as if he were about to ask a question. Henry resisted the impulse to open his eyes. Instead he lay in his self-imposed dark until he heard Hinshaw retreat, and the door shut; then he rolled over, and buried his face in the pillow.

He slept late, as he had been told, the next day. When he awoke, it was to the soft clanging of the doorbell, and voices downstairs. For a few moments he lay listening, as though to distant music; then, with a thudding heart, he knew at once that one voice was Rachel's, another Hinshaw's, and the third, lower and less certain, belonged to Miss Fielding.

He swung himself out of bed and flung open the door of the wardrobe to search for his clothes. He dragged his trousers on and reached for a shirt; but it was impossibly difficult to button, and he was obliged to rest for a few seconds, bracing himself against the foot of the bed, light-headed with exertion. There were footsteps along the landing, and the door opened: 'Henry,' Rachel murmured, 'art thou awake? Oh! Lie down, thou must not overtax thy strength.'

'I am perfectly all right. I heard voices – was that . . . ?' Miss Fielding moved into view, behind the little woman in grey, and he stopped. Suddenly he was aware of how loosely his clothes hung on him, and how his fingers were shaking.

'I see you are still not ready to receive visitors,' she said. 'Forgive me. I will write, instead—'

'No,' he said, as she turned to go, 'no, I am glad to see you. If I had been expecting you I would have—'

'Well then, thou must sit down, at least,' Rachel interjected, 'and I will fetch thee some beef tea. And,' she added, turning to Miss Fielding, 'thou must not stay long, he is still very weak. I shall leave the door open, so I shall hear if either of you calls.'

'Thank you,' Miss Fielding said.

'Hmm. Ten minutes, no more.' She looked at them both rather sternly as she left, as though they were children.

Miss Fielding looked about for another chair, saw that he had taken the only one, and sat down on the bed. 'No,' she said, as he started to get to his feet, 'I am perfectly comfortable here. How are you, Mr Latimer?'

'I am well,' he said. 'Or at least, I am recovering. Have you brought a message – a letter?'

She said, overlapping, 'They were afraid for you, at first. When I first came, they told me you would die. It seems a miracle to see you awake, after so long.'

'Are you here because— Did Sir Edward send . . . ?'

'What? Oh – no. He does not know I am here. He has

gone to London. He has not written to you, then? No, I suppose he would not.' She gave him a look that held more understanding than he would have liked, and added, 'Cathermute House will have to be sold to pay his debts, and the factory . . . I do not imagine he has time to be angry with you, if he ever was.'

It was not a consolation. He looked away, despising himself for his own misery. At last he said, 'And you? How are you and Philomel?'

'We are well.' But her hands moved in her lap, as though she had caught a gesture before it escaped.

'What is it? What is the matter? Is it Philomel?' He stumbled on her name. If something had happened to—

'No. It's true, we are both well. But she is— I am . . . that is, we are to leave tomorrow. I am to take her to her mother's family in Hampshire. I will stay there with her for just over a month, and then I understand they wish her to go to an institution for deaf-mutes.'

He stared at her. 'I didn't know there were such places,' he said; and there rose into his mind a horrible vision, a cross between an asylum and the school from *Nicholas Nickleby*.

'They are not so terrible,' she said. 'My aunt spoke sometimes of the school on the Old Kent Road. She was happy there. She loved being able to talk to other children.'

'But you are Philomel's governess – surely you do not want—'

'Why should I not? I cannot imagine anything better for a child like Phil. And Cathermute House has never been a healthy place for her, no matter how hard I've tried.'

Henry took a long breath. It might be true; please God it was true. But whatever happened, the little girl's world would be changed utterly. And Miss Fielding's livelihood would be gone – and more, more, of course . . . He tried not to think of how Miss Fielding had looked when she had said, *I stay for Philomel*, or the light that had shone in her eyes as she made the sign for Philomel's name. He could see the shadow of that expression in her face now, with the unflinching anticipation of anguish.

Abruptly he remembered the poker he had wielded in the spider house. He had fought there like a crusader: so sure of himself, so determined to rid the world of evil, so unquestioning, so angry. He saw the glass spraying through the air and heard the satisfying crunch of it underfoot. At that moment he had thought himself a good man. But he had not considered Philomel, or Miss Fielding, or even Lady Ashmore-Percy, whose expensive imprisonment must at least be better than the county madhouse. What would happen to her, the woman with the face of Arachne, in the stinking ward of a paupers' Bedlam? It was his fault. He struck out, foolishly, against the arm of his chair. 'No,' he said, '*no*.'

She blinked. 'I beg your pardon?'

'You love her. Don't you?'

'Naturally I love her,' she said, levelly, 'but that is hardly—'

'Well then,' he said, and leant forward, his voice trembling, 'then you cannot let them take her away from you. You simply cannot.'

She gave her head a tiny shake, frowning. 'I am entirely powerless, Mr Latimer. Even if I thought that it were not the best thing for her . . . There is nothing I can do, nothing at all.'

'There must be something. You must not let her go – you must not, I *forbid* you.' He tried to get to his feet, and found that his whole body was quivering. 'If you love her—'

'If I love her then I must submit to what is right.'

'But it is *not* right!' His voice had grown rusty while he

was ill, like an old man's. 'You may think it is, but you will realise that she needs you – you will realise it too late, and you will be even more powerless than you are now. For God's sake,' he cried, swaying, 'you must not fail her, you hear me? I cannot bear it if I have— If you – please—'

'What do you imagine I could do?'

'Anything! Take her in your arms and – take a carriage to somewhere, anywhere.'

'You are raving mad.' She had risen to her feet; now she reached out for him. 'Henry, you are still an invalid, sit down. I wonder where Mrs Hinshaw has got to with her beef tea.'

'You are not listening! I mean it with all my heart. You must believe me.'

'How can you possibly think—?'

'Because I cannot stand by and let Philomel lose the only person who has ever cared for her. I cannot. When you love her – if someone had told me, when I gave up my daughter . . .' He stopped; he had forgotten how to speak, forgotten everything except the ache in his chest, his eyes and guts and hands, the pain that was more than pain.

Miss Fielding stared at him. Gradually a new expression spread over her face. It was as though a fog had blown away, and she found herself somewhere entirely unexpected.

She said, 'Your daughter? I thought . . .'

'It doesn't matter.' He wished he could gather the words back into his mouth and swallow them.

'I thought that you were childless – that your wife—'

'Died in childbirth. Yes. But I have a daughter.'

There was a silence. It should have changed the whole world, to say it aloud, after so long; but nothing changed, the room was exactly as it was, and only Miss Fielding's frown told him that she had heard.

'But . . . do you mean that she is—?'

'She almost died.' The air in his throat threatened to choke him. 'She would not cry, for a long time. She was blue and – and silent – and . . .' He stopped. He could remember the appalling stillness in the room: it was full of noise, the midwife saying something, Madeleine's weak murmur, the drip of something on the floor, his own heart, but drowning it all out was that deafening absence, the uncrying child . . . He had thought he would suffocate too. And then – oh God, it had seemed like a miracle – Madeleine had reached out . . . the midwife had said, 'You see, I said she would be safe and sound . . .' The wail, thin and weak, but – enough. And slowly the morbid violet of the baby's skin had turned pink, and the midwife had bundled her away, calling for the nurse-maid, and . . . If only he had asked to hold her. But he should not even have been in the room, he was only there on sufferance, pressed against the wall out of the midwife's way, and anyway his attention had turned back to Madeleine and the terrible dark dripping of the bedsheets. He had waited, helpless; and at last he had said, 'Shall I call a doctor?' and the midwife had bitten her lip and nodded. By then Madeleine's eyes had closed, and she did not respond when he said her name. He wanted to tell her that she had been right, hours before, when she'd said that something was wrong – that she had been right, that she knew best, that he would always, always listen to her if only she would just stay here with him . . . But the blood kept running out of her, and by the time the doctor arrived there was nothing to be done. And the child – the baby—

'What is she called?'

He shook his head. He did not want to remember. He did not want to see the nursery door in front of his eyes, and smell the queasy miasma of dirty napkins and gruel. In the days after Madeleine's death he would stand there for hours, unmoving, and listen. He never knocked. He would wait until, among the nurse's footsteps or the turning of pages or the falling of coals, he heard the child raise her voice; so that he could be sure she was, at least at that moment, alive. He could not bear to go inside. It was on the second or third day that he received the letter from his cousin, and showed it, heavy-hearted, to Argyll. Then it was only a question of waiting until the funeral, when it would all be over. Sometimes he hoped she would die; sometimes he would jerk awake from a doze in his chair, crying out, his face wet, because he dreamt that she had.

'They took her away,' he said. 'I haven't seen her since she was a few days old.'

Miss Fielding did not move. He sat down, stiffly, and laced his fingers together. 'A household with two bereaved men, and no children,' he said. 'Naturally it was not suitable. Better for her to be looked after by a woman. A mother. In the bosom of a family. My cousin lives up in the North – he is a lawyer, a wealthy one – and his wife is . . . there are five children, and another one expected. I could not . . . my daughter would not be . . .' He did not trust his voice. He looked up at the ceiling, blinking; above him the shadows of leaves wavered in the grey light. He could see the words in his cousin's writing: *My wife has always wanted a daughter, and it seems that the Almighty has disposed her heart so as to answer your need. I propose that we should raise the child as our own. There will be no difference in our treatment of her; neither in our love, nor our care, nor our provision for her. You may thus be relieved of a burden, knowing that she will be a blessing to us.* He had read it three times, and it took every drop of self-control he'd had not to throw it on the fire. He had despised his cousin's pomposity, his reference to the Almighty; and how dare he write so dismissively of a burden? The baby was his, Henry's, his daughter, and the only living flesh that remained of Madeleine . . . But he sat with the letter on his knee, and when he had grown calm again he knew that he had no choice. He could imagine the kindly disbelief on his friends' faces if he dared to suggest that this empty, woman-less house would be better than his cousin's: if he wanted to deny his daughter their cheerful, noisy nursery and five rollicking boys, the garden scattered with hoops and balls and fishing-rods, their games of soldiers and hide-and-seek, their puppy . . . Perhaps even then he had held out a last hope that Argyll would snort and throw the letter back in his face; but Argyll had hardly taken the time to read to the end before he said, heavily, 'Aye, lad, I suppose we must thank the Lord for his mysterious ways . . .' And so Henry had written to accept the offer.

He had hated them, and he had hated them even more when they arrived, the day before Madeleine's funeral. He hated them for their pity, for their kindness, for the way his cousin tugged at his nose and coughed when his wife hurried up the stairs to the nursery, her face rigid with the battle between tact and joy. He turned away, determined not to strain his ears for his daughter's cry. The next day there had been the funeral, subdued guests pressing his hand, the smell of lilies, a sick void in his stomach. He had wanted them to be gone. But when at last the guests had left, and Argyll had disappeared to drink whisky alone in the library, he watched his cousin put on his hat and gloves and almost begged him to stay – for one more day, one more hour. He looked up and saw the nursemaid carrying the baby down the stairs. One reddish fist protruded from the folds of the shawl. The nursemaid said, 'She's asleep, at last.'

'Best not wake her, then,' he'd said, and turned away. If

he touched her – if he bent over that tiny crumpled face
– if she woke, and opened her eyes . . .

'Oh, Henry,' his cousin's wife said, 'surely—'

'It's all right. Thank you for coming,' he said, shaking his
cousin's hand. 'I am more grateful than I can say.' Perhaps
he made it sound sincere, because neither of them flinched.
His cousin nodded, and patted his back, and ushered his
wife out of the front door after the nursemaid. He thought
that he had got it over, but at the last moment his cousin's
wife hesitated and stretched out her hand to him. 'I am so
sorry, I understand how difficult it must be. We will write
every week,' she had said, 'and *any* time you want to visit . . .'
He took his hand away. They had both known already that
he would not visit.

And then they were gone, and his daughter with them.
She might as well have been underground, in the Argyll vault,
in Madeleine's arms; at least then he would not have had to
imagine Madeleine's face if she had known he would give
their only child away. Or he would not have had to wonder—
Oh God, those nights when he could not sleep for wondering!
Was she awake? Was she crying? Could an infant grieve?

He said, 'I wrote to them, a few weeks before the gala. I
told them that they should consider her their daughter. To
say that it was best if they never told her she wasn't. That
is, if she lives to the age of understanding. They say she is
a sickly little thing.' He drew his hands apart, stared at them,
and laid them palm to palm as if he were praying.

'Why?' Miss Fielding asked, at last.

'I thought I could begin again. I was starting a new life,
at Cathermute, with Sir Edward. I was – foolish.' He looked
up at her, and knew that she could hear perfectly well the
words he could not say. 'Except that . . . maybe it *is* best,
even now. She will be happier.'

Miss Fielding bowed her head. 'I am sorry,' she said.

It should have been a relief to tell the truth, but he felt the treacherous prickle of heat under his eyelids. 'So am I,' he said. He turned his gaze to the window, the green trees and lush, dusty flowerbeds. He knew that she was right: she had no power at all to keep Philomel by her side, no hold on the little girl except love, and that was worth nothing.

A minute or so passed. At last Miss Fielding got up in a rustle of skirts. 'I am afraid I must go,' she said. 'I only came to say goodbye.'

He held out his hand. She took it. 'Forgive me,' he said. 'I should not have pitied you.'

A gleam came into her eyes; but all she said was, 'You may pity me all you like. And I shall do the same for you.'

'Will you— Will you give my love to Philomel?'

'Of course.'

'And – if you felt like writing to me . . .'

'I shall certainly write, if you wish me to.'

'Thank you.'

She squeezed his hand, then let go. 'I can hear Mrs Hinshaw,' she said. 'I had better leave you to rest, or there may be some very Quakerly plain-speaking.'

He tried to smile; and he maintained the effort as she walked to the door and pushed it further open, and turned to give him one last look. 'Goodbye,' he said, and raised his hand in one of the few gestures of fingerspeak that he was sure of.

'Henry,' she said, 'it is not too late. Anyone may make a mistake.'

'I don't know what you mean—'

'She is still your daughter. She is more your daughter than Philomel ever was.'

He gave a laugh that felt like splinters in his throat. Of

course Philomel was not his daughter; just as Sir Edward had never been his father, or his friend, or his lover. He said, 'I know. Goodbye, Miss Fielding.'

She seemed on the brink of adding something else; but at last she only nodded, and left, and a few moments later he heard Mrs Hinshaw's voice, and Miss Fielding answering.

He had no desire to listen. He bent his head, put his hands over his eyes, and wept.

Sometimes, in the days that followed, Henry wished he had not woken at all. He felt as though he were treading a long path with no goal at the end but his old life, or whatever remained of it. His healing was slow, full of fits and starts and small relapses; so by the time he was returned to his former state of health they had reached the fat, rank end of the summer, full of what he would always think of as Quaker skies, warm and still and grey. Slowly his horizons broadened, and his daily walks took him out of the Hinshaws' enclosed garden – which was modest, of course, compared to Cathermute House – and along the river, with its gravel shallows and overhanging trees. In the afternoons he read, alone, working his way through Hinshaw's library, often letting the volumes drop into his lap. It was a life of waiting: he chafed under it, but he did not want it to end. He could not presume on the Hinshaws' hospitality longer than his infirmity required, but he flinched from the thought of leaving. If only he had something – someone – to go home to; but there was only Argyll, and the empty house, and failure.

But when at last he steeled himself, determined that he would make plans to depart by the end of the week, Hinshaw forestalled him. They were in his study, after dinner, and Henry had been staring unseeing at a book of history, when

Hinshaw put his pipe to one side and cocked his head at him. 'Thou art better,' he said, 'thank God.'

Henry glanced up, not quite glad that Hinshaw had given him this opening. 'Yes. And thank *you—*'

Hinshaw held up a hand. 'I have been thinking about thee, and thy affairs. Thou shalt leave soon, and then what wilt thou do?'

'Go home,' Henry said, and wished that the word did not ring so hollow.

There was a pause. Hinshaw said, like a teacher prompting a pupil, 'But thou dost not wish to. Thou art like a man preparing for the gallows. No, I am not faulting thy resolve, I am merely observing what is in front of my eyes.'

Henry swallowed. 'I must return to London,' he said.

'Must thou?'

'That is where my living is. And my home.'

Hinshaw regarded him, expressionless. 'What family dost thou have there?'

'My father-in-law,' Henry said, and then shrugged, to cover the pause. It was a very short list.

'I thought I heard thee say once that thou had'st a cousin, near York. Thou wast brought up with him, thou said'st, like a brother.'

'Not exactly . . . That is, he is much older than I am. He never took very much interest in me. And now – I do not even write to him, any more.' He slid the ribbon marker of his book through his fingers, avoiding Hinshaw's eyes.

'I happen to have a friend who knows him. He speaks well of him.'

'Oh. That's good.'

When he glanced up, Hinshaw was watching him, with the shrewd glint that Henry had come to know. 'Wouldst thou consider moving up to the North, away from thy father-in-law?'

'I don't know why I would—'

'Humour me, and answer the question.'

'You are kind to take an interest,' Henry said, and the resentment he had not felt before rose in his throat. 'But it isn't that simple. I work for Argyll – my father-in-law – in his shop. My only skills are – well, I have none, really. I can't transplant myself very easily. And Argyll . . .' He bit his lip. Actually he was sure Argyll would be willing to see him go – relieved, even. 'I don't have enough to live on without some kind of job, and I will not ask my cousin to find me a post.' Dismayed, he heard himself raise his voice. 'No, I must return to London. I do not look forward to it, but it's honest, at least, and I'd rather that than cadge a living as my cousin's office-boy. If you don't wish to insult—'

'Hush,' Hinshaw said, without blinking. 'Thou mistak'st my intent. I have another proposal for thee. Wilt thou listen, and let me tell thee?'

Henry nodded.

'I have another friend who runs a school for deaf-mute children. It is not far from York, five or ten miles at most. It is a delightful place. I think it would lift thy heart to see it; the children get a better education than many at our foundation schools, and study more than the usual subjects. My friend is keen to equip them for worthy work, as artisans or clerks or teachers themselves. And he is looking for good men who might be able to help him – who do not have to be teachers already, as long as they have enquiring minds, and some education' – he put a faint weight on the words – 'and, above all, a facility with fingerspeak. Now I believe thou know'st very few signs, yet, but thou hast experience of deaf customers in thy father-in-law's shop, and if thou wast willing and diligent, with a little time thou might'st learn enough to start with.'

Henry sat speechless. It was not what he had ever wanted. But it was no worse than returning to London, and taking up his old work in the shop . . . A teacher, he thought. A teacher of children like Philomel . . .

Hinshaw waited. As the pause grew longer he showed no sign of discomfort; instead he sat back and filled his pipe again, lit it, and gave an unselfconscious grunt of pleasure.

'I don't know,' Henry said, at last. 'I must think about it.'

'Naturally.'

'I should have to write to your friend myself, to know more.'

'Certainly. I shall give thee his address.'

'I'm not sure I would be good at it.'

'Thou canst never know in advance, of course.'

'And – if I were to take it – I would want to know what he thought I should teach. I have a sound basis in literature, but the other subjects . . . I suppose I might learn about other things. I should like to, in fact. I am all too aware of the limitations of my knowledge. What would he require? Geography, history, botany . . . ?'

'I should think thou might'st be able to find out.'

'I would have to confer with him before considering how to tackle a programme of study. Even once I was proficient in fingerspeak, there would be a great deal of preparation to be done. And then there would be the question of finding somewhere to live.' Nowhere too near his cousin; nowhere where he might risk running into his daughter, and hearing her call his cousin *Papa*, and having to look down into her small face and pretend he did not know her . . .

'I dare say I could ask another Friend to find somewhere for thee.'

'Not that I will necessarily take the post. I must think about it.'

'Quite right. Thou must take thy time,' Hinshaw said, and smiled.

In spite of Rachel's offer to help, Henry packed his own things two or three days before he was due to leave for York. He piled them into his old suitcase as quickly as he could, on top of the belongings that had been mouldering there for weeks, ever since he'd left Cathermute: the fine suits, the gloves and handkerchiefs, a couple of gilt-edged books that he had bought and hardly opened, the edition of the *Telverton Argus* that contained the announcement of the gala. When he arrived in Yorkshire, he promised himself, he would throw away anything that would not be of use in his new position. Until then, there was quite enough room to add his serviceable clothes, supplemented with a few second-hand shirts that Rachel had bought for him. On top he placed his picture of Madeleine and his writing-case. Apart from his comb and razor and tooth-powder, that was all he needed.

But the day before he left, he found himself dragging the suitcase out from its place and rummaging inside. He had been restless since he woke; outside it was raining, so he had no inclination to go for his customary walk. After days of wholesome religious texts he was desperate for one of the bloodier Shakespeares, or a sensational novel, or a Gothic romance – none of which, he suspected, would be allowed over the Hinshaws' threshold. Then, abruptly, he had remembered that a few days before the gala he had purchased a volume of Miss Rossetti's poetry, and never opened it. That would do. And he flung open the lid of the case and dug under his folded shirts, searching for the book by touch.

A stiff corner of paper slid under his thumbnail, and he pushed his clothes to one side. But what he had felt was not *Goblin Market*, it was the bundle of his cousin's letters. A few had been opened; the rest were still sealed. He bowed his head. He had forgotten that they were there. Or had he? He had certainly not wanted to remember.

He hesitated. The letter on the top of the pile was the most recent one; the last one his cousin had sent . . . What good would it do to read it? He could recall perfectly his own last letter: *I have important work to do here, and must not allow other concerns to distract me.* How insufferable he had been. And Charles was known for bearing grudges – that was, many said, what made him an excellent lawyer; would he choose a scathing retort or icy agreement? Or, worse, the heaping of coals of fire, the polite sting of, *Thank you for your offer of money, but please do not trouble yourself, I suspect you are rather more in need of it* . . . ? Henry clenched his jaw. Well, he had deserved it. If ever his daughter read his own letter, and saw how easily he had— No, he would not think about that. And partly to distract himself, partly out of a desire to know the worst, he set his fingers to work on the envelope.

My dear Henry, his cousin's handwriting said, *I am pleased to hear from you after such a long silence. I have always felt that you were a man without direction, and I cordially wish you every success and prosperity in your new position. However, you will forgive me if I observe that enthusiasms may wane, and speculations fail, and nothing is certain in this world; and so I regard it as my duty not to take anything you have said as entirely final. Let me say only that while we love little Madeleine as we love our sons, we are conscious of the inescapable truth of the matter, namely that she is your daughter; and we have no desire to lie to her, even if we could do so in good conscience. I may have been too eager to reassure you that she would be welcomed into the bosom of our family, and that you need have no fear that she would be less loved because she is not our flesh and bone. If I have, forgive me. We will never seek to seduce her affection and gratitude away from its proper object – that is, yourself, as well as the memory of her mother; and if you are not yet in a position to welcome her filial feelings, she must simply wait until you are.*

For a moment the words danced in front of Henry's eyes. Cordially, he thought, with two 'l's . . . And he heard Miss Fielding's voice: *She is still your daughter.*

Tomorrow he would be only ten miles from his cousin's house – tomorrow, and for days after, for weeks, perhaps the rest of his life . . .

Something else spilt out. He bent to pick it up. There was another letter, in a looping hand that he did not recognise. *This is hardly worthy to be called a postscript; I only wanted to tell you that Linnet (that is what we call her, she is too little for Madeleine yet) is sitting up now, and she laughs and points her finger when she hears birdsong. She is still delicate but growing stronger, we hope. Here is a drawing that Andrew made of her.*

He unfolded the piece of heavy paper. His daughter looked up at him, entirely unfamiliar, smiling. He held the paper very carefully, making sure that his fingertips should not smudge the pencil marks. He stared at the small, pudgy face. There was a sharp ache in his throat. It was grief, of course, mixed with hope, and shame; but he did not know whether the shame came from his trust or his mistrust, both so appallingly misplaced.

There was a rap at the door. The sound had a heavy patience that suggested the knuckles had been knocking for some time. He said, automatically, 'Come in,' but he could not lift his eyes from the paper.

'One would think thou wert a prisoner,' Hinshaw said. 'How many paces is it from that wall to the window?'

He blinked and looked up; it was extraordinary that the room had not changed, that the walls and window were still in exactly the same places, that Hinshaw himself was as sturdy and sardonic as he had always been. 'I'm sorry,' he said, with an effort. 'Did I disturb you? I won't do it again.'

'That is not what I meant. What ails thee?'

'Nothing. Only I have packed all I can, and I can't find anything to occupy myself.' He saw Hinshaw's eyes slide to the paper in his hand, and he slid it convulsively into his pocket. He was not ready to let anyone, even Hinshaw, look at it.

Hinshaw nodded. For a moment Henry was sure he would ask another question; but at last all he said was, 'Thou hadst better get outside, then. Wear thyself out. Rachel says exercise does thee good, and tomorrow thou'lt be sitting longer than thou wouldst want, I bet.'

'Yes,' Henry said. 'Only it's raining—'

'Not any more,' Hinshaw said. 'Go.'

Henry nodded, and struggled to his feet. He did not say anything to Hinshaw; was grateful, almost to tears, that Hinshaw would not be offended by a lack of conventional courtesy. He did not even look round as he staggered through the door and down the stairs, suddenly desperate to be out in the open air, and alone.

The rain had stopped, and it was a mild, stagnant day. For the first mile or so he hardly knew where he was, but at last he glanced from side to side and saw that he had taken a different path from the usual one. Instead of downriver, he had chosen the way that curved north, along the Telverton road, and now he was walking through the outskirts of the town and up to the high street.

He had not been into town since the flood, and it gave him a shock to see the boulders still scattered here and there, the buildings that had collapsed and been abandoned through lack of funds to rebuild; he had not realised the extent of the damage, he had thought only of the factory, and of himself. But the strangest thing was the noise, or the lack of it. Of course there was still the usual cacophony – the carriages and horses, the banging and shouting, the ordinary hubbub of people about their business – but it had a sort of cleanness. It was like, he thought, smelling manure after the stench of gangrenous flesh: it was unlovely, but it did not hint at a world that was rotten. He looked up at the smokeless factory chimney. The air was clearer, too. What had Hinshaw said? *I will rejoice from the bottom of my soul if the factory closes.*

He did not walk past the factory itself, or Sub Rosa, although he stood for a time at the corner of Clovelly Street, staring at the stripped windows and the bare rooms inside. He had no inclination to go any closer: what would he see through the windows but his own failure, and the bloody handprints he had left upon everything he touched? He took the road that led out of Telverton, up the long hill and into the village; and there, after he had passed the row of cottages with their overblown late-summer gardens, and then the church, he came to the gate of Cathermute House.

It was closed. He could not see if anyone was in the lodge. It was very quiet. He had not meant to pause – had not meant to come this far, before he turned for home – but now he stood watching and waiting; as though Sir Edward might know he was there, as if he might relent and stride over the grass towards him, holding out his hands. Nothing moved except a few browning leaves that blew across the drive.

He took hold of the bars of the gate. The cool metal was

slick against his palms. The sensation brought something to mind, something distant, but for a moment he could not think of it. If he could only get into the house, and be welcome there . . . He forgot his cousin's letter, and his daughter; as he grasped the gate, waiting, hardly breathing, he forgot everything but Sir Edward's mouth, his hands, the light in his eyes. It hurt, and yet he did not want to move. It was not too late, he thought. There was still something to be salvaged, even if it was only friendship – and perhaps now they might be equals, now that Henry was not his employee, and Sir Edward was ruined.

Ruined. The word brought him to his senses, and he rocked back. *That* was what it had reminded him of: the factory gate, just before he had climbed over it.

He could not undo what he had done. He was going away, and his daughter was waiting for him, and Sir Edward was far away, in London. Whatever Henry had felt for him – and it had been love, he thought; love, no matter what else it was mixed with – Sir Edward had not returned it. He had not been worthy of it.

Henry took a deep breath and held it, as he might have braced himself for the first touch of a scalpel. Then he turned and walked away, his neck aching from the effort not to look back.

He crossed the river by the little stone bridge and struck out through a patch of woodland. He meant to follow the waterway, but the path swerved aside, and he did not pay enough attention to where he was going; a little while later he discovered that he was more or less lost. It took him a good hour's walk to discover his whereabouts. But at last he came to a steep grassy slope and saw that ahead of him, on the other side of the river, were the beginnings of the town, with the factory chimney like a gnomon beyond; and to his right, downstream, was the hamlet where the Hinshaws lived.

He began to scramble down towards the riverbank. Where the watercourse curved he was obliged to step over debris from the flood, scattered high on the gravelled margin: broken reels and boxes, tools wedged against overhanging roots, and a lattice of splintered, waterlogged planks. On the other side of the water, caught in a knot of brambles, hung a clump of pages from an old blank-book, washed clean of writing. Whatever words had been written there, they had dissolved in the flood and been carried by the spate to the sea.

Then, just beyond the bend in the river, he came out onto a flat area of sward among trees – a sudden, green-enclosed chamber, open on one side to the ripple of water over chinking stones. The river glittered as if it were sunlit, although clouds still covered the sky. He stepped forward to see if there was a way through; and then, as a breeze lifted sweetness from the damp grass and cooled his face, he stopped. He could hear . . . for a second he thought he had heard a voice, and in that space between two heartbeats he knew it for Madeleine's – or Linnet's, laughing. His hand went to the pocket of his jacket, where the drawing of his daughter sat against his heart.

He blinked. There was a cobweb suspended in front of him; it was so fine he could only just make out the cross-lines that gleamed with nacreous light. At its centre there was a knot of black, its legs poised on the radiating threads. The web filled with the breeze like a sail, and he heard the lovely Aeolian whisper as it bounced a little on its anchor-lines.

He raised his hand. It was trembling. He held it there, a finger's breadth from the spider, his mouth dry, his knees weak. Echoes sang in his ears.

Then, with the same effort of will that had turned him

aside from Cathermute House, he stepped back. He moved very carefully, inch by inch, until he was sure that no hanging silk had snagged against him, no unseen creature crawled onto his collar. At the edge of the clearing he took a final breath, listening to the unearthly notes of air and water, but here they were so faint he could hardly hear them. There was only that yearning, which was the knowledge of love, and love lost.

Then he turned and scrabbled up the bank on undignified hands and knees, to find another way home.

Acknowledgements

The only time I regret working with so many fantastic people is when I come to write my acknowledgements, because it makes it impossible to list everyone who deserves thanks. I genuinely cannot think of anyone who has contributed to *The Silence Factory* to whom I am *not* grateful – so here, first, is an enormous thank you to everyone who has worked on it in any capacity. You have all demonstrated so much talent, creativity and passion, and it has been an honour to see my book blossom under your touch. Thank you.

That said, some books are harder to write than others. *The Silence Factory* took several years of my life (and possibly several years *off* my life) before it assumed its final shape, and without the invaluable help and support of a few particularly amazing people I would probably still be wrestling with it.

There are probably a lot of agents who can be relied on to point out that a first draft is a bit of a mess, but I imagine only a few can do it with the tact, humour and general brilliance that Sarah Ballard can. I am profoundly grateful both for her incisive judgements and her ability to communicate them with such grace; without her support I would have felt even more despairing, at moments, than I actually did. Thank you.

The same can also be said of my fabulous editor, Suzie

379

Dooré, who was confronted with a second draft which was, frankly, *still* a bit of a mess, and responded with character-istic acumen (not to mention wit). Thank you so much for your transformational magic – it was, as always, a joy to work with you. Thanks are also due to Carla Josephson, who contributed a huge amount to that editing process. It must be rare for any author to benefit not from one but two such fantastic editors.

I was also lucky enough to get feedback from other readers whose contributions were enlightening, useful, and some-times profoundly thought-provoking. Some people who worked with me on this book did so by giving freely of their personal experience and history as well as their knowledge and expertise, and it was an absolute privilege to try to take that on board. Thank you.

Thanks too to everyone at HarperCollins and at United Agents, especially Eli Keren; to Eleanor Jackson at DCL; to Micaela Alcaino (you absolute genius); to Ariana Sinclair and everyone at William Morrow (and argh, I am still morti-fied I forgot that Teams meeting!); to my lovely friends and family, especially Nick; and finally to anyone and everyone who has read this far. Thank you.